"This searching, humane novel debut contemplates God, the cosmos, and humanity's place in it all… thoughtfulness powers the novel, which unfolds in clear, engaging, at times playful prose… Wald proves an engaging, empathetic storyteller."

BOOKLIFE REVIEW BY PUBLISHERS WEEKLY

"Harmony and clarity are found as four men pursue happiness in tandem in this endearing" [and] "soulful novel."

FOREWORD/CLARION REVIEW

"Delightful, compelling, and thought-provokingly realistic."

MIDWEST BOOK REVIEW

"An outstanding debut… Five-plus stars to *The Overexamined Life of Jacob Hart*. It's a literary triumph for those seeking a read with both substance and uncommon depth. We can't recommend it highly enough."

PUBLISHERS DAILY REVIEW

"Stellar. *The Overexamined Life of Jacob Hart* is a thought-provoking, heartfelt, and inspirational story told with depth, nuance, and emotion. Jacob Hart is a complex and compassionate soul who is worth rooting for. We will be hearing more from this talented author. Highly recommended."

SHELDON SIEGEL, NEW YORK TIMES BEST-SELLING AUTHOR OF
SPECIAL CIRCUMSTANCES

"If you have ever thought about the big questions, the meaning of life, religion, and your place in both society and the universe, in other words you live an 'examined life', then *The Overexamined Life of Jacob Hart* is for you. Page by poignant and humorous page, Wald weaves a magical world out of the ordinary, much the way Hermann Hesse did in his classic, *Steppenwolf*, appealing to readers young and old. This book is a very satisfying journey in Paradise."

NEAL KATZ, AUTHOR OF OUTRAGEOUS, RISE TO RICHES: THE VICTORIA
WOODHULL SAGA VOLUME 1

The Overexamined Life of Jacob Hart

the
Overexamined Life
of Jacob Hart

a novel

Jerry Wald

Torchflame Books

VISTA, CALIFORNIA

For information, address Top Reads Publishing Subsidiary Rights Department, 1035 E. Vista Way, Suite 205, Vista, CA 92084, USA.

ISBN: 978-1-61153-593-8 (paperback)
ISBN: 978-1-61153-507-5 (ebook)

Library of Congress Control Number: 2024905504

The Overexamined Life of Jacob Hart is published by: Torchflame Books, an imprint of Top Reads Publishing, LLC, USA

For information about special discounts for bulk purchases, please direct emails to: publisher@topreadspublishing.com

Cover design, interior illustrations: Teri Rider
Book layout and typography: Teri Rider & Associates

Printed in the United States of America

Author's note:
This is a work of fiction. None of the characters are real people. The reader should not impute personalities, views, or anything else to any actual person, living or dead. Any resemblance is entirely coincidental. Any depiction in this novel of a corporation, business, university, city, rail division or similar unit, body of water, or any other entity, topic, person, place or thing, is also pure fiction and not intended to be factual.

Just enjoy this work for what it is. That is, complete make-believe that hopefully provides food for thought.

Special thanks to the Harry Chapin Foundation for permitting me to use words from the following iconic tune:
CIRCLE
Words and Music by Harry Chapin
© 1972 Ampco Music
Transferred © 1986 Harry Chapin Foundation (Renewed)
All rights administered by HARRY CHAPIN FOUNDATION
Lyrics Reprinted with the Permission of Harry Chapin Foundation
All Rights Reserved

If you've enjoyed this book, please consider leaving a review for me.

For Dena
With Love On Our 40th Wedding Anniversary

Four men
Wrestling at the apex

One a dreamer, another devout,
The next a scholar, the last the chief

Fluttering
Through the hourglass of inevitability

Flittering
Amidst majesty, grandeur

Flurrying
To ageless rhythms, eternal order

Flickering
With divinity

Paradise for the taking
To wrestle to the ground

Sometimes

PROLOGUE

Jacob Hart fretted over the long road in his rearview mirror, the diminishing runway ahead. After six decades of toil and churn, he still had unfinished business.

His eyes were piercing blue, his skin wrinkled in the expected places. What remained of his hair was more salt than pepper. The journey had been choppy, but he remained strong.

Though Jacob lived a good life, it was not the one of his dreams. How could it be that he knew so little after so long? This gnawed at him as the sands of time continued their relentless descent through the hourglass.

He was a man of commitment who worked harder than most his entire life. At school, Jacob had holed himself up studying at the college library day and night. Throughout his career as an engineer with GoldOrb Diversified—a sprawling conglomerate nicknamed G.O.D. by bull market loyalists—Jacob earned a reputation for excellence in his craft but was known for less admirable traits as well. Be that as it may, he navigated the best he could within the jagged boundaries carved by societal forces rather than his heart, leaving him at times satisfied and at other moments anxious, wondering if he had missed something important.

Jacob played by the rules. Sacrifices were routinely made, obligations completely met. Taxes paid when due, to the penny. And time, precious time, evaporated as he donned his helmet and sped further down the road.

In his mid-fifties, Jacob's heart began sending subtle recommendations. He'd feel a light pushing sensation on his chest even though nothing touched him. The cardiologist prescribed the usual rigmarole of tests up to the point covered by insurance. He looked simultaneously bored and harried as he gave the prognosis. "You're a moderate risk. There's some chance, though not likely, that you'll have a cardiac event in the next ten years."

"Not exactly what I wanted to hear, Doc."

"Look, Jacob, time stands still for nobody. Lighten the stress, hit some golf balls. That'll do the trick."

Jacob christened the unwelcome pressure in his chest his "Early Warning System." But the doctor's advice fell on deaf ears. *Medical mumbo jumbo,* he concluded, as he continued to cascade through the American Dream. There was no alternative but to keep accelerating. *I'll slow down later. For now, I've got to get the job done, take care of my family.*

So, Jacob sacrificed for tomorrow, saving up to retire early to an undefined nirvana. "My plan is to get rich slowly," he lectured Lizzy. "Do it the right way without cutting corners. We'll be glad we did."

Lizzy was cheerful, kind, and pretty, with beautiful curly hair. Jacob felt like an ogre in comparison. As usual, he was being too sensitive. His reserved nature and intensity complemented her optimistic, carefree approach.

The couple had twins: Walter and Michelle. Lizzy was a nurturing mother and Jacob a stoic father, doing what needed to be done to ensure their stability and safety.

Despite his unexpressed affection, Jacob loved the twins and Lizzy dearly. But marriage was peculiar. *You learn more about your wife than you ever thought possible to know of any human being,* he reflected in that common spousal anthem. *Yep, you understand more about her than she knows herself.* And yet, Jacob never discovered Lizzy's affair.

When the kids had grown and tomorrow finally arrived, Jacob was emancipated from GoldOrb. But much to his chagrin, he felt scorned by the oracles of the day. He was labelled "privileged" and "complicit," just another well off, old White guy. His accomplishments served as proof that he was the oppressor.

Jacob vented to his neighbor, separated by a wall of flowering azaleas and a political schism. "To say I'm annoyed would be an understatement. I never inherited a dime. All I ever did was work my butt off, pay my damn mortgage, and put the kids through school." He interpreted the pained expression on her face as encouragement and gathered steam in righteous indignation. "I did exactly what I was supposed to do while others sat on their asses grabbing freebies from the government. Now they call our meritocracy a myth and belittle me. Who changed the rules?" Jacob understood that he was embellishing, that the situation was complex, but it felt good to get it off his chest.

He wouldn't make this mistake again. Within days, the community grapevine was abuzz with venom. "Jacob is an ignorant bigot who succeeded on the backs of the poor," gossiped a young social worker who lived around the block. "Thinks he's special, counting his stash while playing the victim card. What an ingrate!"

The rebuke stung and Jacob's Early Warning System wailed. Sure, he was born White. But he didn't come from money and worked to exhaustion for his modest pot of gold. He prided himself in playing by the rules of a system he had no role in creating. *This is a bait and switch,* he stewed.

Jacob complained to Lizzy that labeling him as privileged was unfair, diminishing his sacrifices and accomplishments. And how could he have acted complicitly when he struggled alone? As was his lifetime habit, he then upped the ante. "Why, if there is a God in heaven, would He have allowed this so-called unjust system to continue for so long?" God was always at the forefront of Jacob's consciousness.

Still, in the quietest moments of reflection, he admitted to himself that the neighborhood blowback contained threads of reality. *Perhaps I didn't look around enough, wasn't up to the demands of the task,* he considered. *But who the hell was? Not God, that's for sure.*

There was nothing he could do at this stage in life one way or the other. So, he clammed up, felt misunderstood, also vaguely guilty, and moved forward to cash in on the dream he had strived so hard to attain. Jacob sorely needed to believe that he had rightfully earned his holy grail. His sanity depended on it.

PART I

The Book of Jacob

*"Go confidently
in the direction of your dreams."*

—Henry David Thoreau

CHAPTER 1 – LIZZY

What was the hula girl doing at a frigid baseball game in Ithaca when the Jewish batter got beaned? Sounds like a lame question from a Borscht Belt comedian, right? But this was no laughing matter. It was the moment I first laid eyes on my husband.

I made my way to upstate New York for one simple reason. I needed to flee as far away from Honolulu as I could. I'd do anything to escape being suffocated by my parents' chauvinistic attitudes and puritanical oppression. Even trudge through two feet of snow.

When my Cornell application asked why I wanted to attend, I told the hideous truth: "To get away from paradise. It's my personal hell." That paradox differentiated me as a keeper. To the admissions folks, I was a unicorn. A darned good female student willing to emigrate from the tropics.

I spied my true love from the grandstand in the second inning of the Cornell-Colgate game. My roommate and I were downing peppermint schnapps while doing the human wave with the rest of the fans as he stepped up to bat. The pitcher looked miffed that he was crowding the plate and responded by smacking him in the head with a fastball. Jacob was wobbly, but his coach yelled, "Take first, take first. Shake it off, boy!" Dazed yet determined, Jacob gathered himself and trotted down the line, paying no attention to the smirking pitcher. I'll never forget the resolute look on Jacob's face.

Cornell lost 7–3, but who cares? What's important happened the next morning at the college hospital. The cute guy who'd been beaned checked in with a nasty headache. And me, I inspected student IDs and registered patients for three bucks an hour.

When Jacob handed me his card, I studied the picture and looked up at him. It wasn't love at first sight, but definitely a crush waiting to happen. He was so handsome with those bright blue eyes, a perfect ten. So, I struck up a conversation about the game. "Do you have a dent up there?" Not exactly Romeo and Juliet, but our lifelong tango was launched.

Over the years, Jacob would ask, "Was our rendezvous preordained or random?" He was always wondering about impossible things. Personally, I didn't care. Kismet or chaos, I was grateful for that lump on his noggin.

I won't get into the details of our courtship. Basically, it centered on studying books and bodies. We made love most every day in every way, and my Jacob was both passionate and gentle to the point of ecstasy.

When we weren't fooling around, Jacob studied. He was the consummate problem solver and went by a mantra that I have heard maybe a million times: "For every problem there is an answer, for every issue a solution."

Time and again, over then back. "Problem, answer; issue, solution." "Problem, answer; issue, solution."

If I repeat this again, I swear that I'll puke. Looking back, I should have nipped his crazy attitude in the bud and landed another punch right where the beanball did its damage. But I stayed quiet while Jacob continued his quest, working as hard as anybody in the entire engineering school for his beloved answers, his sacred solutions.

Don't get me wrong. He left time for me too, which was flattering and fun. We dated for three years and decided to elope rather than return to our homes so far apart. My parents were furious but powerless.

We honeymooned at a beautiful lake deep in the Colorado Rockies, staying in a cabin on the shore. The water sparkled like sapphire gemstones and was surrounded by towering mountains with impossible snow-covered peaks. "This is nothing short of paradise," Jacob exclaimed. "I only wish we could spend our lives here." I agreed. This was indeed paradise, unlike my home back in Hawaii.

It's not like I didn't give my parents a shot. We sucked it up for a ten-hour flight so that Jacob could meet them. My mother cornered me in the kitchen and whispered, "I still love you, but you broke my heart. You stuck a knife in it with this Jewish boy." Dad acted all chummy when Jacob was around, but comatose when he left. "This one will use you, so be careful Lizzy. All he cares about is money. He'd murder God again for a lousy buck."

My folks were true believers of the worst order. They were also polished fakers, and Jacob missed the dark vibes. He was blinded by the light of the Hawaiian tropics, calling my home the Paradise Motel, as if we were still in the Rockies. Well, this was a property he needed to vacate. He didn't understand the isolation he would come to feel there if we stayed. And he couldn't comprehend that my family hated him for being Jewish, a religion he harbored so many doubts about. Oh, the irony.

After this disaster, our marriage began in earnest. We started with a cheap studio apartment in Minneapolis with a bed that pulled down from the wall. At least it was near GoldOrb, so I could see a little bit more of my busy husband. After several years, we moved to a three-bedroom home in Plymouth, a nice suburb with good schools. We even had that two-car garage Jacob craved, so nice in the cold. Who needed more? The house was old and required tending to, but my Jacob was handy. Our front yard sparkled as he scored points in his competition with the lawn-mowing gladiators down the block. In the winter, he was the first one out to shovel our driveway and then took care of the widow Goodman's house across the street. Jacob did nice things like that without fanfare.

When the twins were born, we decided to raise them Christian. Despite my crazy parents, this was what I knew. Jacob agreed with a twisted look on his face. "I have serious questions about all religions, Lizzy, about God, faith, everything. I'll follow your lead but need to work this out."

Nothing was ever simple, but I don't regret marrying Jacob. He had so many wonderful qualities, large and small. He was funny, kind, and gentle. The man was a great provider. He loved Walter and Michelle to pieces. And he loved me. I know he did. If I were to sum it all up in one sentence, in a single breath, it would be that Jacob was a man we could count on. In the end, I don't think a girl can ask for more.

Our marriage was mostly a bed of roses, but a few thorns clung stubbornly to the vine. Jacob had a problem. The man was a major-league obsessive, and his fixations caused trouble.

And there's something else. I wish I'd found out sooner. But he had to be fine, right? After all, he worked so hard and accomplished so much.

CHAPTER II - JACOB

Jacob never left work early, but today was special. For months he had been searching for a technique to shrink GoldOrb sensors. Finally, he had a breakthrough. *For every problem, there is an answer,* he thought with pride. *Just reconfigure the wiring, that's all.*

His boss was thrilled. Costs would sink while customer appreciation would soar, a clear "win, win" in corporate lingo. Jacob's idea could be applied to an army of GoldOrb products for exponential gains.

"Take the afternoon off," the boss said, patting his ace engineer on the back. "Celebrate! That's an order."

Jacob hesitated, uncomfortable deviating from his routine. But after further prodding, he took the boss up on his offer.

Jacob's enthusiasm grew during his drive home. He was excited to see Lizzy and play with the twins in the middle of the workday. But when he arrived, the house was empty. Lizzy had told him over breakfast that she was taking the kids to the dentist. Still half asleep and expecting to be gone anyway, her plans registered as white noise.

It was rare for him to be alone in the house. He perused a National Geographic with little patience, then roamed about searching for something to do. Eventually, he grabbed a family-sized bag of Fritos and headed to the couch for television.

Hippocratic Happenings caught Jacob's attention. A sexy nurse bursting out of her too-tight, white uniform offered to bathe a handsome burn patient. He was unscarred and appeared extraordinarily healthy. Jacob felt like a voyeur with binoculars trained on a neighbor's bedroom window as he watched the popular soap opera. *How can networks air this trash*, he righteously wondered, transfixed by the flirtation.

He removed his socks and mindlessly munched and crunched to

the point of indigestion. Scooching to the middle cushion, he swung his legs onto the couch, resting his head on a soft pillow at the opposite end, fully supine, balancing the half-empty bag of chips on his stomach.

As the nurse suggestively closed the white laced curtain surrounding her patient's bed, Jacob sighed, lost focus, and dangled his arm from the couch to the floor. He touched something below that flinched. It felt like another hand. Trancelike, Jacob wondered if it belonged to his deceased grandfather, guiding him like he was a small boy crossing the street.

Jacob clasped the hand only to discover that it was impossibly cold and calloused. *This has nothing at all to do with grandpa.* He tried to free himself, but the hand squeezed tighter. Jacob trembled as the room temperature sank. He felt like he was in a freezer.

The soap opera broke to a whimsical commercial enticing Jacob to increase his carbonated intake. While a jingle about living life to the fullest filled his ears, the hand imposed a death grip and began to pull Jacob to the floor. His arm was nearly yanked from its socket. The bag of Fritos spilled.

Jacob was slipping fast. He made a last-ditch effort to pull free, but the adversary beneath him was unusually powerful and twisted his arm beyond the breaking point. A snapping sound echoed in Jacob's brain. "God help me," he cried in agony. It was a secular exclamation, not a prayer.

On the verge of defeat, Jacob felt two new sensations. One jumped on his chest further scattering the chips, another plopped below his knees. Both were soft, warm, and wiggly.

Jacob opened his eyes and saw Michelle hovering over his face with a huge grin, eyes full of mischief. "Wake up, Daddy," she sang. "Get up, sleepy head, or you'll soon be dead." She playfully pinched her father's cheeks.

Walter scratched Jacob's bare feet. "Tickle, tickle, smelly, smelly." In a louder voice, he announced, "Michelle had two cavities, and I had none. Ha, ha, Michelle can never eat candy again. NE-VER!"

"Stop teasing me," Michelle cried as she nestled into Jacob's neck.

Lizzy walked in and smiled. "I'm glad you're home early," she said. "But why are you drenched in sweat?"

CHAPTER III – THE BOSS

My name is John Shepard, and I was Jacob's manager for most of his career at GoldOrb Diversified. To sum up his time here with G.O.D. in a single word, it was... well... complicated.

Lizzy insists he was different at home, but at the office the guy was more indestructible robot than human being. His intensity and schtick rubbed some people the wrong way. But let's start with the good stuff.

Day after day, year after year, and decade after decade, Jacob showed up on time in his khakis, a plaid buttoned-down shirt, and a Timex wrapped around his wrist as if to proclaim, "I'm still ticking despite the licking." There was no flash to the man, no bellowing for recognition like so many of the Broadway wannabes on my staff. Instead, he dug in and took care of business with laser focus solving our toughest problems. He was an outstanding engineer.

He rocked on nonstop for thirty-eight years, never calling in sick, always meeting deadlines, and the caliber of his work was stellar. So, what's not to like? It turns out, plenty.

Jacob created morale problems for my team and migraines for me. He told new employees that he'd never made a mistake. Worse yet, when coworkers approached him for help, frustrated with a thorny project, Jacob would pipe up with his canned response: "For every problem, there is an answer, for every issue a solution." Thanks a lot for that helpful input, Mr. Roboto.

The team called Jacob "Crazy AI" behind his back, giving him the initials of the flamboyant basketball star, Allen Iverson, nicknamed The Answer for his prolific scoring. The joke was that Jacob, with his exasperating motto, was the answer here at GoldOrb. It was also a shot at him for being more like artificial intelligence than flesh and blood. I laughed when I first heard the nickname since there was a ring of truth to it. Jacob resembled a machine. A *very* productive one.

No, he would never win a popularity contest at GoldOrb. People were jealous of his talent. He was the superior engineer. But he rubbed it in with his abrupt style, showing no sensitivity for peers with less ability. He didn't mean it, but that's how he came off.

It's on me that I never gave Jacob honest feedback about his poor impact on morale. When it was time for reviews, I praised his achievements and avoided the hard conversation about office decorum. I even awarded him a special bonus for his ingenious solution that eliminated fire risks from heating coils.

The CEO would not have been pleased. "Tell it to 'em straight," he urged us managers. "That's how they improve. And if they don't up their games, get rid of them." Easier said from his fancy headquarters suite, though, than implemented on the ground floor where the action happens. My approach was to bury problems and inch another day closer to retirement with as little friction as possible.

Jacob was great at his job but too intense and obsessive. Blind to the feelings of others. The same traits that caused his people problems also made him an extraordinary performer. On balance, that's what mattered most for GoldOrb's profits. So, I left him alone and ignored the snickering behind his back by his candy-assed teammates.

Think of it like your cleanup hitter in baseball. The guy acts like a prima donna. But he knocks in runs all day long. Sure, you'd prefer that he play nice and coddle the scrawny utility infielder. Be that as it may, you still love hearing the crack of his bat and watching the ball skyrocket out of the park.

CHAPTER IV – JACOB

Traffic to the Pavilion crawled. Jacob and Lizzy were in Memphis visiting friends, the first time he had been able to escape GoldOrb in two years. On the last night of their vacation, the friends offered to babysit so Jacob and Lizzy could see Travis Upton. Tickets were expensive, but Jacob jumped at the chance.

The parking lot smelled like a backyard barbecue from hordes of tailgaters with fired-up Smokey Joes near their pickup trucks. As Jacob and Lizzy emerged through the smoke, they intersected with a long row of merchandise booths. A vender held up an extra-large black hoodie inscribed in gold with the message, "I Saw the Prophet." He wore a visor with "Travis Tells" emblazoned on the brim. "Half off your second purchase!" he shouted.

People roamed in all directions. They held signs proclaiming God's glory and predicting the coming of the Messiah. "Abortion is murder!" screamed a woman through a cone-shaped megaphone while raising a Bible. "It says so right here."

A man with an oversized Tennessee Titans hat pulled over his eyebrows approached. "Need a ticket, man?" When Jacob ignored him, he pivoted, "How much for yours?" Jacob politely declined and gave Lizzy an ironic smile. "Americana in all its glory," he said. "We enter through Gate C right over there."

They found their assigned seats in the balcony, but the famous preacher was ninety minutes late. In the meantime, one side of the crowd occupied itself by chanting, "T-T-T Travis." The other responded, "P-P-P Prophet." A guy on Jacob's left who was wearing one of the extra-large hoodies rose and shouted, "Now, now, NOW!" Jacob put his arm around Lizzy and shrugged.

Finally, it went dark. A loud drumbeat sounded, and laser beams crisscrossed the arena. Expecting Travis to appear, Jacob was surprised when the White Angels took the stage, fresh off their performance at the Grand Ole Opry the night before. Their cowboy hats and stomping boots were covered with matching rhinestones that glittered from the spotlights. "Here we go," yelled the drummer. "On your feet!"

Jacob's heart pounded with the vibrations as the band performed its latest Christian rock hit to a standing ovation. When the song ended, the chanting resumed:

"T-T-T Travis."

"P-P-P Prophet."

"Now, now, NOW!" screamed the man in the hoodie.

A few minutes later, the people got their wish. A spotlight located Travis Upton walking briskly down the center aisle, clapping his hands with his arms extended over his head. He leapt on stage and took a long sweeping bow. Despite the distance, Jacob could see the preacher's shining eyes and exuberant smile.

"Welcome, y'all!" he shouted. He thanked the White Angels and announced, "We're in for a special treat tonight. The brothers and sisters came to help out." On cue, five people skipped onto the stage wearing hip blue outfits, chic gold earrings in the shape of crosses, and the latest technology to amplify their voices. *They look like they're from Motown of the South,* thought Jacob.

Travis hugged each brother and sister like they were at a reunion and hadn't seen each other in years. He then gazed back at the crowd and shouted, "Say amen, friends."

"AMEN!"

"Oh, that sounds mighty good," said Travis.

"Say it again for us now," sang the brothers and sisters in perfect harmony, extending their arms in unison toward the crowd.

"AMEN!"

"Do you believe?" asked Travis.

"AMEN!"

"Do you submit to the Lord?"

"AMEN!"

"Are we created in His image?"

"AMEN!"

"Do we walk side-by-side with Jesus and not down Satan's sinful path?"

"AMEN!"

"Pray with us now, pray hard!"

"HALLELUJAH!"

Travis led a long prayer fest in a soulful voice requesting that the Almighty bestow all forms of favor upon each attendee. He skillfully interspersed his invocations with heartfelt stories from his past containing important lessons. He then yielded to the White Angels to perform another hit song. The pattern repeated as each brother and sister recited a prayer, supported by fervent Christian rock.

Jacob was mesmerized. He watched in fascination as the audience jubilantly extended their arms to the rafters of the Pavilion during worship. And he was dumbfounded by how many people had tears in their eyes, waving handkerchiefs while the band played. When a prayer was recited, Jacob sat rigidly at the edge of his seat, listening carefully to the words, struggling to make sense of them from his own experiences in the world he thought he inhabited.

Lizzy nudged him. "What's going on with you?"

It was as if she woke him up, and his eyes cleared. "This Travis is slick," he said. "Is he real like these folks need him to be?"

"Let's talk later."

Travis announced, "It's time for healing. God will rid you of your suffering if you believe." A man in a wheelchair was lovingly pushed onto the stage by a smiling brother. Travis hugged and kissed him, another reunion. He handed the disabled man a microphone and interviewed him. The audience learned of poor Billy's impoverished upbringing and near fatal motorcycle accident in the Smoky Mountains.

"I'm paralyzed for life," he said.

"Not your soul," responded the preacher. "We'll make sure of that, Billy."

Each sister cried out a prayer of healing, and the crowd responded, "AMEN!" The White Angels appeared, and Travis implored the audience, "Pray for our friend here like there's no tomorrow. Take away Billy's pain." The guy in the hoodie on Jacob's left jumped to his feet and screamed, "Now, now, NOW!"

Jacob cynically expected the paralyzed man to rise from his wheelchair, but his infirmity persisted. Travis was undaunted. "Your spirit shall soar on eagles' wings," he proclaimed. Billy looked unsure of himself but then nodded as if he had a revelation, raised his head and wiped tears from his eyes. He stared at the microphone and began to sing, first in a hushed tone, then gradually louder, until he finally unleashed a powerful, baritone voice worthy of The Royal Opera House of London. Midway through, the White Angels joined, and the song took on a rock and roll flavor. "I believe," he sang out to the heavens. "Lord, how I believe."

"Well, your faith has been rewarded, my friend," proclaimed Travis. "From now on, you'll be touring with us." Travis handed Billy a check. "The amount is blank. Just fill in whatever you think you need." Billy looked as if he was in ecstasy.

"Feel the love," said Travis in a wondrous voice.

"My soul is saved for Jesus," Billy cried.

Travis got down on his knees and bowed giving thanks, then gazed at the audience with kindness and sincerity. "You shall be saved too," he promised. "Submit to the Lord and your soaring spirit will vanquish your pain, turn it to glory."

"AMEN!"

"AMEN!"

"Now, now, NOW!"

Travis gave a signal, and another smiling brother pushed Billy backstage. He told the audience, "Let us join together in a moment of pure silence. Contemplate what you've experienced tonight, be grateful, submit to God."

At just the right instant, he broke the quiet. "I don't know friends, but The White Angels might have one more song up their sleeves. Do y'all want to hear it if they're willing?"

The crowd gave a thunderous ovation. As the band belted out its finale, Travis joined the lead guitarist to share a microphone and sing along. The brothers and sisters reappeared with the man in the wheelchair. Billy's baritone voice blended in perfectly. During the final few verses, the back curtain rose, revealing a children's choir dressed in maroon robes and white caps and gloves. The youths harmonized flawlessly while swaying and clapping. Travis broke into a joyful dance and the crowd went berserk.

With the final drumbeat, the preacher again dropped to his knees in gratitude. Brothers waved in all directions, while sisters hugged Billy and threw kisses to the crowd. The children in the choir spun around in merry circles. "I'll be back," Travis announced. "Travis tells, tells y'all right now, God loves you!"

"AMEN!"

Jacob checked his Timex just as confetti was released from the rafters. Travis had been on stage for exactly ninety minutes, the same length as the delay. He took Lizzy's hand, and they wound their way through the departing crowd. At the exit, they were blocked by a man with strong smelling cologne wearing a suit and tie. He handed them a small Bible and made sure that they saw his collection plate. "It's for wheelchair Billy," he said. "Give what you can." He pointed to a group of trailers parked outside the stadium. "In case you want to convert, head there. They've got tissues, sandwiches, and someone to help."

Making their way outside, Jacob and Lizzy were stopped again by a logjam of humanity funneling into the street next to the parking lot. A white stretch limousine was inching its way through the pedestrians, horn blaring. A young boy on Jacob's left lost hold of his mother's hand and was nearly trampled by the sea of movement. His panicking mother lurched forward and grabbed him by the collar, just as the limo's side mirror cracked her elbow. As she screamed in pain, Jacob caught a glimpse of Travis Upton in the back seat of the moving sedan, staring straight ahead and holding a champagne flute.

Traffic was gridlocked for miles surrounding the stadium. "What a spectacle!" Lizzy exclaimed. "A people watcher's paradise."

Jacob remained stone silent. The back of his neck was red, and his eyes twitched.

CHAPTER V – LIZZY

What else can I tell you about my love? Well, there was a fun side to Jacob's intensity. You just had to learn to appreciate it.

Take, for instance, his fantasy football fixation. Jacob felt compelled to install a satellite dish crookedly on our roof so that he could watch every game. You'd think he was on the gridiron playing middle linebacker by how riled up he got. What was not a fantasy, but all too real, was the leak in our attic from where the dish was installed.

Next came his birding phase. After months of study, Jacob spent a fortune on the best binoculars and feeders. He ended up attracting squadrons of squirrels and mice instead of anything that chirped and flew. The varmints found their way into our leaking attic and made it their new home.

Jacob then locked in on beer making for one sudsy spring season. His brownish-green concoction tasted like acidic root beer and caused unrelenting headaches. "I guess we're in AA now," he joked. "Alcohol and Aspirin." The pungent brew wasn't worth the painful side effects, so I confiscated his equipment and he moved on.

Once these bursts of activity ended, Jacob completely lost interest and never gave the hobby another thought. Now you see it, now you don't, except for the persistent squirrels, mice, and dripping water from our damaged roof.

"You shift from fixation to fixation," I teased. "Always forgetting about anything but your latest obsession du jour."

"You're my obsession forever," he responded with a laugh. Such a Don Juan romantic.

I only wish that all his obsessions were comical. Jacob was plagued by more serious fixations that affected his life, our lives. And I believe they had their roots in his being an absolute perfectionist, unwilling to stop until he could solve any problem no matter the time or personal cost. His motto, "For every problem there is an answer," blah, blah, blah, sadly caused more issues than solutions.

Jacob's biggest hang-ups were about religion and God. He wasn't a devout man, not in the least, but he was obsessed with discovering the meaning of life, thinking he could solve the mysteries of the cosmos just like he decoded engineering puzzles at work.

And to Jacob, you could not comprehend life without also understanding death. "After all," he reasoned, "Death is the one sure event that happens to everyone. Death is part of life. They're inseparable." My husband, the mortician.

Well, after the Travis Upton extravaganza in Memphis, everything escalated. It was always there, deep inside of Jacob. But now his obsession poured out, enough to fill an ocean, drowning me. It always began with a twisted face. "Lizzy, why in the world do people pray so much when they're in trouble? If they think God will rescue them, doesn't that mean *He* caused the predicament to begin with? Why was Billy in a wheelchair if God didn't will it?"

I didn't know, nor did I care. But my husband devoted countless hours to these questions, feeding the fire. He read the religious scriptures beginning with Judaism, next Christianity, and then Islam. He gobbled up all forms of commentary. Nothing satisfied him. "The inconsistencies, irrationality preached to the masses make no sense to me, none," he'd complain. "How can so much of our world's edifice be built on flimsy reeds, ancient myths?"

"I'm not sure Jacob."

"The liturgy describes endless miracles from an active God high in the sky doling out justice. Is that what's happening in real life, Lizzy? Is it?"

Before I could say a word, try to change the subject, his voice would rise in moral outrage. "What about the Holocaust? Eleven million murders in concentration camps. Six million for being Jewish. Why? Why? Why?! Countless wars and massacres, all in the name of religion, inflamed by preachers with damnation on their minds. There may be wisdom in the folktales, but there's a dark side."

"Calm down, Jacob. Let it go."

But he'd just keep pressing. "If God is praised for the good, why isn't he blamed for the atrocities? If he freed slaves from Egypt, who enslaved them to begin with?"

It was as if each question caused physical pain. For both of us.

Eventually, Jacob would take a breath, giving me a chance to lower the temperature. "Pharaoh did it, he's responsible for capturing the slaves," I said. "Lighten up and be thankful. Isn't expressing gratitude for your freedom the real point?"

But Jacob wore a stubborn expression, and his eyes twitched. "Did God really *choose* a tiny tribe in the desert for unending persecution?" Sad stare. "Should children be clad in explosives in the name of Allah?" Long head shake. "What about earthquakes or hurricanes striking down thousands of innocents?" Voice rising. "Where is God, Lizzy? I can't find Him! So, exactly who should I be grateful to?" Red face.

By this point, I'd be spent. I think what bothered my husband the most was that other people could still embrace religion and their Lord without agonizing over the contradictions. "I wish I could be like them," he'd say time and again. "Life would be so much easier to just go along and not think so much."

But, of course, he could never follow the pack, not my Jacob. Don't get me wrong; he raised legitimate points. He was sincerely seeking truth without an agenda, like an innocent child who repeatedly asks his mother the same question over and over, believing sheer repetition would yield the answer. And I loved him for that. But oh, how excruciating it was. What was the point of obsessing over the unknowable? Others feel doubts too but get on with their lives, adopting those parts of religion which help or rejecting it altogether. Whatever, dammit, just whatever.

But it got worse. Jacob decided he wanted to go to a monastery in Michigan for two solid weeks, depleting his rare vacation time, our precious family time. "I won't utter a single word, making space for uninterrupted contemplation," he said with childish hope in his eyes. "And I'll be assigned a spiritual leader to guide me on my journey."

I was furious. "Why don't you just go on a pilgrimage with Travis

Upton, you idiot. You're wasting time and money. And who's supposed to take care of the kids all day and do every crappy chore while you're gone?"

But after venting, I saw the deer-in-headlights look on his face and felt his probing sincerity. My fixated husband couldn't come to grips with anything unless he saw it all the way through to his all-consuming answer and solution. And Lord, how I wanted him to figure it out already. I was sick and tired of the routine. Despite my anger, I also felt sorry for him, and a little guilty. Maybe he could solve his elusive quest in solitude with a stranger wearing a robe. "Go retreat to Neverland with the monks," I relented. "Get it out of your system once and for all. I don't want to spend another minute talking about any of this." This was the biggest mistake of our marriage, hands down.

When Jacob returned, he spoke nothing about an epiphany and pledged to never burden me with his obsession again. "I refuse to let the meaning of life impede our lives, Lizzy," he vowed. "I'm over it."

I mockingly replied, "Thank God, praise the Lord, AMEN!" But I also suspected that Jacob's fixation lingered. Jacob had not discovered *the answer, the solution.* I hoped that once, just a single time, he'd let it go.

Jacob's obsessions were squeezing me out and suffocating me simultaneously. He didn't mean it, but between religion, and his other preoccupation, make that GoldOrb, I felt marginalized. There was a cost to his work ethic and high marks on the job. Marital tension. I felt ignored while he searched for his beloved answers and solutions at GoldOrb. I was nothing but a second fiddle headed toward middle age.

I tried to reason with him. "Let's enjoy your success, buy a bigger house, see the world. Get that fancy car that the neighbor drives."

But Jacob was adamant that we save our money and retire early. He assured me, "We'll have a good time then, Lizzy."

In the meantime, I did the dirty work. I cleaned the house, washed the laundry, and brought in a little extra cash with a boring part-time office job. I saw myself as a low priority, far below what mattered most to Jacob. Truth is, I was wrong. He unconditionally loved me. But that's how I saw things during the hard times.

Don't misunderstand. I loved Jacob, despite his flaws. He was a fine husband, a good man that I could rely on, and I would marry him again in a nanosecond if we were to transport back in time. But without his fixations, his need to tackle the impossible, our lives would have been better. And I wouldn't have met somebody else.

I met Jimmy at my yoga class when Jacob was away at the monastery. He was a nice guy coming off a divorce, athletic, and handsome. After class, we went for coffee. Another classmate said she'd join us but never showed up. Jimmy looked needy and fidgeted endlessly before getting to the point. "Why don't we do some hot yoga at my place?"

I hesitated, deluding myself that this was innocent. "Sure, I wouldn't mind a little more exercise," I said.

At Jimmy's apartment, I took off my sweater to get started, but he surprised me, stripping the rest of my clothes off before I could blink. I readily succumbed. We practiced yoga moves and so much more. I needed a break from Jacob, his ruminations and intensity. I wanted to feel appreciated and craved pleasure here and now. The affair lasted several weeks until I broke it off.

I never confessed to Jacob. Why risk our marriage when I still loved the man? What good would it have done to hurt the twins? This was the toll for Jacob's inability to let things go, his penalty for seeking so hard that he lost something important in the process. I was weak and deserved blame. But after Jimmy, I was completely faithful.

Time passed and our lives calmed. Jacob toned down his obsession with God, religion, and death—at least with me. We focused on sharing the normal activities of a good life. Restaurants, strolls, movies, and an ongoing Scrabble game. He was sweet and considerate, my best friend, my true love. Jacob would take a bullet for me and I for him. My transgressions with Jimmy faded from memory, dwarfed by the good times with my family.

We celebrated our thirty-fifth anniversary on Cape Cod in perhaps the most wonderful week of our marriage. The weather was glorious, the beaches pristine, our relationship solid as a rock. This was testament to all we had done right, which far outweighed the warts. We were still in love, still having fun. Jacob was still my hero.

Why couldn't this go on forever? Why did I have to get sick?

CHAPTER VI - THE BOSS

Near the end of Jacob's career, GoldOrb's head honchos began a campaign to lay off expensive talent. I was summoned to headquarters to meet with the vice president of human resources. We sat in a swank conference room while she eagerly marched to the corporate beat over a cup of steaming latte. Staring at a printout listing the names of my staff and their salaries, she said, "This Jacob fella has been here forever, and with all those raises you doled out, his wages are out of line. I seriously doubt he's worth it." She asked her assistant to fetch her a refill, enjoying her opportunity to play chess with the lives of people she had never met. "The CEO wants them gone," she exclaimed. "We need to cut payroll, meet Wall Street projections."

Well, I knew a little secret. Jacob cost GoldOrb even more than she thought. A long time ago, a pal from the benefits team confided that Jacob was on some sort of expensive drug. "It's for mental health," he said. "But this is off the record. HIPAA, privacy rules, you know."

I couldn't have cared less. HIPAA was nothing but a funny word. What mattered was that GoldOrb's medical budget absorbed the cost, not my department. If my cleanup hitter needed a few steroids to keep bashing homers, that was fine by me.

So, I resisted the queen grandmaster, promising to halve my department's travel costs instead. In my mind, laying Jacob off would be age discrimination, plain and simple, not to mention complete disloyalty to a long-service employee. I was also sympathetic to his plight. It would be impossible for him to land a good job anywhere else at this late stage of his career. He was no longer a man of privilege in the business world except here at GoldOrb. For any other company, he'd be a persona non grata, begrudgingly hired despite his age as a consultant at a fraction of his pay.

Oh, who am I kidding? I mostly resisted to avoid discomfort. I was a coward, hoping to ease my way to my own retirement with as little tension from my staff as possible. Fester was my middle name.

I had almost forgotten my meeting with the VP when the news hit. It started with a rumor that the company had polluted the Chicago River. Sadly, one of our old factories near the shore did everything by the book. We awoke generations later to discover that the rules and science had changed and that we might have been emitting toxic chemicals. Our stock price tanked.

Then another story broke. GoldOrb, known for its upstanding corporate citizenship, was accused of an accounting irregularity that I don't begin to understand. Somehow, our numbers guys concocted a way to inflate the income from our services to increase profits for Wall Street, while deflating the same stuff to lower taxes. The headlines read, "GoldOrb Cooked the Books." The company fired its treasurer even though he wasn't directly involved, hoping to satisfy regulators lusting for blood. The shares plummeted some more.

The mood in the office was in the toilet, and guys like Jacob were easy prey for the bean counters, fueled by the CEO's rampage to cut costs. I could barely hold out and even feared for my own cushy job if I didn't find a way to reduce my staff.

Amid this turmoil, Jacob walked into my office, looking exasperated. "Listen, John, I'm wondering if I should be embarrassed working here nowadays. Decades of dedication leave me associated with GoldOrb scandals."

"Go on," I encouraged, wondering if he was giving me an opening.

"I've been thinking about my life lately and, you know, Boss, GoldOrb has been a huge part of it. Am I a good man if my company is bad?" His voice took on a pleading tone. "Did I do the right thing working here all these years?"

I too fretted about GoldOrb—make that my job. But I had not connected the company's reputation to my personal legacy. And I certainly didn't feel implicated by *G.O.D.'s* flaws like Jacob did. "You shouldn't take this so personally," I said. My lame feedback obviously fell on deaf ears.

Conversation mercifully shifted to our long tenure together, and we reminisced over the early days. I reminded Jacob, "The company flew straight as an arrow. We were invincible back then." Jacob nodded but still appeared upset and looked like he had more to say.

Finally, I got it out there. "Can I be blunt? Are you looking to retire, Jacob?"

He flinched. "Well, I … err … I just … I just might."

Jacob looked flustered as he studied me for a reaction, I shuffled meaningless papers that had decorated my desk forever, calculating how pleased our top brass would be to rid the company of his salary. I was willing to protect Jacob's job. But, if he wanted out, I certainly wasn't going to stand in his way.

"Listen, Jacob, I'll be straight with you," I uttered in a sympathetic voice. "I'd consider leaving too, but haven't saved enough, and my kids are younger, still in college. GoldOrb might be in a nosedive, and maybe it's humiliating, just like you say. You need to do what's best for you. I'll understand."

I held my breath and eyeballed him for a reaction. "Should we fill out the paperwork?"

Jacob looked at me sideways, and his eyes twitched. "I'll get back to you tomorrow with a decision," he said. "Once I run it by Lizzy." I think he was disappointed, expecting that I would try to assure him that GoldOrb was fine and convince him to stay.

As promised, he reappeared in my office the next morning. He still looked shaken, but his message was succinct. "I spoke to Lizzy. I'm out of here."

It was awkward. I thanked our best engineer for his service but neither of us exchanged the pleasantries you'd expect. I guess we both felt steamrolled by events beyond our control. Ah, life with *G.O.D.*

When I announced to the team that Jacob was retiring, a few fakes fussed that they'd miss him. Mostly, there was an atmosphere of relief. I overhead one of my younger underachievers say, "AI is leaving. Hip, hip. Time to loosen up around here."

Twelve unenthusiastic souls attended Jacob's retirement lunch at a run-down grill a few blocks from the office. Jacob ordered his steak, medium rare, but it was served well done. During toasts, his colleagues repeated one after the next that he was our best engineer, a technical guru. But I cringed at their lukewarm tone and apathetic body language.

I then rose to speak, thanking Jacob for his tireless devotion in seeking "the answers, the solutions." People laughed. I called him "my right-hand man" and meant it. I closed, looking directly into Jacob's eyes with all the appreciation and friendship I could summon. "Come back anytime, Jacob. Stay in touch, don't be a stranger." And with that generic invitation, his longtime service had ended.

That night, for one of the few times I can recall, I couldn't sleep. My conscience was in overdrive. I knew I was a rare survivor in corporate America. I had an uncanny knack for reading the tea leaves. For finessing my way to survival in the nick of time, depending on the course set by the CEO, the whims of customers and world events outside anyone's control. I always sought the easiest path. I envied Jacob for his unswerving and blunt dedication to excellence without a political bone in his body. I would miss my cleanup hitter. GoldOrb Diversified had taken another blow.

CHAPTER VII - JACOB

After his tepid sendoff from GoldOrb, Jacob tried to settle into the retirement phase of his American Dream. He and Lizzy would make up for lost time. "Let's go places while we're still young," he gushed. "Rome, Sydney, Anchorage, and, of course, Jerusalem. I must see the cradle of religion."

But like so much else in Jacob's life, it ended up being a dream. Lizzy became nauseous and started losing weight several months after he retired. She was in no condition to travel. Her tests revealed their worst fear: cancer. The doctors believed they could control the spread, but Jacob worried, witnessing how she suffered.

Lizzy was pulverized by her well-intentioned medical team, first with lethal chemicals and then ineffective surgery excising body parts. Jacob supported her every step of the way. He hated being a caregiver but did so dutifully and with love, receiving the scars and rewards that only a caregiver can understand.

After a year of torture, Lizzy was spent. Taking hold of Jacob's hand from the hospital bed, her few remaining curls resting on the pillow, she looked like an angel. "I love you, Jacob, but I can't stay. Please understand." With tears in her eyes, she issued her final instructions: "Meet someone to be happy with. Live your life and guide the twins when they need you. Then come find me when your time comes. I'll be waiting."

Jacob held her but couldn't speak. He knew that her body and spirit were broken. Finally, he whispered, "I understand, my love." Two days later, Lizzy died.

Jacob sunk into a stoic tailspin, silently berating himself for delaying what mattered in life until it was too late. His obsession over the meaning of life, of death, boiled to the surface. He wanted to know where his love had gone and what awaited him.

His grief also took tangible forms. He kept a vigil for his wife by continuing to set each night's dinner table for two. Of course, now there was an empty plate next to his own. Jacob understood that this was not a recipe for a lifted spirit, but it seemed right. As usual, he could not let go.

With this constant reminder of Lizzy, he seldom tasted his food. Sometimes, he sat paralyzed, deep in thought over questions grieving spouses ask:

Why did Lizzy leave me?

Could I have treated her better?

What should I do with the rest of my life all alone?

And, of course, Jacob sought answers from the universe:

Did God intend to punish me?

But why through her?

Jacob's Early Warning System sounded its alarm during these moments of harsh reflection. That soft pressure on his chest, invisible, pushing, reminded him he would be next soon enough.

After dinner for one at this lonely table for two, Jacob would retreat to the living room, sit in his battered recliner, and watch the news. Broadcasters could barely contain their exuberance as they reported the latest wildfires, hurricanes, and mass shootings. Flippant tweets from the White House at two in the morning were dissected as if they deserved frantic analysis.

Nothing remained that Jacob had confidence in. Not the government, not the business world, and certainly not religious institutions vying for power while concealing sex scandals. *Lizzy is dead, and the world is off its rocker.*

Sometimes, the news reports caused Jacob to speak out loud, shaking his head in frustration. "Cultural wreckage, a societal wasteland, wrecked, wasted." He sensed deep in his bones that society was nearing the brink of disintegration unless the depravity could be reversed. "What happened to old-fashioned values?" he whispered. "Maybe I'm overrating the good old days, but I don't think so." He knew he sounded like a crotchety old man, but his anxiety grew as he fretted about how the twins would cope in a shattered community. And he worried about himself, knowing it was crazy to be spouting off to an empty room.

While most friends through marriage deserted him, Jacob was not completely alone, nor was he the type of person who needed barrels of companionship. He had a few buddies that he met for pizza or went to a ballgame with. And, of course, there was the professor, his dear friend for over half a century, whom he spoke with regularly. Where would he be without the professor's Chicago real estate tips? *A lot poorer and still working*, thought Jacob.

Jacob also received loads of love from his dog, Hunter. Lizzy had shocked him when she brought the golden retriever home as a gift on the first day of his retirement. "He was so cute and cuddled right up to me at the shelter," she said. "He handed me his squeaky toy like he knew me."

"You've lost your marbles," Jacob scolded. "What do we need a pet for now, at this stage in life? We're going to travel the globe, not walk down the block to pick up turds."

But his smile at the wagging tail and the exuberant tone in his voice told Lizzy everything she needed to know. "We can do it all, Jacob. There are professional dog walkers to step in while we're away."

"I guess everyone's a professional nowadays."

Lizzy ignored the sarcasm and paused, deep in thought. And then, in a cryptic line Jacob would rehash a thousand times, she said, "Hunter will keep you company when I'm gone." At the time, he assumed she meant Hunter would be there for him when she was out shopping or having lunch with friends. But now he wasn't so sure. *What did she know? How long was she feeling sick?*

What Jacob soon embraced as a verifiable fact was that his wife gave him the perfect retirement gift. Hunter would lie under Jacob's dinner table for two, nibbling on leftovers and spills. The inseparable pair would then move to the living room where Hunter would sit contently next to the recliner while Jacob cringed at the cultural wreckage unfolding on television. The loyal canine made them an automatic twosome, providing comfort and friendship.

In a rare moment of impatience while Lizzy was still alive, Jacob yelled at Hunter for digging up a chunk of the lawn. "Go easy," Lizzy said. "Dogs have emotions just like people." Though Jacob had scoffed at her in the heat of the moment, he came around to the view that this beautiful creature inhabiting space in his home loved him with all his retriever heart and soul. And Jacob felt the same.

Jacob also kept in touch with the twins. He knew he could count on Walter and Michelle, but also understood the reality that they were grown up and busy, busy as hell. *They have their own lives now,* he reminded himself. *I don't want to be excess baggage.*

He worried about Walter, sensing that his son's marriage was on the brink of failure. And he fretted that Walter's career was like a treadmill to nowhere. The rich opportunities that Jacob had taken for granted during his career with GoldOrb had mostly disappeared. Instead, good jobs were now jettisoned half-way around the world where labor was cheap or eviscerated by technological breakthroughs. Jacob recalled his neighborhood rebuke. He speculated that perhaps he *was* privileged in a certain sort of way, that maybe he patted himself on the back too much for his achievements. *I was lucky. But it seemed so hard at the time.*

Michelle was doing better than her brother. She had a good job and someone who loved her—her partner, Gracie. As hard as he tried, Jacob still struggled with his daughter being a lesbian. He remembered the insults hurled at "queers" in his youth. As times changed, he too became accepting, but could not fully deprogram his ingrained bias when he saw his daughter hold hands with another woman. His attempts to fight the discomfort were all too obvious.

On the first anniversary of Lizzy's death, when Jacob felt particularly isolated, he phoned the twins, hoping they could stop by for a visit. Michelle returned his call the next day. She was on a Caribbean vacation with Gracie. "It happened last minute, Dad, but I'll call as soon as we get back to the States to set something up." Jacob winced, thinking of the two lovers strolling the beach hand in hand. *You out of touch old fool,* he scolded himself. *Stop it.*

Walter, however, answered the phone on the first ring. "The kids' allergies are acting up," he said in a beleaguered voice. "Nothing serious, but I'm bouncing between pediatricians and drugstores while wiping noses. Juggling overtime at work too." He hesitated and cleared his throat. "Maybe next month will be better, Dad. Yeah. That should work." No date was offered.

Jacob assured Walter that he understood, hung up the phone, and stared into soul sucking space, feeling regret over the stark role reversal. After the many years when it was Jacob who had been overly burdened, it was now his son's turn. He nursed a few beers until his mood improved to melancholy. *This is natural, all I deserve,* he thought as he stroked Hunter behind the ears. *We still love each other.*

No longer stressed out from his own job, Jacob decided to stop taking the colorful pills. He had been on medication since the twins' tenth birthday at Lizzy's insistence, but she was no longer there to object. *No more job, no more tension, no more dreaming,* he reasoned. *For Pete's sake, I'm old now and those crappy pills are expensive and don't do anything but add extra pounds.*

He made other changes too. Jacob met a few new people and tried some different things outside his comfort zone. He even sampled a shady massage parlor on a long weekend with the professor in Manhattan at his friend's urging. He could not get comfortable and barely escaped with his dignity.

And then there was that awkward fix-up with the widow Goodman's niece. Jacob's dinner date spoke over him the entire night, emphasizing her points with a hyperactive index finger and conspiratorial winks. When the server approached the table with the bill, she disappeared to freshen up. Once Jacob paid, she returned to render her candid feedback with an exaggerated shrug. "Jacob, you're nice, but I like to slip while you like to slide."

What did that even mean? Jacob had no idea, but it hurt his feelings as he struggled on, following a routine that seemed to slip and slide to nowhere in particular. *Another day, same old song. Play it again.*

But the monotony soon ended. It began happening on Wednesday nights. On other nights, Jacob would lie awake for hours, thinking about life, about death, mostly about Lizzy. He then moved on to obsessing over privilege or cultural wreckage. He tossed and turned, self-flagellating with imponderables:

Was privilege part of the wreckage?

Were both intended by God?

Was there a master plan, or was life a feather fluttering this way and that at the whim of the breeze?

Sometimes, he gained control over his spinning mind, reasoning that he had lived a good life, at least according to standards set by others. But any sense of satisfaction was uneasy and offset by the troubling feeling that he was like a tiny mite whose time was almost up, still fluttering about without a clue.

Wednesday nights, however, were different, and Jacob looked forward to them. They were unpredictable and exciting, offering him an escape from drudgery and ruminations. Jacob even wondered if they might lead to his coveted answer, his sacred solution. Was he getting closer to God, to the meaning of life? But he was also deeply troubled by what was happening to him as his Early Warning System sounded the alarm.

CHAPTER VIII – WALTER

S eriously, Mom's funeral made me somber, but I didn't feel as much grief as I expected. Yes, I'll miss her. And of course, she was a great mother. But let's be real. Mom is in heaven now and that's a far better place than down here. And, to boot, she is no longer in pain from her cancer. My minister captured the situation perfectly: "Our Lizzy is smiling up above, an angel watching over us, basking in the love of Jesus Christ. She has been rewarded for her goodness. May we all experience such peace when our time comes. Amen."

I believe there is a better place that awaits us with all my heart and soul. Mom, I'm happy for you and will think of you at church every Sunday. I'm glad you are no longer in agony here on Earth. Hurting like me.

The funeral was like a carnival where I was forced to endure my crazy relatives. And Dad was all over me, as usual, trying to simultaneously give me space, but make sure I listened to his advice about the rewards of hard work. Talk about counsel that no longer makes sense.

Don't get me wrong. I feel terrible for Dad, all alone now. "Have faith, Dad," I consoled. "She's with God now."

He shot me that funny stare that makes me feel six years old. "The only thing I know for sure is that your mother is gone. I have absolutely no idea where she went, or if she's anywhere at all."

I feel bad for Dad, but let's keep things real. Dad has had a good life. I'm sorrier for myself. I know how self-centered this sounds, but I am crunched by obligations. I'm committed to a bad wife, a nonbeliever who only worries about the color of her toenail polish, and whether people admire her expensive sweaters and her ever changing hairdo. We hardly communicate—unless she's criticizing me. She has run up over twenty grand on the credit cards and expects me to pay with my lousy job. I can barely afford the double-digit interest as my suffering compounds.

I don't know how Dad accomplished so much while I struggle. Am I just not up to the challenge? Maybe old guys like Dad were given a leg up to my detriment. I must stop thinking like this. Keep moving forward. Faith, faith, faith.

Trust in the Lord is the only way for me to even tolerate my lookalike sister. She was inconsolable, tears flowing like Niagara Falls, during Dad's eulogy. Michelle has always been an embarrassment, so why should the funeral be different? In grade school, she was the dorky, undersized twin who nobody wanted to hang out with. She had the same face as me but adorned with braces and acne. Then, in high school, she was nerd number one, studying twenty-four-seven and trouncing me on report cards. My friends mockingly called her my better half. But I think of her as my sinning sister.

She's a sinner all right. Michelle is a shrink specializing in sex therapy for lesbians. She spends her time counselling girls who like girls. Despicable. And she's a pervert herself—an abomination before God.

And oh, how she flaunts it. She attended the funeral with another woman dressed in black, whom my sister introduced to everybody as Gracie, *my dear partner*, as if there was nothing wrong with the whole scene. Honestly, I'm horrified by the image of these two women doing it, one with *my* face.

Focus, focus, focus. A dead-end career, a crummy wife hemorrhaging cash, my sinning sister, Dad alone, and Mom gone. Faith, faith, faith. It will deliver me. Faith!

My mind was a spinning roulette wheel with the pea ball heading toward black thirteen when Michelle approached. She gave me a hug and pointed at Dad. "Oh my God, just look at him, so fragile and lost," she said in a wavering voice. "He was always busy at work, but that's gone. And now his best friend has left him. What are we going to do, Walter?"

I stared upward like she needed to get a grip. "The answer is right in front of Dad if only he'd embrace Jesus. Mom is in heaven now with our Savior, a better place than here."

Michelle cringed, her usual reaction to anything I say. I guess I can't mention Jesus, or even heaven, without receiving a subtle rebuke from my sinning sister. Tough luck. Deal with it, brat.

I took a deep breath and exhaled slowly, ridding myself of her obvious disapproval. "Dad wants to get things on the calendar so that we can see each other more," I said. Michelle nodded as my voice grew frustrated. "He asked to go fishing, but I don't even have a rod. He suggested a few baseball games, but I can't stay awake during those bore fests. I know he needs me, but jeez."

There was that look again from my sinning sister, but I ignored it and shared my hope. "Maybe he'll join me on Sundays at church. I told him he's invited anytime."

What I didn't mention was that I can't be a substitute for Mom because I'm up to my eyeballs with troubles of my own at home and work. I also feel a tinge of resentment in the pit of my stomach that I'm trying to manage. I find it hard to square Dad's requests for togetherness with his long absences when we were young. He spent most of his time at GoldOrb or grooming the lawn, his head in the clouds. Michelle had the same father. Surely, she sees the irony.

But that's only part of the story. I care deeply about Dad, far more than I let on. He's a good man and I love him. It's just hard for me to say it out loud. Plus, God's commandments couldn't be clearer. I am obligated to honor my parents. Talk about conflicted feelings. I might see my minister about this.

While my brain was in free fall from this civil war of emotions, Michelle preached at me with incomprehensible psychobabble about Dad's delicate mental state and the role Mom played in anchoring him. "Mom tethered Dad to the real world," she lectured. What in the world was she implying?

She then made her pitch. "Walter, neither of us can do this alone. You and me, we need to work as a team to help Dad. Let's share info and be there for him, for each other. Like Dad says, 'For every problem there is an answer, for every issue, a solution.' That's us now. We're his answer, his solution." Beside her stood Gracie, gesticulating her approval like a cheerleader. Go Michelle, go Michelle, ra, ra, sis, boom, *bleck*.

I reluctantly agreed. I was miffed that the two girls teamed up against me, but they had a point. My minister was sure to tell me the same thing. He's big on families working together. But did Michelle really have to use Dad's motto to seal the deal?

And so, I fear that Jacob and Lizzy's twins have once again become joined at the hip. Inhale deeply, *ugh*. Exhale fully, *yech*. Faith. Faith. Faith.

CHAPTER IX - MICHELLE

W e all have just one life to live and it's here on planet Earth. My stock advice to patients is, "Imagine yourself ten years from now looking back. Will you be satisfied with your choices, how you spent your days, your narrative? Make the most of the present!" It's not exactly an original insight, but people forget.

I think that's why I cried so hard at Mom's funeral. My time with my mother has ended. I will no longer see the person who gave me life, cared for me as a child and, most important, accepted me for who I am. For exactly who I am. When I look back ten years from now, Mom will be missing from that part of my life.

I wish I could believe she is in heaven, like my brother does. But I see nothing in this world that justifies it. Mom is simply gone, gone forever. And in her stead is a painful void.

So, it's time to assert myself. Help Dad. Heal my family.

I can do this. Things are going well for me. I'm so fortunate to have Gracie as my partner during this time of acceptance. I told Gracie, "Pinch me," when the Supreme Court recognized gay marriage. "I can't believe it." She was more cautious, rightfully predicting, "There'll be blowback," as she uncorked a bottle of pinot. "But here's to progress."

I also have a great job where I earn a good salary helping women just like me. We were born this way and should be proud of who we are. If God exists, *She* created us in *Her* image. Why can't Walter understand?

Gracie and I live in a nice place, have made fine friends, and can do whatever we wish. In fact, we have plans to vacation in Italy later this year. I refused to visit the Vatican, however, telling Gracie, "It's the refuge of old men in pretentious robes who somehow remain empowered to fabricate God's will. They've caused wars and persecution. And they can't find it in their hearts to fully accept us." I guess I inherited dear old Dad's skepticism.

Gracie is more open-minded and I love her for that. Ever the voice of reason, she responded, "What would you suggest we replace religion with to fill the vacuum? It gives people a moral compass." Before I could complain that I am plenty ethical without it, she said, "You've got a strong sense of empathy and were educated with good secular values. But that doesn't work for everyone. Religion can shine the light."

Gracie is Jewish and loves to attend Sabbath services. "It works for me," she continued. "And you don't see me waging war or persecuting people in the name of religion." Hearing Dad's ever-present voice, I remained dubious, but kept it to myself.

I was rehashing these thoughts at Mom's funeral while the minister confidently assured us of her salvation. Sadly, I wasn't thinking clearly enough that day, which is usually a problem when Walter is around. My twin brother wears a chip on his shoulder the size of Gibraltar when it comes to me. I'm clueless about how to improve our relationship. But I am committed to our family. He is my blood, my other half, and I love him. And somewhere deep inside, after penetrating through his ultra-religious haze, he loves me too. At least I hope he does.

Well, now this theory will be put to the test. We have a huge project to work on together. It's called Dad.

I can't say for sure, but when I think back to childhood, it's quite possible that Dad had a psychotic episode. It happened on our tenth birthday. Mom had the flu, so he took Walter and me on a long hike while she stayed home to rest. He prepared peanut butter and jelly sandwiches loaded with gooey fluff and packed twinkies for a special treat. We had an amazing time, the three of us, and even Walter seemed happy despite my being there. Dad was so much fun.

The next day, I snuck up behind Dad and put my hands over his eyes. "Guess who?" I asked. "Here's a hint. It's someone who had a lousy time yesterday. Let's never do that again." Of course, I was joking, hoping to win attention.

But when I took my hands away and Dad looked at me, he seemed ashamed. "You've got that right Michelle, never again."

Dad sounded serious, and I was crestfallen. That night, I overheard him quietly telling Mom in the kitchen, "I lost them for over an hour. Please don't talk to them about it. I'm too embarrassed. I don't want this to be a permanent stain in their memories."

Was I in the Twilight Zone? We never left Dad's side on the hike, not for a minute. But I was young and unsure of myself. Maybe I didn't hear right. And I wasn't supposed to eavesdrop. I had snooped on Walter and his friends too many times and was warned that I'd be punished if I didn't stop. So, I decided not to mention what I overheard to Mom.

I asked Walter if he noticed anything strange, but he parlayed this into another opportunity to ridicule me. To say once again to my face, his perfect mirror, "You are a moronic worry wart." I have fond memories like this galore. I think *I* need a shrink.

What I'm sure of is that Dad began taking medicine. Several months after our hike, I discovered a pillbox buried in his sock drawer while nosing around. It held colorful capsules in little compartments for each day of the week. Shoot me, but I still poked around, feeling a rush of excitement as if I was a detective.

I had no idea what the colorful pills were for. A few years later, I worked up the courage to ask Mom about that day. She wore a defensive look on her face. "Maybe you didn't get so lost on that hike. Dad was mistaken, but he's fine. He works so hard, and if it was anything, call it anxiety. There's nothing to worry about."

I suppose I came to share Mom's optimism. Maybe Dad was a little uptight, but he seemed fine. He never let us down. And when I got a little older, we had deep, interesting talks about hard questions. Dad was logical and laser focused. Were those colorful pills all that he needed? By the time I graduated college, the hiking episode was a distant memory.

And now here we are. A threesome without Mom, our family's center of gravity. I suggested to my brother that we needed to step up our game. My vague questions about Dad's mental state, dormant for so long, were resurfacing. I thought he was okay, but he seemed overwhelmed. Helping Dad was simply the right thing to do. Walter begrudgingly agreed, but not before we reenacted our dysfunction in front of Gracie.

Walter, Walter, what to do about Walter? I don't know what's going on with his marriage, what's happening at work. The vibes are bad. Sometimes I think he hates his life and takes it out on me. Gracie reinforced my view. "He looked at me with such disdain that I didn't know if I should leave the funeral and wait in the car," she said. "That sweet-faced brother of yours has some serious issues to work through."

My poor twin is overburdened by life. I also know that there is sunshine somewhere deep inside of him.

There's nothing but this moment, no time like the present. I'm going to take this on and be proud when I look back ten years from now. I'll keep tabs on Dad and work with my brother. They both need me. Oh God, I miss my mother!

CHAPTER X - JACOB

On Wednesday nights, after thirty nostalgic minutes watching Frasier or Seinfeld, Jacob would prepare for bed. He hoped to discover a new show for a little variety but kept returning to the soothing embrace of sitcoms from his past. "They're like me, at least the old part," he murmured to the mirror as he washed up. "It sure would be fun to have a new series where Seinfeld sees Frazier for therapy. I'd tune in." He brushed his teeth, combed his thinning hair, and gazed into the mirror again. "How did this happen? Who the heck is that staring back at me? And who exactly am I talking to?"

After these rituals, Jacob climbed under the covers and instantly began dreaming as the scene transformed from comedy to horror. The dreams always began with Jacob in peril. The causes varied. Once, in a medical development to defy all odds, he was stricken with the same cancer that killed Lizzy. The doctor speculated that it was caused by toxic drinking water from old pipes in the house. Or perhaps poison gases seeping up from beneath the basement foundation. But damn if it wasn't the exact same disease. "What an unlucky couple you are," remarked the physician as he prepared to dissect. "One in a million."

In another iteration, Jacob was back in college playing in the baseball game where Lizzy had first laid eyes on him. In the dream, the errant throw by the smirking pitcher flew at superhuman velocity and hit him between the eyes. Jacob lay comatose, the fallen bat a few inches away. He heard his coach urging, "Take first, take first. Shake it off, boy!" But trotting to first base was impossible. The sheer force of impact cracked Jacob's skull and left him on the brink.

And in the version of the dream which haunted Jacob the most, he was in a movie theatre enjoying a wacky comedy featuring both

Seinfeld and Frasier as astronauts. Jacob was laughing uncontrollably when a teenage boy with uncombed hair and a dripping nose strolled to the front of the theatre and took a bow. His tee shirt contained a picture of a twisted snake with the words "Liberty or Death" stitched above the serpent's fangs. The boy pulled out a high caliber rifle and opened fire in all directions. Jacob was hit. Lying on the sticky floor in a pool of blood mixed with buttered popcorn, he slipped into a coma. His last cogent thoughts were, *Cultural wreckage, a societal wasteland.*

Most people would awaken from such dreams with a jolt, staring at the ceiling until regaining a semblance of reality. But Jacob plummeted into a deeper trance. In each dream, the dying Jacob would wrestle endlessly with a burning presence that seemed intent on consuming him. The smell was always the same: burnt animal flesh. *These could be the ancient sacrifices described in excruciating detail in the Bible,* he thought. *I'm a new offering.*

"Not yet!" Jacob screamed, sensing that he was in a contest of wills. He refused to be incinerated until he understood what it meant to die. Conversely, what it meant to live. *There is an answer, a solution to everything,* his subconscious insisted as he resisted the higher power.

The struggle escalated and Jacob was confronted with unearthly sounds, piercing wails in an unknown language. He was now bound by charred ropes, the surrounding earth scorched by the flames. It was as if he was trapped in the middle of an active lava field on the only spot which had not yet combusted. He smelled the toxic sulfur.

But Jacob continued to resist, repeating his beloved anthem in his mind. *For every problem there is an answer. For every issue, a solution.* This struck the omnipotent force as a hilarious thing to believe for someone in such a predicament. Unworldly laughter assaulted Jacob from impossible angles. He wondered if he had amused the Heavenly Father, enticing him to finally visit. Or perhaps it was Antaeus, the ancient god who wrestled mortals to their doom.

Mortal combat would have to wait though as the dream took another turn. Jacob became aware that the Omniscient One was considering his request, his obsession for knowledge. A piece of fruit appeared next to him. It was a red orb, much larger than the biggest apple imaginable, more beautiful, far sweeter. But Jacob was still bound to the seething ground and couldn't reach it.

Would he be allowed to taste the ambrosia? It was packed with unabridged awareness, not mere glimpses and missing ingredients like the fruit Adam and Eve wrestled from the Tree of Knowledge. Perhaps it was time for an upgrade from God and maybe Jacob had been chosen to learn *the answer, the solution* to the meaning of life. He would soon be anointed a prophet.

The red orb shook and began to slowly roll toward Jacob, to be tasted if only he could free himself. Jacob smelled the sweet scent. He tried to will it even closer. And that's when it burst, the juice stinging his eyes. The remains of the fruit quickly evaporated from the blistering heat, while Jacob writhed in agony.

The dream entered its last phase as daylight streamed through Jacob's bedroom window. From the smoldering landscape, a ladder appeared, and Jacob was freed. He climbed twelve steps to a new vision of a crystal blue lake encircled by mountains with soaring peaks covered in snow. The air was so crisp it felt like velvet. Trees and flowers of every description surrounded the shore, offering a kaleidoscope of colors. The gentle breeze infused Jacob's heart with hope. He even sensed Lizzy, her essence, her love. It was the most serene place Jacob had ever inhabited, and he wanted to remain there forever. He was in paradise.

Screech! Jacob's mind exploded from a high-pitched cacophony. A thousand indecipherable voices spoke to him at once and none of them were human. What struck him each time was that the sound blast wasn't meant to wake him from the dream. Instead, it was intended to drown out a veiled message of critical importance emanating from paradise. But awaken him it did, like the bugle call to rally a brigade of troops at dawn. Jacob's dream was finished, and Thursday had begun.

Jacob sat up in bed and squinted at the sunlight. The thousand indecipherable voices were replaced by another rousting call, this time from his Early Warning System. The emotional stress from his fading dream had taken its toll. And it did so time and again as the screeching voices wrested him back into reality. As he tried to calm himself, Jacob's thoughts were always the same. *I'm close, getting closer.*

CHAPTER XI – THE BOSS

Jacob's absence has made my heart grow fonder. After he retired, I learned firsthand just how hard it is to score runs without your cleanup hitter in the lineup. Yes, it's true that he could be a tad abrasive and rattled the fragile egos of some lesser engineers. But with twenty-twenty hindsight, I keep returning to the same conclusion: the dude got the job done.

Without Jacob, we hold hands and have kumbaya moments here at GoldOrb. The problem is, touchy feely doesn't improve the bottom line and I'm taking heat again from the C-suite, this time over our fading results. Jacob's retirement has been my occupational hazard.

I also scolded myself over that uninspired farewell salute we gave him for his years of devotion. It left a bad taste in my mouth. And then Lizzy got sick and died right when they were ready to make dents in their bucket list. Tragic.

I felt sorry for the guy, a little guilty too. Heck, we worked together forever. It's not like he ceased to be a human being just because he left the company, although sometimes I think that's what happens when someone retires. So, I broke the silence and invited him to catch up over a few brews. When I called, Jacob sounded relieved, like he needed a break. "I'm surprised to hear from you, boss," he said in a distracted tone while the evening news blared in the background. "Let's do it."

We met at his favorite pub, Lee's Tavern. The place was old school, no frills, just like him. The lighting was dark, the carpet worn thin, and the air musty. We were seated at a table nicked up with illegible scratches as if to proclaim it had witnessed a lot but would keep our secrets. Despite its rustic appearance, the tavern boasted a crew of regulars, which always creates a friendly vibe.

The waitress was welcoming and brought our drinks pronto along with crisp onion rings—the house specialty. I raised my glass for a quick toast. "To old friends in new places." But it sounded unconvincing even to me, and our conversation dragged. Here's a guy I used to see every day, but now, face-to-face outside GoldOrb, it seemed we had nothing left in common. We both stuck to stilted formalities.

"How are the kids, Jacob?"

"Good. All grown up now. Hot weather we're having for this time of year in the Twin Cities."

"Climate change, I guess. Hey, the Timberwolves look tough if they get better bench play."

Yep, it was tough to melt the ice even with global warming. And Jacob appeared uncomfortable, like something was eating at him. I finally asked, "Who are you seeing from GoldOrb nowadays?"

He frowned and shrugged his shoulders. "Nobody really, but I'm glad you called. I've been wondering if the company's going to turn it around. I'm still reading bad press about the Chicago River and that accounting mess. Guess we worked for the Evil Empire."

Our talk sure perked up from there. We gossiped about the never-ending stream of frenzied newspaper clippings while Jacob wrung his hands and looked at me like maybe, since I was still the boss in his eyes, I had gathered new pearls of wisdom to lighten the blow. Jacob seemed even more troubled over his legacy now than when he retired.

GoldOrb's predicament had begun to gnaw at me too. Actually, it was more like a punch to the soft part of my gut, which was expanding every day. Here I was preparing for my own retirement in a few years. Could I really sail off into the sunset, basking in the glow of a career well done while my employer's reputation nosedived? Jacob and I were in the same boat on this one. Hopefully, not the Titanic.

I stopped nursing my beer and took a few chugs, thinking long and hard before answering, while Jacob peered at me deeply and sincerely, reminding me of an innocent child looking to a trusted adult for comfort. I recalled how we skirted around this topic when he first threatened to leave GoldOrb, but we never had the conversation it deserved. Finally, I assured him, "You, of all people, can hold your head high. Walter and Michelle should be proud of their old man. I don't remember you dumping waste in a river or cooking the books."

Jacob seemed like he needed more convincing. "Look Jacob, you've helped produce useful things that customers enjoy," I said. "You served honorably. Believe it. I sure do."

I also assured him I had been in meetings with the CEO many times over the years and still had faith in this titan from the world of capitalism. "He's off the charts intense," I shared. "But honest."

This was the same speech I was using to convince myself. This time my arguments kind of rang true, other times not as much. It's a tricky thing who you work for.

While I was struggling with what to say next, Jacob got practical. "I just hope our pensions are safe."

"Yes, let's hope G.O.D. can pay the bills," I replied.

He then confided that he wouldn't go hungry. "I've made some savvy real estate purchases in Chicago with my oldest friend, the professor. They've performed handsomely." Jacob looked proud of the investments, but prouder of the long friendship.

I'm always interested in improving my portfolio and asked for details. "What factors did you consider when choosing the property? What were your mortgage rates? Your expected returns? How do you know when to sell?"

Jacob again looked proud. "I rely on the professor. He's got my back."

He kept talking, but it seemed he was now having a conversation with himself, not me. "I wish GoldOrb's problems were my only ones. I can't seem to find my way to an answer, a solution, just a swirl that gets blared out in my mind."

I just smiled, not knowing how to respond. We had downed several drinks by then and I assumed the alcohol was doing his talking. It was definitely doing my listening.

But I sensed that I was the lucky one. At some point, after enough drinks, alcohol numbs me up just like it should. Unlike Jacob, I can stop caring about the hard questions that he constantly agonizes over. I know that he's the better man. Maybe I'm the happier one.

CHAPTER XII – JACOB

Jacob enjoyed reuniting with his boss, but the feeling of camaraderie quickly faded as he obsessed over his recurring dream. All he wanted was to fall asleep, transport back to the idyllic mountain lake, to paradise, and discern the message without unfathomable voices drowning it out. *Could this be the solution to life, to death? I am close, far closer to the answer than I was at the monastery.*

Despite his hope that he was on the brink of something monumental, Jacob accepted the reality that another day without a breakthrough had begun. If his dreaming pattern held, he would need to wait until the following Wednesday to make progress on the drama unfolding in his subconscious.

In the meantime, Jacob recalled the dreams in vivid detail, wondering, *Was that hell or heaven, or both?* He harbored serious doubts about whether these places existed but nonetheless speculated over which direction he'd be assigned on judgment day if heaven and hell were real. *Please let it be heaven. Lizzy will be there.*

Jacob paced the house with Hunter shadowing, wagging his tail as if it was a game. He asked his companion, "Am I loony tunes? A few cards short? This is hard to bear without Lizzy." The dog lifted his ears as if considering the problem from all dimensions. He gave Jacob a lick.

Except for his canine companion, Jacob kept his Wednesday night extravaganzas secret. He didn't seek professional help, knowing it would begin another onslaught of counselling. He had endured therapy years ago at Lizzy's insistence after the hiking episode with the twins. It culminated in an excruciating dispute with his insurer as to whether the out-of-network sessions and colorful pills were covered for reimbursement. *I don't need that hassle or the damn meds.*

He considered confiding in Michelle. *My daughter the psychologist,* he thought with incongruous pride. But he was too embarrassed, rationalizing that she was a specialist for sexual matters, not in what might be ailing her old man. The thought of her professional focus, her personal essence, made him sigh. *Yet another problem I still need to work on as the clock ticks. She's a good kid.*

Finally, he found an unlikely source. The idea came from the widow Goodman, who was worried about him being alone in that big house now that Lizzy was gone. Stopping by with homemade cookies to thank Jacob for fixing her mailbox, she mentioned the rabbi from her temple. "He's brilliant! An expert in matters of the heart," she advised. "He was there for me when my husband died. Maybe he can be helpful to you."

It had been eight long years since Jacob last attended synagogue for a bar mitzvah. While hesitant, he concluded that the widow's suggestion was worth a try. *After all, my problems touch religion and God,* he reasoned. *Who better than a rabbi to speak with? And, if it doesn't work, I'll never see him again.*

The B'nai Chai Synagogue of Minneapolis, or "BC" as its members called it, was a physical contradiction. It had a boxy concrete exterior from the Brutalist architecture school: grey, drab, and boring. But the inside was the opposite, erupting with royal blue carpeting, stained glass skylights and vibrant artwork depicting iconic biblical scenes. The sanctuary was spacious and comfortable, with soft lighting and a state-of-the-art sound system, creating the perfect mood for prayer and contemplation. Spirituality beckoned.

Upon entering, Jacob was greeted by a short woman seated at a desk and immersed in a crossword puzzle. She introduced herself as Sophie, the rabbi's secretary, and brought Jacob to a small meeting room. "You're in for a treat," she said. "Rabbi Friedler is a brilliant scholar. And such a mensch!"

The rabbi was waiting. He was in his mid-fifties, small and frail, with thick black bifocals. He was busy stroking his long shaggy beard, apparently deep in thought. Between the glasses and hair, there wasn't much left of the rabbi's face to see, except for warm, intelligent eyes peering out through the dense lenses and putting Jacob more at ease than he expected. Jacob also detected a hint of melancholy in those eyes, but maybe he was attributing his own mood to the religious scholar.

Sophie brought soft drinks as the men settled in. They tried to break the ice discussing baseball and where they grew up. Neither excelled at small talk, so Jacob quickly took the plunge and told the rabbi his strange story. "I'm not a religious man, Rabbi. But I'm here because my recurring dreams are tied up with questions I have about life, about death."

"Yes, yes, go on."

"I'm afraid that despite my advancing age, I haven't learned much."

"Oh?"

"But now I'm dreaming, and I think there's a message."

The rabbi listened attentively as Jacob detailed the near-death traumas of his visions, the lava field, red orb, mountain lake and a thousand screeching voices drowning out something vital. Jacob appeared to be earnest, also at wits' end.

The rabbi stroked his beard while Jacob spoke, removed his glasses, and stared into space. When Jacob finished, he said, "There's much to unwrap, my friend. I want to help. Together, we'll make progress."

Jacob sat straight at the edge of his chair, intensity radiating from his eyes. The rabbi awkwardly reacted with an attempt to lighten the atmosphere. He struck an ironic pose and quipped, "It makes sense that you're having dreams. After all, your name is Jacob."

When he saw a slight frown appear on Jacob's face, the rabbi reversed course, looking serious. He recited for Jacob a long passage from the Talmud about people who roamed the Middle East thousands of years ago, replete with underdogs, miracles, and salvation. "This tale should console you and provide guidance," he concluded. "Things happen for a reason. Have faith, Jacob. You must have faith."

Jacob thought he saw the rabbi wince as he continued to emphasize the need for faith. "I can tell you're a good man, Jacob. You can do it if you believe in yourself, in God. He'll light the way just like in the story." Again, Jacob detected pain in those kind eyes.

Jacob hesitated while he contemplated the rabbi's advice. The metaphor that the rabbi teased from the ancient text struck him as obscure. The tale seemed obsolete. It provided little comfort, and he could not understand how such a smart man as the rabbi believed otherwise.

His frown broadened as he considered the rabbi's instruction about faith. *Funny, this was Walter's advice too. Is faith the answer? But faith in what? Judaism? Christianity? Islam? Buddhism? Something else? And exactly how do you acquire it? Is it really as simple as the rabbi makes it sound, like flipping on a light switch?*

Jacob lowered his head and rubbed his neck, not realizing how tight it had become. The rabbi had struck a chord. He rehashed past conversations with other religious people over faith. Jacob often sensed he was being judged. That lurking behind the civil interchange over beliefs was a veiled attack on his character for his inability to flip the switch to the on position. *If I can't find faith, if my heart won't cooperate, I am judged to be morally deficient. Does the rabbi think I'm lacking in a fundamental way?*

But all Jacob said to the rabbi was, "I've tried and tried and failed." He felt like he was confessing a sin. "Maybe I'm lacking the right stuff."

The rabbi flinched as if Jacob's admission caused him pain. But he recovered quickly and tried a different tack. He advised Jacob that regardless of his capacity for faith in the Almighty, it would do him good to join the community at his synagogue. Jacob was always welcome, and would find it helpful to be among friends, working out life's mysteries together instead of alone. Stroking his beard, he smiled warmly. "Be part of something bigger than yourself. We work as one, love together, and perform good deeds for the less fortunate. That's the pathway to the answer you're seeking."

Jacob hadn't expected the meeting to morph into a recruitment campaign. While pondering how to redirect the conversation back to his tortuous visions, the rabbi deftly suggested, "In the spirit of performing good deeds, you might ignite a spark by donating to my Fund for Life, an account for rabbinic matters. Many BC members find God through acts of philanthropy even if they have trouble accepting all the stories."

Jacob snapped out of his reflection mode, feeling annoyance, not elevation. The rabbi's request left a foul taste in his mouth. He did not want to be confronted with earthly economics at the very moment he was seeking higher truths.

The conversation soon petered out. There would be no eureka moment for Jacob at BC, not after the introduction of money into the spiritual realm. Upon departing, he again detected that downhearted look on the rabbi's face. Perhaps the rabbi understood Jacob's dissappointment as the men said their goodbyes.

That night, alone with his frozen dinner of mac and peas for one at the table set for two, Jacob reconsidered the rabbi's comments. The notion of connecting with the community to explore the ultimate while helping the needy resonated. *With Lizzy gone, it wouldn't hurt to have a positive outlet.* Hunter seemed to agree as he cuddled at Jacob's feet.

But in the end, Jacob rejected the idea. It was in his DNA to work things out quietly, away from the crowd, especially when the group's basic tenet was to rally around a religious vision, an aged text, that Jacob had such doubts about. *I can join a bowling league or take a class for community, donate somewhere else.*

Jacob was unable to flip on the switch. His heart was not in it. He would continue to confront his Wednesday night fright shows starring himself as the main attraction in solitude. His switch was locked in the off position as he stumbled in the dark with no faith at all.

Jacob speculated that perhaps, and only maybe, he was tapping into profound enlightenment through his dreams. *If only I can break through, taste the red orb,* he thought. *One bite and I'll know.* But more often, he felt bewildered and regarded Wednesday nights as his own personal horror movie, his night out. *Possibly out of my mind.*

Despite his trepidation, Jacob did not want the dreams to stop. Not until he could interpret them. *For every problem, there is an answer,* he reminded himself. *For every issue, there is a solution.*

This confidence, combined with his never-ending obsession about life, about death, and his willingness to crash through brick walls regardless of the cost, led Jacob to raise the stakes. He speculated that revelation was more likely to occur somewhere else, a great deal further than the rabbi at BC.

Jacob decided to fly to the Colorado Rockies, his honeymoon utopia resembling the transitory paradise in his visions. Perhaps this was the home base of his mysterious dreamscape. He would merge his dreams with reality there. *The answer must be hidden in plain sight,* he thought. But first, there was an important economic matter to take care of.

CHAPTER XIII – THE HOMELESS MAN

I was jumping out of my brain when I met the old White dude, as in gone, gone, gone. My butt was firmly planted on Livertie Avenue next to my tipped over shopping cart, dented and rusty. No friends, no family, nobody. Just trying to stay warm on the cold concrete. I had to take a piss so bad it burned. There was nowhere to go except right in front of people as cars drove by, windows up, doors locked. You try living this way. You ain't gonna do any better.

So, while I'm forcing myself to hold it in 'til I burst, he shows up looking shell-shocked, like he never saw boarded windows, swirling trash, and drugged out hookers. "Wreckage," he muttered in a nervous voice. "Wasteland." Whatever, man. It's home sweet home to me.

The White guy walked straight up to me stiff and stern and looked through me like an x-ray with intense blue eyes. "Let's grab a cup of coffee," he said. "How 'bout it?"

Getting a closer peek, I thought he was gone, gone, gone, just like me. His eyes were burning and moist, twitching at the corners. But I wasn't gonna turn down his offer over looks. There was nothing I wanted more than a free helping of hot joe, along with indoor plumbing. "Hell yes," I responded. "Let me hide my cart so that White hobo on the next corner doesn't steal my stuff."

We dragged our sorry asses to the Dandy Cafe across the street and sat at a beat-up counter that should have been trashed years ago. The fat waitress was grouchy when she saw who she had to serve. She glared at me, cold and hard, but she kept her trap shut when she saw the White guy and brought us drinks with two big chunks of apple pie that he ordered. If I had walked into Dandy's alone, I would've gotten the backside of a boot.

After I took a leak that lasted a week, I could think clearer. The White guy introduced himself as Jacob and asked if I liked sports. White folk seem to think that's all we talk about. But I cut him slack, thinking he was trying to be friendly, that's all. So, we talked up the Vikings number one pick, his speed and size. Whatever, man. Who cares? It was his dime.

He squirmed in his seat with his eyes blinking at the speed of sound. That's okay, everyone looks edgy around me. I'm iced up at this point. It only hurts when I breathe.

He also seemed uncomfortable with himself. I don't know why, but I thought that me and this stranger from another part of the universe shared something.

Jacob asked where I came from, so I gave my usual story. That I grew up in Hyde Park, Chicago, and made my way to Minneapolis up highway ninety-four for a construction job with my uncle. I put a sad look on my face. "Uncs, he got sick. Things didn't work out after that." I always blame my uncle.

The part about Chi Town was true, but everything else was fibs. I forgot to mention that I like to drink booze from a crumpled burger bag. and can't be counted on for a single damn thing. Keeping numb is the only way I can get by. I'm not even up to being a beggar except on the good days when I have enough energy to draw a sign: "Vietnam Vet Starving." I wave it as I limp by stopped cars for coins or maybe a buck.

I don't know if Jacob believed my story or was even listening. The guy was somewhere else. I could tell he had his own problems and meant no harm. Again, he muttered, "Wasteland," as if he took whatever was bugging him personally.

I'm thinking this fellow was as weird as grilled spinach wrapped around a popsicle and then he proved it. With eyes still twitching, he yanked out his wallet and handed me crisp hundred-dollar bills, just like that, while I'm forking in my last mouthful of pie. One, two, three, four, five of them. "I'd rather give this to you than the Fund for Life," he said. "Anyway, you deserve something from me. Give yourself a break from the wreckage."

I never held this much bread in my life. After I stuck the bills in my pocket, he lectured, "Don't spend the money on booze."

Sure thing, Pa, I thought. *I'll stick this in my college fund.* But I kept the sarcasm to myself and thanked the man.

When we left the Dandy Cafe, I noticed that Jacob stiffed the ugly waitress. *What goes around comes around bitch.* Then, off we rambled into the night, to our different parts of the galaxy, only a few miles apart.

A few hours later, I got to wondering if this whole thing with me and Jacob was a dream. Was I hallucinating again? But no. I reached in my pocket and felt the bills. One, two, three, four, five. It was the real deal, made me squeal.

And here's the best part. This was only the start. The White dude kept coming back to replay the scene. Coffee, apple pie, strained conversation and, yes, yes, yes, the dough. Five hundred beautiful green ones.

Each time Jacob handed me the cash it was confusing, like I was the one doing him the favor. "Take it. I want you to know that I didn't do anything. This doesn't move the dial but take it."

And then came the lameness. "Don't buy liquor."

Sure thing, Pa.

Back on Livertie Avenue, I thought about what Jacob said. I couldn't tell if he meant that he didn't do anything and was innocent. Or that he felt guilty for doing nothing when he should've done something. Whatever which way you slice the apple pie, my job was to help him feel better. Nice work if you can get it. Truth is, these old White guys need to give something up 'til it hurts, or this ain't ever getting fixed.

Little did Jacob know, but the money helped me in another way. I'm not supposed to talk about it, but I think it flipped my switch back on, helping me regain my telepathic powers. I had TP back in Chicago, before those two MFs gave me all that hell. "Get a job, spare a dime!" they yelled.

Me and this Jacob, we had a secret connection. The guy was crazed. You could see it on his face. Why can't he just let it be? Why can't I?

Maybe when I regain more TP, we can talk about it, man to man, mind to mind, no matter the distance. We'll figure out an answer, a solution. Until then, I better stay near my cart and lay low. Feel the warmth of the hooch. I Hope nobody robs me.

CHAPTER XIV – JACOB

Jacob departed for Colorado the next morning with unyielding determination to pursue his premonition. He would spend this Wednesday night in a new neighborhood closer to the epicenter of his recurring dreams. He was hopeful yet skeptical that the change of scenery just might yield his precious answers to his questions about life, about death.

He understood that he might be criticized, that skeptics might harshly judge his sojourn in pursuit of an epiphany. But Jacob saw it differently. *Don't millions of people venture far from home on holy pilgrimages?* Besides, there was nothing to lose. *Even if there's no cosmic breakthrough, I'll get some R and R.*

When planning his itinerary, Jacob found an enticing bed and breakfast located steps from a beautiful mountain lake immersed in the Rockies. It was called the Paradise Inn, named for its proximity to Lake Paradise. The place reminded Jacob of his honeymoon spot and, of course, of his beloved Lizzy.

Jacob dropped Hunter off at the Doggone Lodge and headed to the airport. Upon landing in Denver, he rented a car for the last leg of his journey. He still had two hundred miles to go, but the road was fast and the scenery breathtaking. He thought about the slum where the Homeless Man lived, wishing he could magically transport the dilapidated neighborhood along with his new friend to this vast openness and splendor. *Why are people forced to congregate in squalor, one on top of the next, when there's so much room with a view out here? Is this God's plan?*

He arrived at Lake Paradise late afternoon. Before reaching the Inn, he drove through the cozy, rustic town that shared its name with the lake. Main Street boasted a row of quaint shops, fine restaurants, and art galleries. A drugstore, auto garage and local accountant populated the outskirts of town as commercialism invaded the grandeur to service the practical needs of vacationers and a vibrant retirement community. Jacob recalled that unwelcome mix of economics and spiritualism that troubled him with the rabbi but now accepted it. *This is the nature of things, even in nature.*

The Paradise Inn stood between Main Street and the lake, the best location in town. Jacob checked in at a small office in front of the building. The Innkeeper seemed to be waiting for him. He sported an unkempt white beard and ancient dried out skin. But his green eyes were remarkably bright. He sprang up from behind the rickety counter. "I'm Merle Yoder," he said. "I reckon you're Jacob. Yes, indeed. Yes, indeed."

The Innkeeper seemed ecstatic that Jacob had finally arrived. He advised that breakfast would be served at eight-thirty sharp and urged him to get out on Lake Paradise before dark. It sounded like an order. "The Inn has kayaks, so grab one and start paddling. You must, you must. This is God's country." He pointed Jacob in the direction of his room and instructed him once again with singular focus, "Don't waste time, get out on the lake. Hurry. You don't want to miss it. Yes indeed."

Jacob found the man odd but had fond memories of kayaking as a boy and decided to follow the innkeeper's plan. He made a quick stop in his room to drop off his suitcase. There was one double bed covered with a frayed duvet. An old desk sat crookedly in the corner with nothing on it but smudges. Scattered cobwebs hung over the curtains and a few dead moths lay in the corner of his tiny closet boasting a single hanger. *Location, location,* he assured himself, trying to justify the hefty price.

He then lost confidence. *What the heck am I doing at this dive? Is that Innkeeper a fruitcake? Am I?* But he had travelled too far to give up. He forced himself to keep moving forward as he left his room and headed down a narrow path leading to Lake Paradise.

Jacob's mood brightened when he reached the shore. The pictures drawing him to Lake Paradise were fabulous but still didn't capture the full essence of the location. He was entranced by the sunlight piercing through the soaring trees to create an infinite prism of colors, the perfect backdrop to the clear blue waters. Towering mountains with jagged snow-capped peaks reaching to heaven encircled the lake. This was the scene of dreams, maybe his dream.

Jacob found a beat-up kayak with the Inn's name on it and began rowing, feeling shaken but excited. He now praised himself for his boldness, not just letting the weight of life collapse on top of him.

But as he paddled, moving further from shore with each stroke, nothing happened. He just rowed, and rowed some more, alone on the water, muscles stressed, doubts creeping back in.

When he reached the middle of Lake Paradise, Jacob stopped to rest and enjoy the view. He focused on the mountains, in awe of their sheer size and diverse shapes forged by nature. A feeling of inspiration filled his heart. *I wonder if they're alive,* he speculated. *Perhaps in a different way than we know.*

Jacob's attention shifted to the water. He leaned over the side of the kayak, hoping to see his reflection. It was as if he was gazing into a perfect mirror, the water so clear, so mesmerizing. Jacob could make out the features of his aging face while his questioning eyes looked back at him, rippling with the movement of mild waves. Concentrating on his reflection, he heard loud chirping. A flock of black and white birds had arrived and were circling above the kayak, serenading him, as if with singular purpose. How had so many appeared from nowhere?

A moment later, still peering into the water in a trancelike state, Jacob was staring into Lizzy's eyes, through the depths, the impenetrable, into eternity. Not a word was spoken, but it was the most intimate moment of his life. They held each other's gaze until dark, the kayak gently swaying on the water, the mysterious birds watching from above. As the sun set and the sky took on a purple hue, Lizzy gave Jacob the longest kiss of his life. Their lips never touched but their hearts melded as she gradually receded into the darkening waters. When she vanished, the birds were gone.

There was nothing left for Jacob to do but paddle back to shore under the evening sky in bliss and confusion. He returned to his room and retired to bed. Staring at the blinking emergency light on the ceiling, he thought about his encounter with his love. And then he fell into a deep, peaceful sleep.

Breakfast the following morning was scrumptious. The old innkeeper offered an overflowing spread of homemade breads, smoked salmon, cheeses, and fruit. Pouring Jacob some coffee, he pierced through to Jacob's very soul with those burning green eyes. "You had the time of your life on Lake Paradise, didn't you?! Yes, indeed. Yes, indeed."

CHAPTER XV - THE INNKEEPER

People get paralyzed over lame details that don't matter. *They don't matter!* What cereal to buy? Which outfit to wear, red or green? Should I text, email, post, ping, or pick up the phone? They spend their days on minutia, ignoring the big picture.

So, let me fill you in with the truth. The Earth is a puny speck, a microscopic afterthought under Goliath's fingernails. And guess what else? We are not alone.

If you need convincing, buy a telescope, go out in the pitch dark at Lake Paradise, and take a gander at the billion trillion stars twinkling in the ever-expanding universe. I said a billion trillion! With a *B* and a *T*. I don't even know how to write that number with so many zeroes. Nobody does.

So, you don't have to be Galileo to discover that life exists under those other suns. And you don't need to be Einstein to conclude that they have found their way to planet Earth. That's right. Aliens are right here, right now, hanging out under our very noses. Yes indeed, yes indeed.

Just talk to my friends in Roswell, New Mexico. They'll set you straight. I was born there and saw things with my own eyes that you wouldn't believe. Mama Yoder used to say, "I didn't raise you to be no fool, Merley. If you done seen it, then it done happened." And plenty of people saw *it* in Roswell. Saw *them*.

Well, I've also gotten an eyeful at Lake Paradise. That's why I bought the inn. It makes me feel part of something bigger. Something closer to the truth. Funny, that's what my minister lectured about on Sundays back in Roswell.

And yet, people of faith, whatever that even means, protest and scoff. "You're an old fool," they say. "Get new glasses." But what's the difference between my sightings of the supernatural and their epic tales from the Bible? At least I felt it, right now, right here. I'm not just repeating verses about what some distant ancestor claimed happened eons ago.

When I saw the shores of Lake Paradise turn into a lava field for no earthly reason, people avoided me. "The old Innkeeper fell off his scooter," they mocked. "It's dementia." Yet, those same critics believe wholeheartedly in a burning bush and revere the bearded man who stumbled upon it. If that isn't a double standard, I don't know what is.

So, let me tell you what else I've seen. One time, I was out in my boat in the pitch dark and spotted a flock of black and white birds swarming above the middle of the lake. There was a glow rising from the water, illuminating the creatures. They were flurrying this way and that when they should have been asleep in their nests.

Another time, the waves shifted directions, moving backward. That's right, in reverse. The water flowed from shore to center, right where that light was coming from, under the hovering birds.

And then there are the sounds. I can sometimes make out alien voices, like nothing you've ever heard. A thousand of them. Yep, something from another planet is out there in the middle of Lake Paradise. It makes me feel good to be near it, at peace with the cosmos. Yes indeed, yes indeed.

It's also attracting people to visit me. There's a certain type of guest who checks into the Paradise Inn once in a while. You just know he isn't here to stroll in the woods or catch trout for dinner. I call these people "seekers." A few have been certified lunatics, but most are earnest, just unsettled and confused, like any sane person ought to be.

Anyway, this guy Jacob checks in and I knew right off that he was a seeker. He was preoccupied and intense. It was like he travelled here for a critical mission that even he didn't understand.

After we did the paperwork, I asked how long he'd be staying. He looked confused. "I don't know. As long as it takes, I guess." Now who but a seeker says that?

Sometimes when a seeker shows up, I get premonitions. It's like a frequency from the middle of the lake transports into my brain. What entered my mind this time was that Jacob needed to get out on the water pronto. The signal was strong.

I don't question why I'm in tune to the paranormal. I just hear the music and follow the beat. Yes indeed, yes indeed.

After Jacob dropped off his luggage, I was glad to see him head toward the lake like I told him. Like *it* told me. But I had no idea he'd stay out there in that uncomfortable kayak longer than any guest ever has. It was already getting dark, so I decided to take my motorboat out for a spin to make sure everything was okay.

While I was revving up the engine at the dock, Jacob reappeared ashore. He didn't even acknowledge me. He just rose from the kayak, rubbed his back, and walked past me zombie-like to his room with a peaceful smile on his face.

Yep, there's something out there in the middle of the water, and Jacob tapped into it. And I made it happen.

In the morning, Jacob sat silent at breakfast. He picked at my homemade banana bread and looked at me with a strange expression, studying me. I told him about my favorite sites like I do for all my guests, where to hike and fish, but he didn't care. Sometimes that happens with the seekers. Instead, he settled his bill and grabbed his belongings. Right before leaving, he gave me a bear hug. "You helped me more than you know, old friend. It was paradise to be near Lizzy."

I don't know who Lizzy is, but that's beside the point. What matters is that this seeker discovered what he was after, and I helped. I feel proud that I do people a service running the Paradise Inn. Most guests visit for great fun and astounding views. And those who are seekers, at least the lucky ones like Jacob, connect with something otherworldly, from one of those billion trillion stars.

But I'm growing old and weary. I miss home. I just might sell the Paradise Inn when I find a buyer with the right attitude, pack my bags, and return to Roswell.

Before I do, I'm going out to the middle of Lake Paradise at night, just like Jacob. I want to see ET one last time. Yes indeed, yes indeed.

CHAPTER XVI - JACOB

O n the Wednesday night following his return from Lake Paradise, Jacob climbed into bed with trepidation. Would there be another horror film featuring him in the lead role after he turned off the lights? But Jacob enjoyed a perfect night of rest. His recurring dreams had ended.

But he obsessed over the dreams and what happened at Lake Paradise. Were they messages? *Yes.* Did he need to change his life? *Likely. What am I holding onto anyway?* Would he find more of his answers and solutions at Lake Paradise? *Maybe.*

Jacob fixated over relocating. He created detailed lists of the pros and cons of moving to Lake Paradise. Cost of living, distance from the twins, contrasting altitudes and attitudes, even the effect on Hunter were studied. *What about the healthcare system in the boonies? Can I make a few new friends at this stage in life?*

The results of his analysis were close, but even as Jacob tallied them, he understood that something else was at play. Jacob had discovered where Lizzy was, just offshore, in the heart of paradise where their eyes locked together as one. And if she was there, weren't the answers about life, about death, there as well? *I guess I have enough faith to take this leap,* he mused. *I'll flip the switch on this one time. The signal is remarkably strong.*

He sold the Minnesota house for a fair price and bought a cabin on the shore of Lake Paradise with the help of a scrupulous agent. The cabin was built of sturdy oak, had three bedrooms and a remodeled kitchen. Each window offered panoramic views. While his new home was more expensive, Jacob didn't hesitate. He could easily afford it from those crafty real estate investments he had made with the professor.

Before relocating, Jacob updated the twins. Walter was encouraging. "I'm proud of you, Dad, for being brave, taking bold steps. I have faith and trust in the Lord that this is for the best." There was a tinge of relief in his voice.

Michelle, however, could barely contain her worries. "Dad, don't rush into things. Stay here with me and Gracie instead until you sort it out. Please, please come. We'll talk." Of course, she knew her stubborn father would refuse.

Jacob told both children, "I must follow my dreams." Neither twin understood just how literal he was being as he packed his belongings and made the trek out West with Hunter.

From the moment Jacob pulled into the cabin's driveway, he knew he had made the right decision. The house was in perfect shape, the surroundings surreal. He could make his way to the water within minutes. And there were multitudes of nearby trails to explore.

Jacob soon spent entire days at one with nature, becoming part of the landscape, breathing in tranquility. Hunter was eager to hike with Jacob anytime, anywhere. The canine expressed unbridled joy, unleashed in the crisp mountain air, chasing squirrels, and detecting enticing scents from all directions.

Jacob felt liberated and perhaps even spiritual. He called his new home "God's country," a place where he could literally see the workings of a higher power in the majestic nature. He fixated over the connection between the two. *Were God and nature the same? Was the solution hidden in the connection?*

Lake Paradise touched something deep within Jacob that had been missing. He wondered if it was his soul. He then considered the consequences of having one. *Does a soul prove God exists? That we are eternal, in His image?*

Jacob's questions remained perpetual, as was his devotion to Lizzy. He maintained his mealtime vigil, keeping that extra place setting for her. After gazing into his love's eyes through the waters, he understood she had never left him. They were both part of paradise, in the different ways that apply to the living and the dead. But he missed her.

While Jacob spent considerable time in solitude, this was not

Walden Pond, nor had he become Henry David Thoreau. After all, it was still a vacation destination with plenty to keep him busy.

Jacob made friends with several locals. He met a group of retirees for weekly breakfasts at Paradise Donuts, where he mostly listened to the banter, dunking sweet pastries in his bitter brew. Oftentimes, he became preoccupied with his usual thoughts about life, about death, as the conversation flowed around him. He couldn't help it. *I've come a long way from Minnesota,* he reflected. *But wherever I go, I'm still me.*

Jacob also stayed in close touch with his oldest pal, the professor, and gained a pair of unlikely new friends in the rabbi and CEO. The professor was his link to the past, his boyhood chum who helped make him rich in adulthood. The rabbi and CEO were newer cronies, each willing to probe endlessly with Jacob over the imponderables that fixated him. *I'd love to get the professor, rabbi, and CEO in a room together,* he thought. *The stories they could tell.*

Once a year, the twins would visit—separately, of course. Jacob and Hunter tried to make them feel like royalty. His children seemed to relax and breathe deeply in the fresh mountain air. But Jacob also sensed that they struggled with the inevitable pull from their lives back home, unable to completely immerse themselves in his paradise.

Jacob reciprocated, flying back to see Walter and Michelle each summer. He wanted to spend quality time as a unified family, but old grudges persisted. Jacob visited one week with Walter and spent the other with Michelle, keeping the peace but missing something important in the process.

He also made time while in Minnesota to visit the homeless man, to resume their ritual of coffee, apple pie, and cash. Nothing seemed to change in the bleak slum so distant from paradise.

During Jacob's first week at Lake Paradise, he planted a beautiful weeping willow in the backyard. Each spring, the tree flowered, and the aroma wafted through the cabin's open windows. It reminded him of Lizzy's sweet scent, of rebirth, and an eternal order so magnificent that it could not be comprehended. But he still endeavored to understand it. Lord how he tried.

Seven years later, the tree had grown tall enough to provide soothing shade to accompany its sweeping charm. It was under the weeping willow that Hunter was buried. Jacob tried to console himself that his canine companion had not disappeared. *He's still part of the world, just in a different way,* he reasoned. *Like Lizzy.* But this theoretical construct that he had labored so hard to devise did nothing to ease his grief. Instead, Jacob broke down and sobbed uncontrollably as he placed Hunter into the ground.

Prior to Hunter's death, Jacob believed that his relocation was a success. But where was his answer, his solution? What had he really learned in seven years? Time was evaporating and Jacob was still wrestling, at the tip of the apex, balancing precariously on the highest mountain peak as it soared toward heaven. Inch by inch, Jacob ventured closer to the sun, to the blistering heat, to the ultimate, with a vengeful Antaeus standing guard.

Jacob's world was on the verge of conflagration. Hallucinations were gathering like thunderclouds at the gates of paradise.

PART II

The Rabbi Chronicles

"It is a mysterious thing, the loss of faith—as mysterious as faith itself."

—George Orwell

CHAPTER 1 – THE RABBI

The rabbi knew he was overreacting. Nobody can bat a thousand. Taken in isolation, the misstep was a blip. But after twelve excruciating years, it was the final straw.

His encounter with Jacob the dreamer, months before Jacob moved to Lake Paradise, had been a disaster. Instead of helping, he made matters worse by asking Jacob to contribute to his Fund for Life. The rabbi had full discretion to spend donations on whatever he deemed helpful for the congregation. It was not a coincidence that the money benefited him too. *What's good for the rabbi is good for BC,* he rationalized, supported by his wife's spirited encouragement. His self-loathing soared as he recalled his disingenuous advice: "Many BC members find God through acts of philanthropy even if they have trouble accepting all the stories." *Poor judgment, no class,* he ruminated. *Jacob knew the score.*

And he liked Jacob. He perceived a refreshing innocence and sincerity in the perplexed man. There was depth to this dreamer in crisis. The rabbi's job was to help people like Jacob find meaning. He browbeat himself for his selfish failure.

After Jacob left the synagogue, the rabbi instructed Sophie, his loyal secretary, to hold all calls. He rarely did that, wanting to be fully accessible whenever congregants needed him. Sophie looked curious, but simply responded, "Yes, chief." The rabbi knew she hungered for gossip, but mechanically walked to his office in silence and shut the door with uncharacteristic force.

Once alone, he sat paralyzed at his desk. The only time he moved was to stroke his long shaggy beard, his fingers traversing through the thick bush like a theologian from a bygone era. His wife, Mia, called this habit the "sacred stroke." She joked, "I can tell you're bothered when you fondle your face. The more strokes, the bigger the problem." Mia was sensitive to the pressures her husband faced as leader of the ever-expanding BC religious community. Getting serious, she spoke with admiration in her voice. "I know you are talking to God for guidance when you do the sacred stroke. So, I'll lie low and give you space."

The rabbi appreciated her unwavering support. Mia was the model wife in many ways. But as his vigil continued, he couldn't help but feel that she was also a big part of the problem. He needed more space than she could imagine.

The rabbi finally rose from his desk, only to stretch his arms and move to the beat-up couch in the corner of his office. This was a change of scenery, nothing more. Again, he sat comatose, sunk in the cushions in harsh introspection, as day turned to night. The only proof that rigor mortis had not set in was again his unrelenting sacred stroke.

He was surrounded by a vast collection of treasured books. The rabbi had read them all, marking them up in the margins in red ink with his own carefully considered observations. He never placed a book on the shelves unless he had devoured it, found it insightful and thought it might prove useful for future guidance. This man of books loved to preserve his literary jewels.

Pictures of the rabbi's family were scattered on the bookshelves. Prominently displayed was a photograph of his beloved parents, still in their prime, long before the tragedy. There was also a picture of beautiful Mia on their wedding day and a photo of their only child, Hannah, clutching a stuffed baby panda. Hannah and her little Binxie were inseparable. Hannah's name meant "grace" in Hebrew, a quality the rabbi and Mia hoped to instill in their daughter. The rabbi let out a long sigh. *If only I could go back in time to make things right.*

To visitors, it seemed as if the rabbi's perfect family was smiling at him, reaching out from the picture frames to embrace the wise man. This was a mirage. He felt no joy, only paralysis and self-contempt.

Next to the snapshot of his parents was an antique pocket watch in mint condition. It was pure silver and kept perfect time despite its age. The rabbi's parents had proudly presented the timepiece to him when he completed his studies at Divinity school. Inscribed on the casing was a love note: "To our beloved son, a work of God doing God's work."

The pocket watch was not only a treasured memento from his deceased parents. It was also, at one time, a symbol of everything the rabbi stood for, all he believed in. It served as proof of a higher order, of the Hebrew God. And from God, the rabbi took his marching orders.

How did he attach such significance to a mere artifact? The answer could be found in his favorite book from Divinity school called *Natural Theology*, by William Paley. He removed the book from the shelves and gazed sadly at the fervent red markings he scribbled in the margins as a student long ago.

Back then, he enthusiastically embraced Paley's view that an intricate instrument like his very pocket watch proved the existence of a creator possessing intelligence and purpose. Certainly, no animal could have produced something this complex and artistic. Instead, man, a superior being, was responsible, and the motive for the creation was to keep time.

Likewise, when a mere mortal beholds the sheer complexity of the human body, the intricate workings of the eyes, the brilliance of life-giving organs functioning in synchrony, it is equally evident that a creator endowed with wisdom and power far superior to man was responsible. Just as man produced the pocket watch, Paley concluded that God created man. And the rabbi agreed, heart and soul. The rabbi went on to embrace the teachings of the Hebrew Torah, which he believed was handed down from the Lord and explained His purpose for man's creation.

The rabbi's parents raised him with these beliefs, and he was a good, obedient son. The pocket watch analogy was his final springboard to a robust acceptance of faith. It provided him with theoretical fortification as he zealously marched into the clergy to the religious beat of the ticking antique.

Stroke, ponder, stroke, ponder, stroke, ponder. The rabbi slumped further into the couch and shook his head wearily. He beat himself up over the leaps in logic he carelessly took in the name of faith. He had flippantly disregarded Paley's critics, who argued that the complexity of the human body can result from evolution and other forces besides a Divine creator. And he ignored the fact that Paley believed in Jesus and Christianity, not Judaism. After more sacred strokes, he cleared his throat, let out another mournful sigh and stood, leaving a dent in the cushion.

The rabbi walked to the shelf robotically, placed *Natural Theology* back where it belonged and picked up his cherished pocket watch. He inspected it, as he used to do when seeking inspiration. He removed his glasses to see it better, to take a closer look at his parents' loving inscription. Tears filled his eyes. *I'm so sorry Mom and Dad.* He then gently placed the keepsake on the floor, lifted his right foot high in the air, and slammed down on the antique with all his strength.

The rabbi's mind reflexively shifted to the shattering of glass by the groom at a Jewish wedding, the traditional last step in the ceremony, and the many times he had happily shouted, "Mazel Tov!" to bless the moment. His smashing of the pocket watch sounded the same.

But this was not a joyous occasion. The rabbi had destroyed his most treasured possession, his talisman. Shards of glass surrounded him as he stood hunched over, eyes cast down to the floor. And while in that pose, the rabbi softly uttered, "Mazel Tov," in a shaky voice to nobody but the books and pictures staring out at him in disbelief.

Roots of purpose sprouted in his heart. He picked up the phone and called Jacob. "I want to meet again, my friend. We have more in common than you think."

Jacob took the call while nursing a late-night glass of wine in his recliner. He sounded surprised and unsure how to respond. He took a sip, reached down to pet Hunter, and finally said, "Why not, Rabbi? Let's give it another go."

CHAPTER II - MIA

I was packing our suitcases when Sophie phoned to report that "the rabbi" would be home late. After all these years, she still calls him by his official title and that's okay. But when I think of my dear husband, he is Aaron Friedler. And "the rabbi" too, of course. There was still so much to do that I didn't give Sophie's call a second thought.

We are travelling to Napa Valley with the synagogue's board of directors and some influential contributors. We depart early tomorrow, which is perfect since we'll still have time for fun in the sun.

Our trip was advertised by the temple as "a retreat." Sometimes we call it that, other times we label it "a mission." Mostly it will be a glorious vacation.

We'll spend a week at a working farmhouse in a vineyard that boasts an infinity pool overlooking the California countryside. I heard it's five stars. Wow! The BC travelers will play together, pray as one, dine on French cuisine with home-grown wine and, most important, bond.

We have the best programs. On the first day, we'll take a class called "Meditating Merlot." We'll be led by a master guru in a newly renovated part of the farmhouse designed for quietude, while sampling the best reds in the Valley. We also booked a cooking class with a popular chef from San Francisco who adds cinnamon and a hint of chocolate to his exotic creations. Yum! And then it's off to Palmar Vineyard, producer of the best Cabernet in the country.

Of course, there will be loads of free time. We can ride bicycles through the vineyards, swim in the infinity pool or do some good ole shopping. I love hunting for antiques with the ladies. They have great taste and can spot a bargain anywhere. Sometimes, they buy me a gift just for tagging along.

Yep, I'm excited. Not only will I be with people I love, but I've got a little secret that makes the trip even better. It won't cost Aaron or me a penny. The flight, hotel, meals, even the wine tour and cooking class, are on the house. The rabbi and his wife always travel first class while our members pay just a little more to bring us along. If we fall short of money for some crazy reason, no problem. Aaron's Fund for Life pays the rest.

It only makes sense, doesn't it? We're the leaders of BC. Our flock needs us to guide it on the pilgrimage. We provide the inspiration, the religiosity. We are the exemplars. I do whatever I can to make the trip a delight for everyone and Aaron shares his brilliant insights. For us, this is work, work, work. So why should we pay?

I do, however, play a little game that only Aaron knows about. I like to record our freebies in my Book of Balloons. This is where I keep track of the fun things that we receive that nobody else does, our extra perks. Ha, I'm like an accountant, but this isn't taxable. And let me tell you, it adds up fast. Imagine being treated like this for doing what you love while helping people. Not bad for a girl from a family that struggled to put food on the table.

Don't get me wrong. Religion is important to me too. I love singing the prayers out loud while Aaron leads the service. During the week, I hum the catchy tunes and they put me in a happy frame of mind.

But I have a secret. I don't care about the lofty teachings that Aaron obsesses over. He's so cute with that sacred stroke. All his philosophies are too serious for me. I say just go with the flow and don't think so much. It's more about the joy you get from religion and the happiness you spread. And to be paid these extras? Well, that's a miracle!

Anyway, I was doing the best I could to zip my suitcase over four pairs of shoes when Aaron finally limped through the door looking like he'd been mugged. My husband is not the tall, dark, and athletic type on a good day, but he seemed even more run down than usual. The California weather and dips in the pool will do him a world of good.

While scurrying around the house and making last-minute changes to my wardrobe, I asked Aaron how his day went and why he was late. It looked like he was unsure how to respond. Finally, he answered, "There are four hundred and fifty families in the temple and over fourteen hundred souls. I'm up to my eyeballs meeting their needs. Things happen day and night." He sighed and bowed his head in exhaustion. "Day and night," he repeated, talking to himself as much as to me.

It looked like something important was eating at him, but he kept telling me about the usual synagogue affairs. "The BC board wants me to weigh in on architectural plans to expand the building. And the CEO was at it again, making sure GoldOrb gets loud applause for funding the renovation. Honey, I'm frazzled. Sorry I'm late."

I gave Aaron a quick hug and brought him a plate of leftovers from our synagogue luncheon. The food was donated by Emanuel's Eatery, the hottest vegan restaurant in town. There was plenty remaining, so I filled up a shopping bag and brought the food home for dinner. Ha, another entry for my Book of Balloons.

I could see that I needed to pump Aaron up for our vacation. "Just eat, enjoy, I've got packing under control. Should I throw in a bathing suit for you? I know you love the whirlpools and schvitz."

"Whatever," he responded, looking withered, as if he had already been in the steam bath far too long.

"You'll be able to relax, take it easy in Napa Valley," I cajoled. "I'm so excited, I can't wait!"

Anyone could see that my husband was bedraggled. He barely sleeps nowadays. And when he does catch a wink, he wakes up screaming. Two nights ago, his pajama shirt was soaked with perspiration as he sat up in bed. "I can't recall each detail, but the dream is recurrent and horrible," he confessed. "It happens in the synagogue's basement. A surgeon wearing a black mask is trying to cut out my heart with a sharp scalpel. His green eyes flash out at me brighter than is humanly possible."

Yikes, what a doozy. Such a nightmare for my poor Aaron. I wondered if there was more to the dream that he wasn't telling. But this vacation to wine country will do the trick. He needs a break and a little pampering, that's all. We'll be surrounded by admirers and can bask in the healing warmth they reserve for their beloved rabbi … and for me, his loyal wife.

I haven't told Aaron the big news yet, but we have another BC trip in the works. There's talk of a mission to Morocco to view religious sites and connect with Jews from Casablanca. While in Africa, it just makes sense to hop a few flights for a safari and to tour Victoria Falls. And, yes, it will be on the house for the rabbi and his wife. More to add to my Book of Balloons.

I love being the rabbi's wife! I love my life!

CHAPTER III – THE RABBI

The rabbi lay awake in bed staring at his sleeping wife, watching her breasts gently rise and fall with each breath. She was still so beautiful. Unlike many women her age, Mia retained her petite figure. Her skin was soft and smooth, and when she smiled, her dimples radiated. He used to tell her, "You've got dimples the size of the moon." The rabbi admired how peacefully she slept, rejuvenating for her big day of travel.

She'd been enthusiastic and supportive from the very beginning. She was the perfect rabbi's wife, a wonderful *rebbetzin*, as she was fondly called by the older Yiddish speaking members of the congregation. Unlike so many spouses of clergy who eschewed the attention, the scrutiny, the entire blessed scene, Mia reveled in the spotlight. Her cheerfulness was contagious and complemented the rabbi's studiousness and contemplative nature. But Mia's effervescence no longer lifted the rabbi's spirits. *She goes too far. Both our perspectives have clouded.*

As often occurred during these sleepless periods of high anxiety, the rabbi dwelt upon his past and how he had gotten to this juncture. As a boy, he knew he was different. Sadly, the children made sure he learned that lesson the hard way. He was that too small, too skinny, too freckled target dressed in the wrong clothing. No Levi's blue jeans for him. His parents bought baggy, off-colored pants from the clearance rack instead, adorned with an uncool gray label on the back pocket that proclaimed his peculiarity to the world. It might as well have read "Bullseye."

He was also brilliant, which made it even harder to fit in. The rabbi was doted on by his teachers while ostracized by the students. He would have chosen sides with the kids in a heartbeat.

The playground became his personal war zone. The rabbi was picked last when the boys chose up teams for baseball, basketball, and football. You name it, he was the afterthought. He ate lunch with a few other misfits in the school cafeteria as he read the adoring note from his mother, eyes lowered, head down, shamed. The message was taped to the plastic baggie holding his sandwich: "I love you, Aaron. Enjoy your tuna fish."

Dennis Rodstein took notice and smirked. Even now, lying in bed with his wife, a lifetime removed from the humiliation, the rabbi could still smell the fresh cut grass that his face was anchored in while the school bully gave him a severe wedgie. How the girls laughed. Rodstein hammed it up for the captivated audience. "Nerdy momma's boy has more skid marks than highway twenty-five. Smells like he never wipes. Guess he needs dipes." The rhyme threw the children into fits of laughter as they chanted, "Look what Aaron is wearin'!" No spelling bee victory or prize in the county's math competition could compensate for this debasement.

But life had its upsides and kept the boy on course. The rabbi's parents were steadfast in their support, and this meant everything. His dad provided classic counsel often reserved for the too small, too skinny, too freckled, too smart. "The kids are jealous, Son. Someday they'll look up to you when the tables turn and your intelligence shines through. You'll see!"

His mother joined the rehabilitation project, hugging the boy tight. "I'm so proud of you and your accomplishments Aaron. You have the talent to be an important leader." And then he'd catch a whiff of the ultimate salve. "I'm baking chocolate chip cookies."

As usual, the rabbi's father was his rock, his mother his redeemer. His love for them was boundless.

The rabbi also felt at home at his parents' synagogue. The adults were nice to him and made him feel appreciated. He loved the biblical stories, especially about Jacob's dream. The notion of angels ascending and descending a staircase to heaven captured his imagination. Even as a boy, the rabbi believed dreams held great significance.

While other children played outdoors, he gobbled up everything there was to learn about Jewish customs and rituals, all in a nourishing environment with no one to antagonize him. The synagogue was his boyhood refuge.

During prayer service on Saturdays, the rabbi watched his mother reciting the verses while bowing and swaying. He could see from her ardent expression that she believed each word with every fiber of her spirit. And when he prayed like his mother, replicating her movements, the rabbi's father draped his arm around the boy's shoulder. "This is a beautiful service. I'm proud of you, Son."

These blissful moments inspired the rabbi. The gifted child gradually matured into a devout young man intent on becoming a religious leader. He would emerge victorious over his playground demons, just like his father predicted. And he would do so in step with the will of God. He felt empowered, enthralled.

Tossing and turning in the dead of night, the rabbi relived these emotions. Eventually, sorrow replaced them. He couldn't escape from the homicide, the suicide.

Mia rolled over and put her arms around him, still in a deep, regenerating sleep. He felt a sense of security and warmth from his wife, much like he experienced when his father embraced him at the synagogue long ago. Finally, he calmed his mind and drifted to sleep, the couple intertwined as one like thousands of times before.

A half hour later, the rabbi kicked Mia in the knee screaming, "NO, NO, GET AWAY!" He was strapped down in the BC basement and the black-masked surgeon with flashing green eyes was readying to operate. The surgeon's scalpel nicked his chest and was on the verge of penetrating deeper. Dark red blood percolated from the incision. He had to escape. The kick was hard enough to stir Mia but didn't hurt. She mumbled softly to the rabbi from her sleepy haze, "Rest sweetly, my love. California here we come."

Mia was oblivious to his anguish. She rolled over and fell back into her gratifying slumber. No need to dream. She was living it.

Inches away, the rabbi stared at the ceiling in terror. For him, the bedroom had become a torture chamber, his mattress a hospital gurney. He ruminated over his nightmare, still believing that dreams mattered.

With each recurring episode, the masked surgeon's scalpel had inched closer before he could awaken. At first, he roused when the surgeon picked up the deadly instrument from a nearby metallic table. The next time, he awoke when the masked man raised it, and so on, until this latest dream where the scalpel grazed his chest, the surgeon's green eyes burning with desire. At this rate, the rabbi's beating heart would soon be sliced from his body.

He had to escape the bedroom. He kissed his sleeping wife and went downstairs for a glass of water. He then proceeded to the living room, turned on the lights full blast and picked up a magazine. But the rabbi couldn't concentrate. Instead, his mind locked in on what happened a few hours earlier, reliving the sound that his cherished pocket watch had made as he smashed it to pieces. *Mazel Tov, Mazel Tov,* echoed in his brain.

He was twisted in knots. He had always been a pleaser and couldn't bear to disappoint anyone. He pleased his parents. He pleased his teachers. He pleased his congregation. He pleased his wife. *And I thought that I pleased God,* he considered with a feeling bordering on contempt.

The days of making everyone happy were over. It was time for the rabbi to focus on himself. Otherwise, the surgeon's scalpel would finish the job.

The rabbi resolved not to lead the BC retreat to Napa Valley. He knew that Mia would be upset, the congregation shocked. Nobody would be pleased, but he was out of options. He was on the brink of a seismic change, and it somehow involved Jacob, the dreamer.

CHAPTER IV - HANNAH

I t was a fairy-tale beginning. A thousand people celebrated my baby naming in a large reception hall near the back of the synagogue. The room boasts an oversized ornate clock, like the one at Grand Central Station in New York. "Gratitude to God" is inscribed on its face and beneath that appears a message from the CEO in smaller print: "A gift from GoldOrb Diversified."

The food came from Katz Caterers, a new deli in town. They got a tax write-off and an advertising blitz from their generosity. Mom gushed with joy as if the Almighty was pleased with the free pastrami and knishes.

There's a picture of the tumultuous event hanging in my parents' living room over the sofa. Mom and Dad wore outsized smiles while holding little me with a throng of strangers crowding us, staring in, suffocating me.

In my early childhood, people treated me like royalty. They said I inherited Dad's brains and Mom's looks. "What a fusion," an older lady with a triple chin doted, wrapping her arms around my glowing mother. "The rabbi's daughter won the genetic lottery."

The compliments were endless, and we basked in them. When I walked to my seat for religious services, trailing Mom down the center aisle of the sanctuary, the tiny princess at the heels of the queen, I heard whispers:

"She's gorgeous, just look at her."
"I hear the little lady is a genius like the rabbi. She'll skip a grade."
"Wait until she's older. Boys will swoon."
"I love her dress, her shoes, her ponytails, her!"

The compliments enchanted my little girl ears while Mom and

Dad feasted on the accolades. They loved the congregation, and they thought they loved me. So, my parents beamed with pride when their two favorite things merged.

And let's not forget how they preached family values, reciting chapter and verse from the Torah to support allegiance to the tribe. I was living proof that the rabbi and rebbetzin put their money where their mouths were. Yes, we were the model clan. And I was the ideal child on display for all to see. For everyone to *kvell* and gossip over as they peered into our fishbowl.

I think you can tell from my tone that we didn't live happily ever after. The fairy tale began to unravel when I grew from cute to awkward as a teen. This was near the time of my bat mitzvah when the whole congregation celebrated my parents by hoisting them into chairs and carrying them around the building while I quietly munched on kugel.

Mom still wanted to dress me in ribbons and curls, but when high school arrived, I insisted on cutting my hair short and wearing dark buttoned-down shirts over my flat chest, tucked into tight black jeans. I also began hanging out with kids my parents didn't like.

The whispers from outside the fishbowl changed:

"*The princess is becoming a prince.*"

"*She looks like a boy, oy, oy.*"

"*I heard she befriended that Rodstein girl, the one who causes trouble.*"

"*The rebbetzin told me she's beside herself with what to do about Hannah. She's asking for advice.*"

It felt like everybody was talking behind my back.

Dad tried to reason with me. He came into my room and sat on my bed doing the sacred stroke. "Listen, Hannah, we are leaders of the community with an image to maintain."

"Yes, Dad."

"People are worried about what they're seeing."

"Okay. Noted."

"You have to clean up your act right now."

How, how, how?!

It was typical. Dad always bent over backward to preserve his reputation. He wanted me to genuflect to the crowd along with him.

My full rebellion started at sixteen. It happened at a BC party hosted by two big shots for their twenty-fifth wedding anniversary. They were renewing their vows, and Dad was to officiate. I was invited, even though I had nothing to do with these people. Desperate for Mom and Dad to stop parading me around like a trophy, I refused to go. But then Leslie Rodstein told me she was related to the "newlyweds" and would be there. So, I caved.

Dad's face got all contorted when I mentioned Leslie. I heard that he didn't get along with her father back in the day.

Leslie and I hated the boring music and slow dances. So, we hung out in the bathroom. Nothing was premeditated, but we ended up in a stall together and nature did its thing. We made out while feeling each other up, exploring all the curves. A few minutes later, our shirts were unbuttoned, just in time for one of the biggest mouths at BC, Mrs. Kepler, to enter. She heard us in the stall and knew exactly what we were doing. Her face was ablaze with moral indignation, make that sheer excitement, as she flushed us from our cubby hole. Word about the rabbi's daughter spread like a plague.

Back home, Mom and Dad confronted me. They reacted as if I had murdered them and slit the throats of our holy ancestors who preceded us. I had shamed them and, of course, was grounded forever.

Dad forced me to accompany him while he called the CEO of GoldOrb, Mrs. Kepler, and other prominent congregants. His ears were bright red. "I want to apologize for my daughter's abhorrent behavior," he groveled. "She's right beside me now. I'm so sorry, and she is too." After he made his last call, he stared darts at me. "This must never happen again, Hannah, do you hear?! Do you?! You have a *responsibility*."

I understood why my parents were angry. What I did was natural, but where I did it was wrong. Still, I can't comprehend why they didn't try to talk to me about the serious changes happening in my life, other than to lecture me that they were embarrassed. They didn't care about me or who I was becoming. They weren't concerned about anything other than our sacred status. Mom called us "exemplars." Well, it's hard to be a model of virtue for the entire community when it turns out you're an awkward teenager, completely confused about your sexuality.

I won't bore you with the whispers that slashed my confidence, how everyone looked away in mortal judgment as I trailed my mother down the same center aisle that I did as a small child to applause. Nor will I dwell on my parents' radio silence at a time when I needed kindness and guidance. I did not choose to be the rabbi's daughter. I did not ask to be a lesbian. God made me this way.

Dad reacted to my new reality with distance and distraction. Was it all because of what I did in the bathroom? Was there something else? And Mom built a high wall with barbed wire to separate us. She busied herself with BC congregants and events, leaving me to work things out alone.

The beloved princess had become the pariah in the fishbowl. The fairy tale was over. Therapy was beginning, and it would last a long time.

CHAPTER V – THE RABBI

Mia stretched with satisfaction from a good night's sleep. She vaguely recalled that Aaron suffered a nightmare, sighed for the poor dear, and made her way downstairs to find him.

Her husband was in the living room staring into space. "You better get moving," she said excitedly. "Gotta go!"

Aaron's face was ashen. "I can't travel to Napa Valley. I don't belong." No matter how hard he tried, he couldn't explain his decision further.

Mia stared at him in astonishment. She had known that something was eating at him. *Maybe a midlife crisis,* she speculated. Deep down, a small voice tried to get her to listen. *He hasn't been himself for a very long time.* She had repeatedly disregarded the warning signals with unbending optimism, reasoning that the rabbi had continued to meet every challenge. He was a fine husband, a good man, and helped many a congregant through his own crisis, her hour of need. *So, he has a few nightmares,* she assured herself. *He's fine.*

"Aaron, this is crazy."

"No."

"Please, we can't play around. We've got a flight to catch."

"I can't. I don't belong. NO!"

From the hardened look on Aaron's face and locked-in tone of his voice, Mia understood that she would be unable to coax him into changing his mind. Not in the few minutes before the taxi to the airport was scheduled to arrive. Her only recourse was to lead the group to California without him.

Flabbergasted, she remained practical. There was so much to love about their elevated status as rabbi and rebbetzin. The spiritual and material bounty were elixirs. It made no sense to jeopardize everything just because her husband was in an irrational funk.

Out of options and time, she looked at the rabbi sternly. "I'll go without you, but you're acting bizarre, irresponsible. Our lives are glorious, and I'll do whatever it takes to protect them." She would tell anybody who asked that the rabbi had a bad case of the flu. "So, your job is to recuperate and get over what's ailing you. This can't happen again, or people will talk. When I return, you'll be good as new. You must. For both of us. For all of us. We need our rabbi."

Mia was strong and capable. But her irrepressible positivity and infatuation with her lifestyle clouded her vision. This was not a one-shot deal to be cured like the common cold.

The rabbi looked crushed by his wife's admonishments and the guilt he felt over disappointing her. He nodded his head but gave Mia no assurances. Without making eye contact, he said, "Travel safely."

With the honk of the horn from the impatient taxi driver, Mia left. The rabbi could breathe again, but there would be no lasting relief. He suffered unrelenting remorse over abandoning his wife and responsibilities. Doubts bombarded him. *Am I really rendezvousing with this Jacob, a stranger, instead of going on the retreat? What about my wife, my career?*

Invisible forces were at play that the rabbi could not control. Impulses were emanating directly from his beating heart, the organ so vulnerable to the masked surgeon of the night. *A person can only push so far, clinging to the past, when his spirit aches to be released in a new direction,* he thought. And in this case, the rabbi's primal instincts signaled that his path somehow led through Jacob.

They met at Lee's Tavern the next evening, the same bar where Jacob reunited with his boss. The rabbi didn't want to host a second meeting at the synagogue since he was feigning illness. He told Jacob, "You decide when and where. It's your home turf this time."

Lee's Tavern was not the type of establishment that the rabbi frequented, but when he entered and felt the amiable atmosphere, he thought it was perfect. He also was relieved to see that there weren't any BC congregants in the place. *People talk,* he worried.

The owner escorted them to a small wobbly table in the corner. When the waitress ambled over and greeted them, the rabbi held back, waiting for Jacob to order. Jacob requested a Corona with a lime and the rabbi piped up, "Make that two," not really knowing what type of alcohol he even liked other than the sugary red wine he drank on Friday nights after making a blessing.

The rabbi stared at Jacob, weighing what to say next while doing the sacred stroke. Finally, he removed his thick glasses and spoke. "Jacob, thanks for agreeing to see me again. Listen, let me just get it out there and apologize. I should never have asked for a donation to my Fund for Life when you came looking for help. It was selfish. It would mean more to me than you could imagine if we could get back on track and try to work things out for you."

Jacob shrugged. "You actually did me a favor, Rabbi, so no big deal. You got me to thinking about charity. I found a needy person on the streets, a homeless guy down on his luck."

The rabbi hesitated, processing Jacob's cryptic response about the homeless man. Again, he liked this guy. Jacob was a decent human being and the rabbi intrinsically trusted him. He needed to unburden himself, away from the BC fishbowl where he had to be perfect. *I have no friends there. Not real ones who I can talk to.*

The rabbi sipped from his mug, noting the bitterness. Still, he kind of liked it. The beer made him feel alive in a strange sort of way. To Jacob's astonishment, he chugged the rest, working up enough courage to take a leap. "Jacob, let me tell you something that might surprise you," he said in a quivering voice. "Perhaps you'll be more at ease with your own life if you know you aren't alone in your doubts, your nightmares. The long and short of it is that I, too, have no idea what to believe." The rabbi paused, looking like he had confessed a felony. "At one time, I had all the answers. Such hubris. But that day has come and gone. I lost my faith twelve years ago from a calamity. Since then, my friend, I've lived a lie. I'm a leader without conviction. A wise rabbi who knows nothing. A total fake. And, like you, nightmares haunt me."

Jacob, an introverted man with scant experience in heart-to-heart talks, was tongue tied. He looked paralyzed, then mystified. Finally, he blurted out in a high-pitched voice that was intended to be sympathetic: "What! How can that be?! You're the rabbi. You are *leading* those people!"

The rabbi sobbed, causing the table to wobble in synch with his heaving. Jacob scanned the room in panic and urgently signaled the waitress to bring another round of Coronas. "Hurry. Make it fast." Then, turning again to the rabbi, *"What?!"*

CHAPTER VI – THE NURSE

I won't forget Mr. and Mrs. Friedler. Never!

He checked in at age sixty-three, young but in bad condition. They thought she'd be fine living on her own. Just lonely. But she needed to be with her soulmate. And it turns out that she suffered from the same curse. While her disease struck later, it destroyed her mind faster. So, Mrs. Friedler joined her husband on the fifth floor just a few months after he got here.

Let me tell you about Sunnyside Nursing Home. From the outside, it looks all nice, modern, and spic and span. Even *sunny*, like they want you to think. But once you get to know the place, it's more like a mausoleum, except the corpses walk the halls. And the owners don't give a shit. They just line their pockets, charging sick old people until they go broke while paying us peanuts.

Floor five is the last place you want to go. That's where my station is, with cheap plastic plants and reeking disinfectant. Me and a few other nurses from south of the border, one a "Dreamer" and another without a hint of papers, spend our day chasing too many residents to handle with too many problems to fix. They all have Alzheimer's Disease. I told my daughter, "Shoot me if I get it, put me out of my misery fast." *Dios Mío.*

Mr. and Mrs. Friedler were the only married couple on my floor. Their son with that long beard fixed their room up nice. I heard he was the rabbi of a big important place a few miles from here. I never met one before, but I liked him. He always made time to talk to me, not like a lot of the visitors who are in a rush to get the hell out of here. They treat me like another plastic plant.

The rabbi brought pictures to hang on the wall in his parents' room. "Don't you remember this photo?" he asked. "It was taken on my graduation day from Divinity school and is in my office too." Both Mr. and Mrs. Friedler wore huge smiles in the photo and had their arms around the rabbi, looking proud.

The rabbi then pounded something in the wall by their door. It was made of colorful tinted glass and reminded me of a church window, or those pretty lamps from fancy furniture stores, only smaller. "It's called a 'mezuzah,'" he said. "My parents had one at home and touched it for good fortune and to show respect to God whenever they walked in and out of the house. They can do that here."

"What a great idea to help mamma and pappa feel at home," I replied. "It's beautiful." And sure enough, while we were still talking, his mom and dad approached the mezuzah, one after the other, touched it and then kissed their hands while smiling at their son.

The rabbi visited often. The three of them would escape to a quiet courtyard overlooking a garden. The rabbi positioned himself between his parents, just like in the picture. He put an arm around each one, hugging them close. Some of my other residents on floor five have no visitors.

If only the garden scene could have lasted, but it never does here at Sunnyside. The Alzheimer's got worse. Mr. Friedler barely spoke and didn't seem to understand me anymore. Worse yet, this nice, gentle man turned violent, which was a real problem for us since he was still strong. I mean no disrespect, but where I come from, we'd call him *"loco."*

In the meantime, his wife remained mild and sweet, but was also sinking. She could no longer dress herself and had trouble with a fork and spoon, let alone holding onto her bowels until we could get her to the bathroom. We put her in diapers while she screamed words in a language we didn't understand.

It was like Sunnyside's drinking water was poisoning the rabbi's parents. I wondered if either of them even wanted to live.

Doctor Stern from floor one examined them and issued an order: "Monitor the situation." That meant we had no clue what to do. Nobody would. That's life, death. *Vida y muerte.*

I'm not going tell you every gruesome detail of what happened next. I can't bear it, even after all this time. But let me just say that as things continued to "progress," as the doctor likes to call it, meaning as they went to hell, Mr. Friedler became more violent, even dangerous, throwing food trays and disrupting singalongs.

Once, the rabbi called and asked to speak to his father. Mr. Friedler punched the nurse who was trying to hand him the phone. He gave her a bloody nose while profanity spewed from his mouth. "Get the fuck away from me, bitch!" he yelled, as the phone crashed to the floor. The rabbi could hear everything. I picked up the receiver and told the rabbi, "It's under control. Everything's fine." It wasn't.

Mr. Friedler behaved better at worship services on Saturday mornings. When the leader sang a prayer, he'd stop acting out and join in. He bothered some people, standing at the wrong time or praying too loud, but I thought it was good. Funny thing about those prayers. Sometimes, they're the only things left that people on floor five remember.

After more "monitoring," Doctor Stern prescribed some happy pills with the rabbi's approval. Drugging Mr. Friedler helped a bit. Plus, he'd always calm down when the rabbi visited and hugged his parents.

While Mr. Friedler was a handful, we could count on him being kind to his wife. Somehow, he still knew she was special, so we didn't worry about him trying to hurt her. He'd sit with her peacefully in the hallway and it looked like he was trying to protect her. When he started with the happy pills, he would remain content by her side for hours before roaming the halls, looking for trouble.

But now it was Mrs. Friedler's turn. She stopped talking and cried like a baby when she needed something. She had an old rag doll that she clutched all day long. She would sit there forever yanking its hair, fondling its eyeless sockets. She'd shriek when we took it away to feed her.

Mr. Friedler, while no longer as violent, thanks to the happy pills, lost control of his bladder. And he began repeating the same phrase over and over:

"The Lord is one. The Lord is one. The Lord is one."

He might have been right, but it drove us nuts. The rabbi explained that the words were part of an important Jewish prayer but grimaced when his father recited them like a tick.

I admit it. Sometimes I walked away from the rabbi's parents. I just couldn't cope. Our staff was bare bones. I was overwhelmed and underpaid. This was out of my league.

We invited the rabbi to a big meeting to be sure he understood what was happening. The cheap veneer table in our stuffy conference room served as a border. He sat alone on one side while floor five's staff talked at him from the other. The poor man kept stroking his beard and wiping tears from his eyes. He clutched the edge of the table like he was holding on for dear life, lost in this land of the dead known as Sunnyside Nursing Home.

When we finished the lecture, the rabbi was nice enough to thank us. "You're doing God's work for the elderly," he said. But the little man left Sunnyside slumped over and defeated. I couldn't blame him. It's rough enough when it's a ninety-year-old granddad. But when it's both of your parents at the same time and they are young, well, that's torture.

When his pretty wife with the dimples stopped by, she lifted everybody's spirits. But she didn't come often. "This is my lodestone," the rabbi explained. "Mia has her own life to live, and we need to keep up appearances at the temple. She's maintaining a presence."

I was picturing the rabbi with a heavy boulder on his back, slouched over, climbing a mountain, when I entered the Friedlers' room for my routine bedtime check. Something was different. The picture of the rabbi and his parents from graduation day had been removed from the wall. It was lying on the floor, smashed to pieces, with shards of glass sparkling against the tiles. I looked up at Mrs. Friedler's bed and noticed that she was on her side and still. A razor-sharp blade of glass sat near her pillow. It was smeared in red. And then my mind understood what my eyes were telling me. She was lying in a pool of her own blood with her neck slit open.

Mr. Friedler sat nearby on his own bed, staring at the vacant spot on the wall where the picture had been, reciting:

"The Lord is one. The Lord is one. The Lord is one."

I screamed for help, but nobody came. Next, I called Doctor Stern, but he didn't answer even though I knew he was in the building. Out of options, I gently placed Mrs. Friedler in a wheelchair and rushed her to Doctor Stern's office. He had fallen asleep with a book on his lap. When he comprehended the emergency, he sprang into action, but it was too late. "DOA," he announced as he closed her eyes. "Poor woman." We never called an ambulance.

When I returned to the room, Mr. Friedler was gone. Missing. How? But the bathroom door was open. I looked in and there he was, lying dead on the floor. Another pool of blood. The same shard of glass.

I called the rabbi, and he rushed over. He saw the bloody mess, fell on the floor and stayed there without moving or making a sound. When he finally rose, I told him the last words his father uttered.

The rabbi's jaw locked. He repeated, "The Lord is one," several times in a soft, trembling voice. When he finished, he walked over to the beautiful mezuzah he had brought for his parents to enjoy. This gentle man punched the colorful glass to pieces. I wonder if he needed stitches.

It's still a mystery whether the rabbi's parents planned to kill themselves. Doctor Stern got defensive when I brought it up, like he missed something he should have known. "No chance!" he lectured angrily. "They didn't have mental capacity, neither one. The picture frame must have fallen, launching a random chain of events. This was all a freak accident." I wasn't convinced.

If you were to read the obituaries, you'd think that what happened was normal. That old age had taken its toll, only twice, nothing more. Well, I'm proud to have helped keep the secret along with Doctor Stern. The rabbi had pleaded that we remain silent. "I don't want my congregants to learn of our family's shame," he said. "My parents deserve to die with respect. And Mia ... oh, Mia." He wiped his eyes and lowered his head.

A few hours later, the rabbi arranged for that undertaker friend of his to collect the bodies and do the paperwork. The undertaker didn't ask a single question. The man understood what needed to be done and moved fast.

I wanted to talk to somebody, but the only other person who knew the full story was Doctor Stern. When I went to see him, his face flushed. "Drop it," he said. "Nothing happened. Do you understand? *Nada.*"

He was nasty but right. Staying quiet was the least we could do. This nice family had enough grief. The rabbi would have been tormented if the story was gobbled up by the newspapers or made its way through gossip channels at their temple. Imagine the headline: "Prominent Rabbi's Father Kills Wife and Self in Bizarre Murder-Suicide."

And just think of the grilling we'd have faced at Sunnyside. Should Doctor Stern have prescribed the happy pills? Where was the staff when the murder happened? Why did I move Mrs. Friedler and leave Mr. Friedler alone? There would be more investigations than shards of glass from the smashed picture frame and mezuzah.

No, thank you. This was a tragedy, but it was nobody's fault. We did the right thing by not making noise.

Funny, but we never saw the rabbi's wife again. Maybe she was furious with Sunnyside and didn't want to speak to us. Who can blame her? Or maybe the rabbi was still carrying all the burden. I remembered his comment: "This is my loadstone." What a good man. *Un buen hombre.*

Even now, I'm disgusted to tell you that the owners of Sunnyside Nursing Home wouldn't give me time off for the funeral. I heard it was standing room only. People still talk about the rabbi's heartfelt eulogy, proclaiming his love for two remarkable parents. I doubt many in the crowd knew Mr. and Mrs. Friedler like I did. They certainly never visited them at Sunnyside.

May Mr. and Mrs. Friedler rest in peace. *Descansa en paz!* May their Lord, their precious "one Lord," watch over them in heaven. *En el paraíso!*

CHAPTER VII - THE RABBI AND JACOB

The waitress rushed over the new round of beers that Jacob urgently ordered and placed them on the wobbly table in the corner of Lee's Tavern. It was an extraordinary moment in the establishment's history. For at that table sat a frail little man with a shaggy beard and thick glasses wailing between convulsive gulps. Across from him was Jacob, wringing his hands, his forehead glistening with sweat and eyes twitching.

Patrons frequented the bar to talk boisterously about inconsequential nonsense. They bragged of sexual conquests and game winning bowling strikes, or lamented the latest Timberwolves defeat, the missed call by the referee. But at the wobbly table, the rabbi and Jacob were on the brink of a profound conversation, if only the rabbi would stop crying and Jacob's Early Warning System would deactivate.

Finally regaining his composure, the rabbi attempted to answer Jacob's probing question: *"What?!"* Moisture clouded his vision. "I loved my parents. They were my heroes and bowed down to God and his dictates. Well, if there is one Lord in control, He made them suffer and killed them in a gruesome way."

The rabbi took another break to steady his emotions while Jacob waited in silence. With one hand wiping his tears and the other doing the sacred stroke, he found the fortitude to continue. "Let me just say it out loud. My loving, demented father murdered my precious, senile mother. The weapon was a sharp piece of glass from a shattered picture frame holding a photo of me with my parents on graduation day from

Divinity school. After Mom died, my father committed suicide with the same blade."

Jacob looked stupefied but stayed quiet and inhaled his beer. He could see that the rabbi was gathering himself to confess more. "They left behind a shell of a son, the esteemed rabbi. I felt an obligation to my wife and congregation to carry on and protect my family's reputation. So, I kept it secret. I've tried to continue as if nothing happened, but the religion I preach rings hollow. Nothing comes from my heart."

The rabbi looked as if a burden had been lifted as he filled in the missing details. He wondered what it was about Jacob that enabled him to tell the truth after twelve long years of living a lie.

Jacob listened with genuine sympathy, trying to make sense of it all. He also chimed in when the rabbi seemed like he needed a break to share his own sorrows. "Lizzy and I finally had time to do things I put off too long. See the world. Instead, cancer got her." Now it was Jacob wiping his eyes. "It's as if she was being punished. But how can that be, Rabbi? She had a heart of gold. She put up with a lot from me."

"That makes it all the worse how I treated you the other day at BC," the rabbi responded. "You sought help, but I fed you a song and dance with my hand stretched out for money that I didn't need. You're a good man seeking answers. I'm nothing but a fake selling snake oil."

The rabbi looked exhausted. Jacob could see how he browbeat himself over things beyond his control. "Rabbi, I hope this conversation is helping," he said in an encouraging voice. "I guess this is like a confessional. Maybe the Catholics have it right."

The rabbi first chuckled meekly at Jacob's awkwardness, but his laughter grew in intensity until he was guffawing like a lunatic. He had often counseled congregants that the line between laughter and tears was blurred. He steadied himself again, feeling looser from the comic reprieve. "Jacob, I know you're seeking answers to hard questions. So, let me share what I've learned after four years of religious studies in college and five more at Divinity school, delving into the mysteries of our existence. I've spent my life poring over the words of countless sages accumulated over thousands of years. Not only Jewish wisdom, but the teachings of all major faiths and scholars. Socrates. The Gospel. Tillich. Nietzsche and those meshuga existentialists."

Jacob sat at the edge of his chair. He looked spellbound.

The rabbi looked at Jacob with kind eyes. "Let me save you time and a splitting headache, my friend. There are no answers to man's relation to the cosmos. None. Zip. There are only questions. Anyone who tells you otherwise is a counterfeit soothsayer and sitting right across from you is Exhibit A."

Jacob found the feedback eye opening coming from such a learned man, not that it would end his lifelong obsession to overcome the human predicament. But he set aside his impossible questions, his improbable dreams, for the time being. "Rabbi, I just want you to know how sorry I am about your parents. It wasn't your fault." Losing the awkwardness, he tried to reassure the rabbi that he made the right decision to remain on the pulpit. "You did the best you could. Like you said the other day, there's value in community, in people coming together to work things out. You have done great deeds, sir."

"Thank you," the rabbi said with no conviction. "If only it were true."

No matter what he tried, Jacob could not break through the iron clad barriers the rabbi had erected over twelve years. The unfairness of it all enraged him. "Rabbi, how come an innocent person like you self-flagellates over something outside his power, while so many people commit one obvious sin after the next with no remorse? Surely you see the irony."

The rabbi's eyes glimmered with affection. A friendship was blossoming.

As the alcohol continued to work its magic, the men laughed at how they were different yet the same. Jacob was a seeker still striving toward his first revelation. The rabbi also was a seeker. But the bearded man noted a fundamental difference. "Unlike you, I thought I knew it all and spouted off. I was Mr. Big Shot, instructing people with fables from a place of authority. I ran the marathon with countless souls following my lead, only to find I made a wrong turn at mile twenty. Now, it's time to suffer the pileup while I slam the brakes and change course."

He guzzled more beer but looked all too sober. "Jacob, I'm once again seeking, just like you. But there are complications. Marital and institutional chains around my neck. Consider yourself lucky to have never found what you thought was the answer. Because, like I said, it doesn't exist."

Jacob empathized with the rabbi's dilemma. The man was trapped under the weight of doctrine he no longer believed. But Jacob didn't agree with the rabbi's assessment that he was the fortunate one, not when he still didn't have a clue after a lifetime of searching. He stretched his arms wide for dramatic effect. "'Tis better to have loved and lost than never to have loved at all."

The rabbi laughed like a madman again. And this time, Jacob also became hysterical. A party had broken out at the wobbly table in the corner of the bar.

The men could have gone on for hours. Jacob had a million questions and ideas to discuss. The rabbi was the perfect companion to bounce them off. Who else but a clergyman would be willing to spend day and night dissecting the very topics that obsessed Jacob?

But it was closing time, so Jacob put aside his inquiries and waved for the bill. The waitress stopped by and gave the rabbi a shy smile. "I hope you feel better sir, real soon."

The rabbi looked at his wristwatch to check the time, which reminded him of the treasured gift from his parents he had smashed to pieces. *Mazel Tov.* He turned serious and thanked Jacob for the evening. Jacob said, "Back at you, Rabbi. Let's do this again soon. We have a lot more to talk about."

Meanwhile, far, far away under a billion trillion stars, Mia and a few of the BC congregants were enjoying what had been advertised as a mild and spiritual bicycle journey through picturesque vineyards. The hills were not steep. But they might as well have been the Himalayas for Mr. Shep, one of the older congregants on the retreat whose belly sank over his belt buckle from years of overindulgence at local delicatessens.

Mr. Shep was winded from the first incline and walked his bike up the next. "Go ahead, Mia," he encouraged. "I'll catch up with you."

When Mia looked over her shoulder a few moments later to check on his progress, Mr. Shep was lying on the pavement with his head resting at an impossible angle against the curb. His right arm was caught between the spokes of the front tire, while the back wheel of the bicycle spun haplessly, parallel to the road.

CHAPTER VIII – MIA

A stupid bicycle ride through the vineyards ruined my glorious vacation. Poor, poor Mr. Shep! The doctors said he had a cardiac arrest and expected the worst. I phoned Aaron in tears to report that he was in critical condition. Aaron was slurring his words as if he had been drinking, but that's ridiculous.

We discussed the steps to take under Jewish law if Mr. Shep died in California and we needed to transport his body back home. "Fly here in the morning," I pleaded. "Everybody's calling for the rabbi."

There was a stubborn tone in his voice. "I can't come. I no longer have spiritual capacity. It would be a lie." He was stammering again. What in the world was going on with my husband?

On the somber flight home, alone with my thoughts, my worries multiplied. Was Aaron having a breakdown? I tried to remember the name of the psychologist who specialized in treating clergy. Jared Bloomberg, I think. I decided to call him but was skeptical. After all, I think therapy may have caused more problems than cures for Hannah. Still, what other options did I have?

Looking out my window at the specks below, I wondered where in this vast country my daughter might be. But this wasn't the time to think of Hannah. I needed to keep my focus on Aaron, to wake him up. He was my rock and my redeemer, everyone's source of inspiration. Aaron needed to get his act together so that he could conduct the funeral if Mr. Shep died. More importantly, so that he could resume being our beloved rabbi, the wise pillar of strength that we all rely on for guidance and solace during times of sorrow.

Aaron picked me up at the airport. I looked into his kind eyes and saw the wonderful man I had married long ago. But his jaw was locked the entire ride home.

The first shot was fired the instant we walked through the front door. Aaron looked ashamed but determined. "Mia, I need to resign as rabbi immediately. My heart isn't in this. I can't lead the flock when I don't believe a word of what I'm saying."

I was angry and scared and tried every which way to state my case. But he just shut me down, rejecting my ideas a split second after I got them out.

"Do you need a longer rest?"

"Even a sabbatical won't help, Mia. We've taken these boondoggles every few years and I'm a mess. The only thing that'll work is to get out, start over."

"But how will we make ends meet?"

"We have plenty of money and you know it. I've been paid handsomely and with all those extra favors, we might spend less than people in public housing. All the while, decade after decade, we saved."

"But we deserve to be taken care of for what we do."

"We've been rewarded tenfold. We can afford to make a change. I must resign. I'm a fake. I'm shot."

Aaron stared at me like he was making an accusation. Some of what he said hurt, as if we didn't earn the perks. Like I was greedy and sought them out. Well, here's my question. Why should a doctor or lawyer make more money than my husband?

But what got me furious was that Aaron had made up his mind without talking to me. His decision affected both of us. I deserved better after faithfully standing by his side for so long. I couldn't hold it in any longer. "You are obligated to me and your community. You can't walk away like a coward now that you have money. That would be immoral, a *grievous* sin." My voice rose with indignation. "I've given you everything, putting myself second. How dare you, you hypocrite!"

I lost control over my emotions and escalated our argument past the boiling point. "This is my life too," I said. "You're ruining it like a spoiled brat. I love who I am, how people treat me, how we help. What's wrong with you?"

My gentle Aaron, who never raised his voice to anyone, screamed back at me, at himself, at the world. He didn't say any words, he just shrieked in misery. I never heard anything like it.

Stunned silence followed. Neither of us could move. Finally, he composed himself enough to say, "The two of us have been in this damn fishbowl far too long. Everyone thinks they own us. That they're entitled to our lives. And to the soul of our precious child."

He pointed his finger at my face accusingly. "Mia, we take too much and revel in it. I have nothing left."

I felt like I was flailing in a freefall. This man I love, this respected leader, a scholar, my very hero, was melting down before my eyes. But it still didn't add up. Something was missing.

"You're not telling me the truth, Aaron, at least not all of it. You know how to navigate the fishbowl. It may not always be ideal, but there's so much to love that it's worth the circus, the parade, and yes, even at times the charade. There's something else." And then I asked in a flat voice, "Is there another woman? Is that what this is about? What were you doing in your office after hours?"

I was crazed and had lost control over what was coming from my lips. We both knew there was nobody else. My Aaron was as faithful as any husband who ever lived.

He understood and raised his hand for me to stop. "Enough. I give." Eyes cast down, shoulders all but drooping to the floor, he admitted that he indeed owed me the truth. I braced, but nothing could have prepared me for it. And when he gathered his final ounce of strength to tell me his secret, I learned for the first time what really happened to his parents at Sunnyside Nursing Home. About the murder-suicide. The rabbi's loss of faith.

I don't remember more. I don't recall how I responded. Did I hug him? Did I lash out angrily that through his silence, he had been living a lie, we had both been living a lie, for twelve long years? That he deceived me. I just toppled in a heap on the living room floor at my husband's feet.

When I revived, neither of us spoke. We retreated to separate rooms for the rest of the night. I can't explain it, and I'm not proud of it, but I somehow fell asleep. I have no doubt Aaron remained awake the entire night.

Early the next morning, I woke up from the vibrations of our garage door. Aaron, my husband, my true love, the rabbi, had left. On the kitchen table sat a note, wet from his tears:

My Dear Mia.

I love you and always will. But staying here will cause too much pain. Please don't think of me as a coward. Consider me instead a man who has sustained a near fatal injury to his beating heart and must heal before it's too late. Before the heart is cut from my body.

Mia, when you penetrate to the essence, the problem is that I don't believe in God anymore. I don't know what to believe. I tried to hold it together for you, for everyone. That was my downfall. The strain from my deception has become too severe.

I will send the CEO a resignation letter. You have the right to be angry. But perhaps, if you can wait until I heal, we'll resume a different life, a better one.

I know this isn't what you want to hear. You deserve the best. You should still be queen. In my eyes, you always will be.

I'm so sorry. Please, please wait for me.

With all my love,

Aaron

CHAPTER IX - HANNAH

As I entered high school, my shame was magnified under the BC microscope by a thousand people snooping and judging:

"What did you say the rabbi's daughter did with that Rodstein girl in the john?"

"She's a whore, a deviant. Can you believe it?"

"The poor rebbetzin doesn't know what to do about Hannah."

"The rabbi had his head buried in his books, didn't know what was happening under his own roof."

Each whisper opened a fresh wound. It was impossible to mature into who I needed to be, who I really was, and to gain an understanding of my sexuality.

My parents forced me to see a psychologist who specialized in advising members of the clergy. You'd be surprised by how many of them are overwhelmed or plagued by other problems you wouldn't expect.

Obviously, Mr. Bloomberg was the wrong fit. My parents could have at least done some research to find an expert in what I needed. But they trusted he'd be discreet, which was the first order of business for Mom and Dad. He had scant experience with adolescents, let alone lesbianism, but knew how to counsel a rabbi.

I spent endless hours on a long suede couch, three feet from his reclining chair, bombarded by clichéd inquiries:

"How do you feel?"

"How did you feel?"

"How will you feel?"

"Do you feel better after telling me how you felt?"

"Do you need a tissue?"

Mr. Bloomberg tried but was ineffective. He didn't help me cope, couldn't mitigate my pain, and counselled nothing of importance about how to move forward.

But I can't write my time on his suede couch off completely. Mr. Bloomberg conveyed something unintentionally that was critical for me to hear from another adult. What he said will stick with me for my entire life.

It happened when I told him in an emotional outburst that I had to get out of the house, escape the entire scene, before it killed me, or I killed me. I meant it too. Suicide was on my mind.

Mr. Bloomberg looked frazzled. "Good. We're making progress," he said. "Now, breathe in deeply. Exhale fully."

He was clearly worried as he peered up from his notepad and into my eyes. "Look, Hannah, your parents are good people who mean well and try to help others. They're also misguided. They, too, need therapy." He immediately looked away like he went too far.

Finally! It was the first time an adult told me even a semblance of the truth. Everybody else praised the rabbi and rebbetzin, showering them with gifts, seeking their blessings. Mr. Bloomberg's cryptic comment gave me a dose of reality and legitimized my feelings. "They're also misguided. They, too, need therapy."

I often replayed the conversation in my mind as I watched my mother continue her personal celebration. Intoxicated by the adulation, the perks, she ignored me. Her silence was deafening. Doctor Bloomberg explained, "Perhaps she doesn't know what else to do for you and is waiting it out, giving you space. Don't forget, she sent you to me, which means she cares." I refused to listen as I watched her party on without me.

Dad wasn't enamored with the superficialities like Mom. His singular focus was his work, doing the sacred stroke while scouring the holy books for meaning to share with his followers. But Dad had no clue how to be a father for a kid like me. In one of our more intense moments, he told me, "The only way I can do my job is to be a model citizen, to behave in a perfect way dictated by scripture. Otherwise, how am I to be taken seriously as a teacher of sacred wisdom? Your job, Hannah, is to do the same." The message was clear: I was failing him.

This wasn't the sagacious parenting a shaky adolescent like me needed at a critical juncture. It also didn't help when Dad left a photocopy of a page from the Torah on my bed, with Leviticus 18:22 circled in red: "Do not lie with a male as one lies with a woman; it is an abhorrence." I wanted to slit my wrists.

Fortunately, I was smart and tested off the charts on my college entrance exams. That landed me a slot at the University of Pennsylvania, far away from my troubles. It was there I began to heal, to create my own identity. I also made some good friends. People I shared things in common with, without the pressure of being tagged "the rabbi's daughter." I could attend a college basketball game in whatever garb I pleased without all heads turning in my direction as I walked down the aisle to take my seat.

Believe it or not, I majored in psychology. So many of us with difficult childhoods gravitate there. We feel like experts having gone through our own personal hell and want to help others drive out their demons. Mr. Bloomberg would be proud.

I returned home during my first summer break and hated it. I was back in the fishbowl as the ugly stink fish. That was the last time I stepped foot in my parents' home. For the next three years, I got a job with the university and stayed away.

Mom and Dad seldom visited. BC obligations took priority, even during Parent's Weekend and Homecoming. Again, Mr. Bloomberg's unintended comment gave me perspective. "Misguided ... need therapy." Thank you, Mr. Bloomberg, wherever you are.

They did attend my graduation and seemed genuinely proud that I earned cum laude. Dad looked different. Sadder somehow, troubled, less sure of himself. What was going on with him? As for Mom, we still inhabited different planets. They fit me in for the day but booked a flight back to Minneapolis early the same evening. "There's so much going on at BC," Mom exclaimed.

"What a surprise," I said, clenching my fists.

After my graduation ceremony, we went for an early dinner. My parents made no attempt to talk to me about anything of consequence, keeping the conversation about themselves, their members, their world. They only wanted to discuss the goings on at BC, not my four years at college, not my goals or achievements, certainly not who I was. Waiting for them to give me the consideration that I deserved, I grew livid behind a veiled smile.

Mom finally lit the fuse after the server cleared away our dishes. "When you come home, we have a nice boy to fix you up with, the son of a BC macher." Dad nodded his approval.

I looked up to the ceiling in absolute disbelief. They still didn't get it. Standing up in furor, I uncorked in a loud, angry voice, "You have no idea who I am and don't care! A boy?! A boy from BC?!" People at nearby tables stopped eating to glimpse our dysfunction. "You couldn't even spend a single night with me. Get back to your precious mirage. I'm out of here."

What happened had been building up inside of me for a lifetime. The ticking time bomb had finally detonated. My parents looked embarrassed as I slammed my fist on the table and stormed out, leaving them to pay the bill and make their way to the airport.

I stayed awake, angry at myself for causing a spectacle. But I was also proud of my newfound strength. In the morning, I composed a letter which I suspect was catastrophic to Mom and Dad. My goal was to never see them again, and I made that clear. We needed to go our separate ways so that I could preserve myself and prosper.

I went on to earn my PhD in psychology, also at the University of Pennsylvania, and again graduated with highest honors. It was there that I met the love of my life. She's brilliant, yet gentle, beautiful inside and out. She still struggles with her family for acceptance but understands that my past was worse, a complete rupture. I've never told her the details, nor has she pressured me. That's not her way. "Besides, it's all about the future, not the past," she said. "Our future!" For the first time, I shared something in common with my mother. I loved my partner, my life.

After graduating with my doctorate, the school hired me to stay on as a professor. I love the world of academia and can spend days on end researching, probing different theories and philosophies in the workings of the mind. I want to shape young adults for the better.

In the spirit of new beginnings, after my flareup with Mom and Dad, I changed my name but not its essence. My new identity reminds me each day that I am the same person, but in a better place with a wonderful future.

I also hired a private investigator who was a savant with computer systems to keep my secret safe. It was expensive but worth it. He changed my social security number, license, phone, credit cards, you name it. When he was done, he bragged, "Hannah Friedler has left the building."

"I doubt my parents will look for me," I responded. "But if they do, let them fail!"

CHAPTER X – THE RABBI AND JACOB

The rabbi met Undertaker Black one week after he was hired by BC. The undertaker kicked off the partnership, inviting the rabbi and Mia to an exquisite French restaurant to introduce them to his wares. It was Mia's first entry in her Book of Balloons. From then on, they worked one or two funerals most weeks. They were excellent at their craft and performed seamlessly together.

Mia laughingly labelled their relationship "symbiotic" in honor of their cozy connection in the industry of the dead. The rabbi served as the consoling figurehead, providing poignant eulogies honoring the deceased. He gave sweeping assurances to grieving families:

"Your beloved is in heaven with God now."

"She'll be rewarded with peace, eternal rest alongside the angels."

"He will live on in us, in our memories and good deeds."

While this eloquence played out in the clouds at fifty-thousand feet, Undertaker Black managed the mundane with somber aplomb, positioning chairs, digging graves, lowering caskets, and lining up cars behind a rented hearse for the deceased's decorous escort to a final resting place.

Before long, Undertaker Black was swimming in profits from the rabbi's referrals. And when a grieving family approached the mortician first searching for a clergy to orate from high above, Undertaker Black returned the favor.

It was therefore only natural that the rabbi tapped into this symbiotic relationship when his parents died. He called Undertaker

Black in a panic after leaving Sunnyside Nursing Home.

"There's blood everywhere."

"Aaron, calm down, I got your back. Just tell me what happened."

The rabbi explained how his father killed his mother, then himself, but choked up before he could make his plea. He was paralyzed by heartbreak and fear that news of the murder-suicide might spread. Could he still effectively serve his congregation with a tarnished image? And what of his beautiful, optimistic Mia? Did she deserve such pain? Did his parents deserve to be dishonored?

No appeal was necessary. Undertaker Black instinctively understood the delicate nature of the situation. "They died of natural causes, Aaron, a sad coincidence, but nothing more. I'll make sure we properly honor your mother and father. Please accept my condolences."

Twelve years later, after leaving a tear-stained farewell note to Mia, the rabbi now had two people he could realistically reach out to. His old crony the undertaker, and his new friend Jacob. One to help with the nuts and bolts of his escape. The other to assist with theoretical backing from fifty thousand feet.

Fleeing from his house in the early morning, the rabbi phoned Undertaker Black first. The undertaker sounded astonished by the news but pledged complete loyalty. The rabbi needed a place to stay to soul search, and the undertaker had connections. "I have an idea where you can go without bumping into acquaintances," he told the rabbi. "Grab breakfast while I check on a couple of things. I'll get back to you. Hang in there, Aaron, I got your back."

The rabbi next called Jacob and conveyed his story of woes. Jacob could hear the distress in his voice and invited him to breakfast at a rustic dive minimally nicknamed "the Canteen." "We can both make it there in fifteen minutes if traffic is flowing, Rabbi. The coffee is strong. We'll talk."

The rabbi was touched to the core. Here was a guy he barely knew a few weeks earlier willing to drop everything to lend a hand, an ear. And just as incredible, it was Jacob whom the rabbi reached out to in crisis, instead of anybody from BC. *They'll just gossip. So many of them count on me, but I can't depend on a single one.*

Traffic cooperated and the Canteen's coffee was as advertised. The rabbi spoke for a long while as he explained to Jacob the events leading to his personal exodus. Jacob listened attentively, but was embarrassed, noticing that in his early morning hunger, he had wiped his heaping plate of eggs, home fries and a blueberry muffin clean, while the rabbi's food remained untouched. The awkwardness between the two men continued, but so did their determination to get past it.

After the rabbi finished his story, he looked bewildered and asked: "Why did this happen to me?"

Jacob had been obsessing over the very same words in trying to understand why Lizzy had died prematurely. In his lifelong pursuit for meaning, he never found a satisfactory explanation for why the universe dealt out so much random suffering. Explanations that he had grappled with sprang into his mind as he began to probe. "Rabbi, do you believe in the free will theory to explain why good people like you must endure agony? That God gave us the gift of freedom. It's up to us to use it as we please. If pain results from our personal decisions, so be it." Jacob looked genuinely confused. "Rabbi, does this make sense? Does free will help you deal with what happened with your parents, and now with Mia?"

Jacob meant to say, "You're a good guy, rabbi, and I'm sorry these awful things happened to you. You don't deserve it. How can I help?" But the free will theory tumbled from his mouth reflexively.

Raising theodicy would have been absurd for anyone else. Some men would have remained stoic, even resorting to jokes to hide the pain. But for the rabbi and Jacob, a deep philosophical discussion was exactly what was needed, a springboard to explore their feelings and make conceptual sense of their damaged lives.

They were both entranced by the age-old question: "Why do bad things happen to good people?" The rabbi knew that this simple inquiry was an Achilles heel for believers in an all-powerful, benevolent God meting out justice, as depicted in the Bible. He therefore devoted untold hours studying theodicy back when he was a true believer, and the free will theory became his mantra. "After all, without free will, we'd be robots, puppets, dummies sitting on the ventriloquist's lap," he'd counsel. "But with the Almighty's gift of freedom comes consequences for our actions, hence the bad."

But now, sitting across from Jacob at the Canteen, the rabbi cringed. "I used to pontificate, believing that I was providing useful advice to congregants. What was I thinking?" He stroked his beard in angst. "The Germans murdered unthinkable numbers. Rwandans and Cambodians were slaughtered in genocides. What happened to the free will of the victims? And, what of natural disasters? That tsunami in the Pacific killed two-hundred and thirty thousand unsuspecting souls. It wasn't their free choice to have their plans for the day suffocated. No human benefited from the gift of free will as waters engulfed them." He choked up as he thought of the murder-suicide at Sunnyside Nursing Home. "And my parents, my dear mother and father ..."

Jacob quickly interjected to complete the rabbi's point, not wanting to reenact the weeping scene at Lee's Tavern. "It's all intellectual gymnastics that can't withstand scrutiny or reality," Jacob said. "The free will theory is a rationale concocted by very smart, well-intentioned people to provide an explanation to those who are grieving while protecting God and their myths. Alzheimer's destroyed your parents' free will. It wasn't a necessary consequence of their gift of freedom. I'm so sorry, my friend."

The rabbi had secretly harbored the same sentiments for many years, and his doubts grew over time. He couldn't reconcile the theory with stories in the Bible that glorified an omnipotent God intervening over free will to distill justice, or with countless prayers asking God to act. He could no longer contort his soul to keep within the confines of doctrines he now rejected. Freed from these "intellectual gymnastics," as Jacob put it, he could now be angry at God, if He even existed. He felt a vague sense of liberation mixed with guilt.

Picking at his eggs, the rabbi considered other justifications he would apply to counsel suffering congregants. "I would tell them that we are mere mortals, imperfect beings. How can we possibly question the intentions of our omniscient Lord, the supreme power? To do so is hubris. If bad things happen, there is a good reason. But we're incapable of grasping it and must have trust in God."

He grimaced as he remembered uttering these words to a young mother who accidentally killed her toddler while backing her minivan from the garage. The child died of brain damage. The mother was later institutionalized.

The rabbi looked ashamed. "I knew that the argument was metaphysical. You either believe it or not, but it's impossible to prove one way or the other." He spread his arms in futility. "I no longer believed it when I counselled the poor woman. I'm sure she sensed I was faking it."

Jacob looked exasperated, forgetting the rabbi's dilemma, and sinking further into his own obsessions. "Here's the problem, Rabbi. Like you said, it's 'metaphysical.' None of this can be proved. And the justifications contradict each other. The same people who declare that free will explains why God doesn't intercede reverse course at the drop of a hat and pray for Divine intervention or urge us to trust God's plan. They proclaim, 'God willing' and 'God forbid' all day long as if He's pulling strings from above. As if He's in control but unreadable like you say."

"'Man proposes, God disposes,'" the rabbi added softly. "That's what the hip ones say."

Jacob's eyes twitched. "Catchy, but aren't they speaking from both sides of their mouths again?"

Jacob's Early Warning System flashed red. He was frustrated with the contradictions and his lifetime incapacity for faith. He wondered if his Wednesday nightmares were some sort of manifestation of his shortcomings. "I wish I could believe this, dammit, but it's not credible. I know a theologian would find me simple-minded. But man, I just don't get it!"

The rabbi looked sheepish, knowing that he was one of those theologians. And he felt ashamed for preaching these ideas long after he stopped believing them. *I'm being punished,* he thought, immediately grasping the contradiction. *I'm left to deal with the murder-suicide and estrangement from Mia without a satisfying explanation.* The rabbi had lost his faith.

Jacob stared across the table and saw how pale the rabbi had become. "I hope I didn't cross the line with my comment about theologians. I just get exasperated with unprovable labyrinths, but mostly with my inability to embrace them. It would be much easier if I did."

The rabbi sat up and took a sip of coffee. "You didn't hurt my feelings. I need to talk this through with someone who understands. This is helpful, even cathartic."

With this feedback, Jacob was tempted to dive deeper into the unknown. He wanted to steer the conversation toward the ultimate defense, the "clincher for God," as he labelled it. That is, bad things don't really happen to good people after all. Instead, all human actions are recorded in Providence and there's a settling-up upon death. Kindness is rewarded with a beatific afterlife in heaven, and evil is punished in the fires of hell. *Just another impenetrable defense, more metaphysics incapable of proof,* he thought. *It numbs peoples' minds to the reality that bad things indeed happen to good people every which way here on Earth.* With these silent thoughts and the rabbi looking on, Jacob again chastened himself for lacking the capacity to believe. For being skeptical about whether his Lizzy was in heaven.

He wanted to share these feelings with the rabbi if they could even be put into words. But when he looked across the table again, his companion appeared even more overwhelmed, his pain raw. He decided to tone it down. Still embarrassed by how quickly he devoured breakfast, he told the rabbi, "Our plates are asymmetrical. Mine is empty, yours is full. Let's lighten up, take a breather. The blueberry muffins are fantastic."

The rabbi nodded and began to eat. Blueberry muffins were his favorite. From theology to the bakery, these two understood each other.

While the rabbi worked toward symmetry in their breakfast plates, Jacob told him about his latest Wednesday night dream and a colossal decision he had made that very morning. "I'm travelling to ground zero to get to the bottom of my visions. I'll be staying at Lake Paradise in Colorado, about four hours from Denver. The scenery looks outrageous. I've got a feeling Rabbi. Maybe my moment is at hand."

The rabbi looked concerned. "Whoa, that's a long way to go my friend."

"Look, I know this might seem unconventional," Jacob responded. "But my subconscious is talking, and I need to listen. I'm still solid as a rock, at least when I'm awake."

The rabbi remained disconcerted. But his mind flipped to his own nemesis, the masked surgeon brandishing a scalpel. Questioning Jacob's plan would be hypocritical, so he decided to be encouraging. "If dreams were a Rorschach test, Jacob, I'm afraid we'd both be sent to the loony bin. This dream of yours is of biblical proportion. I wish you well in your quest."

Jacob smiled. "Maybe your dreams are biblical. After all, you're the rabbi. But mine are more likely in the realm of Stephen King."

As if on cue, the rabbi's phone rang. It was Undertaker Black. "Listen, Rabbi, I have an idea. I want you to go to Boulder, Colorado, to work things out. My family owns a big cemetery there with drop-dead breathtaking grounds. There's a vacant house where the groundskeeper used to live until they outsourced the work. You can stay there for as long as you wish."

"I can't impose like that," said the rabbi. "But I'm touched."

"No, no, don't think like that. The way I'm looking at it, you'll be doing us the favor. Business is slow in Boulder, and we can't figure out why. My family wants you to consult for us while you're making new plans. You bring a lot of inside information to the table and we'd love to hear your views."

The rabbi acquiesced and expressed his gratitude, but the undertaker wasn't finished. "One more thing, and I hope you don't find this presumptuous. I bought you a flight leaving in a few hours." He gave the rabbi the necessary information before hanging up.

The rabbi was flummoxed by his partner's generosity. And looking at his new friend Jacob sharing breakfast with him, he felt doubly thankful.

I now have two symbiotic relationships. As he finished his meal, the rabbi told Jacob the strange coincidence. "I guess we're both Rocky Mountain bound. Maybe we'll see more clearly a mile above sea level."

This, of course, set the two men off again with their own brand of metaphysical gymnastics:

> Jacob: "Is it fate that we're both going to Colorado on personal quests at the same time?"
>
> Rabbi: "Or random chance? But the odds, what are the odds?"
>
> Jacob: "Does God care that we're doing this?"
>
> Rabbi: "Does He exist?"

Jacob ordered four blueberry muffins to go and handed two to the rabbi. "Take them for the plane. We might as well start our journeys with a little nourishment. Bon voyage, Rabbi."

CHAPTER XI - THE PSYCHOLOGIST

M ia Friedler, *the rebbetzin*, paid me a visit that I won't forget, not in a million years. She phoned telling me, "We have an emergency with the rabbi affecting the whole community. Drop everything!"

I was slightly annoyed … and curious. I agreed to juggle some appointments to make time for her in the afternoon. Truth be told, there was nothing to shuffle. I'm not particularly busy these days. My clergy connections have grown stale along with me. Many of my associations are now retired, moving to pastoral settings where their need for counselling has been replaced by relaxation and solitude. Maybe I should head off into the sunset too.

I recalled treating Hannah, the rabbi's daughter, years ago when she had that unfortunate incident in the temple bathroom. I reviewed her file to prepare for my meeting with Mia. My notes were sketchy, but I got the gist of it. Hannah was a good kid in a rough situation. I thought she'd come through in the end. Like many teens, she needed a fresh start to figure things out. College away from what she called the "fishbowl" would do the trick. "The further the better," I scribbled. I also gleaned from the file that I had reservations about her parents.

When Mia arrived, she was agitated. I ushered her into my office, asking if she'd like a soft drink or tea, trying to put her at ease. She declined and sat on the same suede couch her tearful Hannah occupied years earlier. I began with small talk, telling her that I could see the mother-daughter resemblance down to the dimples, when she blurted out between tears, "Aaron has left me. What will I tell the congregation? What will people say?"

My first instinct was that the rabbi was having an affair. A lot of hanky-panky happens. The stories I can tell … but won't. There is a seductive energy when one person is perceived to be in a position of authority possessing mystical wisdom, while the other is vulnerable and needs help. Especially when sessions occur off hours in a cozy office with comfortable furniture. Yes, things combust. Trust me. I've heard it all.

I gently told Mia, "Take as long as you need to collect yourself, then get it off your chest. You'll feel relieved and I'll be in a better position to help."

Oddly, she launched into a blunt soliloquy about how she loved being the rebbetzin:

> "Okay Mr. Bloomberg, here's the deal. I love that my husband is the esteemed rabbi. People wine us. They dine us. We're treated like celebrities, royalty, the center of attention.
>
> And my husband is their spiritual leader. The man with answers. He marries congregants, buries them. They seek his blessing, mine too. We get to be in the room for the most intimate phases of their lives.
>
> But the best thing, Mr. Bloomberg, is something nobody talks about. I see it in their eyes. People may not be able to touch and feel God directly, but they can cast their loving glances upon the next best thing. The mediums—yes, us. I feel a thrill from the sparkling gazes at me, hoping to connect to the Lord.
>
> And for this, we spend nothing. We're treated to everything, and people thank us. *They thank* us!
>
> I love my congregants. I love helping them. And I bask in the glory of being their exemplar.
>
> It's over now, Mr. Bloomberg. The rabbi is gone. How can BC go on? How can I?"

I was dumbfounded. I've been treating clergy for my entire career, and nobody ever explained it this way. Most of my patients from the pulpit were simply burnt out, or had witnessed too much sadness, catching their own personal bouts. They were good people trying to lend a hand, but in over their heads from life's vast sea of challenges.

Was Mia's insight valid, or delusional? She seemed panicked about losing her coveted station in the community, not her husband. And what in the world was that about "basking in the glory?" I also noticed that Mia failed to mention her unique opportunity to practice her faith while simultaneously making a living, as if religion itself was an afterthought.

My mind shifted back to Hannah. The kid was smart and sweet on the inside, pretty on the outside, but in considerable pain. I was seeing the source firsthand. I switched topics, hoping to learn how Hannah was doing. Maybe she was connected to Mia's current crisis. "Have you told your daughter yet?"

Mia looked startled by the question, maybe even miffed that I had the nerve to pile it on like this. Her eyes lowered, and she began to cry. "I wouldn't know," she confessed. "Hannah wrote a goodbye letter saying she never wanted to see us again, that we should stay away."

That wasn't the answer I expected. I thought the family would have reconciled by now, especially with the emerging acceptance in the liturgy over sexual preferences. Surely the rabbi and his wife weren't still rejecting their sweet child as a biblical abhorrence.

To disguise my surprise, I jotted down a few notes while my mind raced. *Mia, the rabbi, Hannah ... They're good people, right? What the hell is going on?*

We worked our way back to the rabbi. "Why did Aaron leave you, Mia?"

"I don't know. He just picked up and left. Now what should I do, Mr. Bloomberg?"

"You've got to tell me more if I'm going to help."

Mia's resistance was normal. She took a few minutes before reluctantly nodding in agreement. She inhaled deeply as if to steel herself, pushed to the edge of the couch, and told me what happened at Sunnyside Nursing Home. If I was stunned before, I was near paralyzed now. In a flat controlled voice, the rebbetzin said, "My husband kept the murder-suicide secret for twelve years. He was trying to hold our wonderful lives together. I love him so. How could we lead others and set an example if the story of his parents leaked?"

Bingo. Somewhere in all this swirl, she said the magic words: "I love him so." But it was garbled up with everything else.

I hate to admit it, but I was getting angry at my patient, maybe at life. I know a professional isn't supposed to bring personal emotions to counselling, but I didn't seem to have a choice. My feelings were on autopilot.

Thinking back about Hannah, I now remembered with greater clarity the misgivings I had about the family. Well, the dysfunction was now on display here in my office. Somehow, the endless admiration bestowed on Mia by her congregants had corrupted her mindset. She had been on an unrealistic, unsustainable high and was about to land hard. Her husband's predicament was worse. He had fallen head-first from a cliff.

Mia tore through a box of tissues while she continued to pour out her heart. Again, her primary worry didn't seem to be Aaron or Hannah. She instead was lamenting the thought of no longer being rebbetzin.

We were out of time. The session ended as they all do, with Mia wanting a quick fix. "What should I do Mr. Bloomberg? This can't wait."

Giving my stock answer, I responded, "It's far too early in the process to know. We need to talk more, delve deeper."

Mia wanted results at warp speed, so I made an appointment for her to return in two days with instructions to bring along the goodbye letter from Hannah. And then I asked a question, implying that it was going to hurt. Like a slash from Occam's Razor as it cut through the fog to the heart of the matter, to the simplest answer. Perhaps I even wanted to inflict pain. "Mia, don't answer now but think about it for our next session. If you could still be rebbetzin and an exemplar, would you choose that life? Would you take it, knowing full well that you'd never see Aaron or Hannah again?"

This was indeed a loaded question designed to slice. Worse yet, I signaled my feelings with a tone of accusation in my voice. Mia was speechless as the ancient razor cut deep.

A professional isn't supposed to do this. To judge the patient after one visit. To attack her. Instead, the patient should be encouraged to discover her own conclusions and devise her personal plan of action after months, if not years, of therapy. I was ashamed by my malpractice. I had accused Mia with a faux homework assignment full of hurtful innuendos at her greatest moment of vulnerability.

And the rebbetzin knew it. Her cheeks flashed red and her eyes blazed. She rose without saying another word and gave me the finger as she stormed out, slamming the door.

CHAPTER XII - THE RABBI

During his breakfast schmooze with Jacob, the rabbi functioned within a semblance of normalcy. He was diverted by theodicy, instead of his personal odyssey. After the men said their goodbyes, it was a different story.

Preoccupied, the rabbi headed toward the drugstore to buy a toothbrush and deodorant. He had forgotten these essentials in his haste to escape his house, his wife, and his life so early in the morning. *Can I really leave BC, throw away my career? What about Mia? Am I a coward?*

He kept returning to the same crushing predicament. *I've been running on fumes too long, living a lie.* He could not resume that life. The surgeon's scalpel would amputate his very heart.

He was suddenly overtaken by fatigue and pulled the car to the side of the road. Resting his head on the steering wheel, he feared he was about to have a nervous breakdown as traffic whizzed by. His phone rang and snapped him out of it. He was certain that it was Mia calling from the airport. He also understood that he couldn't resist her. If he answered, the rebbetzin would talk him out of resigning and convince him to return home, which would be the end of him, of them. He lacked the strength to argue. His only recourse was to ignore her calls and the countless messages she would soon leave on his voicemail. *I feel like I'm cheating on her.*

The rabbi pulled back onto the road to run his errand. When he left the drugstore, he craved more coffee, his only hope of making it through the day. The Java Hangout was around the corner, so he stopped in to grab a cup, hoping that the world's most popular psychoactive drug would clear his mind.

While reviving his senses amidst a dozen strangers staring robotically at their laptops, the rabbi composed his resignation letter. He would send it to the CEO. The two men had worked on countless synagogue projects together, with the rabbi supplying spiritual insights, the CEO providing capital and management skills to get the job done. He was confident that the CEO, the most powerful man at BC if not the entire city, would handle the matter appropriately. With the caffeine infusion working its wonders, the rabbi finished the fateful correspondence, dropped it at Federal Express and drove to the airport.

The security line was long and chaotic. When the rabbi finally reached the front, a guard frisked him, checked his bag, and confiscated his deodorant. "Too many ounces," he instructed. "You can keep it, but you can't fly."

With his case a little lighter, the rabbi proceeded to the departure gate where he learned that a thick fog had rolled into Denver. He boarded several hours later and found his shrunken middle seat in coach, where he remained squashed between a loud snorer and an oversized leaner for the duration of the flight. At least the rabbi could enjoy his blueberry muffins from Jacob.

The plane landed at Denver International at half past ten and the rabbi headed to find a taxi to Boulder Paradise Cemetery. Several drivers rudely refused, thinking something was wrong with this bearded man with bloodshot eyes headed to a graveyard so late at night. Finally, he found a cabbie desperate for the fare. The driver kept glancing at him in the rearview mirror while they rode in silence.

Forty minutes later, they reached the main gate of the cemetery, and the rabbi instructed the cabbie to drive through. "We need to find the groundskeeper's house," he said, as if this was a normal request. In the reflection of the mirror, he saw frightened eyes. "Sorry Mister, this is the end of the line. Christ, I'm not driving into the cemetery. Grab your case and hoof it from here."

The rabbi knew it was pointless to argue. *I'd feel the same if I was behind the wheel. I'm acting bizarre.* He paid his fare and added a generous tip despite the abrupt ending to the ride.

There was no choice but to complete the journey by foot through the vast cemetery grounds. No living being waited to escort him. The rabbi turned more frightened than the superstitious driver.

He checked the time. It was midnight, the witching hour, a time to be safely tucked in bed. *How has my life become a B-rated horror film?* He tried to calm himself, remembering that he had performed innumerable eulogies in just this setting. *I always enjoyed the quietude, the tranquility of cemeteries.* But his rationalizations rang hollow in this dark isolation.

Undertaker Black had told him that the groundskeeper's house was in the middle of the cemetery next to a large, white brick mausoleum. The rabbi reasoned that he'd find it if he proceeded down the long dark road leading into the cemetery from the main gate. It was still foggy, but scattered lampposts vaguely lit the path.

He passed grave after grave in slow motion, thousands of them in all directions. Headstones poked up from the ground to announce beloved parents, grandparents, and children, their names and birthdates memorialized. A particular slab under a yellowish flickering light caught his attention:

HERE LIES BELOVED
"GRANDAD" ZACHARY WHIT
JANUARY 9, 1876 - JUNE 22, 1948
MAY HE REST IN PEACE FOR
ETERNITY
UNDER THE PROTECTION OF
OUR LORD

The rabbi was startled. June 22 was Hannah's birthday. He whispered to the ghosts, "My only child is dead to me," and trudged on, shoulders stooped.

Fifteen minutes later, amidst an ocean of tombstones, the rabbi heard a ruffling sound. He turned toward the noise and saw a freshly dug grave, open for business, awaiting its deposit the next morning. The rabbi was relieved when he spotted two rabbits scurrying about near the hole. Believing these gentle creatures were the source of the disturbance, he turned back to the road. It was then he spied a homeless man bedding down for the night on a rectangular patch of grass.

For a split second, the grass reminded the rabbi of his childhood humiliation when the Rodstein bully drove his face into the lawn. He fought off the memory to focus on the situation at hand. There was no choice but to continue walking past the stranger.

The rabbi gave a respectful nod, but fear stopped him from speaking. The homeless man also looked scared. "Be careful here, sir," he slurred. "You shouldn't be out in this darkness. Nope, no way. Not if you've got a choice."

The rabbi waved meekly. There was nothing more to be said at this hour, in this strangeness. He resumed his trek, stopping to look back several times, afraid that the homeless man was trailing him. But there was no sign of any living being. Just more graves, more tombstones, more open patches awaiting inevitable death.

Finally, he approached an intersection, and a sign came into view: "Turn Left for Mausoleum." Never, in the history of the world, had a living person felt such relief from this message. And, when he obediently headed left, the rabbi saw the ghostly illumination of the white brick building. The groundskeeper's house was nearby, just like Undertaker Black promised.

Home sweet home was only a few steps further. As the rabbi approached, he heard a creaking sound. The front door of the groundskeeper's house was wide open, swinging in the breeze. *Come on in, come on in,* he heard from a petrified corner of his mind. *Come on in and take your shoes off.*

CHAPTER XIII – MIA

never want to receive another letter! Aaron's farewell note might as well have been laced with anthrax. And Hannah's, the one Mr. Bloomberg asked to see, was a missile, not a missive:

Dear Mom and Dad:

I NEVER want to see you again! Our relationship is irretrievably broken. This became obvious to me with your graduation visit. I wanted change, but you were the same as always.

The fact is we are bad for each other. Whenever I'm with you, I feel inadequate and hurt. And every time you see me, I embarrass you. I'm not the daughter you wished for, not good enough for the minions you need to please.

Since you can't accept me for who I am, you'll destroy my life if I let you. My life has value, and it's mine, not yours. You are no longer allowed in.

I bet you're happy. Just think of it. Now you can spend even more time at BC without losing even a minute for your lesbian daughter the abhorrence.

I'm going to change my name and everything about me. Don't try to find me. Until something changes, you are dead to me.

I'm sorry that you couldn't love me.

Hannah

When the missile arrived, Aaron wanted to drop everything, hop on the next plane, and work it out. I disagreed, reasoning that Hannah needed time, a cooling-off period, that's all. "She'll come to her senses," I assured my husband. "Let's not force the issue." I emphasized that her letter said, "until something changes," leaving the door wide open.

"You're parsing words," Aaron replied. "This sounds serious." But he relented, pouring his energy into his BC obligations and studies.

If we are being totally honest, I felt the pull of important events happening at home. Zaide Mandlebaum's funeral, the Hirsch's fiftieth wedding anniversary and the Lubenstine bat mitzvah. Our presence was imperative. And the CEO wanted to treat us to dinner at the General's Club. What a place! How could we turn down an invitation from our biggest donor? "Time will heal our rift with Hannah," I repeated over Aaron's obvious discomfort.

Well, time proved me wrong. We panicked after several days of not hearing from our child. We tried to call but her phone was disconnected. We contacted her roommates. Nothing. We reached out to her friends, at least the ones that we knew. No response. We searched for her Facebook page. Deleted. We received her latest credit statement. No charges. We called the college, but they refused to release information without her approval even though we paid the tuition. How backward was that?

We hired a private investigator who specialized in finding runaways. He reported back wringing his hands. "Your daughter has disappeared off the face of the map."

And Hannah, my only child, stayed away for good, breaking my heart. I can't make up for the years we lost. They've vanished and won't return. Now Aaron has left too.

The doorbell jarred me out of my self-flagellation. It was the CEO and, lo-and-behold, he had another letter. It was from Aaron:

> *My Dear Congregants:*
>
> *With a heavy heart, I have decided to resign as your rabbi immediately. Thank you for giving me the opportunity to serve BC for these many years. I will*

*always treasure the time we spent worshipping and
learning together, making the world better.*

*The sad truth is that I am no longer up to the task of
leading this great congregation. Please know how hard
I have tried to be the best that I could be for you.*

*This is a difficult time for me and the rebbetzin. I
will forever be in your debt for treating Mia with the
kindness she deserves while I go away to heal.*

Yours truly,

Rabbi Aaron Friedler

The CEO scrutinized me while I teared up. He was looking through
me, judging me, just like Mr. Bloomberg.

I was shellshocked and shamed. How could Aaron have sent this
to the CEO without showing the letter to me first? And he made it
obvious to the entire world that he had left me, abandoned all of us.
There it was, in black and white.

I did the best I could to hold my emotions in check. I thanked the
CEO for personally delivering the letter and made my plea. "Please
don't share this with anyone. The rabbi will be fine, and we'll be back
leading the temple in no time."

The CEO looked conflicted but worked out whatever was bothering
him and gave me a hug. "Listen Mia, whatever you need I'm there
for you. Your husband has been a pillar for the community. We are
indebted to him."

"He still is a pillar," I insisted. "This will pass."

The CEO paused, looking like he wanted to emphasize his next
point. "Mia, I have an observation to share that I've learned over the
years at GoldOrb. Sometimes, no matter how much you want to hold
on to something, you must let go, move on, and embrace change."

"But not now," I begged. "Now isn't the time."

The man still seemed like he was making a calculation in his mind.
"Okay Mia. I'll keep Aaron's letter quiet for two weeks. We'll tell people
that the rabbi travelled to Israel for an emergency meeting, still isn't
feeling well, or whatever you wish. But after that, if he isn't back, we

need to come clean and make an announcement. For the good of BC. For your well being too."

I must admit that Aaron and I never felt completely aligned with the CEO. He was our largest contributor by miles. But he didn't believe in religion, once calling the story of Passover "smoke and miracles." He assured us in business jargon that the services Aaron led were "probably a net positive for the community," but added, "I have strong doubts about the substance." What the CEO never said was that he was using us to advertise for GoldOrb Diversified, the CEO's *almighty*. His donations were a cheap way to connect with influential congregants and reach our large community with commercial messages. The CEO worked for GoldOrb twenty-four seven. Aaron and I tolerated this, believing that his contributions to BC likewise transformed him into "a net positive."

But, in fairness, he always supported the rabbi, and they worked well together. We became friends despite our differences. The CEO seemed sincere in wanting to lend a hand now. He was my only ally.

"Aaron will come around, you'll see," I said. "We'll be in touch."

"Okay Mia, let's hope so."

The CEO departed with a dubious expression on his face. *Let it go, embrace change,* I repeated in my mind. Was there another choice? My world was crumbling.

Alone again, I held a letter in each hand. One from my estranged daughter, the other from my missing husband. *I ignored their cries,* I lamented. *What was I thinking?* Silence lashed at me. Loneliness ripped my heart. I lifted my arms half-way up reaching from one wall to the opposite, my wingspan stretched wide as if I was nailed to the cross. Weighing each letter on the scale of justice, my guilt was confirmed.

With my spirit crucified, I thought of Mr. Bloomberg's comment about Occam's Razor. It seemed so confusing during our session. Well, now I understood. The fabled blade had slit my wrists and my lifeblood was pouring in a single, simple direction.

Toward my family.

CHAPTER XIV – THE SECRETARY

S tationed at my desk outside the rabbi's office each day, I've seen it all. You'd be astounded by what takes place right in front of me as if I'm an inanimate book on his shelf. Screaming matches, power plays, make up scenes, laughter, and tears in the house of God. It makes my job interesting.

Well, today ranks on my all-time list. It started with the rebbetzin calling, before I could even take off my coat and ease into work with my crossword puzzle. Mia always sounded cheerful, but this morning there was desperation in her voice.

She directed me to schedule a meeting with the CEO and the full board of directors, the twelve most important people at BC. "It has to be today," she demanded. "This is an emergency."

I asked if the rabbi was okay, and her response jarred me. "No, he isn't, not at all."

I miraculously reached everybody and scheduled the meeting for one o'clock. A few directors needed to phone in, but most dropped everything to attend in person. When you tell people there's an urgent matter involving the rabbi, they salute and reshuffle their calendars.

There was one hitch. We only had a single hour to meet in order to leave time to get to Mr. Shep's funeral. Everybody was going. We felt awful about what happened to him on his bicycle ride through Wine Country. I recalled that the rabbi cancelled his trip at the last minute following his meeting with Jacob Hart and holing up in his office. Was this all related?

When I reported back to Mia that the meeting was booked, she thanked me. "Sophie, you've been a faithful secretary and friend. I'll be going to the funeral too. Poor Mr. Shep. Poor me."

We met in BC's board room, where I had soft drinks and pastries waiting. Long ago, the CEO instructed, "There must always be good refreshments no matter the topic. That's how you get things accomplished." Everyone arrived on time except the rebbetzin of all people. When she walked in a few minutes later, people stopped talking and stared.

The CEO broke the silence, welcoming the BC board and rebbetzin, but then relinquished the floor. "Let me turn this over to Mia. She called the meeting." Looking around the room at each director, he added in a sympathetic voice, "Mia, I want you to know that we're all here for you."

My job as secretary was to take notes, but Mia asked that I put my pen down. She looked like she was already at Mr. Shep's funeral. "Thank you for dropping everything in your busy day to be here," she said. "You'll find my message surprising and disturbing too. Please, just listen until I can get it all out. It's possible you might know something important."

She paused and peered around the room looking vulnerable and alone as everyone nodded encouragement. One of the board members on the speakerphone said, "We love you, Rebbetzin." Mia replied, "Well I love you all. But the rabbi and I need to leave, and I'm formally submitting his resignation. Let me request that you not ask why. All I can say is that the rabbi is traumatized and can't go on here. My place is with my husband."

There were gasps of surprise as Mia wiped her eyes. She looked over to the CEO, desperate for him to fill the vacuum. As if on cue, the CEO pulled out a piece of paper for visual effect. "Listen up. This is a copy of the resignation letter the rabbi sent me yesterday. I was planning to keep it quiet for two weeks, hoping he'd change his mind. But as you heard, it's effective immediately. We are grateful to the rabbi and rebbetzin for their tireless devotion. Mia, we'll do everything in our power to help. Just name it." All heads turned to Mia, nodding in agreement.

The CEO's kind words gave Mia time to recompose. She cleared her throat. "My friends, you are the closest people to the rabbi and me in the whole world. He's in dire straits and I'm worried sick. He left me without saying where he was going. If any of you know, please, please tell me."

The room was in shock. I thought to myself what courage it took for the rebbetzin to share her secret. It had to be humiliating. There she was telling everyone that her husband had left her, and she didn't even know where he went. Her open wounds from the fishbowl were on display for all to see.

Our hearts went out to her. Person after person told her with tears in their eyes how much they loved the rabbi and rebbetzin. We all pledged to help. But nobody knew where the rabbi went. And these were the people he spent all his time with. I guess it shows just how well this poor, sweet, little man of intellect hid his demons. The meeting ended with Mia thanking us, despair written all over her face. Not a single pastry was eaten.

I offered to drive the rebbetzin to the funeral, and she seemed relieved not to have to attend alone. While in the car, she assured me how much the rabbi appreciated my service. "You've been the model secretary, Sophie. Dependable, but more important, faithful. I consider you my friend." She then broke down and sobbed the rest of the way. All I could do was stay in my lane and keep us safe. I had no words to help. None existed.

When we pulled into the funeral home's parking lot, there was a long black hearse near the entrance, emphasizing the mood of the day. The rebbetzin looked like she didn't want to get out of the car. "Sophie, my life is over. Each person at the directors' meeting will start long lines of gossiping dominoes cascading down in all directions as the entire town discovers my disgrace. What am I to do?"

I took her hand, but it made no sense to lie. I told her she was right, that everyone at BC would hear the news. "But so what?" I said. "People only want to help. Anyway, you need to worry about your family, not anybody else, or what they think."

Mia flinched. "Yes, that's been my downfall."

I know it sounds funny, but the funeral was a beautiful affair. We missed the rabbi leading it, but the people who spoke captured Mr. Shep's spirit. He was loved by his family and praised for his wry humor and sentimentality. I knew him well, and he was always a gentleman, unlike the prima donnas who bull rush past my desk, ignoring me in their intense pursuit of the rabbi's attention. Mr. Shep was kind and considerate, deserving of a loving sendoff.

When the memorial service ended, Mia understandably didn't want to loiter and make small talk. So, I put my arm around her shoulder and we quickly headed toward the exit. But there were people everywhere who wanted to greet the rebbetzin and inquire about the whereabouts of the rabbi. Even in our obvious rush, she was surrounded and bombarded with questions:

"Why didn't the rabbi give the eulogy?"

"Didn't he and the Shep family get along?"

"Is your husband okay?"

"Where is he?"

Oy! I wished for her sake that she could turn invisible.

Finally, we broke free, but a bottleneck had formed at the door leading back to the parking lot. Standing there was Undertaker Black handing out small white slips of paper with driving directions to the cemetery burial plot. The undertaker appeared dignified and respectful, with a proper touch of remorse. But as he saw us approaching, his forehead began to glisten with sweat and he looked like he'd rather be anywhere else, even in the coffin.

Mia stiffened. I turned toward her to see if something was wrong. Her eyes were locked on the undertaker. She uttered under her breath, "His partner."

She instructed me to wait in the car. Still focused on Undertaker Black, she grabbed him, knocking the white slips of paper to the floor. She held on to him for dear life, pulling him away from the crowd toward a long hallway that led to his office. There was nothing discreet about it. I heard the undertaker's door slam shut as I left the building.

While waiting in my car, I thought about how much time Undertaker Black and the rabbi spent together. I used to think of them as "the odd couple." Maybe they were indeed "partners" like the rebbetzin suggested in a way that I hadn't considered.

When the rebbetzin emerged a half hour later, my car was the only one left in the lot. She opened the door with purpose and buckled her seatbelt. But she didn't say a word until we were almost back. Finally, as if she was talking to herself, she said, "This is drop dead crazy." I never saw her or the rabbi again.

CHAPTER XV - THE RABBI

The rabbi felt like he barely survived a collision with a Mack truck. Everything hurt. His back, legs and shoulders ached while his head pounded. He needed more sleep, but sunshine streamed through the bedroom windows while birds nesting in nearby trees sang praise to the new day, urging him to arise.

He stayed in bed a few more minutes, reliving his exodus from Minneapolis. He had used his last ounce of courage to walk through that swinging door. Once inside, he stumbled to bed without changing clothes, unsure if he'd ever wake up again. *I was creeped out of my skin,* he recalled.

He had somehow survived, and the groundkeeper's house felt different in the sunlight. It was surprisingly luxurious with a kitchen that boasted an array of state-of-the art appliances. As he poked around, he found a note from his host on the kitchen table:

Dear Rabbi Friedler,

Welcome to Boulder Paradise Cemetery! I hope your travels were peaceful.

I'll stop by later. For now, make yourself at home. The fridge and pantry are stocked and there are fresh towels in the bathrooms. The coffee is an organic Kona blend that we love. Help yourself to anything and everything.

I look forward to meeting you in person.

Yours truly,

Judd

The rabbi was astounded by the abundance of food. There were rib steaks for barbequing, chocolates, fine wine, and aged cheeses galore. Undertaker Judd was throwing a symbiotic party.

After touring the rest of the house, the rabbi walked outside. The serenity was palpable. *My faith in the quietude and tranquility of cemeteries is restored,* he mused. Gazing east, he was treated to the sun rising over the horizon, ushering in the new day with life affirming colors and warmth. *I might have watched a sunrise but can't recall when. It's glorious.*

Staring out at the endless graves and tombstones separated by well-groomed lawns as far as he could see, the rabbi reflected again on his shock from the night before. *Was there really a homeless man bedding down between graves? Did that happen?* He believed it had.

He strode back inside and grabbed a quick breakfast, still acclimating to his new abode. He then prepared another meal, poured a fresh cup of coffee in a second mug, and went out to find the homeless man. He retraced his steps and before long nearly stumbled over him, lying on the same patch of turf.

This time, the rabbi did more than nod to the stranger in fear. He smiled at the only other living human on the vast grounds. "Good morning, sir. I have more food than I know what to do with. Help yourself to breakfast." Now it was the homeless man's turn to be speechless as the rabbi continued. "I'm Aaron Friedler. I wish we could have chatted last night, but it was late and, to be honest, I was startled."

The homeless man sat up and rubbed his eyes. One of his front teeth was missing. He looked frightened, perhaps worried that the little man would call the police for trespassing. But the rabbi was reassuring. "Have the coffee while it's piping hot. It's Hawaii's finest."

The homeless man took a sip and stretched awkwardly. It looked like he had forgotten how to have a simple conversation but gave it a try. "They call me Sutcliff Hand. I grew up in a small town south of here. Tried to make it to the majors but blew out my arm in Triple A."

"Sorry to hear," the rabbi responded disarmingly. "I wasn't good at baseball a day in my life."

Sutcliff smiled and continued. "I had a hot fastball but not anymore.

Made my way to Boulder to find work. I thought the cemetery would be safe to spend the night, if you can get over the ghosts." Sutcliff didn't mention that he was mixing painkillers with cheap whisky and had been fired from Boulder Machines a month ago.

The rabbi sensed overpowering sadness in the homeless man's eyes, his beaten down shoulders. Life had taken its toll at an early age. He reflexively recited in his mind the anthem of the lucky. *There but for the grace of God go I.* But he now rejected the message as irrational. *The grace of God? Come on! Why didn't God bestow his grace on this young man? If the Lord lifted me up, wasn't he also responsible for Sutcliff's fall? And what about my parents?*

Nothing made sense anymore. And yet, the rabbi could not imagine failing to be thankful. He needed to express gratitude. But to who? He was lost in contemplation when the homeless man asked, "What were you doing rumbling around the cemetery so late? Are you crazy, man? I'm only here cuz I got no choice."

The rabbi responded with comic sincerity. "I know the owners of this cemetery and will be living here for a while, near the mausoleum. You're welcome to have a bed."

The homeless man looked flummoxed, unused to any form of hospitality. "I best keep outside. Thank you for the coffee and breakfast, sir." He paused and lowered his head. "And for talking to me."

Sutcliff finished his breakfast in silence. His body language signaled that he needed to be alone. *Maybe that's part of his problem,* the rabbi speculated. *Or his path to redemption, just like for me.* The rabbi excused himself and returned to the house to wait for Undertaker Judd.

He grabbed a book from a shelf in the second bedroom, found a comfortable chair and stared out the window at the immaculate grounds. Two minutes later, he fell into a sweet sleep. There was no surgeon with a scalpel.

Undertaker Judd visited in the afternoon. He was young, charming, and sported an expensive haircut. "Greetings Rabbi. My cousin in Minneapolis thinks you walk on the Great Lakes. The place is all yours. Just let me know what you need."

The rabbi insisted on paying for the accommodations, but the undertaker refused. "No worries, Rabbi. I hear you've done a lot for my cousin. This is on the house, our thanks to you." He then moved his hand through his perfect hair. "But all the same, if you see something at my cemetery that needs improvement during your stay, let me know. Business could be better."

After the undertaker departed, the rabbi felt depressed. *Maybe I'm destined to be a funeral consultant. I'm not qualified for anything else. And I miss my wife.* But he resisted the negativity and fell into another sleep until his stomach roused him for dinner.

The rabbi wanted to cook the steak on the patio grill but didn't know how. He had never lit a barbeque before. So, he prepared a simple sandwich and brought it outside, this time to watch the sun setting out West. The sunset was every bit as inspiring as the sunrise. *What have I been doing with my life? I never made time to view these daily miracles, always meeting in a stuffy room instead, or scrutinizing small biblical print for new meaning.*

He reflected on the similarities of sunrises and sunsets. They looked identical at that singular moment when Helios balanced at the tip of the horizon, whether ascending or descending. And the feeling of awe was the same. The rabbi pondered the irony. *Is there a hidden meaning, a connection between beginnings and endings?* For the first time, he was considering nature the same way he studied sacred writings. *With each inevitable end follows a new start, a sunrise.* He decided to make watching these two key moments of the day a ritual.

He climbed into bed a few hours later and again his thoughts turned to Mia, wishing he could cuddle with her, feel her warmth. He had kept his phone off the entire day to avoid a conversation. His wounds were still too raw, and he was overwhelmed by guilt. *She doesn't deserve what I can't deal with.* Finally, he fell asleep, but this time he turned from side to side subconsciously reaching for his wife.

A few more days passed this way at the groundskeeper's house. The rabbi had moments of worthwhile reflection but became lonelier while his guilt escalated. On his third night, the pattern was broken by a loud scream in the distance. He tried to repress thinking about how unprotected he was, alone in the middle of the cemetery late at night. *My imagination is in overdrive, that's all,* he reasoned, as if he was reassuring his beautiful Hannah when she was a toddler. But the scream permeated his thoughts.

Again, came a fitful sleep. But a short time later, there was a loud pounding at the front door. A man yelled, "Open up, open up right now!" The thumping intensified. "Unlock the door!"

The rabbi was shaking so violently that he could barely put on his robe. He crept to the door and glanced quickly through the peephole, jumping back before he could see anything as the door thundered again. *The lock won't hold. Then what?*

When he regained enough courage to look out again, the rabbi saw the homeless man with a wide smile that highlighted his missing tooth. Behind him stood Mia.

CHAPTER XVI – MIA

Undertaker Black's expression was a mixture of fright and embarrassment when our eyes locked while he was handing out driving directions at the funeral parlor. *He's the man with directions all right*, I thought. *Directions to Aaron.* Call it "rebbetzin intuition."

After I escorted him to his office, the undertaker couldn't look me in the eye. He first claimed ignorance and next that he was sworn to secrecy by my husband. I clarified that as far as I was concerned, if something happened to the rabbi, it would be his fault. Not to mention that he was interfering with our marriage. I then stared him down.

Finally, he blurted out, "I was just trying to help."

"Go on. Tell me everything."

I couldn't fathom what I was hearing as he confessed their plan. "Boulder Paradise Cemetery?!," I repeated in astonishment. "The groundskeeper's house?! Have you two lost your minds?!"

The rest of my day was a blur. After leaving Sophie, I drove to the liquor store and asked the owner to recommend a gift for a friend who did me a huge favor. He retreated to the storage area and returned with a bottle of aged scotch that he cradled like a baby. "This one is smooth and smoky," he instructed. "A prize for someone who knows his stuff."

My next stop was Mr. Bloomberg's office, where I apologized, handed over the bottle and gave him a hug. "You saved me," I said. "Enjoy this peace offering. Bottoms up." I still thought he was out of line but thank God for his razor.

And now, here I am reunited with my husband at the groundskeeper's house in the middle of a cemetery half-way across the country. After comparing notes with Aaron, it sounded like we both starred in the same B-rated horror film. I wouldn't wish my nighttime stroll through the graveyard on my worst enemy.

I feared the time had come to meet my maker when I tripped over the homeless man in the dark. I let loose a scream like I was being attacked by an axe murderer. But the poor guy calmed me down and led me to the rabbi. I stood behind the homeless man as he knocked on the door. You should have seen Aaron's expression transform from panic to euphoria.

Our reunion was remarkable, again straight from Hollywood, but this time it was a classic love story. Maybe "Ghost." Ha! We embraced like it was our honeymoon, while the homeless man quietly receded into the night. No words were spoken. We just held each other and cried.

Aaron escorted me to the bedroom, and we made passionate, honest love. We became one again. True, we were no longer the rabbi and rebbetzin. But our bond was strong. He told me, "Sleep, my love. The sun and birds will greet us soon and we can watch the world recreate itself at dawn. We'll recreate ourselves too." Aaron slept without tossing and turning.

The morning was perfect. We sat together and watched the sunrise while sipping aromatic coffee. All those tombstones made me anxious, but Aaron observed, "Death is part of life."

"How reassuring," I responded. Nevertheless, I soon acclimated to the strange setting that was to be the focal point for our healing.

We decided to stay a month. We watched the sunrise and sunset every day, in awe of the eternal rhythms of the universe, a reminder that there was something bigger than just the two of us with our silly troubles. That we, like the world, could begin anew.

We also worked on our marriage as if we were in therapy. I took Aaron's hand and said, "We're starting over and it's scary. To get it right this time, we must share every thought. Nothing's off limits." I wasn't casting blame but remained shaken by his dark secret that had thrown us into a tailspin.

Our conversations were difficult and intense. I apologized for being self-centered and refusing to see that the very thing I thrived on, being the rabbi's wife, was hurting Aaron. I was having the time of my life at his expense. "It was unintentional, but I see now that I was dense and selfish," I admitted. "Worse yet, I let you lie awake in anguish while I dreamed my sweet dreams." I wondered how many other couples had the same problem. One spouse happy and clueless, maybe even on purpose, the other one stoic, absorbing grim burdens in stone silence.

But I wasn't guilty alone. Aaron also made oversized mistakes that needed to be called out. "I know your heart was in the right place," I said. "You were trying to protect your family, satisfy BC."

"Yes, true," he responded with his head lowered.

"But how could you have kept secret what happened to your parents? Twelve years, Aaron! Was your plan to deceive me with silence until our time for burial in a place like this?"

By this point, my voice was shaking. Aaron had tears in his eyes. "I was trying to be all things for all people," he said. "I'm sorry."

Our morbid location, eccentric as it may seem, turned out ideal. We set aside time to share, reflect and relax. The sunrises and sunsets provided natural structure. We worked it out as soulmates again, ready to relaunch and take on the world.

Well, I'm being a bit optimistic. In all candor, we were petrified. We had spent our entire adult lives as the pampered rabbi and rebbetzin, embedded in the cocoon of our adoring community. We had no idea what to do now, no training or skills outside the clergy. It's not as if my husband was a handy jack of all trades, equipped with a manly tool chest.

Aaron put on a strong face. "We need to live our new lives for a while, Mia, see how it goes. Get comfortable in our new skin." How can you argue with that? He also pointed out that we were "privileged," as they say. We had plenty of money for a soft landing while we explored our options. "The world is wide open to us," he continued.

Well, he was right. These platitudes made sense. But what about the details?

We also needed to address another sore topic. Make that Hannah. "I'm to blame," Aaron said. "Our child needed me, but I was worried about appearances and a rarified religious edict that locked her out."

I disagreed for the thousandth time. Hannah's absence was more my fault. The thing is, I loved my daughter. I also loved BC. I thought our child should make herself fit in like we did. She was part of the family, part of the clergy team, part of our image, end of story. I was wrong, and the penalty is an open wound where our daughter should be.

We didn't know what else we could do to find her. By this time, we had hired several additional detectives. The last one summed it up: "She disappeared with some serious help. This isn't an amateur's handiwork." We resolved to hire another PI but feared that Hannah had to make the first move. I wanted to scream.

During our third week at the cemetery, Aaron received a call from a man named Jacob, who coincidentally stayed at a place called Lake Paradise a few weeks earlier. It was in the mountains several hours from the Boulder cemetery. Jacob loved the location, labelling it "God's Country." As I learned more about Aaron's new friend, it sounded like they were clones in some ways.

I eavesdropped while they chatted over the speakerphone. This wasn't your run-of-the-mill conversation among man buddies. One minute they discussed Darwin, with Jacob asking, "How can you square the Bible's creation story with evolution? Science proves it's a fable." Next, they dissected God's habit of rewarding and punishing descendants for the behavior of ancestors. Jacob pounced again. "So, let me get this straight, Rabbi. If I sin, my unborn grandson will be disciplined by the Lord, even if he's virtuous? And if I'm righteous, my descendants will reap the fruits despite their evil ways? Rabbi, that's unfair."

My husband, the rabbi I used to know, would have gently set Jacob straight, spinning out rationalizations with more gyrations than a dancer in a Broadway musical. Most likely, he'd carry the day, teaching that the story served as a metaphor. "Don't be so literal," he'd counsel. "Only the lesson from the creation story matters." For the most recalcitrant who were unwilling to accept allegories, Aaron might prod, "Well, I hear you, but you should know that you're pushing back on thousands of years of teachings by our best minds, not to mention your own ancestors and traditions."

Aaron was always polite when correcting people. He reasoned, "Guilt delivered with love is powerful."

But my, how times had changed. The new Aaron voiced his own doubts, confirming Jacob's skepticism. "Darwin and science must be respected," he agreed. "Creation didn't happen in seven days. Man evolved from the ape over millions of years, long after dinosaurs roamed the planet. I'm not saying God didn't create our natural world or set evolution in motion. But the story didn't unfold like the Bible tells us."

Jacob sounded animated. "I agree, but 'In the Beginning' is the single most important part of the Bible. If we can't take creation literally, did any of it really happen? If not, if it's all abstraction, we might as well read an insightful novel instead, or update these religious texts. Certainly, we shouldn't fight wars or reject science over metaphors."

I was thunderstruck when Aaron concurred in silence. My king of metaphors had abdicated his figurative throne. And I was dumbstruck as he abandoned other long held positions with ease. "These notions of intergenerational punishment and reward are ethically bankrupt," he told his new friend.

I could see why the men got along and was happy they found each other. Heavy philosophy has never been my thing and Aaron needed a buddy to air out his evolving views with, now more than ever, as he attempted to recreate himself from trauma.

While Aaron would have preferred living in his mind to examine the unknowable day and night, we needed to take care of the mundane. A call to the real estate agent to sell our house. Another to the storage company for our furniture. I cancelled our newspaper, mail, cleaning service, the internet, and trash collection. The hassles of change are endless.

Aaron also called the CEO to apologize for his abrupt departure. The CEO assured him, "Rabbi, you built a strong institution. We'll survive, but BC misses you. I miss you." The CEO wanted to fly out on the company jet for a visit, but only after we were ready. "I'll give you space," he said.

Undertaker Judd stopped by several times during our stay. He was nice but appeared more like a polished businessman than even the CEO. He pumped Aaron about how to improve the cemetery. Aaron advised him that the grounds and facilities were outstanding. But Judd kept his face stern until Aaron told him what he really wanted to hear.

"I'll do my best to introduce you to some clergy leads when I'm back on my feet." Judd looked like he struck gold.

We didn't mention the homeless man to the undertaker but searched for him several times. We hoped to invite him for dinner and to spend the night. But the poor guy vanished.

Our time for pause and reset passed quickly, which spoke volumes about the persevering strength of our relationship. Imagine being stuck in the middle of a cemetery for a full month with only your spouse. That is, while you are still alive. If we could get along here, we could make it anywhere.

It was finally time to leave, but we still didn't have a plan other than to tour the Rockies and keep thinking. What a privilege.

Aaron suggested we follow in Jacob's footsteps and make Lake Paradise our first stop. When I called for a reservation, the innkeeper sounded eccentric but welcoming. "You won't believe it when you see it," he said. "Yes, indeed. Yes, indeed."

CHAPTER XVII – THE RABBI

The rabbi came to breakfast clean shaven. Mia acted like she had seen a golem but steadied when she detected a hurt look on her husband's face. She touched his red, irritated skin. "You're ten years younger without the beard," she said. "Smooth and sexy." Aaron reverted to the sacred stroke with nothing left to run his fingers through.

They drove off from the groundskeeper's house in a peppy red Maxima rented in Boulder. They felt like youngsters beginning a jaunt through Europe after college graduation.

The rabbi opened the sunroof. "What a concept. We can go wherever we wish, stop for as long as we want. Nobody to worry about but ourselves." He turned on the radio to find classic rock.

Mia heard the rejuvenation in her husband's voice as the wind blew her hair. "I don't need to be on a retreat or mission with crowds of congregants to have fun. I'm with you, my beardless wonder, and the mountains are calling."

But there was also a sense of disquietude. While Aaron and Mia pledged to no longer keep secrets, both harbored unexpressed worries about where they were headed, navigating the world anew while ensconced in middle age. All they knew was the life of the clergy. Aaron tried to joke about it. "We used to be the rabbi and rebbetzin, now we're Bonnie and Clyde … Batman and Robin." Mia hummed the superhero tune with modification. *"Do, do, do, do, do, do, do … Ricky and Lucy!"*

The dynamic duo left their doubts behind as the terrain became mountainous, the driving intense. Aaron gripped the steering wheel until it hurt, realizing that even a slight veer at the wrong time would mean instant death. But with each hairpin turn and switchback came more magnificent scenery. Their ears popped and so did their eyes.

While they had travelled to beautiful locations in the past, the focus was always communal. They had never been singularly immersed in nature like this, with awe-inspiring mountains, untouched aqua lakes. They could see into infinity through the clear, crisp air.

When the driving eased, Aaron again considered whether he had missed something fundamental during his tenure as rabbi. He lowered the radio volume to talk. "Looking at these wonders, something is stirring my soul, a new sensation. Is it possible there's an entirely different way to find meaning?"

Mia could barely speak. Her spirit too was moved by the grandeur, but her response mechanism was to enjoy the ride, have some fun, feel the joy. She'd leave the dissection of the moment, the intellectualization of the experience, to her husband.

She tried to keep the mood light. "We're on the right path dear, but hold on to that steering wheel, or we'll discover the great unknown before our time. Turn the radio back up and play some music." Aaron, of course, began dwelling over the great unknown as they rocked on.

They pulled into several lookouts to better enjoy the scenery. One area offered an easy trail leading from the parking lot. It was the first time in their married lives that Aaron and Mia hiked together alone. Aaron continued to consider the implications of being so close to majesty, feeling roots of inspiration sprouting from natural order. Did the endless study and detailed rituals comprising his former life ironically block him from the very awe they were meant to facilitate?

Mia's hike was easier. Delight filled her heart as she inhaled deeply enjoying new scents and world class views. "This is eye candy," she told her husband.

After a few more jaw dropping stops where Aaron cogitated while Mia rejoiced, they found their way to Lake Paradise for a late afternoon check-in. The innkeeper introduced himself as Merle Yoder. Aaron flinched, noticing the man's gleaming green eyes. *They resemble the surgeon's eyes,* he thought. *But this man doesn't frighten me.*

The innkeeper didn't seem to notice and asked where they were from, what they did for a living. These were not complicated questions.

But it was the first time the couple was confronted with such inquiries since Aaron's resignation. They responded simultaneously.

> Aaron: "I'm no longer working. Just seeing the world, trying to figure things out."

> Mia: "He's the rabbi of a big temple in Minneapolis. This place is awesome!"

The innkeeper smiled at the disunity. "Interesting, interesting," he mumbled to himself. "One a seeker, the other out for fun."

In a louder voice, he launched into his long-rehearsed dialogue about the facilities as he escorted them to their room. Aaron and Mia fell in love with the place. It was a little beat up and neglected. But as they wandered the spacious grounds, they sensed something spiritual. They also swooned when the innkeeper pointed out the path leading to Lake Paradise. "What a view," Mia exclaimed. "Wow, wow, oh wow."

"There's more to it than that," the innkeeper responded. "Yes indeed, yes indeed." Aaron couldn't tell if the innkeeper was talking to them or himself.

They stayed four nights. Each morning started with breakfast hosted by the innkeeper. Unlike Jacob, they savored the meals and had long conversations with the old man. The innkeeper was obviously eccentric with his talk about aliens and Roswell, his green eyes burning out of their sockets. But they also found him engaging and sweet. And his recommendations for tours and restaurants were outstanding.

The rabbi asked if he remembered Jacob's recent visit. The innkeeper looked excited. "Now that one was a seeker, his soul on fire. He seemed desperate but found what he was looking for out there on the lake. Yes, yes, he found it. Just like I did when I arrived. I seen it too."

Mia wondered what the innkeeper meant by "seen it," thinking that he intended to say "felt it" instead. Not wishing to dive into semantics, she asked, "So what's it like living here?"

"It's paradise all right, just like the name," he responded. "But my time has come. I'm too darn old to keep running this place. I want to see it again, see it one last time at night before I head home to New Mexico."

Before they could digest this comment, the innkeeper looked at them like a lightbulb flashed in his mind. "I bet you two haven't gone fishing a day in your lives. I'll take you myself after the other guests clear out for the day."

The rabbi looked hesitant, but Mia exclaimed, "You'd win that wager, but not after today."

They met at the shore an hour later and climbed into the innkeeper's small motorboat. The innkeeper pulled out slowly but soon accelerated. The rabbi and Mia were enthralled as water began splashing up the sides of the craft in mirthful dances. Refreshing spray pelted their faces while they propelled through nature.

The innkeeper navigated to his favorite spot and cut the engine. He handed out fishing poles and helped them hook the bait. "Sit tight and wait for a bite," he instructed. "Just keep still, take it in. The less talking the more you'll sense. You'll be at one with it. Yes indeed, yes indeed."

Aaron's overactive mind triggered. *What a notion. Transcendence without prayer or chatting up a storm with a crowd.*

Mia embraced the calm and left herself open to possibilities. While Aaron was wondering what the innkeeper meant by being "at one with it," she yelled, "I have a bite. Holy Toledo." The innkeeper helped her reel in a good-sized trout struggling against her pull as Aaron nearly fainted.

Aaron grilled the fish for dinner on a barbeque outside their room that the innkeeper helped him light. He was surprised by his feeling of empowerment ignited by the flames gyrating beneath Mia's catch. Nothing ever smelled or tasted so delicious as they dined outside in this remarkable venue.

Later that night, Aaron called Jacob to thank him for recommending Lake Paradise. Jacob's response shocked him. "Glad you like it Rabbi because I've got news. Hunter and I are moving there. I just put a down payment on a cabin with a million-dollar view." There was silence on the line as if Jacob was weighing whether to say more. Finally, he added in a softer voice, "I think I found what I was looking for."

Aaron was unsure how to respond. *How can he make such a big decision based on a single day's visit?* He had an uneasy feeling about

Jacob's state of mind but knew he couldn't change it. He opted instead to be supportive. "That's big Jacob, huge. I'm happy for you. This place has a magnetic pull. I feel it too."

After the call, Aaron and Mia rehashed Jacob's plan from all angles as only a husband and wife can do. "He doesn't know a soul out West," said Aaron with a baffled expression. "It's risky, impulsive."

"Maybe he should find a big city," piped in Mia. "More people to meet, a diversity of activities, culture."

But Jacob's courage was undeniably admirable. He was taking a bold leap while so many choose lives of quiet submission, passively anchored in what no longer works while dreaming of escape.

Although they were discussing Jacob, they were nibbling around the edges of questions confronting their own lives. How should they recreate themselves? Where should they live? Finally, Mia blurted out a barely formed musing that was floating around the outskirts of her consciousness from the moment they had arrived at Lake Paradise. "What do you think it would be like to own the Paradise Inn?"

Aaron looked contemplative as she enjoyed this moment of pure reverie. "Are you serious?"

"Serious, delirious, my love."

CHAPTER XVIII – MIA

My life has become a reality TV show. Not American Idol or The Apprentice, but surreal nonetheless. The latest episode following "An Odyssey To Boulder Paradise Cemetery" began with my innocent comment about the Paradise Inn. Aaron asked if I was serious, and I responded, "Serious, delirious, my love." Let me repeat the word "delirious."

Obviously, with my silly rhyme, I was conveying that I was serious about charting our future lives, but more than 99 percent joshing about being an innkeeper. I was having a little Walter Mitty fun.

Not another word was spoken about the Paradise Inn or Jacob's move out West as we turned to planning our travel itinerary. We decided to depart after breakfast for the open road. First stop would be Rocky Mountain National Park. We'd see as many of these natural landmarks as possible in a month. Yellowstone, Tetons, Grand Canyon, here we come! I went to bed excited over the heart-to-heart conversations we were sure to have as we plotted our future amidst wonders of the world.

But my dumb husband had a different itinerary. The first I heard of it came at three in the morning with someone banging on the door. I was petrified, particularly when I discovered that Aaron was missing. This was probably how he felt when the homeless man pounded at the front door of the groundskeeper's house in the middle of the night.

When I looked through the peephole, there was the old innkeeper's eyeball staring back at me. "Hurry along, hurry along to my office," he said from the other side of the door. "Sometimes these things happen late at night. Yes indeed, yes indeed."

I arrived disheveled and groggy, mostly out of my mind with concern. But the scene was strange, not scary. Aaron was wearing his pajamas and a baseball cap. He was hunched over a card table, poring over a document like he used to study Torah. He looked up and exclaimed, "Mia, you've never been so right. I've been working this out with the innkeeper for half the night. We are of one mind now." The two men looked at each other like small boys unable to keep a wonderful secret for a second longer. Aaron blurted out, "He's going to sell us the Paradise Inn! The price is fair."

The men giggled with glee. The innkeeper wore an insane smile on his face with his gleaming green eyes dancing a crazy tune, only to be matched by my husband grinning like a toddler while eyeballing me through his dense glasses with innocent sincerity.

The innkeeper chortled, "You seen it too. That's why I want you to have the place. I know you seen it."

There "it" was again. "It." I still had no idea what the innkeeper was so enthralled with. I also couldn't tell if he was even talking to me, or just Aaron, or maybe somebody or something else altogether. I was late to this party, the last prune in the box, the one on the outside looking in through the foggiest windows ever. The two men were jubilant, while I barely functioned.

"Excuse us," I said. "Aaron and I need to talk."

"Ah, ah, take your time," replied the innkeeper. "I'll see you both at breakfast, if not sooner. Yes indeed, yes indeed."

Back in our room, Aaron looked sheepish as it dawned on him how furious I was. "Let me explain, here's the thing," he said. "When you talked about owning the place, you said you were serious. Even delirious with the idea. So, I got to thinking—"

My Medusa stare froze him mid-sentence. "You fool. Have you lost your mind? I wasn't serious, just having fun, imagining the unimaginable."

I let that sink in as he hopelessly searched his face for his missing beard, and his mind for words. "But Mia—"

"Did you forget everything we worked out? What happened to your promise not to keep secrets? Let me get this straight. You just get up in the middle of the night and go off to change our lives in your PJs without cluing me in?"

"I wasn't going to act without you," he said in a hurt voice. "That's why the innkeeper came to get you while I finished reading the contract. I was excited by your idea and Jacob's courage to take a leap. I couldn't sleep, so I stepped outside for a minute to see the stars. It was as if the innkeeper was waiting for me. I love Lake Paradise and this inn is special. We could center our new lives here."

I was flabbergasted. Aaron envisioned me, the rebbetzin, magically transforming into the "hostess with the mostess." And picture him, the rabbi, toting his wrench to fix that leaking faucet in room six. PLEASE!

He was undaunted. "We can host religious gatherings and if the visiting priest or rabbi needs a little counselling on the side, who better than me to give it?"

He waited for an answer, but only got an icy stare.

"And the inn would be a natural destination for weddings, anniversaries, you name it. You'd be my partner Mia, like always. You could cook up a storm for breakfast and hold court."

Aaron hesitated. He could see that he crossed the point of no return with that last remark and tried to adjust on the fly. "Well, I would help you serve food, of course." Stutter. "And you're great with people. We'd be treated to fascinating encounters every day." Stammer. "In our off hours, we'd be living in paradise. What an adventure."

I glared. My husband had thought things through, but alone again, inside his mind, while shutting out his fricking chef and hostess.

There are times in a long marriage where you aren't sure if you should hold your spouse in a loving embrace or murder him. A small part of me was thrilled that Aaron still had the gumption to leap at pursuing a dream. But my furor dominated any feelings of endearment. Aaron took my flippant "serious, delirious" remark and ran solo. Instead of working through a life altering decision as a couple, he ventured out in the dead of night to meet with the innkeeper. He left me snoozing while he planned our future with a man whose sanity I seriously question.

Aaron looked baffled and shaken, unable to read my conflicted emotions. As he awaited my verdict, I relived other painful reality television episodes from our past. The nightmare at Sunnyside Nursing

Home. The twelve-year secret. Our daughter gone missing. A coffee shop resignation letter. The groundskeeper's house. And now we are to be hoteliers. To think we were once exemplars, the picture of stability that others sought to emulate.

I had to get away from my husband. "Run the inn alone, you delirious jerk," I shouted. Before Aaron knew what hit him, I bolted and raced down the path to Lake Paradise.

The moon lit my way as I followed a trail that led to a small, secluded beach. I sat in the soft sand staring at the water as I rehashed our conversation. The idea was absurd, although I must admit that I was intrigued by "holding court" during breakfast. And Aaron was being creative, devising ways we could use our former skills. But this was too fast, the idea was outrageous, and I was out of patience with his solo act.

I swear that I'm not narcoleptic. Well maybe just a little. People kid me that I can sleep anywhere, any time. I gained my reputation on the Fourth of July, dozing off to the 1812 Overture while fireworks burst in the night sky. Well, now I can add Lake Paradise to the list. As I began to relax, listening to the endless waves as they meandered to the shore, I drifted off, leaving the absurdity behind.

I'll never know if what happened next was real or a dream. As I lay on the soft forgiving sand, I looked up at the night sky. Black and white birds hovered far off in the middle of Lake Paradise. The moonlight cast an eerie glow on them as they flitted and fluttered. Why weren't they ashore, fast asleep in their nests? Casting my eyes on the water, I saw that the waves had switched direction and were impossibly moving backward toward the middle, another optical illusion. From a far corner of my mind, I heard a soft voice repeating, "You seen it, you seen it." Was it the innkeeper?

And out of the midst he appeared in his small motorboat with a kind look on his face and his green eyes gleaming brighter than the stars. "Your husband is a kind man. You are deserving too, Mia. This is my gift. Yes indeed, yes indeed." And then this Moses of Lake Paradise came ashore, lifted me like a small child, gently placed me in the boat and returned me to the inn.

In the morning, I woke up in our cozy bed with Aaron beside me. I took my husband's hands, looked into his eyes, to his very soul, and said, "Let's do it."

CHAPTER XIX – THE PARADISE INN

Aaron and Mia deliriously toured the National Parks, reveling in nature's miracles. Old Faithful, El Capitan, Arches, Hoodoos. They saw it all. The splendor was the perfect backdrop for those heart-to-heart talks that Mia felt were crucial for their future. After a month, they were inspired soulmates ready to conquer the world.

On their final afternoon before returning to Lake Paradise to begin their new lives, they hiked a remote trail hugging a narrow river. There were no soaring mountains, plunging waterfalls, or mystifying geothermal activity to thrill the senses. But the location teemed with life.

A mile in, they rested, dipping their feet in the cool water while admiring the surroundings. Waterlilies opened wide to greet the sun. A mosaic of yellow, red, and purple flowers bloomed on the riverbank, while bees and butterflies rippled about, and herons hid in the tall shrubs. A family of turtles sunned on an ancient boulder protruding from the water, ignoring the darting fish below. It was a mystery how the granite monolith had found this unlikely resting spot, or by what means these immobile creatures scaled it. The swans, ducks, and geese didn't care as they glided by.

Mia rested her head on Aaron's shoulder as she watched two hawks soaring above, wings spread wide in the clear blue sky. "I love this place," she said. "It makes me calm and happy."

Aaron wrapped his arms around his wife like he would never let her go. "This wisp of a river isn't on the map. But even here, everything is interconnected, a microcosm of the universe, a miracle. I hope that's how we'll feel about our new home."

Mia smiled and took Aaron's hand. She led him barefoot to a small clearing with soft pine needles covering the ground. "Let's make like the birds and bees. I'll love you in Lake Paradise just like I've loved you everywhere else we've been." She touched her husband in a way only a loving wife knows how. It was a moment of passion they would remember forever.

Nor would they forget the interruption. While buttoning his shirt, Aaron saw a bear rumbling toward the river in search of trout and other tasty morsels. How could such a massive creature move so quickly? Mia's mood swung from bliss to caution. "Let's play it safe and scram. Put your shoes on quick. I don't want to be interconnected with that beast's stomach."

"Just look at the indiscriminate lethality of nature's sublime rhythms," said the rabbi with awe in his voice.

"Come on already," shouted his wife. "I said quick!"

Over dinner, they relived the adventure. Mia couldn't stop rolling her eyes in disbelief. "Who would ever have predicted that the rabbi and rebbetzin would end their vacation fleeing from a bear after making love on pine needles? Inconceivable!" She then smiled wryly at her husband. "We still got it."

Aaron nodded his agreement and took her hand. "What a trip this was. Passion, excitement, spirituality. I'm rediscovering God in a whole new way, a simpler one."

Mia smiled at her husband's ever-growing spirit. "The parks have been a romp," she replied. "Time to take what we learned and move forward, change our name to 'the Hiltons.'"

But when Aaron and Mia returned to their new home, they were confronted with horrible news. The old innkeeper had drowned in the middle of Lake Paradise. The owner of a nearby art gallery on Main Street reported, "It was a tragedy all right. Nobody could understand what the old coot was doing out there late at night."

They took the loss hard. "We barely knew the man," said Mia. "And yet, I sense he helped us profoundly."

"He'll be in my heart forever," replied Aaron as he wiped tears from his eyes. "The innkeeper passed us the torch. I'm determined to prove he was right entrusting the Paradise Inn to our custody."

They decided to renovate the property as a tribute to the innkeeper while recreating themselves. To start, they blanketed the floors with bright new carpeting and converted the rooms to "luxury suites" with the best cable channels, internet capability and latte makers. The walls were given a fresh coat of paint and decorated with large portraits of magnificent landscapes. Two plush robes initialed "PI" were placed in each suite's closet.

Mia announced the commercial strategy. "Let's infuse a spiritual atmosphere into the premises to attract the right clientele." They did so by adding a reflection pool with royal blue and gold tiles to a tranquil area off to the side of the inn. Visitors could luxuriate in comfortable chairs surrounding the pool while contemplating the ultimate. At dusk, they piped in soft music and offered complimentary cabernet with hors d'oeuvres.

Guests could then amble over to a new stone labyrinth added to the back of the inn, encircled by gardens and a white brick wall. Mia sprinkled Buddhas and good luck charms throughout the area signifying love and peace. The labyrinth was the perfect place for a circular journey to the ethereal center. After dark, scented candles in a variety of colors lit the path through the maze.

The new "Hiltons" capped off the update by adding a huge antique cabinet to the lobby. They populated it with books of inspiration. A plaque was placed on the heirloom to commemorate the old innkeeper. It was inscribed, "May our friend rest in peace as his dream lives on."

Aaron and Mia were ecstatic with the finished product. They had produced a landmark for retreats, missions, and family events. Mia joked, "If you build it, they'll come," which is exactly what happened. There were seldom any vacancies during the travel season for this top-rated accommodation.

As Aaron predicted, Mia became a natural hotelier, doling out the charm. She perfected a recipe for cinnamon scones and served them warm with all variety of eggs and fruits. And she "held court" with the guests, creating an atmosphere of cheer while giving sage advice about area attractions. Sometimes, Mia even accompanied them on shopping jaunts.

I'm the luckiest man in the world to have married this woman, thought Aaron. He knew Mia missed being the rebbetzin. But with her indomitable spirit, she had wholeheartedly embraced her new life.

Aaron's counselling business thrived. Throngs of clergy leading sojourns to the inn craved relief from the stress of their jobs. "Guess I wasn't the only one," he told Mia. "Being an exemplar is an occupational hazard and the boatload of sorrow they witness takes its toll." His sensitivity and vast experience proved invaluable for providing sound counsel. Mia said, "You're Mr. Bloomberg of the Rockies."

Aaron also didn't forget his commitment to Undertaker Judd. He recommended Boulder Paradise Cemetery to visiting clergy from Denver. "Tell Undertaker Judd that the groundskeeper sent you."

The inn became popular for destination weddings. Aaron conducted ceremonies at the reflection pool for free. Nevertheless, many couples insisted on handing him a check. Aaron accepted the donations, but he re-contributed the money to charities for Alzheimer's disease to honor his parents. Mia recorded the donations in a new section of her Book of Balloons.

Jacob's cabin with the million-dollar view was located ten minutes from the Paradise Inn. He was a frequent visitor for dinner and Mia grew fond of him. She had a vague concern that he was wound too tight but was thrilled that her husband had a close friend nearby to wrestle with over the mysteries of life. *Still not my cup of tea,* she thought.

Jacob often brought Hunter along. The friendly canine loved circling the grounds for hours as if he owned the inn, adding another dimension for guests to enjoy. After he tired, Hunter would sleep peacefully besides the men without a care in the world as they hypothesized and conjectured. Even the whimsical held profundity for these two.

Jacob: "I envy Hunter. Who needs consciousness with the

accompanying anxiety and suffering when you can be scratched behind the ears and feel bliss all day long?!"

Aaron: "I don't buy it. Tempting as it sounds, I choose life in all its complexity. With awareness comes the opportunity for meaning."

At this critical juncture in the conversation, Hunter was known to yawn and pass gas.

In her spare time, Mia enjoyed observing the guests. Besides clergy, a sprinkling of politicians, athletes, and celebrities strolled the grounds, lured by the inn's stellar reputation and location. Mia was particularly intrigued when she laid eyes on a blond bombshell, famous for steamy romance scenes, circling the labyrinth in high heels. "It's like we're back at BC, only better," she told Aaron when they were preparing for bed. "We rub elbows with fascinating people from all walks of life, not just a single religion, one location. Our little lives in this small town have become downright cosmopolitan."

Aaron was amused by his wife's reaction to a voluptuous porn star. He wisely kept silent, again grateful for his awareness.

The Paradise Inn was a triumph. The old Innkeeper would have been proud. Yes, indeed. Yes, indeed.

CHAPTER XX - THE CEO

B C did not completely vanish from the rabbi and rebbetzin's lives. Instead, its most prominent member became a regular guest. GoldOrb Diversified operated a factory in Denver and the CEO made it a point to combine business trips with visits to Lake Paradise. The man hopped the company jet out West like ordinary people board the commuter rail.

The CEO would stay a day or two, fascinated by how successful the rabbi and rebbetzin had become in their new endeavor. Enjoying a glass of wine with them at the reflection pool, he smiled. "Listen, you two can come work for me anytime. GoldOrb needs people who think outside the box, stretch, take risks to disrupt."

The corporate jargon struck Mia as funny. "I'm in. It's a natural fit for us to work for a company bearing God's initials. We'll replace your HR department with a Spiritual Resources Group."

"Cheers," said the CEO, raising his glass in approval. "It'll be the first of its kind in corporate America." He thought of all the grief his HR department had caused during his tenure. *Maybe she's onto something.*

On one of these executive visits, Aaron invited Jacob to dinner. Jacob accepted without hesitation. Despite being retired, *G.O.D.* pervaded his thoughts. He had never worked directly with the CEO but relished the opportunity to meet the company's leader.

The CEO took to Jacob immediately, impressed by his longtime devotion to the company. But the evening turned awkward when the rabbi and rebbetzin stepped away to assist other guests and Jacob peppered him with questions:

> *"Do you run a complete meritocracy at GoldOrb? I don't recall any minority engineers on my team."*

"Can you achieve diversity while maintaining the highest quality?"

"What about the accounting scandals and pollution reports? If the company's reputation is soiled, it'll tarnish my career. Do you feel the same?"

"Is my pension secure?"

The CEO scratched his head deciding how to respond. Jacob's brand of interrogation struck him as odd, but he also felt good natured mirth swell up inside him. He appreciated Jacob's obvious earnestness and candor. The guy cared deeply about his legacy at GoldOrb, a legacy the CEO intended to protect with every fiber of his being.

The CEO also understood that this was not the place, nor did they have anywhere near the time, to explore Jacob's concerns. "Jacob, you can hold your head up high with pride," he said in a strong, confident voice. "GoldOrb is fine on all fronts. Guaranteed!"

Jacob's brow furrowed. He looked like he wanted to drill down for details. But the innkeepers returned, and conversation naturally shifted to other topics.

During dessert, it was the CEO's turn to tread on a sensitive matter. "How's Hannah?" he asked. "Any progress?"

Jacob lowered his eyes. The rabbi and rebbetzin were uncomfortable talking about their daughter. He therefore sidestepped the topic of children and seldom mentioned Michelle and Walter.

But now the subject could not be circumvented. Mia teared up. "It would make our lives complete to reconcile. Hannah should be part of our new world outside the fishbowl." She tried to say more but her voice faltered. Aaron stepped in for her. "The thing is guys, we've regained a huge part of our lives at Lake Paradise, but not what we want the most. We still can't find her."

The CEO silently considered the fateful decision that he and his wife had made long ago to not have children. His friends' torment seemed to buttress that choice. But he also could see the deep love that the rabbi and rebbetzin felt for their wayward daughter. *Something is missing from my life,* he thought. *Sandra feels the void even more.*

There was a sense of relief when Hunter approached the dinner table after making his rounds. The dog's appearance caused a break in the conversation and the rabbi used it to switch topics. "How's it going at BC?" he asked the CEO.

"We're surviving, but the new rabbi can't fill your shoes," replied the CEO. "He's a little light on substance, but a decent enough fellow. Why, after we agreed on a starting salary, he insisted we reduce it by 20 percent to contribute to the homeless." The rabbi and rebbetzin nodded politely but looked uncomfortable.

After supper, the CEO retired to his room. He emailed Jacob's former boss, John Shepard, to gather intelligence about this interesting retiree with so many questions. "Loved him!" replied the boss instantly. "Outstanding engineer and loyal. Gave him our toughest problems, and he always delivered."

The CEO wasn't surprised and wondered why the company let Jacob retire so early. He was unaware that his underlings had misinterpreted his own edicts to cut costs.

The next morning, he sent Jacob an email urging him to stay in touch. He made it a practice to seek out people beyond his cocoon. *I need fewer yes men and more folks who'll tell it to me straight.* Jacob seemed to be just that type of guy.

Jacob stared at the CEO's email from his cabin. He dashed off a friendly response a nanosecond later but couldn't resist ending his reply with another meaty topic. "What do you think of the cultural wreckage inflicting our nation and does it affect GoldOrb?"

Jacob understood this was a tad eccentric but couldn't help himself. *Guess I'm unfiltered nowadays.* Little did he know how the CEO would react.

CHAPTER XXI - HANNAH

My childhood was toxic, but I've escaped to calmer seas with great reasons for optimism. I live with the love of my life in a safe and accepting environment. My career as a psychology professor is thriving. And I've even rediscovered religion.

But honestly, it's not a clean sweep of positive energy. Truth is, I'm at a crossroads. Time is marching by and I feel an emptiness where family belongs. I want to get married and adopt a child. And I think I may be ready to see my parents again. On my terms this time.

I haven't talked to them since I changed my name. I'm different now. More mature and stronger, comfortable in my own skin. Maybe I'm ready to restart a relationship.

My partner gently prods me to reach out. "It hasn't been a bed of roses with my family either," she said. "But keeping open channels beats erecting a wall."

She's right, although she doesn't understand my past or why I'm clinging to my anger. I still haven't told her all the details. "You'll tell me when you're good and ready," she said. "But you, of all people, know that suppressing your emotions is harmful."

The rabbi from my temple also emphasizes reconciliation. I love the place. I attend incognito as a normal congregant, not the rabbi's embarrassing daughter. Nobody scrutinizes me, expecting me to be what I'm not.

For so long, I remained bitter and disconnected from religion. But now, I'm part of the community, something bigger than myself. Look, there are times I question the biblical miracles. And I abhor the ancient treatment of women and sexuality. But let's put this into perspective. Without organized faith, there would be a vacuum the size of Jupiter.

I'd rather be ensconced within this spiritual community that performs acts of charity than stand alone, focusing solely on myself.

Besides, I like rituals. They serve as pointers for living an ethical life, reminders for being grateful. I feel a sense of continuity with my ancestors, observing the same customs they practiced a thousand years ago. The beautiful poetry and prayer melodies echo through time. What's the alternative? Surely not Darwinism, walking solitaire in the footsteps of apes in a godless world.

Funny, these were the same justifications Mom and Dad pummeled me with long ago in praise of BC. Maybe they were on to something. But BC was horrible, my adolescence terrible, and my parents tone deaf to my needs.

Let it go. Let it go. You can't truly grow if you don't let it go.

When my new rabbi talks, I listen. Last week, he gave a passionate sermon about the Ten Commandments. I braced for the body blow, anticipating what was coming as he locked in like a laser on the Fifth: "Honor thy father and thy mother." He delved into this topic for thirty excruciating minutes, giving every possible reason to respect your parents. "Regardless of their mistakes, you owe it to them," he preached. "And to yourself."

My guilt exploded. I bet nobody else in the assembly had changed their very identity to avoid their mother and father.

That night, I took a small step. I went on the website of The B'nai Chai Synagogue of Minneapolis. I couldn't believe my eyes. Mom and Dad vacated BC without a trace. All I found was an old note from the CEO thanking them for their extraordinary commitment. Somebody must have forgotten to remove it from the site. There was no mention of where they went.

I googled their names, but my search yielded nothing. No synagogue advertised my father as its rabbi. My eyes glanced over a short blurb about an Aaron Friedler from a small town in Colorado, but he wasn't a rabbi. Anyway, my parents would never move to the sticks.

As I teach my students, we repress painful memories that seem unfixable. And when they force their way to our consciousness, we procrastinate addressing them, diverting our attention to the small details of our daily lives. The easy opportunities that we can manage supersede the manure to wallow in.

So, it's not that I intentionally abandoned my search for Mom and Dad at this nascent moment. But I let it fall to the end of my long to do list. With so much else happening, it was easy to relegate my parents to the back burner. Yep, repress, procrastinate, don't step in turds, repeat.

I stuck to the same pattern with Candis, one of my Psych 101 students. It wasn't copacetic, not cool at all. Candis was a small-town girl from Idaho having serious trouble adjusting to college life in the big city. She was bright but needed extra handholding.

The kid was upset with her C minus on our Sigmund Freud exam and requested help. When she came to my office, I tried to coax the bigger picture out of her, asking what other courses she was taking, how she was managing. She told me about her math and economics classes. "I'm holding my own with solid Bs," she assured me.

Since freshmen are required to take four classes, I asked what else she was studying. Her jaw locked. "I'm taking US History. The teacher is a snake in the grass."

"Excuse me. A what?"

Candis blushed. "No, it was my fault. I'm sorry, I'm sorry, it's not true. Forget what I said about the professor. Please!"

There was clearly a problem here. When I probed for details, she clammed up. But she had already signaled telltale signs of distress. Candis seemed full of rage, vulnerable and embarrassed at the same time. For all my training, there was nothing I could do to help.

For the rest of the visit, I tutored her. Like I said, she was smart and soon mastered Freud. She just needed a little coaching outside the large classroom setting.

After she left, I made a visit to our department head. Dean Plager yawned as I expressed my concerns about Candis. He asked, "Do you have anything to go on other than a hunch, female intuition?"

"Candis wouldn't talk," I said in a defensive tone. "But something's not right here."

Despite extensive sensitivity training required by the university,

Dean Plager dismissed me with a condescending wave. "I'll report this up the chain. You've done your part."

Candis did not attend my next psych class. A week later, I found out she quit school.

My mind spun into overdrive. *Did I let her down? Could I have helped another way?* I assured myself that I followed school protocol, suspecting that Dean Plager was a useless, misogynistic bureaucrat. I decided to let things cool down and figure out a way to deal with the mess later.

That's my lot in life. Repress, procrastinate, avoid stepping in turds, repeat. But repression isn't amnesia. All those memories that I struggle so hard to contain don't vanish. They float around in the back of my mind and emerge at the wrong time. Like now, when things are going great, and I don't need to create trouble for myself. Like now, as I wonder where my parents are.

CHAPTER XXII – THE RABBI AND JACOB

W hen a rocket ship blasts off, there is an enormous burst of energy as the missile shoots high into the sky, defying gravity, shattering the status quo. Flames trail, a testament to the combustible power required to break inertia. But soon after the booster rockets ignite and decouple, something amazing occurs. The craft begins to effortlessly glide through space. Smooth sailing ahead.

The three new residents of Lake Paradise were on the same trajectory. It took enormous effort for Jacob, Aaron, and Mia to uproot their lives and resettle out West. But after paying the heavy toll of disruption, they too began to cruise smoothly in the crisp mountain air.

Each season at Lake Paradise offered unique charm, rotating one after the other with a cadence impervious to human trivialities. During winter, sheets of snow blanketed the mountains, declaring their purity. Towering white cathedrals sprang up around Lake Paradise delivering profound messages through their stillness. Spring ushered in renewal with chirping birds, budding trees, and blooming flowers, as sweet fragrances replaced the chill. On rainy days, waterfalls would appear from nowhere high in the mountains, artistically carving the landscape before plunging through underground channels to the lake below. During summertime, herds of animals roamed vast meadows which separated the mountains. They feasted without a care while tall grass blew forward and back under the heated sun. And autumn was best of all, the trees offering an impossible panoply of colors before conceding once again to the cold.

Jacob and Aaron's friendship grew season upon season, year after year. Each sensed the other's fragility and provided support and companionship. They challenged one another to grow intellectually as they pursued their lifetime quests for meaning.

In all that time, the men clashed only once, and it was almost undetectable. No harsh words were exchanged, and outward emotions were tempered.

They were debating an old topic, the existence of God, in a new way. To Aaron, the premise that God existed had become obvious again, and his voice took on an uncharacteristically didactic tone as he stroked his regrown beard. "When I look in all directions at Lake Paradise and observe the mountains, the majesty of nature, the breathtaking symmetry and order of our world, I can arrive at no other judgment. A higher power created this grandeur, and I'm fortunate to be part of His design."

Jacob gave his friend a teasing glance. "So, you're back on the Paley bandwagon like clockwork, eh Rabbi." But he was frustrated by his friend's close-minded attitude despite the unprovability of his assumptions. "Fine Aaron, you've landed with the pocket watch theory again, and sometimes I lean in that direction too. But you haven't begun to explain the Creator's purpose. And you, of all people, know there are other explanations besides God for what you see here. Like a cataclysmic explosion combined with billions of years of elemental forces and evolution."

Jacob paused, waiting for Aaron to interject as usual, but his friend said nothing. With a slight twitch in his eyes, he continued. "And even if we accept your conjecture, you've left other questions unanswered. Are God and the universe one and the same, or did God create our natural world and stay separate from it, maybe even isolated? And if He created it, who created God? Was there a creator of the Creator? And what would his purpose have been?"

Aaron well understood the never-ending mazes, detours, and roadblocks, but shrugged like they no longer concerned him. "Does it really matter if we ever solve the mysteries? Maybe, *the answer* is to make a choice of what you believe and accept the web of contradictions."

He paused, knowing how difficult it was for Jacob to make that choice, to "flip the switch on," as Jacob liked to say. After a few sacred strokes, he added, "I believe in God from my heart, not my intellect. I don't know His origin or purpose, but my soul craves faith in a higher power. To be part of a plan. To be grateful to Him. Without God, my life would be diminished. Jacob, that is my choice."

Jacob pursed his lips. *Diminished*, he thought. He said nothing but felt the sting of the word. *Diminished.*

Aaron could see that something was bothering his friend. He wished that Jacob could find the peace he had finally chosen. But Jacob's stubborn expression annoyed him. "Do we really need to keep debating?" he said. "For once, just try to appreciate the things you have, the knowledge you do possess. This is the human condition, Jacob, and you need to accept it. If you keep trying to get closer to the sun, you'll get scorched."

Jacob's eyes twitched as he repeated the word "diminished," this time out loud. He then fell silent, reduced to that exact state, trying to control his emotions. When he spoke again, he sounded defensive. "Aaron, I'm lost here. If I flip the switch on, accept God and show Him gratitude as you say, am I to flip it back off the next moment and ignore His responsibility for evil? There's a disconnect that I can't get over."

Aaron's impatience grew. "I get it Jacob. But for once, just a single time, can you please not go there?" He was lecturing now. "Both good and bad make up the gift of life that we should be grateful to God for. That's how it works!"

Jacob looked as dubious as the day the two men first met at BC but kept his voice as steady as possible. "We need to stay rational, logical, that's all I'm saying. Let's keep digging, like always. You, of all people, know that 'the unexamined life is not worth living.'"

"And the overexamined life?" Aaron asked in a sarcastic voice.

Aaron immediately looked guilty. "I'm sorry. Let's give it a break today, settle our thoughts." He wished he could help Jacob find inner peace but couldn't put his feelings into words in a way that wouldn't hurt his friend further. *No matter how hard you wrestle, logic isn't the same as wisdom.*

The men fell silent until Mia interrupted. "Jacob, can you bring Hunter by in a few hours? A little girl with a huge cast on her arm checked in and she loves dogs." As Mia walked away, she smiled maternally and mumbled under her breath, "Break it up you loveable nerds."

Mia's intervention worked and the rare moment of discord passed, a forgotten needle in the haystack. Smooth sailing and good-natured debate soon resumed at Lake Paradise.

Wednesdays were the barometer of just how good life had become. Wednesday used to be the time Jacob was haunted by epic nightmares. But here at Lake Paradise, you could feel his joy, literally hear it, as a jubilant beat echoed against the mountains at sundown. The source was a drum circle led by a retired musician who had retained his passion for the art. Encircling him sat Jacob, Aaron, and several locals eager to accompany him with their own bongos, pots, and pans.

The sounds of the tantalizing staccato easily reached the Paradise Inn. Guests strolled to the lake and surrounded the drummers, the vibrations coursing through their bodies. Pretty girls broke into dance as the sun dipped, celebrating the appearance of the North Star.

Aaron felt an electrical charge course through his body as he banged away. "I love sunsets to begin with," he yelled to Jacob. "But watching it disappear, kissing us goodbye while we hammer in unity, is magical. We put this sunset on steroids."

Jacob looked ecstatic. "I guess the answer we've been searching for all these years is to become hippies. Who would've thought a rabbi and engineer would hang out like this?"

"Let's wear tie dyes next time," Aaron half joked.

Between songs, Aaron turned contemplative, recalling the rehabilitative sunrises and sunsets at Boulder Paradise Cemetery. With an observation that only Jacob would be receptive to during this party atmosphere, he said, "I think what we're sensing is the power of community. There's an invisible force when people come together, whether it be for prayer, meditation, even banging the drums."

Jacob smirked, wiping away sweat on his forehead from his musical workout. "Once a rabbi, always a rabbi. I suppose you feel the same power of community at the fifty-yard line of the big game."

"I sure do," replied Aaron. "I used to feel it at services too."

After a spirited rendition of Rhythm of the Saints, the drum circle disbanded, and Aaron and Jacob headed for Chinese food at Wang's Dumpling House. Mr. Wang knew them by name and made it a practice to recommend a variety of dishes from his homeland that they loved to share. That day's offering was mushrooms mixed with rare Chinese vegetables cooked in his top-secret sauce.

"Very spicy," he warned several times as if he was seeking their signatures on a consent form. "Hot, hot, hot."

"Bring it on," replied Jacob smiling.

Jacob was still on a high while he ate. "I counted twenty-five people hanging out with us tonight!"

"Mick Fleetwood draws a few more," replied Aaron using his chopsticks like drumsticks. He then turned serious. "I've got big news. I doubt you're keeping track, but Mia and I have been running the Paradise Inn for almost seven years."

"Whoa, that went fast."

"We're throwing an anniversary bash next month for loyal guests. The CEO is jetting in. You must come."

"I'm in," Jacob responded. "Just be sure to invite the porn star."

As the heat from Mr. Wang's peppers began to dissipate, Jacob recalled the rundown condition of the inn. The improvements made by Aaron and Mia were impressive. Visiting the place was one of Jacob's greatest pleasures. They deserved a grand celebration, and he wanted to be part of it.

But he remembered a scheduling problem. The professor was coming for his first visit and would be staying with Jacob at the cabin. The party was happening on the last night of the professor's stay.

"Problem solved," Aaron exclaimed. "Bring him along, it's a must. Your oldest pal is sure to have juicy secrets about you."

Jacob shared Aaron's enthusiasm. He had still never been in the same room with his best friends. *The rabbi, CEO, and professor,* he thought. *What a threesome!*

Unfortunately, one crucial person would be missing, and Aaron looked upset about it. "It would be perfect if Hannah could join. We hired yet another private investigator, but he failed. Mia cried all night."

Jacob nodded in sympathy but soon became distracted. Lizzy was on his mind. He had only seen her a few times since moving to Lake Paradise, usually when he was anxious, like the day he and Aaron had their dustup. But she had recently been visiting more frequently. Always at dusk, in the middle of the lake, with black and white birds overhead.

Just yesterday, Jacob had gazed from his canoe into his wife's loving eyes, through the depths and beyond all boundaries. Their touchless kiss was overwhelming. His Early Warning System pulsated long after she receded into the darkening waters as he rowed back to shore.

Was paradise a hallucination? After all, how much smooth sailing could Jacob realistically expect? Eventually, that rocket ship gliding effortlessly among the stars reenters the Earth's atmosphere and plummets, encircled by flames.

The men said little more as they finished dinner, each absorbed in his own thoughts. When Jacob returned to his cabin with visions of Lizzy dominating his mind, he found Hunter dead on the kitchen floor. Reentry had begun.

PART III

The Professor's History

"Education without values, as useful as it is, seems rather to make man a more clever devil."

—C.S. Lewis

CHAPTER I - THE PROFESSOR

Jacob met Samuel Lerner, the professor, a half century before he befriended the rabbi. "There's nothing like a friend from way back when," he'd gush when talking about his lifelong companion.

They collided in second grade. Jacob was obediently waiting in line to march single file into the school cafeteria. The professor, full of boyish amusement sprinkled with mischievousness, shoved the unsuspecting lad in the back. Jacob ricocheted off a tiny ponytailed girl, knocking her to the ground, as he slammed head-first into an open locker. When he recovered, he confronted the professor, striking a popular wrestling pose he learned on television. "I am Dick the Bruiser," he proclaimed. "And you will die."

The professor laughed with joy, a boy completely in his element, and kicked the posing Jacob in the knee. He was aiming higher but missed the jeweled target. Jacob absorbed the blow, charged, and the boys tumbled around the floor until the teacher strode to the ruckus and screamed, "Break it up! Back in line or I'll have your parents come get you. Alphabetical order." A lifelong friendship had begun.

Through the decades, each combatant declared victory. Even into their sixties, Jacob and the professor bantered and exaggerated over their famous battle. Jacob, reverting to pre-adolescence, would take a jab. "You kicked me like a wee baby girl. I won even after your sneak attack and could do it again if you want to give it a go, right here, right now." During this sacred moment, the retired engineer thought little about uncovering the secrets of life.

The professor, an Ivy League scholar, covered up and counterpunched. "Have you ever heard of a karate kick, big dummy? You were lucky I only glanced your knobby knee. Sorry you got stuck in the locker."

A more mature translation for their juvenile dialogue reverberating through the years would be, "I love you, man. You understand where I come from and are like a brother." These were words never spoken.

It was an odd couple relationship. Jacob was serious and introverted, known for his abundant obedience and curiosity at school. He was a polite young man who did what was asked of him in class and attended to chores at home.

The professor didn't follow the rules. He was popular with students, but not teachers. He teemed with natural ability but preferred to apply it to shenanigans and playing the class clown.

As far as human nature was concerned, the professor always chose the easiest path. In contrast, his buddy Jacob would dash through a minefield if that's what it took. But somehow there was a chemistry between the two, a gravitational pull that overwhelmed their differences and kept them close.

Jacob found the professor's antics funny and happily followed his lead. They made phonies, played ding-dong ditch, and stacked the deck in strip poker games with unsuspecting kids. On Halloween, they trolled the neighborhood for candy, but the professor was more interested in tricks. He concocted a formula of vinegar and loose dog movements, nicknamed it "stink," and poured the sludge on a neighbor's front porch after grabbing a bagful of sweets. The "stink" spilled onto Jacob's white pants, ruining them. Jacob was spanked and grounded by his parents. To the professor's bliss, his buddy was customarily disciplined, while he remained untouched.

Baseball, however, was serious. The boys devoted their summers to pickup games and dreamed of starting for the Yankees. The professor was bigger than Jacob and a natural athlete, but Jacob held his own with solid ability and grit. They were equally matched.

When they began noticing girls, Jacob and the professor would ride their bicycles to find crushes and tease them. In the middle school love department, the professor held the upper hand. Both boys were cute, but the girls were gripped by the professor's escapades. Jacob was too shy to earn much attention.

Childhood abruptly ended at the start of high school. The professor's father, a chain cigar smoker who washed it down with barrels of beer, died of a massive heart attack. In a memory the professor spent a lifetime trying to suppress, his dad grabbed his chest in agony and toppled on top of the young teen as he watched Three Stooges reruns from the family room floor. The dying man almost suffocated him.

At the funeral, Jacob was terrified by the open coffin. He would never forget the dead man's expressionless face, paralyzed in everlasting nothingness.

Standing at a podium near the casket, the minister spoke in a monotone. "He was an honorable, hard-working man, a nurturing father, a devoted husband." The professor looked on in confusion with a stone face, the pose he imagined a strong man needed to strike at a time like this. He sat between his mother and sister, both sobbing hysterically. As he listened to the minister recount his father's virtues, he relived the family room scene with the dead man smothering him while Moe pummeled Curly.

Prayers were recited. Jacob listened carefully to the beginning of Psalm 23:

> The Lord is my shepherd; I shall not want.
> He makes me lie down in green pastures.
> He leads me beside still waters.
> He restores my soul.

The mourners looked like automatons, repeating the words by rote with respectful voices. Were they paying attention to the meaning?

Jacob was numb. He awaited an explanation from the minister to justify the devastation of his best friend's family, all the time staring in horror at the coffin, at death. But the minister's sermon and anecdotes were clichéd and inadequate. The prayers missed the mark. Jacob's obsession had begun.

Back home, he asked his mother the classic question. "Where did Mr. Lerner go?"

"He's in the ground, honey, ready to turn to dust. End of story."

She waited for a response from her son but only saw clouded eyes.

"Think of this as a lesson," she added in a more positive tone. "Make the most out of your life while you can."

Jacob's mother was from a reform Jewish family that paid little heed to religion. She had become a devout atheist as an adult. She smiled at her inquisitive boy, sensing that she too had missed the mark with her insights. She didn't know what else to say.

As usual, Jacob's father barely listened. He was raised by ultra-religious parents who practiced rituals with abandon while reaping unfair advantages when running the family business. He was happy to escape the contradictions and hassles of this orthodoxy in favor of matrimonial harmony. His job was to put food on the table. Other than that, he practiced detachment. Jacob would not receive the spiritual guidance he craved from either parent.

The professor's mother also had no answers. Her husband died without life insurance, and she could not afford the bills. She was forced to sell the house and move the family to California to live with her parents and absorb their cruel and relentless criticism that she had tried to escape through marriage.

The boyhood friendship derailed. No letters were written, no phone calls made, as Jacob and the professor spent their high school years far apart.

They matured in different ways. Jacob's path was predictable. He was an excellent student, a skillful baseball player, and admired by his classmates and teachers. He was voted "Most Dependable" his senior year for the high school yearbook. Jacob owed his success to solid ability that he stretched to the breaking point with elbow grease and backbone.

The professor gained a veneer of respectability on the West Coast by becoming an exceptional student in the courses that interested him. He learned to charm his teachers and baseball coach to get what he wanted. And his college entrance scores were superlative. Things came easy for him socially, academically, and athletically.

The next time Jacob and the professor met was at the Cornell-Colgate baseball game with the hula girl doing the wave in the stands. The professor was the smirking pitcher who beaned Jacob for crowding the plate, sending him to the hospital and into Lizzy's arms.

CHAPTER II - LIZZY

A few days after I met Jacob, he received a phone call from the Colgate pitcher who aimed at his head. Oddly, Jacob was thrilled. He and the pitcher had a history.

The professor told Jacob that he realized who he had beaned when he read the game's box score. He apologized for, "My wildness on the mound," and suggested they reunite at a boisterous pub in Ithaca. "The cold ones are on me," he promised. "A peace offering."

Jacob looked entranced as he recounted his famous second grade fight. I responded, "I can see why you'd be delighted to get back together with a guy who kicked you into a locker when you were small and crushed your skull when you grew up. Your type of fella."

Jacob paid no heed, thinking that I was trying to be funny. Maybe I was, but I also harbored doubts. The thing is, I was never quite comfortable with this new, make that old, friend of his. First, I was convinced that he beaned Jacob on purpose. And he was too slick for my taste. Good looking and smart for sure, a real star. But he was so full of himself that you could smell the overconfidence.

I also got the distinct impression that the professor was trying to flirt with me, but there was nothing I could put my finger on beyond feminine intuition. "That's just his way," Jacob explained, shrugging his shoulders. "He's always been cocky and flirty with girls, but it means absolutely nothing. The two of us were like brothers." So, I let it go, figuring that if Jacob gave him the benefit of doubt, so should I.

Jacob and the professor liked to meet up in small towns between Cornell and Colgate. I often tagged along, especially if the professor was bringing his girlfriend of the week. I must admit, we had a great time, spirited fun that my Jacob and I could not generate on our own.

The professor loved alcohol and playing tricks that seemed hilarious back then but embarrass me now. He introduced us to "creaming," where we'd drive up to a stranger, roll down the window and ask for directions to the nearest grocery store. If the stranger approached the car, we'd squirt whip cream in his face and snap a photo with the professor's Polaroid. The professor then hit the gas for a fast getaway as we yelled, "We have deemed that you get creamed." He'd toss a snapshot of the creaming to the street, a memoir for the trailing victim. We were young and stupid.

The professor bragged that he partied all day long. "Why waste time studying? Life's short!" he'd proclaim, deaf to the fact that other people needed to work hard to succeed. I found his routine tiresome. "He's full of crap," I told Jacob. "I bet he studies in hiding, too proud to admit it. You can light his boasts with a match."

In my estimation, the professor couldn't hold a candle to my hardworking—and wee bit awkward—Jacob, who holed himself up in the library until closing time. Sometimes he sat trancelike, he was concentrating so hard. I loved Jacob for putting in an honest day's work. He was the man I could rely on.

Even so, the professor lived up to his hype too. There he was goofing around noon and night. And there he also was, the Valedictorian of his graduating class. Number one at Colgate, astounding. He matched Jacob blow for blow with academic honors. Yet the two were opposites.

The next stop for the professor was a PhD in U.S. history from the University of Chicago. I found this remarkable since he never showed the slightest interest in the subject. Jacob's next destinations were the marriage canopy and GoldOrb Diversified. *G.O.D.* was lucky to have him.

When I think back about the professor during our college years, there may have been some depth to him, but it was drowned out by his pranks and outsized personality. He was never serious and refused to talk about his family. Jacob defended him, as usual. "Cut him slack, Lizzy. He lost his father in a gruesome way. I'm still trying to get my arms around it myself."

The men never discussed their feelings. For whatever reason, they chose superficiality, arguing about who kicked whom and where the blow landed. Isn't that usually the case with men and their dumb macho instincts? Neither Jacob nor the professor could open up and confront his demons. Little did I understand at the time how furious the demons were. Little did I see what they would ultimately unleash.

CHAPTER III - THE PROFESSOR

The professor gradually learned to exude an air of sophistication by imitating the elite scholars at the University of Chicago. He also mastered the nuances of U.S. History with ease.

It wasn't that he was particularly interested in America's past or wished to forge new academic ground. Instead, he was intent on building his pedigree as an esteemed academic. He sought to create the aura of an intellectual gentleman donned in an expensive tweed jacket. He would be the smartest man in the room, the most cosmopolitan, the sexiest too. More than anything else, he coveted the fringe benefits. The financial, social, and physical rewards owing to the irresistible scholar.

He did not see Jacob much during graduate school, but they kept in regular contact by phone. The friends scheduled calls during lunchtime to chow down while catching up. The professor's voice travelled cocksure over the phone lines. "I just can't see myself slaving away in the corporate world. I'll teach at an Ivy for an hour or two a day, tops, research for another few, maybe, and we'll call it a day. Summers are for sun and checking the tan lines of foxy teaching assistants and coeds. That's what I'm talking about, Jacob!"

Jacob responded from somewhere deep within the salt of the earth. "I'm pounding away at GoldOrb. The pile on my desk only grows, but I'm learning a ton and creating things people need." Jacob waited for the professor to ask a question, but it never came. "Anyway, the boss is decent, but the rest of my team like to complain more than perform. It sure is sweet getting that paycheck though."

Jacob paused again, wondering how the professor would react to his real news. "I've started stashing away a little extra from each paycheck … for college, yikes. Yep, Lizzy is good and pregnant with twins. You wouldn't believe how big she's getting."

The Professor congratulated Jacob unenthusiastically, noting how long it took his friend to divulge that he'd soon be a father. *I'll never marry, no children for me,* he thought. *I'm a lone ranger on the prowl.*

They continued talking past each other while finishing their sandwiches, sharing little in common at this time in their lives. Still, there was that chemistry, the gravitational pull from childhood. And so, the interchange ended like most.

> The Professor: "You know Jacob, I beat your sorry butt into scrambled eggs once and can do it again, even if I have to travel all the way to big bad GoldOrb for a piece of you."
> Jacob: "Come and get it egg head."

These were treasured moments. Both men hung up the phone feeling lucky to have a buddy from long ago.

While in Chicago, the professor made another friend, Thomas Dumars, a student in law school. They met at a mixer for upper classmen, both disappointed in the scarcity of hard liquor. After downing a few tame beers, they snuck away to the wildness of Rush Street where they inhaled whiskey and rumbled through the night.

Thomas was stocky with charcoal eyes, unreadable except when he wanted to turn on the charm. Unlike Jacob, he was on the same wavelength as the professor. The men jokingly called their relationship the "LL Connection" in honor of Leopold and Lobe, the diabolical genius duo who murderously roamed the same hallowed grounds at the University of Chicago in the 1920s.

This LL Connection wasn't interested in murder, but they reveled in chaos. After too many shots of tequila during a visit to Hyde's Saloon, the professor and Thomas caught site of a youth stalking an old man hobbling with a cane. The kid bumped into him on a poorly lit street corner and masterfully picked his pocket. As the old man limped away, unaware of the theft, the professor and Thomas chased the hoodlum down, forcing him to relinquish the loot before letting him flee. It was time to celebrate, and the LL Connection found just the right establishment, spending their bounty on two hookers.

The professor and Thomas tortured a young homeless man who wandered the streets of Hyde Park. Whenever they spotted him, the professor would get in his face and snarl, "Get a job," while Thomas mocked, "Spare a dime." They made it a habit of blocking the homeless man's path, forcing him to swerve off the sidewalk. To their great amusement, he warned, "Watch out assholes. I have telepathic powers and I'm not afraid to use them."

While Jacob toiled away at GoldOrb and prepared for fatherhood, the professor had descended another level down from "creaming" and spreading "stink." He was all too willing to abandon his facade of sophistication for good old rabble rousing with his new friend. The professor felt a tinge of guilt but suppressed it, refusing to allow moral discomfort to restrain his behavior. He was traumatized as a boy from his father's ghastly demise. Next, he was assaulted by dysfunction in California where his grandparents psychologically battered his mother while his sister crumbled. But he prevailed. It was now his time for conquest as Thomas prodded him beyond boyish pranks to darker behavior.

The professor sometimes justified his escapades by speculating that nobody else truly existed. *Maybe I'm the only one*, he posited. *Nothing else is provable.* This egotism freed him to do whatever he pleased. The professor would toy with this notion of singleness throughout life, more as a narcissistic musing or excuse for his behavior than a foundational belief.

He did, however, follow his conscience when it came to his mother and sister. As they grew more debilitated, he sent money. *Gotta take care of the family,* he reasoned like a mafia boss. A curious yet gratifying warmth swelled from within whenever he wrote them checks.

Thomas Dumars was completely devoid of conscience. Brilliant, ruthless, and ambitious, he planned to use his law degree as a springboard into Chicago politics. This strategy made perfect sense to anyone who knew Thomas. He would indeed make a terrific politician with his big personality and winning smile. More important, he was at home sinking into mud and slinging it. This was a guy the professor admired.

Despite the extracurricular activities, the professor gained valuable knowledge and experience in graduate school to fuel his glide path into academia. He smiled when he needed to, rubbed elbows, and other parts of his body, whenever that was useful, and impressed the faculty at every turn as he mastered his craft.

The professor again graduated with highest honors and received a plethora of job offers. He eventually chose a tenure track position at the University of Pennsylvania, snaring his coveted Ivy pedigree.

Thomas Dumars graduated from law school and took an important job working for the mayor's office. His uncle had connections. He quickly gained a reputation as a player in Chicago politics.

Around the same time that the professor and Thomas launched highflying careers in academia and government, Jacob received a tepid pat on the back from his boss for his fifth anniversary at GoldOrb Diversified, always finding the answer to G.O.D.'s devilish engineering problems. He bought a mid-sized house in the suburbs, tended to the lawn, paid his mortgage, and remitted taxes when due, never late.

But hidden behind this veil of tedium and conformity, Jacob was quietly busy riding the waves of his obsessions, searching for the meaning of life, of death. He told the professor, "My days fly. Work stimulates me. I'm a father. And I am poring over some thorny problems in my spare time."

The professor never asked what those "thorny problems" were. But Lizzy knew all too well as her frustration with her husband's fixations about God, and at G.O.D., grew.

CHAPTER IV – LIZZY

J acob and the professor stayed close as we entered middle age. The boys kept up with their endearing telephone "lunches" every month, and they spent a few weekends together in Manhattan. I let Jacob go thinking he needed a little space, hoping it would help him lighten up, cool it with his fixations. It sure made more sense than two weeks at the monastery or attending another Travis Upton show. For my husband, a weekend in New York was a chance to let off steam. For the professor, it was probably the opposite. A time to slow things down and rest up.

We were getting older, ready or not. I threw a surprise party for Jacob's fortieth at his favorite Italian restaurant with the best pasta in town. The professor flew in to celebrate and sprang out from behind a curtain along with our other friends to surprise Jacob, much to my husband's delight. There the professor stood in a sharp tweed jacket, looking vibrant and classy, smiling at his oldest friend. The only thing missing was a trendy wristwatch. "I have no need to keep track of time," the professor explained. "Schedules aren't for me."

I laughed when I saw that his temples were turning silver. And he had picked up some uppity mannerisms that were hard to take seriously when I thought of him from our college days.

The party was a smash. Jacob was roasted but mostly toasted as a sincere, caring man you could count on. It was true. I gave a speech and cried. The professor spoke of their childhood exploits to the delight of everyone. He then accompanied us home to spend the weekend and continue the celebration.

In bed that night, I joked with Jacob that the professor had usurped the pose of Rodin's bronze Thinker. He had a habit of resting his chin on his hand while heroically driving home one point or another, demonstrating his vast intellectual firepower. Jacob chuckled, "The only thing missing is the pipe."

I wondered if the professor gained any depth to accompany his suave exterior. I also couldn't help but notice how much older Jacob seemed, more weathered by life than his chum. Jacob was going bald, with deep wrinkles around his eyes and on his forehead, but he was still mighty cute.

In the morning, I intended to go shopping and let the boys be boys, whatever that even meant at our age. But they wanted me to stay. So, we hung out, just like the old days, except now we were the old ones.

It was over drinks in our family room that the professor caught us up on his life. He had earned tenure and loved the freedom. "I'd have to rob a bank for them to get rid of me," he said. Jacob looked jealous. Corporate layoffs at GoldOrb were as common as eggs for breakfast.

The professor reported that his job had turned out just as he predicted. "I've taught the same topic forever. No need to prepare squat anymore." He then winked at Jacob. "The girls are even prettier now than when we were students. Except for Lizzy, of course." Always the charmer.

Jacob nodded and smiled ambiguously. He caught my eye with a knowing gaze, both of us realizing that the professor hadn't changed. Not one iota, despite his acquired airs.

The professor was oblivious to our marital mind meld. He looked like he was inhaling his favorite dessert as he continued his brag fest. "Get this. I'm going to Paris next semester to teach US history from the French perspective. Helicopter parents and their little darlings demand international exposure." He was bursting with delight. "I'm paid for a romp at the Eiffel Tower!"

Jacob scoffed, "I guess students need to learn about the cool vacations they won't be able to afford for the next twenty years."

"Oui, oui, my friend," the professor teased. "Oui, oui."

This was becoming painful. All I could think of was how expensive college would be. And now we apparently needed to send Michelle and Walter overseas. Jacob looked mortified, no doubt dreading the brick walls he still needed to slam his aging body through to make it happen for the twins. I worried about my husband's stress level. Privilege had its price.

I was relieved when the professor changed the subject to his biggest news. Striking the Thinker pose, he told us he was writing a book that would cause a stir in academic circles. He called it *Manifest Misery*. The pride he took from his intentional play on words from "Manifest Destiny" was something to behold. Jacob and I congratulated the professor on his cleverness, again shooting each other knowing marital glances. The professor was powerless to camouflage his true nature in the presence of his oldest pal. And his pal accepted him for who he was.

The professor explained that his book did not contain any surprises or breakthroughs in historical research, nothing that scholars didn't already know. "Native Americans still roamed the frontiers before Europeans sailed the ocean blue, and George Washington remained exceedingly tall and our first President," he reported. "*Manifest Misery* doesn't forge new ground in that sense."

But the book interpreted our nation's history with a different emphasis. "I flipped the entire meaning of what it means to be an American on its head, a one-eighty," the professor proclaimed. "When we were young, we were fed the Disney version. Americans were romanticized as righteous and our leaders humane. The world was far better because of us. Our destiny was to lead from a shining city on a hill spreading a beacon of light around the globe. God bless the USA."

Jacob and I were in full listening mode, troubled by where he seemed to be headed. "My book shines the beacon instead on the horrific suffering and never-ending bedlam America has inflicted. We murdered the indigenous inhabitants and stole their land. We pilfered from Mexico, interred Japanese citizens, and banned Chinese immigrants. Our vast wealth that we pridefully attribute to industriousness and our capitalistic creed was generated on the backs of African American slaves still under racial subjugation to this very day."

This was more depressing than college tuition. It seemed he would go on forever detailing our sins and bungles. He held up five fingers. "Vietnam, the Middle East, Latin America, Afghanistan, Iraq...."

"Ugh," I interjected. "Yech." Not exactly scholarly terms, but he was demoralizing me. "Tell us something good."

The professor didn't seem to hear. He looked directly at Jacob as if my husband were personally responsible. "I devoted an entire section of the book to the crimes of corporate America. Business barons control Washington while polluting the planet. Unbridled greed!"

What a mouthful of unbridled negativity. Jacob and I had not considered our past with this cynicism and were trying to digest it.

The professor looked smug. He confided he did little in the way of actual research or writing. "That's what graduate students are for. I own the big ideas."

He also expected his version of history to sell. "There's a lot of pent-up demand for this story. People need the narrative to push agendas. I'm hoping to earn a cool million, maybe more. I'm in talks with a major publishing company in New York."

Apparently, the professor was willing to join forces with corporate America just this once to land a big paycheck. Beyond that, I didn't know what to think. Was this a noble cause from his heart, or did he calculate that his assertions would earn top dollar, while bringing him academic acclaim? And were his ideas really all that groundbreaking?

I knew I should read his book but doubted I could get through it. I also worried about what our children were learning at these vaunted colleges. Admittedly, my generation was brainwashed with a saintly depiction of our country. And I knew we needed to take responsibility for our mistakes and learn from them. But the professor's version sounded too imbalanced, swinging wildly to the dark side. In that way, it resembled the one-sided Disney narrative of our youth.

I braced for Jacob's reaction, thinking he was sure to ask, "How could God have let this happen?" But for once, my husband's focus was elsewhere. He looked insulted. "This is what you're teaching our kids while we spend a fortune on tuition? You mean to tell me that America is 100 percent evil? Did you forget we saved the world from the Nazis, defeated communism?"

Jacob didn't wait for the professor to answer. He just kept torquing. "Are we to ignore our innovative genius that has improved the lives of millions? We're a great country with noble ideals of liberty and the pursuit of happiness." He rolled his eyes as if they were back in grammar school. "Did you forget that in your book?"

I tried to send Jacob more marital telepathy to calm down, but he was pissed. "What happened to nuance? Must everything be entirely black or white when the truth lies in between?" He then pointed an accusing finger at the professor. "You're teaching our kids self-loathing while we parents go broke!"

The professor struck his Thinker pose and chuckled with the air of a superior intellect, inciting Jacob to continue his onslaught. "And what in the world was that you said about corporate America? God forbid someone should try to make money while increasing the standard of living for billions of people around the globe. Do you think it's easy to manufacture cars, planes, and generators that provide light and warmth for entire cities? What about medical breakthroughs? These things don't magically descend from an ivory tower that relocates to France for a semester!"

Jacob's eyes began twitching. They do that more and more these days when he stresses out. "Look Professor, all I know is that I work hard and do some good things at GoldOrb that help people. There are problems, big ones, and greed is rampant. But how can you act as if everything this nation has accomplished is condemnable? What do you plan to replace it with? Socialism? That's never worked. I only hear your complaints, no solutions."

The professor no longer looked so sure of himself. "Calm down, man, stop taking it personally. I know you didn't start the fire."

"I'm not even sure it needs to be extinguished." Twitch.

"Well, it sure needs containment."

The professor tried to placate Jacob for one of the few times that I recall, telling him that he admired how hard he worked. But he kind of took it back the next minute scolding, "You're going to kill yourself with dedication. For what? All you're doing is making the CEO rich."

I was proud of my husband for defending himself but increasingly worried about the weekend. I chimed in before Jacob could get going again. "I have a million-dollar question for both of you. With all these miracles and tragedies, has the United States been a net positive or negative for the world?"

Jacob immediately answered, "Positive. We're a clear plus." But before the professor could weigh in, the twins interrupted, bringing an innocent energy force to the room. I breathed a sigh of relief.

Walter and Michelle wanted to play board games, but couldn't agree between Monopoly, Risk, or Sorry, so I broke the logjam in favor of Sorry. It was shorter and wouldn't spark another debate over profiteering or world domination. Mostly, I was happy for the diversion. What sense did it make to get upset and ruin the birthday weekend when we hadn't been together for so long?

We lightened up and had a grand old time for the rest of the professor's visit. We took in a few movies and ate at our favorite Mexican restaurant, Rosie's Margaritas. The twins were riveted by the professor's stories from their dad's past. "Didn't you get punished for fighting in school?" asked Walter. "What happened to the poor little girl with the ponytails you knocked down?" wondered Michelle. Jacob and the professor looked proud, reverting back to the children they were. All was forgiven.

I kept things low key for the rest of the weekend, although I did find time to ask the professor how his family was. He grimaced. "Fine, fine as always. I'll be going to California to see my mom and sister soon." He abruptly changed the subject to our college escapades.

Shortly before departing, the professor took me aside and peered over his shoulder to be sure Jacob wasn't listening. "Why is he being so noncommittal about the Chicago real estate opportunity? The investment could pay for the twins' college, even that semester abroad." He looked both concerned and unusually anxious. "Sometimes I just don't know if things are completely registering with him. And he's told me some far-fetched stories lately. Listen Lizzy, Jacob should take his foot off the accelerator at GoldOrb. The Chicago idea could help him do that."

I hadn't heard about Chicago and didn't know how to respond. Sure, Jacob was working too hard, but why was the professor telling me and not him? I also had the distinct impression, after all these years, that the professor was still flirting. It interfered with my ability to digest what he was saying.

CHAPTER V – THE PROFESSOR

The professor didn't mention to Jacob or Lizzy that he had only a few dollars left in his checking account and no savings. His lifestyle was lavish, and his mother and sister depended on him for support. He hoped royalties from *Manifest Misery* would solve his financial woes.

Then he met Molly Spicer. A few weeks before Jacob's surprise party, Molly approached after his Roaring Twenties session. Dressed in a halter top and tight cutoffs, she looked both perplexed and adoring.

"Professor, I just love your class," she said. "How can you possibly know so much?" Her expression turned worried. "But I'm having a terrible time memorizing the material."

The professor tingled. "Not to worry. Many students have this problem at first and I have methods to help. Stop by my office at eight o'clock tonight."

Molly seemed relieved. She turned around and waved as she left the lecture hall.

Molly arrived right on time. The office was crammed with books from floor to ceiling. The professor organized them by color, creating a vivid academic display. Red, yellow, and aqua texts adorned the top shelf. Most of the books were masterpieces he had never opened.

Impressive diplomas and awards were strategically positioned on the walls for maximum effect. Nobody could miss experiencing "Samuel Lerner, Summa Cum Laude, University of Chicago." There was also a conspicuous photo of the professor from his younger days in his Colgate baseball uniform winding up to pitch.

But the centerpiece that pulled it all together, adding a sense of power to the intellectualism, was an antique mahogany desk from Belgium, a fine work of art to behold. Behind the wooden behemoth rested a credenza housing a telephone and two small pictures. The first showed the professor with his arms around his mother and sister, a palm tree in the background. The three were smiling in a rare moment the professor wanted to memorialize. The other was an old Polaroid shot of the professor chumming it up with Jacob in college. Viewing the photos together, the professor would often connect them. *Jacob is family too. I'm tough on him sometimes, but like a brother.* He never told Jacob any of this.

The professor invited Molly to take a seat on the other side of the heirloom. After making small talk, he struck his Thinker pose, considering her dilemma. "You know, Molly, I think you have the potential to be a very special student. There are ways to earn extra credit if you apply yourself."

Molly seemed surprised and blushed. But she looked at him with bedroom eyes and softly said, "I'd love to hear more about this opportunity. You are so interesting to me, sir." She told the professor that she needed to leave for an evening dance rehearsal. "I hope you can give me in depth tutoring next time," she said dreamily.

Molly returned to the lair a few nights later. Only a custodian working in the basement remained in the building. She wore the same tight shorts and a shy smile. It was clear to the professor that his candidate had graduated to a keeper.

She put her backpack down and moved closer. *This is what makes it all worthwhile,* thought the aspiring author. He felt that annoying tinge of guilt from an unknown origin but was flush with power and lust. "I have no doubt you'll get an A. Take off your shirt and lie on my desk to show me what an honors student you are. Come Aphrodite. We have a thing here."

Molly climbed on the heirloom and smiled teasingly. "I want an A plus for effort. I'll take everything off for you Professor, not just the top. I'm here to learn from the master."

The professor sighed, "Your wish is my command. Now do it." He began unzipping her shorts.

Molly's flirtatious smile turned into a dagger as she shoved the professor aside, grabbed her backpack and ran from his office. In the backpack was an old cassette recorder spinning like a wheel of fortune.

Blackmail followed, and it was nasty. Molly demanded that the professor bleed cash, or his reputation would be ruined. She'd destroy his carefully calibrated academic career. His book would be condemned to the junk heap of history. After years of taking advantage of young ladies seeking to improve their grades, or who swooned for the charms of the older academic, the professor had met his match.

He panicked for one of the few times in his life and decided to see Thomas Dumars. Who else could he turn to but his long-time LL Connection partner? Certainly not Jacob, who would react like a sanctimonious pilgrim just disembarked from the Mayflower.

At Thomas's suggestion, they met at the Union League Club. Thomas, a long-time member, often conducted private transactions at this prominent venue. Surrounded by elegant wood paneling and immersed in a luxurious leather chair, the professor told him about Molly. "I didn't do anything wrong," he protested. "It's always consensual."

Thomas looked sympathetic. "Take it easy, these things happen to all of us. I bet she was a fox."

"Yes. This fox turned out to be a bitch with fangs."

"Sounds charming."

Thomas's charcoal eyes turned unreadable. "Do you need a loan? The money's yours and I've got an idea to help you repay it."

The professor listened with interest as Thomas elaborated. To nobody's surprise, Thomas had advanced to the highest rung on the ladder leading to the mayor's office. He had intimate connections with the board of trustees for the regional rail division. One trustee was willing to leak confidential information about where they were planning to extend the train lines. The scheme was to invest in real estate nearby ahead of any public announcement.

As Thomas laid out more details, he looked like a general poring over a map to decide where to deploy the troops. "The property will be cheap. Once we buy it and the news hits that the neighborhood is getting a train station, our investment will skyrocket. And our gains will compound as I spearhead gentrification initiatives in the very same neighborhoods."

There was a role for the professor to play in this game. Thomas could not risk putting his name on a deed. It would be too easy for people to discover the plot. But if the professor bought the property in his name instead, the purchase would appear harmless, just ordinary business by a lucky buyer. "Of course, I'm sure you'll want to share your good fortune with your silent partner," Thomas said. "You can also repay my loan for young Molly out of your cut."

The deal was consummated with firm handshakes over vodka. And it worked as Thomas predicted. The professor paid Molly her ransom with an advance from Thomas in return for the cassette. He then bought property in his name with more money funneled from Thomas near an expected track extension site with the help of a shady Chi-Town lawyer and real estate agent.

The men reconvened at the University Club several weeks later. "I'm back on track," the professor reported, looking proud of his play on words. Thomas did not smile. "Seriously, you saved me buddy. Long live the LL Connection."

While the scheme was unfolding, Jacob phoned in for a Saturday lunch shortly before his fortieth birthday party. He had met with a financial consultant that very morning and sounded anxious. While he earned a good salary and had stashed away some savings, his paychecks shrunk under the weight of growing family commitments and taxes. His consultant warned that college for the twins loomed and urged further belt tightening.

"I feel trapped," Jacob confessed. "I'm not sure if I'll retire before cremation."

The professor heard the desperation in Jacob's voice and decided to help his oldest friend by doing the same thing for Jacob that Thomas arranged for him. And Thomas didn't need to know. *I'll just invest a little more on the side with Jacob in the same Chicago neighborhoods,* he reasoned. *My profits are being wiped out by the Molly loan and Thomas's share. I need more. So does Jacob.*

The professor rationalized that he was doing the right thing. He genuinely wanted to help his overburdened friend. He also saw nothing particularly underhanded with the venture. True, he would profit from inside information, but that was a technicality. He would only buy property from people who wanted to sell it at a price they agreed to. *There's nothing wrong with targeting a willing seller*, he reflected. *If I don't invest, somebody else will.*

Of course, he understood that picayune observers might view the transaction differently. He also knew that if there was even a whiff of impropriety, the Mayflower pilgrim would bolt. *What Jacob doesn't know won't hurt him,* he reasoned. *And it will help both of us.* He felt a satisfaction akin to the warmth he experienced when sending money to his mother and sister. *Jacob's family too.*

The professor inhaled deeply and made his pitch. "Listen Jacob, I have an answer to your dilemma. Chicago real estate. I know a terrific location."

"Hmm … that's a new one," Jacob responded in a noncommittal tone. "I didn't know you were into properties."

"Well, I've been studying up in my spare time and I'm onto something big. I'm thinking we share seventy/thirty. My piece comes from finding the property. You keep more of the gains and hold the property in your name because you'll make the down payment. If you need cash later, just borrow against the property as it rises."

Jacob seemed interested. He had accumulated a modest level of savings and thought that he ought to diversify out of the perilous stock market. He feared risky bubbles, another Black Monday. He also hated the idea of Wall Street holding his hard-earned money.

"Any questions?" prompted the professor.

"Nope, I'll think it over. Naturally, I'll have to talk to Lizzy."

"When you give the word, I've got a good lawyer and agent ready to pounce."

But Jacob was preoccupied and soon forgot. He was churning at work and struggling with commitments. His obsessions ate away at his remaining carcass as the solution to his fathomless ponderings continued to evade him. With minimal mind matter remaining, the professor's investment offer would have died silently had Lizzy not prodded him following her talk with the professor.

Lizzy's innocent inquiry changed everything. With her urging, Jacob finally focused. He gave Lizzy his conclusion. "The advice has to be rock solid. After all, it's coming from an Ivy League scholar and my oldest friend." A day later, Jacob told the professor, "Count me in."

CHAPTER VI - JACOB

Ten years later, the venture still thrived. The professor proudly lectured Jacob on the strategy as if he had never heard it before. "Location, location, that's how we manage it. I'll keep picking the spots with my analytic models and intuition, and we roll on."

"I'm still in seventy/thirty," replied Jacob. "Keep 'em coming, buddy."

The professor never told Jacob that the properties were near spanking new train stations. It was easy to hop on, go anywhere, then come back home. "Location, location," he repeated.

Nor did Jacob ask for details. He trusted his oldest friend.

As the twins reached college age, Jacob and the professor owned places on Wilson Avenue, Hampton Street, Ridgeland Lane, and Piccolo Drive. While they bought more later, they lovingly referred to these gems as the "fabulous four."

Jacob's share of the appreciation easily covered tuition, room, and board for the twins. "All I did was pony up cash I didn't want to risk in a bear market," he told Lizzy while tabulating the robust returns. "Because of the professor's knack for choosing the right spots, we'll have financial freedom." Lizzy was delighted that she had motivated her husband to act.

Wanting to express his gratitude, Jacob decided to fly to Philadelphia. "Let's celebrate," he told the professor over a phone lunch. "I'll take you out on the town. Don't even think of arguing, or instead of dessert, I'll kick your sorry butt like I did in second grade. The only difference is how big it's gotten." The professor readily accepted and booked a reservation at a five-diamond restaurant.

Over dinner, Jacob raised a glass, smiling at his friend. "Here's to the fabulous four. My days of indentured servitude will soon be over. Thanks to you!"

Jacob overstated his need for the money. The reality was that he would have eventually made ends meet without the fabulous four. He had a pension from GoldOrb and his savings would have steadily risen. But the extra profits from Chicago provided a cushion few enjoy. "You can't place a value on peace of mind," he told the professor. "Lizzy and I are going to travel the world."

The professor swelled with pride as he shifted to all-out gourmet mode, relishing his eclectic meal. But Jacob was disappointed by the fare. *This frou-frou entrée is artistic but loses every time to a cheap bowl of pasta, or a burger smothered in grilled onions with fries,* he thought. *No matter, he loves it here.*

"Maybe I finally let you off the hook for kicking me, you cupcake," Jacob joked after they ordered dessert. "Seriously, though, I'm grateful."

"Cheers buddy, and here's to dessert," declared the professor.

Over crème brûlée doused with lemon raspberry sauce and a hint of nutmeg, the chef's crowning achievement, the professor shared exciting news. "My good friend Thomas Dumars was elected mayor of Chicago. We used to roam Rush Street in jeans. Nowadays, he dons tailor-made pinstripes from famous London designers while toying with the press." The professor held his head high, basking in a feeling of importance by association.

Jacob was impressed. "I don't know anybody famous, except maybe you, Mr. Author."

The professor struck the Thinker pose and dropped hints about the importance of *Manifest Misery* and his iconic work in academia.

Jacob was appalled when the bill arrived, tucked in a stylish leather folder that was engraved with the restaurant's renowned emblem. Inside was a peace offering of two small chocolates from Switzerland, on the house. *$375! FOR WHAT? We spent as much on this hedonism as their dish washer earns in a week.* But he reminded himself that this was no time to pout.

It was a beautiful evening and the old friends decided to walk off some calories by strolling around campus. A few blocks from the professor's home, they encountered a fraternity hosting a keg party. Jacob and the professor watched the action from across the street. "Old men gaping in wonder," admired the professor. "I wish we could join."

The scene centered on extensive, park-like grounds surrounding the frat house. Booze flowed in all directions as students screamed over blaring music laced with profanity. A frat brother was heaving up nachos in a nearby bush. Three others aimed their streams in synchrony at a large stone with the engraving "Fraternal Brotherhood Forever," one yelling over the music, "This piddle puddle is hilarious!" In the next bush, two boys and a girl were disrobing for oral sex. The professor nudged Jacob, who looked concerned. "No big deal. If there's no penetration, it doesn't count nowadays."

As the old voyeurs continued their surveillance, a contraption was wheeled to the middle of the lawn. It was half inversion table and half gigantic beer bong modified for maximum chugging. The contest was to see who could guzzle the most beer from an extended feeder tube while hanging upside down with feet hooked onto ropes hanging from the top of the device. Any breath would douse the contestant with alcohol.

The biggest, manliest Deltas lined up for the challenge. A large crowd egged them on chanting, "Bottoms up from bottoms up." The winning prize was a visit to the campus emergency room for a stomach pump.

Jacob looked mortified. "This is the cultural wreckage I've been talking about."

"You're past your prime and square," teased the professor. "They're just letting off steam. I've seen plenty worse." He inhaled a deep breath of second-hand ganja smoke as if he could feel the buzz.

"Well, it's okay to have fun, but this crosses the line," yelled Jacob over the din. "Let's get out of here."

As Jacob led the professor away, he thought of the famous Liberty Bell, only a few miles from this chaos. *The crack has ruptured.* He had always taken enormous pride in being an American, but now he sensed darkness invading before his very eyes and felt diminished as a citizen of this societal wasteland.

The next morning, Jacob went for a walk while the professor slept in. Except for a few joggers, the campus streets were vacant. Before long, he found himself back at the scene of the party. The frat windows were open wide with debris hanging out at impossible angles. The front yard was littered with half emptied cups, dirty paper plates, crumpled napkins, and broken bottles. Not a blade of grass could find its way to the morning light. The drinking contraption was broken in two. Jacob could smell the sour, acrid bouquet of vomit, urine, and beer lingering in the air.

A battered white van with *Garcia's Cleaning Service* painted on the side pulled up to the fraternity house. Two middle aged men emerged with trash bags, plastic gloves, and picks. Conversing in Spanish, they began to wade through the debris with shoulders slumped and worn-out expressions. No student greeted them. Jacob muttered, "Spoiled brats," and walked over to help.

Jacob flew home later that day. He would not see the professor again until Lizzy's funeral. Meanwhile, the fabulous four continued to climb.

CHAPTER VII – WALTER

I was racking my brains at Mom's wake trying to remember who the tall, silver-haired gentleman was talking with Dad. He was dressed immaculately, suave, and debonair. He seemed like the type of guy Dad would *not* want to hang with. But he had his arm on Dad's shoulder, and they seemed quite chummy. Who was he?

I didn't have to wait long for the answer. Dad spotted me staring and motioned me over. "You remember the professor, my oldest pal? We've had some great times together, some real laughs."

Well, that dusted off the cobwebs. Of course, I recognized him. The professor had aged but was trim and fit. He looked younger than Dad, like he could still dunk a basketball.

He turned to me with wet eyes, sizing me up, recognition rising to the top of his sharp eyebrows. "Oh my God, Walter! I want you to know that your mom was the best. The stories I could tell. I'm so sorry, Walter."

It turns out that right then and there, Dad and the professor were immersed in a deep conversation about the meaning of life. I gulped down the bitter taste in my mouth. Dad always steers the conversation there, never satisfied with any explanation. He seemed to take pleasure in the torture of smacking his head into granite, repeatedly, for no good reason. And he was sure focused on it now, with death in the air. He needed to understand where Mom went.

Dad told the professor how much time he devoted to this topic. That he had read hundreds of books about religion, even checked into a monastery where he didn't speak for two weeks but returned home unenlightened. He neglected to mention to his friend how furious Mom was. We all walked on eggshells while that insanity was unfolding. Dad apologized to Mom a thousand times, but I guess he remained helpless to abandon his quest. I have no idea why he chooses to make everything so hard when Christ, the one true *solution*, is always present, if only he'd open his heart and have faith.

The professor pontificated. "Jacob, I hope I'm not out of line, but drop the crap about finding revelation already. You can't square a circle."

If only he had stopped with that sound geometrical advice. But no, the professor had to go on, wearing me out. "There are no answers to what you're seeking in religion," he said. "You won't find your solution at a church, synagogue, or mosque. We are men of education and reason. Stop worrying about fables that the religious entrepreneurs sell."

That was more than I could stand. "Religion sets the moral code for society to function," I said. "And keep in mind that we're all being judged." This guy needed to wise up, and fast, before his day of reckoning. Heaven or hell depended on it.

To my surprise, the professor had what sounded like a rehearsed rebuttal at his fingertips. "Some of the most moral people I know are atheists. And how can seven billion human beings be individually evaluated at death by a myth created by man? There can be no judgment without a judge."

Such arrogance. I was furious as hell, which is exactly where this pompous bozo was headed. But Mom's funeral wasn't the place for a scene. Also, like it or not, Dad seemed anchored to the man. No, I wasn't going to create drama. But I did set the record straight in a friendly tone. "Mom was good here on Earth, so she's in heaven now. I take comfort knowing that she's resting with Jesus, her soul restored beside still water. Psalm 23 tells us all we need to know."

Dad tilted his head down, then glanced sideways in that way of his that signals chagrin. He still couldn't accept the truth. But the professor looked me straight in the eye, wanting to engage. "I respect all views, Walter, and I'm happy you feel that way about Lizzy. I always saw her as an angel from heaven. But here's how I see it."

He then blabbed on like he was teaching a class, urging Dad and me to follow along. "You can find peace here on Earth," he said. "You don't need to wait for heaven." It turns out the professor believed in absolutely nothing. "Why make up stories when you can have a good life without them?" he proclaimed. In a self-congratulatory tone, he lectured, "My spiritual needs are entirely fulfilled not through artifice but the art of meditation."

He was so smug about his atheism, his brilliance, his Zen. "Each day, I awaken and sit for an hour, staring into my yard, the atmosphere, infinity, thinking of nothing, feeling the firm ground beneath me. Just being. Alone with my breath. Just … being … breathing. Soon a warmth from within embraces me." He breathed in deeply as if to demonstrate how easy it was. "This is my spiritual light, the eternal truth, peace."

The professor urged us to give it a try. "Take a class, gentlemen. What's there to lose?"

I remained polite but dismissed his nonsense out of hand. Meditation was a fad. The idea of sitting alone with my breath instead of attending church was laughable. Dad, however, looked interested in the professor's offering and, as usual, I was disappointed.

"So, you're saying that meditation provides the answer to life, to death?" Dad asked. "If so, what've you discovered?"

The professor chuckled. "Don't be so two-dimensional, Jacob. It's not like that, and you know it."

I got the feeling the two of them had gone through this routine a thousand times as Dad pressed on. "It sounds like you are saying that the sheer act of meditation, in and of itself, is the answer. But how can that be? Taking deep breaths and chanting 'om, om, om' hasn't shown you where we came from before birth, where we are going upon death, or why."

The professor looked at me with amusement dancing in his eyes and gave a whimsical shrug, as if we were conspirators dealing with my father, a luddite incapable of grasping critical new information.

But Dad surprisingly deviated from script. "I just might give meditation a whirl," he said. "I doubt it's the holy grail, but I sure could use some relaxation right about now."

Astonishingly, for once in my life, Michelle did me a favor. As Dad began to inhale deeply and exhale with intention under the professor's tutelage, she interrupted, asking if we could speak privately. She looked anxious as she pulled me away.

"There's something about the professor I just don't get," she said. "He makes Dad happy for some reason, but I'd keep my distance." Guess my sinning sister was uneasy around a normal American male. Not her style. Then she pulled me into a tight hug, weeping. "We need to have a long talk," she said.

When I finally escaped her mugging, I mingled a bit longer. Just when I had shaken all the hands I could stomach and was itching to flee this brutal scene, the professor approached me from behind. He didn't want to talk any more about religion or meditation. "That heavy stuff is your father's bag," he said with a smile. He asked instead how I was making out at work. Unlike Dad, he understood how hard it was to make a go of it nowadays. "The American Dream is dead for your generation," he counselled. "I see it with my students. You're the victims of my generation's excesses and only a few will become wealthy, either by luck or rigged connections."

I was surprised how tuned in to the new normal this atheist was. Dad's only advice was that I should work harder, grind it out, and pound away. Work, grind, pound. Then grunt and do it again. According to my father, pain was the answer. Well, I was being thumped into sawdust, but it still wasn't working.

The professor said, "There are other ways to make it besides slaving in futility. I have a great investment opportunity in the Chicago real estate market. Your pop is already in." He added that he could loan me the down payment and the property would be in my name.

I was intrigued. After all, the idea was coming from an Ivy League scholar and Dad's oldest friend. I called the professor a few days after Mom's funeral. "Count me in."

CHAPTER VIII – THE PROFESSOR

H e was in a splendid groove. After his close call with Molly Spicer, he had sworn off the erotic fringe benefits of his trade. But as time passed, he could not resist dabbling again, more cautious and older, but happy with his conquests. *One bad apple shouldn't spoil my peaches,* he reflected. He felt that momentary tinge of guilt that visited him on occasion, but quickly dismissed it. *I'm merely a connoisseur of beauty. They all consent.*

Teaching remained a cinch. He never prepared for lectures. Still, his students were awed, expressing youthful admiration for his brilliance, calibrated wardrobe, and panache. *What a fine life this is.*

His portfolio continued to reward him handsomely as the value of Chicago properties held in his own name spiraled upwards. And with each new nugget of inside information about a track extension from Thomas Dumars, he turned to Jacob and Walter on the sly to generate even more profit. His appetite was insatiable.

Manifest Misery, however, underperformed. Other books were published around that time that offered the same essential arguments, but with more eloquence and analysis. "No matter," he proclaimed to Jacob over the telephone during their Saturday lunch. "I gained a measure of fame. My picture is on the back cover and adorns many a student's desk." He lamented the new reality of academics. "I needed to get something out there. 'Publish or perish,' they say."

More royalties would have been welcome, but the professor was dismissive. "I've made a mint with my investments. I bet you and

Walter are happy with the returns, eh? Life is good!"

Jacob enthusiastically agreed. But he wanted to switch topics with news of his own. "Speaking of real estate, I bought a cabin in a slice of heaven here on Earth called Lake Paradise. I'm packing up and moving with Hunter to the Rockies. I felt a higher power, a special insight, beckoning me to be closer to Lizzy."

The professor didn't know what to make of Jacob's special insight about Lizzy but congratulated him. He then reverted the conversation back to his book. "*Manifest Misery* explains the real story behind America's criminal land grab of the western frontier, including Lake Paradise where you'll be living."

Jacob was slightly perturbed by the professor's self-absorption. But the comment reminded him of something he had been wanting to discuss. It was complicated but the professor's book was gnawing at him, in a different way now, even more personal.

"I don't know if you meant it, but your book makes me feel diminished somehow."

"Strange choice of words, Jacob. *Diminished*?"

"Well yeah. If you connect the dots in *Manifest Misery*—our crimes against Native Americans, African Americans, the entire world—these were atrocities that I've profited from. Everything I've accomplished seems tarnished, like maybe I cheated."

"No way," responded the professor. "Lighten up. I didn't say that in the book."

Jacob's voice amplified with consternation. "But what else can I conclude? I keep wondering if I should have done things differently. But what? I voted with integrity, played by the rules, gave some money to charity and a homeless friend. Was that enough?"

"For God's sake, Jacob. You're one measly small fry just trying to get by."

While the professor was curt, he was well acquainted with Jacob's quandary. He had begun receiving subtle judgments from some of his Black students. It was hurtful when people attributed his personal success to privilege, not merit. He was upset that they didn't cut the author of *Manifest Misery* some slack. After all, didn't he expose what the country had done to African Americans? What it continued to do to them? Wasn't he their champion?

But criticism of the professor persisted. A comment to an online review of his class asked, "How can an old White man like Lerner begin to understand our life experience? The complicit asshole is raking in royalties from his book while we suck wind." The harsh judgement received near unanimous backing on the website.

In retelling the incident to Jacob, the professor grew livid. "You know that I grew up without a father. My mother was mentally ill and couldn't care for me or my disabled sister. I made it completely on my own."

He instructed Jacob to stop taking things so personally. His book wasn't intended to undermine their achievements. "Look, *Manifest Misery* says nothing about criticizing good people like you and me who worked hard for the American Dream. It's plain wrong to degrade people, to disrespect us. These critics should take a long hard look in the mirror."

Both men stopped eating as the phone line burned with the professor's righteous anger. "Teenage pregnancies. An army of fathers gone AWOL. Not a peep out of their leadership over unending violence, unless a White cop shoots. Other ethnicities have pulled themselves up by their bootstraps instead of staying on the dole. We shouldn't feel bad about what we've achieved."

The outburst from the seemingly liberal academic surprised Jacob. He recalled the harsh rebuke that he suffered from the neighborhood grapevine in Minneapolis for voicing far less. He was grateful to have a friend like the professor, whom he could speak with openly, even if he disagreed with him. There was a chilling effect in the national spirit that impeded frank communication.

When the professor concluded his diatribe, Jacob responded, "I admit, I have also wondered if the African American community needs to do more to help itself. But the system has been outrageously unfair for centuries. It needs to be fixed without casting blame on the victims for a mess the dominant race inflicted."

"There's no proof any remedy will work," replied the professor.

"Well, what if we make sure that everyone begins the race from the same starting point? The violence and inner-city problems you mention should disappear. Symptoms vanish when the underlying disease is cured."

"I didn't know you were a doctor."

Jacob paused, ignoring the sarcasm but looking confused. "Eventually ... with the right attitudes. That's what I think ... hope."

Jacob went quiet, moving the topic around in his mind like a Rubik's Cube. How could he presume to know anything? He didn't even have a friend who was African American. His entire neighborhood was White. *I've worried too much about me and can't even imagine what it's like for them,* he thought. *I speak in platitudes without a clue. I'm ignorant, maybe even intentionally. Diminished, shrunk.*

The professor was irritated by his friend's silence. He realized that Mr. Corporate America had seized the moral high ground. But he refused to entertain Jacob's observations. "The system might not have been perfect, but guess what," he said. "There were millions upon millions of so called 'privileged' White people with more advantage than me. Well, Trust Fund Timmy the Third, with his mile long head start, fell flat on his face while I smoked him." The professor was a winner in the meritocracy and deserved respect.

At this stage in life, both men craved the contentment that accompanies a job well done. But Jacob no longer shared the professor's confidence. In his heart, where it was impossible to fudge the truth, doubt persisted. *Am I worthy?*

Jacob wanted to continue the dialogue, to relieve his discomfort, his growing sense of diminishment. But the professor went cold. He was finished with the tortuous self-reflection that his friend seemed to live for. His thoughts turned to Candis, that beautiful freshman coed from Idaho who sat in the front row of his class. He had to have her, needed to find a way.

Jacob tried to reel the professor back in with the same question he had been asking in infinite permutations for a lifetime. "How can a God in heaven permit a system that causes such inequality?"

The professor barely heard and cared even less. He quickly concocted an answer to extricate himself from the call. "Simulation

Theory," he said. Jacob could literally feel him smirking over the phone. "You know. Life exists out there in the vast universe which is far superior to man. And computing power doubles every two years. Put these together and it just makes sense that extraterrestrials created a supercomputer to simulate humans. Voila. We are bots with emotions. And the inequality that troubles you is a mere programming glitch, an alien error. Whatcha think, buddy?"

Jacob thought of the old innkeeper. *He'd be interested. Yes, indeed. Yes, indeed.* He accepted the professor's sarcasm with grace, understanding that his oldest friend had reached his saturation point for the ten thousandth time. But he couldn't resist firing a final shot. "So, if we are bots, who created the first extraterrestrials? Was that God?"

"Touché," retorted the professor, thankful the discussion had run its course. *Sweet Candy awaits.*

Before saying goodbye, Jacob reminded the professor of his big news. "When I settle at Lake Paradise, you come visit me and check out the digs. Make a vacation out of it. I'll get a Rocky Mountain High kicking your bot at a higher altitude."

The professor sounded happy to revert to male bantering. "Altitude, schmaltitude. You and an army of aliens wouldn't stand a chance."

CHAPTER IX - THE MAYOR

'

've been thinking about *Manifest Misery*. How did the professor ever birth that piece of manure? The egghead does deserve a little credit though. His asinine work of fiction got me thinking about what recorded history even means. It's peculiar how the exact same facts get twisted into opposite stories over time. The professor enlightened me without meaning to.

He should have written about the Windy City. At one time, Mayor Daley ruled Chicago, if not the entire country, with an iron grip. He was treated like royalty by the press and historians. But Daley and the inept leaders that followed laid the groundwork for our impending financial ruin that will make Detroit look like a walk in the park. Why did they indulge unions with astronomical pensions that no city can afford? I'll tell you why. For votes, power, pats on the back, and more time in office. A half century later, and I've been presented with the tab and blame.

History should be reevaluated with accusing eyes on my predecessors. Just like the professor's damnation of the whole country in his lightweight novel.

I called the professor to vent, telling him that he should write another manifesto about Chicago's fiasco. He pretended to be interested, the fake. With tenure, a published book to his credit, and Molly Spicer gone, he's untouchable. So why lift a finger?

"Interesting Thomas, I'll give it some thought, old man," he chuckled. "Let me get back to you."

That'll be the day. Then, he annoyed the hell out of me, nagging for more real estate tips to fatten his wallet. The academic dick without one just kept begging. "Come on, one more, for old times' sake," he whimpered. Well, it's opium for him but danger for me nowadays. He's a total pain in the ass with his exasperating appeals to our friendship, as if the LL Connection is some cherished memory.

"It's too hot," I told him. "Go make extra dough another way. Maybe write that book about Chicago."

Boy was I ever right to call the gig off. Several months later, a reporter from the Chicago Star requested an interview. She said that she wanted to talk about our horrid pension problems eating Chi-Town for lunch. It was clear the gal had done her homework. She knew the ins and outs behind the numbers that few reporters take the time to understand. "I know it isn't your fault, Mr. Mayor. I want to write a comprehensive story explaining the history of the pension problem, the real history that began decades ago." Music to my ears.

So, naturally, I agreed to meet. This was my chance to set the record straight, to rewrite history with a new ally. My base needed to hear.

I tell you, who would ever imagine that a topic like pensions would become such a shitstorm? But that's the reality; either taxpayers, or retired teachers, cops, and firefighters, lose. It was time to deflect the anger away from me to where it rightfully belonged. Former mayors and dead politicians. I also planned to use the interview to fire another shot at corporate America, my favorite punching bag. The more I could redirect voter anger to GoldOrb Diversified and its asshole CEO for polluting our river, the better.

I was right about the messaging, but wrong about the bitch reporter. She waltzed into my office like she owned the place, maybe even the whole city—my city. Her narrowed eyes were unreadable, but her ears were huge like she could hear things that weren't said.

We started off fine, talking about the pension albatross around my neck as she dived deep into the details. "With falling interest rates and uneven returns on pension investments, you'll need to cough up a significant amount of money soon," she said. The kid was a regular actuary. I admit that I was impressed.

And then she dropped the neutron bomb with an offhand comment. It looked like she was having the time of her life. "Speaking of investments, Mr. Mayor, what do you think of the rise in property values in neighborhoods where the commuter rail extends the train tracks? Any idea who is buying up the property ahead of time? Somebody seems to be making a killing, and it's not the pension fund. Do you care to comment, sir?"

It wasn't only what she said that felt like a kick in the nuts. It was the way she looked at me, right through me, like she knew a dirty secret. Red lasers pulsed from her eyes, and her Dumbo ears seemed to be stealing my innermost thoughts. What did she know?

I stared straight into the lasers and calmly noted that land values, as a financial matter, can be expected to rise when public transportation becomes available. "The theory makes sense," I pontificated, channeling the professor's mannerisms. "With public access comes convenience and opportunity. Simple logic any economist would agree with." I told her that I had no idea who was vacuuming up the property. "Obviously, lucky investors who hit the jackpot."

There was that look again, the same arrogance. She responded with a rebuking tone. "I just may know who the lottery winners are, Mr. Mayor. This is your chance to weigh in if you feel the need."

I kept it civil and navigated the conversation back to broken pensions and how the blame rested elsewhere. She wore a sarcastic smile. "I plan on telling the whole story, sir."

When she left, I called for Tommy Mack, my fixer. "This reporter needs to go on a long vacation," I said. Tommy looked pleased.

Damn that faux intellectual, son-of-a-bitch professor. Always thinking of himself with no clue about the consequences. Just a tiny flea, sucking up enough blood to satisfy his own appetites. I'm done with the geek and his irritating LL Connection.

CHAPTER X – THE PROFESSOR AND JACOB

Jacob's move to Lake Paradise added physical distance, but the gravitational pull and alchemy with the professor made the two men feel like neighbors. Sprinkle in regular phone lunches mixed with soaring investments, and their friendship was as strong as ever, even seven years after Jacob relocated.

After the mayor's rebuff, the professor finally decided to visit Jacob. *My oldest friend would never treat me with such disrespect.* He was curious to witness first-hand the slice of heaven that Jacob raved about.

Jacob sounded thrilled when he called the professor to make final arrangements. "I have the spare room set up for you and plenty of good food. We can spend the week hiking and fishing, mostly catching up. And your vacation will end with a bang, guaranteed. On your last day, we're invited to a shindig at the Paradise Inn for its seventh anniversary. The rabbi wants to meet the author of *Manifest Misery.*"

"This should be intriguing," responded the professor. "I've never met a real-life rabbi."

"He's not practicing nowadays, but you'll love him. And get this. The CEO of GoldOrb Diversified is coming too. He and the rabbi have become two of my best friends. And now they get to meet my oldest."

The professor reflexively scoffed at the mention of a top executive from the boring business world. *Mental midgets.* But he kept his disdain to himself.

Jacob's optimistic prediction for the visit proved half true. Somewhere on the bookshelves in the professor's office, an unopened

Dickens novel with an aqua cover described what ensued. It would be *the best of times, the worst of times* on this tale of two vacations.

The first tale was paradise. The natural splendor so missing from urban life unearthed strong sensations for the professor. He was emotionally charged by the clear blue waters and soaring mountains. He felt awe but didn't consider why.

The friends fished, hiked, and relaxed, just as planned, all the while surrounded by majesty. On a walk down Lordship Trail, the professor thought he had reached the prettiest spot imaginable, but then they continued around a bend and another jagged mountain appeared, sunlight streaming through the trees, colors afire, and he concluded the new venue was even more grand.

"It's called Bishop's Throne," Jacob announced with pride. "They say it was sculpted by ice millions of years before man existed."

"It dwarfs the most magnificent church architecture in Europe," the professor said with uncharacteristic wonderment in his voice.

Jacob proclaimed, "Nighttime's even better. We're in for a treat. There'll be a full moon the night before the rabbi's party. We'll canoe on the evening waters. You'll be changed forever."

The professor studied his friend. Jacob seemed more at peace during their hikes. But he wondered if a counteractive force was lurking. Jacob still had that nervous way about him, blinking rapidly, anxiously. The professor noticed the tic over breakfast and speculated that Jacob's current bout was caused by poor Hunter. Jacob didn't say much about his loss but couldn't control his twitching when he showed the professor the spot under the beautiful weeping willow where he buried the dog.

The professor could not have guessed that his friend was masking other potent emotions. His rendezvous with Lizzy were becoming more frequent. The day before the professor arrived, Jacob had stood beneath the weeping willow grieving Hunter. As he gazed out to the lake, he sensed that Lizzy was beckoning. Jacob joined her in their usual spot, his canoe bobbing beneath a flock of black and white birds. It was their longest, most intense kiss yet.

The men resumed the hike in silence, making their way to a

canyon where antelope grazed in the fresh air. A band of elk examined them from separate feeding grounds. Bishop's Throne hovered in the distance, peering down with approval. Each man was deep in thought until Jacob broke the silence. "I'm still working things out you know, but I feel that *the answer, the solution*, is at my fingertips." His voice filled with reverence. "There's just something about Lake Paradise. This is likely the proof that I've been searching for. Maybe it's God. *Her.* Maybe something else. Maybe. Maybe."

The professor considered Jacob's conjecture about God. He felt a slight flickering within, a moment of kindling and insight triggered by the natural opulence. But after a lifetime of cynicism and a sordid lifestyle, it extinguished before the warmth could take hold. He sat on a fallen tree near a brook that bubbled through the canyon and struck his signature Thinker pose. "I can't make your leap in logic, Jacob, not about a higher order. But I sure can enjoy the view for exactly what it is. Beautiful scenery created by eons of ice, wind, and heat working their elemental wizardry. This is a fantastic place to focus on being, just *being*." He inhaled deeply, meditatively. "I didn't know you believed God was a She." Jacob said nothing but blinked rapidly.

The pattern repeated itself throughout the week. Stupendous views provoking deep conversation without an ultimate resolution. Friends talking past each other. Before the men knew it, there was only one day left until the anniversary party at the Paradise Inn. Jacob and the professor woke up early, both excited that the weather report predicted a perfect evening. The night sky would be crystal clear, the panorama illuminated by the full moon and an unfathomable number of stars. "Yes! These are extraordinary conditions for canoeing," Jacob exclaimed. "We have a big night ahead. The best is yet to come."

After breakfast, Jacob sat rigidly at his computer, staring at the screen with feverish concentration. He was sweating and his eyes twitched furiously. The professor couldn't conceive what had happened to elicit this emotional swing. While sometimes anxious, Jacob had enthusiastically toured paradise with his oldest friend over the last five days, but now he looked suicidal.

"What's up, pal?" asked the professor, pretending not to notice the strangeness. "Do you want me to get the boat ready for tonight? You worried about too much exertion, old man?"

Jacob responded abruptly. "Bad news from Walter. I'll look into it and sleep it off." He blinked several times and then continued as if he was talking to himself. "With dreams come answers, dreams that guide."

Jacob walked into his bedroom and slammed the door. He remained inside for several hours in complete silence.

The professor was incredulous. *What the fuck!* Tale one of his Rocky Mountain vacation was over.

CHAPTER XI - WALTER

C hicago is famous for five alarm fires. Just ask Mrs. O'Leary about her reckless cows. But this time the flames are spreading far and wide beyond city limits to scorch Dad and me to a crisp. Christ, what a hellhole of a mess we're in.

On my drive to my horrible job this morning, I turned on the radio while sitting in traffic. Disembodied voices were hyperventilating about a property scandal in the Windy City. They mentioned a few neighborhoods that sounded troublingly familiar. And that wasn't all. The mayor was implicated, and police suspected foul play with a newspaper reporter.

When I arrived at work, I rushed to my computer and searched the web for details. *Christ.* The locations they reported were the exact same neighborhoods that Dad and I invested in with the professor. *Christ.* The mayor was charged with fraud. *Christ.* Dad once bragged, "The professor knows people in high places. He's great pals with the mayor of Chicago." Christ, Christ, Christ, help us.

A wave of shock ran through my body when I clicked on this article:

CHICAGO MAYOR INDICTED FOR FRAUD
REPORTER MISSING

The City of Chicago is reeling this morning over a stunning array of allegations against Mayor Thomas Dumars for his involvement in a real estate scam. The scheme centered on train track extensions throughout the metropolitan area.

An anonymous source reported that the mayor has been accused of using confidential information

*obtained from a commuter rail insider to purchase
land near track extensions ahead of public
announcements. The property values in these
neighborhoods rose substantially after new stations
were built. The land was bought in other names to
hide the mayor's participation.*

*In another development, the Chicago Star reporter
investigating the mayor has gone missing. Editor
Connor Duffin III confirmed that no one has seen her
for several days and he fears the worst. Her name has
not been released, nor have the other participants in
the fraud been identified.*

The mayor's office had no comment.

Other names? *Other participants?!* Was that Dad and me?

I emailed Dad a link to the article with a note: "Call me after you read this. I'm sweating bullets."

Several minutes later, Dad phoned. In a soft, haunting voice that I barely recognized, he confirmed that these were the locations where we made our money. "Wilson Avenue, Hampton Street, Ridgeland Lane, Piccolo Drive, Harper Blvd., Spangler Street," he repeated several times.

Dad tried to reassure me. "There's an explanation, Son. We've nothing to fear. We're innocent."

But his tone panicked me more. I never heard him sound so strange.

After that, he stopped talking altogether. I could hear his breath, but he said nothing.

"Dad, are you there?"

Silence.

"What's going on?"

No response, just breathing.

"Dad, do we have a bad connection?"

"Dad?"

"Dad, where are you?!"

Finally, in a hushed tone that could be mistaken for reverent if

I didn't know him better, he uttered, "For every problem there is an answer. I will wait for instructions."

What instructions? From whom?

Dad again became eerily disengaged. He tried to console me but was somewhere else entirely. Finally, he whispered, "The professor is here for the week. We'll work it out."

I was going to quit my torture chamber of a job because of our Chicago gains. I had finally paid off my credit cards and even saved a few bucks.

Was it all a sick illusion? Now what? And what was happening with Dad?

Jesus help us.

CHAPTER XII - MICHELLE

I reached out to Walter to hear if he'd been in contact with dear old Dad. I haven't been too worried lately, but I'm never completely off the case and wanted to be sure our sibling tag team was coordinating, dysfunctional as we are. Two pairs of eyes beat one, even if they dislike seeing each other's identical face sometimes.

I was just being cautious. Dad appears to be in a good place. Lake Paradise raised his spirits, fed his soul. And he has some great friends: the professor, an executive from his old company, even a clergyman, although I can't recall his religion. These guys seem to provide a nice little support network. Heck, he even joined a drum circle!

Walter sounded abysmal on the other end of the line. "We may be in enormous trouble, Dad and me. It's all shambles, but that's normal in my sorry life." Walter proceeded to use the good Lord Jesus Christ's name in vain multiple times as he told me what happened. It was quite a bucketful of blasphemy considering the source.

It took me a while to understand. Apparently, Walter and Dad made some horrible investments in Chicago at the professor's urging. This was the first time I heard of it, and I wanted to wring my brother's neck.

I always considered the professor superficial—so full of himself. The embodiment of too slick, too charming, too smart for anyone's good. A real flirt, even with me.

But I have come around to see that there's a better side to the man. He's been Dad's good friend for a lifetime, a link to his childhood. He's provided our father an anchor in his ocean of introspection, especially after Mom's death. Mom once joked that Dad derived weird satisfaction from their friendship. "I think your father lives a bit vicariously through the professor's antics," she confided. "He offers escapism from a regimented life." I agreed, thinking that opposites can be good for each other. The professor gave Dad something that he needed.

There was also a kinder side to the professor that Dad must have tapped into. A camouflaged personality trait that caused me to reevaluate him, to give him some benefit of the doubt once I discovered it. It turns out that despite all his shenanigans and posturing, the professor has been a devoted son and brother.

At Mom's funeral, even though I was trying to avoid him, the professor cornered me and asked for a favor. He knew I was a psychologist and wanted me to talk with his sister, who was going through a rough patch emotionally. Not wishing to disappoint my father's oldest friend, I agreed.

I'm not going to get into the details, but it turns out that when the professor's father died and his family moved to California, his mother became clinically depressed. She was in and out of asylums over the course of many years.

The professor's sister suffered the harsh brunt of her parents' demise. She was constantly criticized and belittled by her grandparents, brought to the brink of her own breakdown. She developed a devastating inferiority complex coupled with paralyzing anxiety.

But the professor stuck by her side. "There are times I wish I was dead," she confided. "Our sole source of support has been my brother. Sam is the only person who gives one iota of love. He sends money we don't deserve."

She also told me what happened when their father died. "He grabbed his chest and toppled on top of my brother. Sam was being suffocated to the laugh track of the Three Stooges." She admired the professor's strength and talents. "Not many make it to the Ivy League with a past like ours."

The professor's sister stabilized, but in a broken condition with little joy. We've kept in touch, and I visited her when I had a conference in California. The professor is her source of strength and holds their small family together despite all of them being terribly scarred.

It's odd that in all this time, Dad never told me about the professor's family. Since his sister asked me to keep our conversations strictly confidential, I have only hinted around to see if Dad would take the bait. I wonder how much he even knows.

After I finished talking to Walter, I told Gracie about the firestorm gathering speed in Chicago, threatening my father and brother. "Let's not jump to conclusions," she counselled. "Maybe there's a better explanation that Walter is overlooking. You know the professor is a complicated person with a good side." I appreciated Gracie's encouragement but remained frightened.

I called Dad several times, but he didn't answer. Sometimes it takes a while to connect.

Oh, how I hope Gracie is right to be optimistic that the professor will come through. Dad and Walter are fragile. They'll be devoured if Chicago winds blow flames their way.

CHAPTER XIII – JACOB

As Walter relayed the breaking news, Jacob was confused, and then panicked—both perfectly rational human reactions. He needed time to process the information. Hadn't he bought properties at the professor's urging exactly where the mayor did through surrogates? Wasn't the professor close friends with the mayor? And now Dumars had been accused of fraud. The connections felt deadly.

He tried to reason his way out of it. Unlikely coincidences occur all the time. Wasn't the professor, his oldest friend, a man he could trust?

Jacob clutched the phone while his son spoke, eyes twitching, mind racing. *For every problem there is an answer, for every issue a solution.*

"Dad, are you there?"

"What's going on?"

Jacob barely heard. His thoughts had shifted to God. He and Walter had made a lot of money from their investments. Had God rewarded them? For what? Now, they might be punished despite knowing nothing of the mayor's scheme? By God? Why?

For every problem there is an answer, for every issue a solution.

"Dad, do we have a bad connection?"

Problem, answer. Issue ... God exists. The rabbi's right. Lake Paradise is proof. God is here. And He doesn't care.

"Dad?"

My son. Lizzy. Lizzy.

"Dad, where are you?!"

The pushing sensations against Jacob's chest intensified as the Early Warning System blared. Jacob heard a tearing sound in his mind, felt something undefinable pull apart. Walter went silent over the phone line while a thousand indecipherable voices filled Jacob's consciousness, like the cacophony from his Wednesday nightmares long ago. Jacob welcomed the strangeness, thinking, hoping, even praying, that dreams would soon arrive, infusing him with a strategy to make things right.

Jacob hung up the phone in a fugue, not remembering his eerie words of assurance to his son, nor his abrupt interaction with the professor that culminated with him walking into the bedroom and slamming the door. Instead, he stared out the bedroom window toward Lake Paradise without making the slightest movement. The most intense trance of his life had begun. And it was really two dreams in one. *Like double mint gum,* his mind inanely repeated. *Double your pleasure, double down, double jeopardy, double, double, toil, and trouble.* Split screens of lunacy, side by side, appeared in his mind.

On the first screen of Jacob's hallucination, the protagonist was the professor. The scene was the middle of Lake Paradise, near where Lizzy had appeared to him.

At first, there was complete darkness, the water looking like black oil. Next, a harsh spotlight down from the heavens pierced the night, illuminating a small raft. On it was the professor, but as he looked as a second grader when he kicked Jacob into the locker.

The spotlight blinked red, and the professor transformed into the pitcher from Colgate winding up to smack Jacob in the head while he crowded home plate. He smiled like a jack-o-lantern as Jacob fell to the ground.

Another flash of red and the professor turned middle-aged with a touch of gray invading his temples, as he appeared at Jacob's fortieth surprise party. He was recommending investments to Lizzy. Lizzy gave the professor a quick kiss on the cheek for his help, and he tried to seduce her.

With a final burst of blood red, the professor metamorphized into the bewildered, silver-haired man now sitting in Jacob's living room. He struck his Thinker pose as he lectured Jacob. "Location, location, location." The words echoed and slowly faded. The spotlight remained deadly crimson for several minutes before flickering out, and the professor was again surrounded by blackness, floating on the raft in silence.

The suffocating darkness finally abated as the raft began to glow. The professor was now tied down to a wooden beam in the front of the vessel, secured by rope made from his tweed jacket. He was a modern-day Isaac bound to a floating altar awaiting his fate, his face aglow with fear.

Swarms of fireflies appeared around the shores of the lake like a plague out of Egypt. Millions flittered near the water, casting unnerving, darting reflections. And the water responded, impossibly reversing course, the waves now moving toward the middle from all directions. The water slid onto the raft, pressing it downward as if it had sprung a fatal leak. The vessel was doomed, the SS *Edmund Fitzgerald* of Lake Paradise.

A furious whooshing sound filled the night air while the waves grew in intensity, soaking the bound Professor, making him gag. The spotlight blinked on again to illuminate a new ghostly presence. It was the old innkeeper, who had tragically drowned in the same waters seven years ago.

The innkeeper's grin lit the evening sky with an electrical charge as he towered over the professor, laughing with glee as a flock of black and white birds appeared. "It's all here now," he exclaimed. "Yes, indeed. Yes, indeed." He began to sing a rhythmic, mesmerizing, and otherworldly tune. The lyrics were unmistakably clear in Jacob's mind:

> *Goats, lambs, Isaac too.*
> *Pay the price, sacrifice.*
> *Bulls, rams, from the pew.*
> *Pay the price, sacrifice.*

The innkeeper pulled a large knife from his belt and sharpened it. A sacrifice was needed to calm the waters, to satisfy a higher power. Terrified, the professor struggled to free himself as the tweed rope tightened around his body like a python subduing its prey.

Jacob, still in his comatose dream state, had a thought. *I paid the price. He didn't.* Jacob began to sway from side to side in time with the innkeeper's rhyming words, repeating them in his mind, while the waves rose still higher, and the raft continued to sink. *Pay the price, sacrifice.* Jacob was now a spectator at the Roman Colosseum witnessing an execution. *Pay the price, sacrifice.*

The dark anthem stopped at the very moment the raft submerged, slowly sinking to the floor of Lake Paradise, its resting place for eternity. Jacob could see the lit grin of the innkeeper as he completed the sacrifice underwater. When the grin flickered out, screen number two blinked on, transfixing Jacob in its glow as *the answer, the solution,* was presented.

CHAPTER XIV - THE PROFESSOR

While Jacob double dreamed in his bedroom, the professor sat in the living room contemplating what to do about his friend's bizarre behavior. He wondered if he should leave Jacob alone or wake him. *Maybe I should go on a hike until whatever's up his ass passes.*

He ultimately decided to do nothing and grab a snack, the standard human response to swirling chaos. The professor munched on aged Vermont cheddar with cashews and flipped on the television. He was immediately bombarded by cable news reporters gleefully talking over each other about the corrupt mayor of Chicago and what they were calling Traingate. Unbridled joy emanated from the agitated eyes of the professional actress masquerading as lead anchor, urging listeners to stay tuned to the breaking story. The news ticker at the bottom of the screen was frantically churning out additional details: *Several people wanted for questioning. Possible ties to Chicago organized crime. Missing reporter's family implores DA to expand investigation.* More dirty laundry was most assuredly forthcoming.

The professor instantly concluded that he would be prosecuted. The police would surely discover his participation in the fraud if they hadn't already. After all, he owned some Chicago property outright, his name in indelible ink down at the county recorder's office with the purchase dates lining up to announce his guilt. The mayor and professor had a long friendship which could not be denied.

The professor understood that the mayor would throw him under the bus without hesitation. Maybe a complete admission with all the unsavory details, the naming of names, would yield slightly less jail time for Thomas. *He's not like Jacob,* thought the professor.

Believing that his own predicament was futile, his thoughts turned to Jacob and Walter. *They don't deserve to be offered up for slaughter. Jacob is family.*

He was struck by an audacious insight. *I can't save my remaining years, my body, but maybe I can rescue my soul.* What an idea. After a lifetime of ignoring his oldest friend's obsession, he was finally scrutinizing the meaning of his own life, to find his own answer, his personal solution, with no time to spare.

The professor found his laptop in the guestroom and began to type. It was a Hail Mary, but the best he could do on the fly. Knowing that the police were certain to be monitoring the mayor's emails, he crafted a message:

> *Dear Thomas,*
>
> *You must be miserable beyond comprehension. That's how I feel.*
>
> *We should never have used insider information for our own profit. I regret it and feel bad for you knowing how many good things you've done for Chicago. I hope you're holding up.*
>
> *I need to come clean with you about something. I convinced my friend and his son to invest even more with me. I should have told you, but I was greedy. Rest assured that they did not know about you, nor what we were up to. They blindly trusted me. Just two regular guys making investments like people always do without a clue about where their money is going.*
>
> *I wanted you to hear it from me and not discover my transgression on the six o'clock news. I'm sorry and hope you'll forgive me. Stay strong, Mr. Mayor.*
>
> *Your friend,*
>
> *Sam Lerner*

The professor knew that the email would seal his fate, jail time for Traingate. His Ivy pedigree would be subsumed by ignominy. *I deserve it, but my brother and his son don't.* His hand shook as he clicked "Send."

CHAPTER XV – JACOB

As the professor's note to the mayor jetted through cyberspace, Jacob's body remained still while his spirit soared. The action on the second screen of his dual hallucination was the vision of a lifetime. The one he'd been waiting for. Nirvana.

He was sitting on the ledge at the highest mountain peak towering over Lake Paradise, watching the doomed academic in the sinking raft below. But something else commanded his attention. Jacob heard a low voice emanating from the core of the lake, ricocheting against the mountains before reaching him at the apex. Unlike his Wednesday night dreams, no high-pitched screeching interfered to drown it out.

The voice was trying to communicate. First, in all human languages simultaneously, like the Tower of Babel, but then gradually whittled down to a single tongue Jacob could comprehend. He instinctually knew that it was critical to decipher what was being conveyed. This was a message of great wisdom.

Jacob was now a prophet on the mountaintop, an old man in a tattered robe, his wrinkled face hidden beneath a long, white beard. He was being commanded to share the message with all humanity. Jacob hoped, even prayed, that he properly understood the low voice, and that he was up to the task laid before him by this omniscient force. *God exists*, he thought with jubilation. *This is the proof. The truth.*

He picked up a sharpie and recorded the sagacity for the masses on a yellow legal pad, believing it to be a golden parchment. Not since Moses delivered the Ten Commandments to the Israelites in the desert had something so awe-inspiring occurred. His feeling of wonderment transformed to lightning pulsating from his heart to his fingertips as he began to sketch the words:

Countless tales, metaphors, myths galore
My imperceptible, imperfect mites

Dwarfed by time, space, omniscience
Scurrying, scampering beneath my master plan ...

It should have taken an eternity to transcribe all the learnings that followed. But it happened in a blink.

Jacob remained in a stupor, gesticulating with praise at the apex. *Such eloquence, such simplicity, such meaning. About life, about death. Yes. Yes. Paradise. My paradise. I am part of it.*

He now possessed the answer, the solution. But there was something he was compelled to do. The voice demanded it, screaming directions at him from all corners of his mind.

When he finished writing, Jacob kissed the yellow parchment and rose to his feet. He peered down at Lake Paradise and abruptly dove headfirst off the peak toward where the raft with the petrified professor and grinning innkeeper had submerged. In their place was the red orb of Jacob's dreams with a small bite in it, bobbing up and down with the waves. Jacob had tasted ambrosia.

In midair, his eyes snapped open and Jacob, now fully awake, headed to the living room toward his oldest friend. The sharpie and yellow legal pad fell to the bedroom floor.

PART IV

The CEO Report

"Every man who has attained to high position is a sincere believer of the survival of the fittest."

—*Philander Chase Johnson*

CHAPTER 1 - THE CEO

Four captains of industry silently convened in the boardroom at GoldOrb Diversified. They gathered around a circular table made of exquisite marble imported from Italy. Their fine leather shoes nestled into an opulent Persian rug while they gazed with admiration at priceless sculptures and paintings tastefully placed throughout the room with a curator's touch. Adrenalin coursed through their bodies. A single chair remained vacant for the alpha male.

He was running late after one of his frequent visits to Lake Paradise. Traffic was congested from an accident between a luxury Winnebago and an eighteen-wheeler. Neither driver could keep his oversized vehicle in the proper lane.

Once at Denver International, the CEO boarded the company jet. They recovered the lost time with the help of strong tailwinds, but traffic from the Minneapolis airport to G.O.D.'s headquarters also crawled. "Too many fricking people inhabit this planet, and they don't know how to drive," the CEO lamented to his long-time chauffeur.

During the journey, the CEO thought about his friends. He was astonished by the improvements the rabbi and rebbetzin had made to the Paradise Inn and even more impressed by their perseverance and adaptability. If they could only find Hannah, their lives would be complete.

His thoughts then turned to that interesting retiree with the probing questions whom he had met over dinner hosted by the rabbi and rebbetzin. The CEO found the former GoldOrb engineer to be smart and earnest. Jacob was also quirky and clearly uptight, but who was the CEO to point fingers?

With a strong endorsement from Jacob's former boss, the CEO

emailed Jacob, encouraging him to stay in touch. Jacob surprised the CEO by responding a nanosecond later:

> *It was great talking. I know you're busy, but when you have the chance, I'd love to keep the conversation going. Don't worry. I won't probe any further about pollution in Chicago or the company pension. I'm worried about a crisis in societal values. What do you think of the cultural wreckage inflicting our nation, and does it affect GoldOrb?*
>
> *Best.*
>
> *Jacob*

As he approached headquarters, the CEO reread Jacob's email and chuckled. It was offbeat and presumptuous, but also refreshing. He wondered what Jacob meant by cultural wreckage. He had his suspicions and planned to talk to Jacob about it.

Clearing his mind, the CEO moved briskly to the GoldOrb boardroom. Small in size, he compensated with overpowering body language and wardrobe. Many companies had shifted to casual dress, but not the C Suite at GoldOrb. The CEO's tie was knotted so tight that it signaled pain, the emotion for the day. He wore a triple starched shirt, a Rolex watch, and jeweled cufflinks advertising the initials "GG."

GG was an abbreviation for the CEO's longtime motto: *Get going.* The initials also stood for his name, Geoffrey Grand. And they reminded him of his "secret pleasure," something he eagerly anticipated for later that night.

The CEO sat erect at the edge of his chair and clasped his hands together in a vice-like grip over the priceless marble table. He scanned the room while his high-ranking executives held his gaze. It seemed like an eternity before he spoke, the silence emphasizing the dire importance of the topic. And then he launched, without any greeting or apology for his tardiness.

"We've let this disaster percolate too long," he said in a perfectly controlled monotone. "How can GoldOrb be blamed for polluting the Chicago River when our plant closed decades ago? What's our legal position and financial liability? Our public relations strategy? And why is Mayor Dumars attacking us?"

The culprit was GoldOrb's first plant, an old watch factory that had its heyday before the CEO was born. The expansive red-brick building bracketed by towering chimneys hugged the Chicago River and had allegedly leaked chemicals into the water.

The watch factory closed when the Japanese gained dominance in manufacturing timepieces. By then, GoldOrb's original business was an afterthought. The company was well on its way toward expanding into multitudes of other lucrative fields circling the globe.

The building wasn't even owned by GoldOrb anymore. The company sold it to a real estate developer who converted the facility into condominiums with premium prices for its waterfront locale.

But Chicago regulators were making threats. This had been going on for a long time and at first seemed like bureaucratic protocol leading to nowhere. But now, Mayor Dumars had joined the fray, raising the ante in public. The CEO's antenna was up as he sought to contain the damage.

With his hands still clasped tight, his tie tighter, the CEO said, "Let's have each of you weigh in with your expertise. We can brainstorm as a team after that. If I'm exaggerating the problem or missing something, tell me."

These were the best minds at GoldOrb, accomplished people in their own rights who wanted to impress the boss. The general counsel was a renowned attorney, winning several high-profile cases before the Supreme Court. The chief financial officer was a genius at manipulating numbers and a master of arcane accounting rules. And the senior vice presidents of GoldOrb's communications and government relations departments brought guile and seven decades of combined experience to the room. The CEO and his captains had seen it all.

They had worked miracles before. They'd kept GoldOrb humming following the September 11 terrorist attacks and the 2008 financial meltdown. They'd also weathered an accounting scandal that caused embarrassing headline news but only a modest fine from the government and a sacrificial firing. They knew how to buy and sell massive businesses at just the right moment and moved workforces across the globe with tactical precision. But they had never encountered a politician like the mayor of Chicago who seemed to harbor a vendetta.

The general counsel spoke first. He gave his high-level views of the law in a gruff voice, laying his glasses on the table for dramatic effect. He threw the phrase "strict liability" around with relish to scare the room. "We can be liable without fault," he explained. The CEO allowed him to pontificate. *As usual, no helpful answers, just more problems.*

The CFO followed with no pomp and circumstance. He was all business and his answer crystal clear. "If everything heads south, if we lose on all legal defenses, our financial exposure will be 1.37 billion. Cleanups require colossal labor and logistical expertise, and the fines are astronomical." The CEO cringed, worried about a freefall in GoldOrb's stock price.

While the team digested this gloomy forecast, the senior vice president of communications chimed in, reminding the CEO of their current strategy. She was the friendliest of the lot and spoke with a soothing upbeat voice. "GG, we're doing everything in our power to lay low, never bringing up Chicago. If the press forces our hand, we deny wrongdoing and emphasize that this happened in another era. Everybody, and that includes the city, thought that our operations were harmless back then. And there were other factories on the river. We weren't the only one."

The general counsel harumphed that these were also arguments the lawyers would make. "But the law may well go against us. Strict liability!"

The CEO showed little emotion despite his intensity. He pointed to the senior vice president of government relations for her input. She was one of the most connected people in the country and spoke with cool confidence. "My sources report that Mayor Dumars has a bee in his bonnet. He could give a rat's ass about pollution. But the city's got a financial disaster brewing and he's desperate for distraction. He wants to show the voters that he's a tough guy, in their corner, while he hides from the fact that he can't come up with enough money to continue paying retired cops, firemen, and teachers their pensions."

The general counsel interrupted her. "I wonder if we're overstating the problem. Any legal action would likely be brought by the state, or perhaps the federal government, not the city. Maybe the mayor is less potent than we think."

She responded looking at the CEO, not the lawyer. "Not a chance. The governor is in the mayor's back pocket and needs his backing for reelection. As for DC, the mayor's influence is absolutely scary."

As the conversation proceeded, all eyes remained locked on the CEO. Every comment was directed for his consumption alone, each participant calculating how to garner favor.

The CEO found this transparent and annoying. It reminded him for the second time that day of the rabbi. The rabbi, too, seemed to be the fulcrum of the universe wherever he presided. The CEO would silently mock the spectacle of BC congregants stumbling and bumbling over each other to make eye contact with the bearded man, to gain his attention, as if he was their conduit to heaven. He understood the pressure the rabbi faced trying to meet their expectations. *Maybe he cracked because he didn't have a release valve, an escape from it all, like I do with my secret pleasure.*

Refocusing on the Chicago River, staring daggers at his team, the CEO spun out the game plan. Part of it was predictable, even generic. He instructed the general counsel to reach out to the best legal minds anywhere to see if there were new creative arguments to add to the company's arsenal.

He directed the CFO to lower the price tag, knowing it was unlikely. "Think about selling GoldOrb products to the contractor we award cleanup work to. That should cut losses. Also, find a way to spread the accounting charge over more years." The CFO looked skeptical.

He then turned to the SVP of communications. "Let's get our head out of the sand and stress the positive. Whenever the river is mentioned, I want the public to hear all the ways we make lives better.

GoldOrb creates great products and can be trusted." She gave him a knowing nod.

The CEO paused for questions and then locked eyes with the SVP of government relations. *This is where we win or lose,* he thought. He directed her to set up a meeting with Mayor Dumars. "Make it one on one, nobody else in the room. And get me personal information about the guy. What's the mayor like, his strengths, weaknesses? Confirm your views as to why he's pushing so hard. What can we offer? Can we promise jobs instead of a cleanup?" Still looking only at her, he directed the team about timing. "I want to see the mayor once we've run down every loose end. Let's schedule it for after we release our next financials to Wall Street. I'll fly to Chicago."

The meeting ended as it began, except the CEO was first to leave. No niceties. He just rose abruptly and departed while the others remained to debrief. And, of course, to gossip over the CEO's surly disposition.

As he marched toward his office, the CEO felt a vague weariness. He was fifty-seven years old and had been operating in corporate overdrive for his entire adult life. While still a dynamo, he fretted over how much energy he retained in reserve. He felt weakened somehow, beleaguered from balancing on the high wire for so long.

And then, for the third time, he considered the rabbi and rebbetzin. *They made a momentous lifestyle change and landed on their feet. Nothing is permanent but change, and Sandra's ready. Can we pull off what they did?*

But as quickly as these thoughts invaded his consciousness, he vanquished them. *GoldOrb is all I know. They'll have to carry me out with my boots on.* Sandra hated it when he said that.

The CEO forced himself to focus. This was no time for daydreams. He had to get going with two days of work to fit into the afternoon. And he wanted to call Jacob to hear more about cultural wreckage. The notion intrigued him. Later, he'd unwind with his secret pleasure.

CHAPTER II - SANDRA

I met Geoffrey at Harvard. He was getting his MBA and I was an undergraduate philosophy major. We didn't have a penny to our names, unlike the hordes of rich kids that paraded around Cambridge.

We both grew up in New York. I lived in Queens, where my mom struggled with depression. My dad delivered mail during the week and took care of household chores that she neglected on the weekend. I was left to fend for myself.

Geoffrey was a Bronx boy. His parents immigrated from Eastern Europe and ran a corner grocery store. They barely spoke English. Geoffrey stocked shelves and worked the register after school, leaving scant time for fun.

Both of our families relied on religion to make it through the day, anesthesia for the pain. My parents followed rituals to the nth degree for their own sake, instead of as the means to the ultimate. What to eat, how to bow, when to leave the lights on or take a dip. "Just obey the rules," my father instructed. "And don't ask why. Who has time for nonsense? We don't want anything bad to happen to us." Mom wore an unhappy look on her face, nodding in agreement. Ironically, the rules commanded her to feel happy each Sabbath. She didn't.

Geoffrey's folks were unwilling to abandon their old country roots. He told me, "They already made enough changes. They like the order to their lives that religion offers."

The most important thing to understand about our childhoods is that we hungered for more. It was like our families concluded we did not quite fit in. But we excelled in school and that was our ticket out.

Geoffrey was a no-nonsense guy, blunt and honest. He was also wicked smart, not exactly unique at Harvard. But what set him apart was unrelenting grit and competitiveness, his take-no-prisoner attitude. If Geoffrey wanted to do something or go somewhere, he made it happen. When he broke his foot, he kept our date to go hiking, hobbling on crutches through the rain. No hurdle would ever slow GG down. He was ambition personified.

We thought alike. After studying untold pages of philosophy for midterms, I worried that the scholarly wisdom was nothing but hot air. *I think, therefore I am? Existence precedes essence?* "Well thanks a whole lot for that useful advice," I complained, my voice laced with sarcasm and anxiety.

But Geoffrey chuckled out encouragement. "It's undeniably stimulating, like a mind puzzle."

"Gobbledygook," I replied. "We need to just make it happen, get going, right?"

Geoffrey nodded with a twinkle in his eyes. "You said it. But you also need to ace your exams."

Religious philosophy posed the same limitations. We became proud atheists instead, believing only what could be proved, things we could see with our eyes, touch with our hands. Geoffrey and I replaced the platitudes and unproven claims with a personal credo that was simple and lined up with science. "The fittest will survive and prosper," I said. "That's us." The cost was Darwinian isolation from our families, from belonging. It hurt sometimes.

Our courtship was quick. Geoffrey moved fast, and I led at warp speed. I fell in love with this unique man who could take me on a magic carpet ride.

Our goal was to capture as much from life as possible, to maximize. We were the worthiest and deserved the best. During this lifetime, it only makes sense to go for it like GG says, make things happen. When you die, you disappear, and the worms crawl in, out, and all about.

Our religious views didn't stop us from participating in synagogue life at BC. We did that for business, for profits. I joked to Geoffrey, "I guess we're serving G.O.D. after all." But he stayed serious. "There's no ethical conflict, Sandra. No hypocrisy if you're honest about intent." He was right. Put another way, BC and the rabbi weren't hypocritical taking our money knowing full well what we wanted, were they?

After graduation, Geoffrey exploded like a nuclear missile into the business world. That's apt to happen with superstar MBAs from Harvard. Not so much for philosophy majors like me.

I lost track of the number of positions he held at GoldOrb, the times we packed our bags and relocated as my juggernaut husband climbed the corporate ladder. I asked, "Will things ever slow down so that we can stay in one place long enough to get to know the neighborhood, make friends?" For the first time, I felt a tinge of frustration.

But my husband took my hand and spoke in a soothing and confident voice. "We'll soon live in a fantastic Minneapolis neighborhood near HQ. We'll stabilize when I am CEO."

He wasn't being cocky or delusional, just stating the facts. I had no doubt the goal would be attained and did everything in my power to help. We were teammates in all endeavors.

Geoffrey's ascent to rarefied heights would have been harder if we chose to start a family. The solution was easy. We kept it a twosome. He got a vasectomy one morning and marched back to work that afternoon. We made a clear-eyed decision to create a different, better life. I assured him, "Life won't be conventional, but it will be wonderful."

Well, that was prophetic. GG was unstoppable and I was there all along, pulling levers from behind curtains. Next thing I knew, I was "Madam CEO," the queen of the corporate world, attending sold out extravaganzas at exotic locations, hanging out with the rich and famous. Heck, we became celebrities ourselves. We've hosted senators and royalty, hung out with rock divas and superstar athletes hawking the company brand.

As Geoffrey predicted, we moved near GoldOrb's headquarters into an enormous mansion. Of course, the two of us didn't need the space. Nobody does. But it sure feels fine when your sleek Jaguar motors up to the security gate and it opens wide for you to enter Xanadu. Tennis courts sit on the side of the house with our pool and rose gardens in back. Mr. Hearst would be envious.

People joke about my husband. "The CEO is too intense, wound tight as a spring, ready to snap," they say. "Just look at how he wears that necktie and clasps his hands." They wonder how I can live with the maniac.

Well, I'll tell you how. Yes, they are correct that Geoffrey is, shall we say, an A plus personality. So am I. That's the only way to conquer, to be the fittest. But nothing is quite as it seems. They don't have the full picture.

As a husband, Geoffrey is kind and sweet, loyal to a fault. He's funny too when he loosens up. And my GG lets off steam with the best of them. He calls it his secret pleasure. I call it what everyone else does. His "Gabbing Gloria" blog. That's right. The CEO of GoldOrb runs a website using a fake name with his real initials. And it's a big time hit. Now you tell me if you wouldn't find it a hoot being married to this character.

I'll leave it to you to decide if Geoffrey, make that GG, make that Gabbing Gloria, is crazy. After all, a CEO with an anonymous blog site is, shall we say, unique. But I would suggest that he's the sanest man in the world. Just read his posts and watch him steer GoldOrb. He's masterful on both fronts.

As you can see, my life is complicated. At times I hear a small voice asking a loaded question. *These endeavors are all his. What about that?*

Look, I'm as smart as my husband, maybe brighter. I'm also every bit as determined, just in a more discreet way. But to reap the bounty from our unorthodox lifestyle, my role is to take a back seat in public and surreptitiously help GG steer the ship. Geoffrey knows it. "Sandra, you're the keys to the kingdom," he said. "You've had my back all these years and I love you."

He's being completely honest. And I love him too, no questions asked. We've had a blast navigating the seas of capitalism, never once springing a leak. But to be frank, the thrill is waning. It gets lonely sometimes wandering the long corridors of Xanadu.

Funny, but not once during my highfalutin education did my philosophy professors focus on the most powerful psychic force in history: *acclimation.* When you live in pain, you get used to it and may even find happiness. But guess what. When you live at Xanadu, you also acclimate, but this time to your detriment. You start taking your wonders for granted and negative thoughts invade your psyche. Milton Friedman and Ayn Rand should have written sequels to their romps with capitalism to help the fittest people decide what to do when acclimation arrives to calm the animal spirits.

I find myself growing anxious over what's next. Is this all there is to life? Do we have a second act?

I sense that Geoffrey is also beginning to feel a void. He tries to ignore it, or gets all macho, defending the status quo, yapping something about keeping his silly boots on so that he can work at the company until he dies. The last time I broached the subject, he said, "It's a midlife crisis Sandra. It'll pass and we'll be fine at Xanadu and GoldOrb, still blogging and kicking ass."

His face tells a different story. He looks so weary sometimes. The world seems different now, and things that used to work to perfection no longer satisfy.

Don't misconstrue. I have few regrets. I still pinch myself some mornings when I awake to this fantasy. But I had more fun climbing the pyramid than I'm having now on the sharp tip of its apex.

CHAPTER III – THE CEO

T he CEO and Sandra enjoyed a catered dinner in their gourmet kitchen. He updated her on how the rabbi and rebbetzin were faring in Lake Paradise. Detecting a wistful look on his wife's face as he raved about their adaptability to their new environment, he quickly switched topics to his new nemesis, Mayor Dumars, and his recent acquaintance, Jacob.

Sandra's eyes narrowed at the mention of the mayor. "The prick sounds like Mussolini."

"Let's hope he suffers the same fate."

"Jacob seems like a keeper though, Geoffrey."

"Yep, there's something about the guy. He interests me. And he'll tell it to me straight."

Sandra had the body of a relay swimmer and the wardrobe of the First Lady. She was a good two inches taller than the CEO and looked like she could inflict serious injury if provoked. But her brown eyes were soft and caring, especially when it came to her husband. "You seem worn out Geoffrey," she said. "The mayor isn't worth it."

After dinner, the CEO slipped away to Xanadu's ninth bedroom at the far end of the upstairs hallway. He had waited all day for this moment.

He plopped into an oversized beanbag chair. From there, he viewed authentic originals of his favorite celebrities. Peyton Manning, Michael Jordan, Tom Hanks, Don Henley, Billy Joel, and the cast from The Sopranos adorned the wall. Each picture was autographed with a personal note to GG. Their smiles inspired him for the task ahead.

The CEO transformed into a new person in this unlikely setting. Psyching himself up for his secret pleasure, he had changed into baggy jeans with a black silk shirt, untucked and half unbuttoned. His Rolex and cufflinks were replaced by a thick golden necklace. His stodgy designer suit and suffocating necktie lay crinkled in the corner of the bedroom.

Sandra poked her head in. Raising an eyebrow at his getup and the mess on the floor, she teased, "My CEO schizo. No time for tidiness?"

But he was the same man as always. He still had that irrepressible urgency to get going, just with a different purpose. As Gabbing Gloria, he banged out nighttime messages to the universe with the same vigor that the CEO fired out corporate directives to his staff during the workday. In both cases, his handiwork was staggeringly precise and effective.

GG had a knack for identifying topics for his blog that struck a nerve. It started frivolously with a post criticizing Lebron James for leaving Cleveland. The CEO was miffed that the basketball legend had the audacity to work behind the backs of management to ensemble a super team in Miami. It was the first time "King James" was taken to task. Gabbing Gloria asked, "What type of king forgets his loyal subjects, Cleveland's fans?"

He understood that there was intense competition for clicks in the age of the internet. So, GG offered a jackpot for visiting Gabbing Gloria. Readers who spent more than three minutes on the site were entered into a lottery. The lucky viewer received one thousand dollars. The CEO was playing to win.

The blog buzzed. Incorporeal snippets about Lebron laced with responsive insights, praises and expletives ricocheted across the sports world. Since then, Gabbing Gloria posted direct hits covering politics, technology, racial tensions and, of course, the business world. The prize money flowed.

GG knew that he was onto something when mainstream social media outlets began quoting from Gabbing Gloria. And a national newspaper discovered the blog, praising it as "scintillation with a punch, inside views for guilty pleasures." There were criticisms too, but they provided free advertising. And no carping could stymie GG's well-placed advertisements inviting readers to "Study Up, Win A Mint."

By the time the CEO had met Jacob, the blog had a huge following. Many viewers were passionate, searching for answers mixed with spice from a trusted source. A few were jerks, trolling for victims to attack. All wanted the prize money.

GG understood the risks. He'd be ruined at GoldOrb if word got out that the CEO by day was Gabbing Gloria at night. But the liberation was intoxicating. Sandra encouraged him, hoping the excitement generated by the blog would break her monotony too.

GG hired one of the best computer minds in the world to ensure that the blog remained anonymous. "We're flying incognito," he assured Sandra. "For all they know, Gloria operates from a basement in Sydney."

As the blog matured, GG struggled to generate new material to stay fresh and relevant. He worried that he would soon grow weary of Gabbing Gloria, the same way he sometimes felt as CEO. *Sandra keeps warning about acclimation*, he thought. *She's in my head.*

This made him doubly glad to meet Jacob from Lake Paradise. *What a source!* About midnight, he clicked the submit button for his new post called "Cultural Wreckage." It was inspired by a long talk with his new friend.

CHAPTER IV – GABBING GLORIA

Post 26: Cultural Wreckage

Greetings crew. I apologize for being in your face today. But this is critical. Mega. We are fiddling while Rome burns. The values necessary to run our Republic are going up in smoke. Think it over, then SCREAM!!

...More guns than citizens! Ask Newtown, Orlando, maybe a shattered neighborhood near you, how that's working out.

...An internet of CRAP! They claimed it would connect us, but instead there's porn, conspiracy theories, lies and hate at our bubbled fingertips.

...24/7 stupidity at fever pitch! Fox, CNN, Rush and the gang stoke fears while serving half a loaf. Biased news for your entertainment loaded with orgasmic disinformation. Translated: It's BULLSHIT! Turn it off dears, take a deep breath, and walk away.

...Reality TV in Washington! We voted in Nero. This is ridiculous folks. We are better than this.

...Bestiality is next! Sexual predators in the priesthood, boy scouts, C suites, Hollywood. I want to cry.

...Homeless people everywhere! Why do human
beings sleep under bridges in the wealthiest nation?

The list goes on... and grows... and multiplies. The Varsity Blues and failing schools. Profanity masquerading as music. Barrel-sized sugar drinks for slurping up obesity and diabetes. Graffiti on Plymouth Rock, the Redwoods, even tombstones for God's sake. Tattoos on asses. Where next?

I CAN'T TAKE IT ANYMORE! THIS IS FREEDOM GONE AMUCK!

So, let's clean up our act. Yes, you have rights, but you have obligations too. Do something nice! A good life begins and ends with values!

Take your time and think about this. Poke around. And remember, there's a thousand dollars waiting for one of you to win. $1,000!

Till we meet again! I love you!

Gabbing Gloria

Likes: *11,354*
Dislikes: *384*
Comments: *1008*

Big Romeo: "*We suffer from ignorance and poor education. Nobody cares, so we are going down. BTW Gloria, we voted in Caligula, not Nero. Pack your bags.*"

Toenails: "*Lighten up, Gabby, you're being a curmudgeon. There's just as much good out there as bad. My glass is half full. Cheer up and smile.*"

Charlie D: "*Just look at the wildfires raging out West. Rome is already burning! The Dark Ages are coming! Reckoning will be a bitch.*"

Little Juliet: "*I agree with Big Romeo. I'd pack my bags to go anywhere with him.*"

Yamish: "*Go girl! Our leaders are depraved. A country that elects garbage is headed to the trash bin of history. Rome is ablaze."*

Chug It: *"Stay out of politics Gloria. And to all you ass wipes out there, don't you see we are trying to restore values by making America Great Again?"*

Lubovi: *"The Messiah is coming to burn away the wreckage."*

Benedict: *"POTUS may be rough around the edges, but he's done a good job. I focus on policies not personality. Clean the swamp and the good ole days will return."*

Paul: *"Frankly, I'm worried. We are tanking, losing our national soul. Which country should I move to? Iceland has hot chicks."*

The Condenser: *"The Blacks, Jews and immigrants are to blame for our cultural wreckage. Go back to where you came from!"*

Pinger: *"Gabby, take your White trash bigoted views about rap and shove them up your ass. I've had it with this site."*

Gilligan: *"You are pointing out the fatal problem ... education. We can't have a democracy without enlightened voters."*

Croncite: *"You're right Gloria. Don't watch Fox, CNN or listen to the CRAP unless you want to be neurotic."*

Evan: *"Hey Gloria. You forgot to single out abortion, the biggest sign of wreckage. I believe in life."*

Better in Blue Jeans: *"Gloria is an alarmist. There are medical breakthroughs and innovations every day. Life is good. This blog is as one-sided as the networks."*

Fallen Angel: *"Fox news tells the truth. My Second Amendment rights are God given."*

Shire Lady: *"Hi Gabby. Just know that the culprit for the wreckage is Satan and those who choose him."*

Myth Buster: *"Well, if Satan exists, didn't your God create that demon? Isn't God therefore responsible for the wreckage too?"*

Shire Lady: *"SINNER! SINNER!"*

Marvel: *"If we keep talking past each other, we're doomed.*

Religion adds values that we sorely need."

Avi: *"I'd love to talk to Marvel about anything. I bet you're virtuous plus hot."*

Marvel: *"718-474-6785."*

Swami: *"This culture problem will wreak havoc when we're faced by an actual emergency, say a global pandemic. Mark my words, and Gabby's."*

CHAPTER V - THE CEO

G was back at GoldOrb headquarters early the next morning, his tie clasped around his neck in place of the golden chain. He was on a blogger's high but exhausted from his late-night vigil in bedroom nine. His post on cultural wreckage was an instant triumph and he credited it to Jacob. *It was as much a tirade as a commentary,* he thought. *The overreactive rantings of an old man ... make that old woman.* Still, Jacob had convinced him that societal values were in freefall, and his readers devoured the notion.

The CEO rarely acted impulsively but, in his excitement, decided to send Jacob an email with a link to the blog:

> *Jacob, after our conversation, I came across an interesting site last night. This Gabbing Gloria character thinks like you.*

The CEO knew it was risky, but just had to share the post with his new friend, to hear his reaction.

Jacob responded in a flash:

> *Wow. She nailed it on the head. I added a comment to the site about God and corporate America. By the way, to switch topics, I'll be visiting my children in Minneapolis next month and would love to talk more. No sweat if you're too busy.*

The CEO welcomed the invitation. He directed his assistant to block out an entire evening for dinner with Jacob at the General's Club.

There was no more time for extracurricular activities. The clock was ticking, and the CEO could tolerate no more diversions. He needed to turn to work, to get going, but couldn't resist a last peek at Jacob's incoming post to the blog:

> *Corporate greed spurs inequities, pollution, backlash ... societal wasteland. But big business also innovates, creates wealth, jobs,*

things people need. Corporations resemble the god, Abraxas.
They are both good and bad.

Jacob's entry created a virtual stir. Comments instantly populated the Gabbing Gloria site with most bashing greedy corporate America, a few agreeing with Jacob's nuanced viewpoint. A handful of followers focused on Abraxas, the munificent yet evil god, abandoning the topic of societal rot altogether.

The CEO's adrenaline pumped as his blog hummed with activity. He was right about Jacob. His new friend was already a valuable resource for his secret pleasure.

A knock on his office door snapped the CEO out of it. He quickly closed Gabbing Gloria from his computer and assumed his position of intensity, sitting straight on the edge of his chair, hands together in a vice-like grip.

The general counsel found him in this customary pose as he sauntered in. "Sorry for the interruption GG. I didn't want to raise this in front of the full team yesterday, but there's a development. We poured through mildewed boxes of old documents from the watch factory and found something."

The general counsel seemed to be enjoying himself, as he raised a yellowing piece of paper to emphasize its significance, his importance. "I haven't concluded that this is a smoking gun yet," he said. "But it was written by the plant manager from the watch factory and shows that leadership possibly knew what they were doing. It's long but I'll read the key passage."

He paused to find his reading glasses while the CEO sat stone-faced. The lawyer squinted at the document, cleared his voice, and read:
I fear it's possible that we are polluting the river. We're not alone.
Other factories have the same processes. But I am concerned.

Anticipating the next question, the general counsel told the CEO that his team already tried to locate the manager to help them interpret the memo. But he retired long ago and recently died.

The general counsel stopped speaking, watching the CEO for his reaction. But the CEO stayed quiet, examining his lawyer. Again, he sensed that the man was extracting a degree of pleasure from the bad news.

Breaking the silence, the CEO asked in his usual steady voice, "How bad is this for GoldOrb legally?"

"It's knotty," replied the general counsel. He launched into a detailed dissection of the memo, parsing words, noting ambiguities. "We're in a trickier place than before," he opined. "Until now, I was under the impression that the company had no awareness that the emissions could be dangerous. This may change the equation, hurt our negotiating posture or reputation. Nothing's definitive."

The general counsel was gathering himself to give a sermon about esoteric strengths and weaknesses of the case when the CEO interrupted him. "Have you talked to outside legal experts yet like I asked?"

He nodded with a strained smile. "Yes. Some have new theories that go one way, while others reverse course. They're still researching. The situation is confused, fluid. But I warn you again about strict liability."

The CEO had difficulty hiding his disdain from the general counsel. Their philosophies and styles clashed. From the attorney's point of view, the CEO failed to appreciate ambiguity. He was always pushing the company to the brink, forcing his law department to get on board to exploit uncomfortable gray zones. It made the general counsel uneasy. He felt as if he was under continuous attack by a bullying powerhouse, forced to defend convoluted laws that were not of his making. "Sometimes we have to slow it down, GG, analyze, reflect."

These were not the words the CEO wanted to hear. He chose compliance when the law was clear. But he also had a business to run at warp speed. *Damn the legal subtleties!*

The CEO asked to see the memo and the general counsel handed it to him like it was a rare jewel. While he examined it, the general counsel's mind drifted to Sandra. He had tried to make a move on the CEO's foxy wife long ago when the CEO was out of town. He always knew when GG was away. All he had to do was check the flight log for the company jet or ask the CEO's administrator for his calendar. *When the cat's away, the mice ought to play,* he thought. *The guy's an asshole anyway.*

But the lawyer misjudged the situation. Yes, Sandra was often alone in that gigantic house, but she showed no interest in his advances, and he aborted before she could decisively discern his design. While she may have had an inkling, Sandra never mentioned anything to her husband. The thought of cheating on GG was ludicrous, unworthy of discussion. This was not the brand of excitement she craved to battle acclimation.

The CEO stopped reviewing the memo and stared at the general counsel. *What on Earth is the man thinking about?* He was a master at reading body language, unintentional phrases. He knew that the general counsel was a great lawyer and valuable to GoldOrb but he didn't trust him.

Still holding the ancient document, the CEO reached a decision. "This fortifies my view that we need to approach the problem delicately and avoid a legal battle in court. I'll try to lower the temperature when I travel to Chicago to meet the mayor. We need to offer up something that GoldOrb can live with that will still let him proclaim victory."

The CEO was irked by the discovery of the old memo and his tone reflected his annoyance. "I don't understand why those boxes weren't purged long ago. What was the point in storing junk? Was it to raise problems for us decades later?" He instructed the general counsel that he would hold on to the note for the time being. "I'll read the damn thing again later."

The CEO did not want the memo to be shared with anyone. He also understood, without a word being spoken, that the general counsel retained a copy. *The guy is a literal hoarder for God's sake.* For a moment, his mind wandered, and he considered writing a Gabbing Gloria post about the pitfalls of hoarding. But he quickly refocused and told the lawyer, "Keep digging. Find something helpful next time."

With the general counsel gone, the CEO returned to his computer. Sixty-five new emails had streamed in. Most were minor or irrelevant, but he scanned them all to be certain. *It's too easy for anyone from anywhere to reach me. I should turn this instrument of torture off.* That vague feeling of weariness washed over him.

The fatigue soon dissipated when the CEO clicked on a message labelled "Highly Confidential" from the SVP of government relations:

GG, I'm hearing ratty whispers. The mayor of Chicago takes low blow politics another level down. He's a rotten apple you can't trust for a single bite.

Bottom line: Be careful when you meet. He's dangerous!

GG was frustrated. Cultural wreckage was insinuating itself in the seats of power throughout the land. And getting in the way of *G.O.D.*

CHAPTER VI – THE CEO AND JACOB

Jacob was completely out of his element at the General's Club, surrounded by moguls and bombarded by invaluable artifacts that meant nothing to him. He wore khakis and a short sleeve plaid shirt for the occasion. His customary business wardrobe usually provided inconspicuous cover but shouted for attention in this chic locale. Checking his Timex, he noted that the CEO was twenty minutes late.

As if reading his mind, the waiter appeared with freshly baked rolls and a general's martini. "The drink is a house specialty ordered for you by your host," he said. "The CEO is running late and said to start without him." Left to his own devices, Jacob would have requested a draft beer.

Alone at the table, Jacob nursed the concoction. His mind was on returning home to Lake Paradise on a flight scheduled to depart early the next morning. He doubted that any of the General's Club's patrons flew coach or lived in a cabin. *I'm an odd duck here but I'll be back in paradise soon enough.*

As usual, Jacob's visit with the twins was tangled. He spent his first week with Walter. His son appeared glum, having been placed on furlough from work while his wife rebuked him. Walter assured Jacob that he was fine, "Nestled in the outstretched arms of Jesus," but Jacob harbored serious doubts.

He stayed with Michelle the second week, where the atmosphere was upbeat. He was happy for his daughter. She had a successful counselling practice and was in love. But as hard as he tried, he couldn't shake the discomfort and would lower his eyes when the two women displayed affection for each other. He honestly liked Gracie, but rarely spoke with her alone. And when they did chat, the conversation was stilted and of no consequence:

"Nice outfit."

"Thanks. It was on clearance."

"That was delicious."

"Healthy too."

As usual, Jacob resolved to work harder at acceptance, wondering if he'd ever succeed. He hoped that Michelle was oblivious to his hangups. *Wishful thinking.*

The alcohol provided Jacob with a small buzz by the time the CEO arrived. On his heels was the waiter, urgently rushing over with another general's martini and a refill for Jacob. Winking at his dinner companion, the CEO instructed the waiter, "We'll have the general's premium banquet for two." He then apologized for the delay. "My board meeting for Faith House was interminable. There are twelve directors, and each needed to hear himself yack. That's not how things work at GoldOrb."

Jacob was intrigued by the name Faith House and asked what they did. The CEO looked unsure of himself. "The place serves the homeless population of Minneapolis," he said. "There are eighty beds, maybe. Residents receive meals and coaching to find jobs, but alcohol and drug abuse is a huge impediment. We were talking today about adding an addiction program."

Jacob wondered if his homeless friend from Livertie Avenue ever lodged at Faith House. As only he could do, he began showering the CEO with sincere and precise follow-on questions, none of which the CEO could adequately handle:

"How long can residents stay without looking for work?"

"What if you catch them using?"

"What percentage find jobs?"

"Which faith?"

The CEO eventually admitted, "I don't know much of what you're getting at, Jacob. I've never been to Faith House or met a homeless man." He waved at a high browed colleague in a polka-dotted bow tie at a nearby table and went on explaining. "Faith House directors gather in a ritzy part of town. I attend board meetings to steer the enterprise and raise funds. We have a gala event coming up, formal attire with an auction, and I'll speak. It's good for GoldOrb's reputation and business development."

As the conversation continued, Jacob learned that the CEO served on five other charitable boards and headed up a local business association. He also met regularly in New York to share leadership practices with other chief executives and travelled to Washington most months to strategize with lobbyists. He spread his arms wide apart to sum up his reach. "I go wherever it's best for GoldOrb. To gain market intelligence, sell products, mostly to find movers and shakers who can help us down the road. And yes, there's gravy. Many of these organizations are for a good cause." It was no wonder he had never been to Faith House and could not answer Jacob's detailed questions.

Jacob struggled to relate. He had been a mere worker bee for his entire career who retired to anonymity after logging his time. He never served on a board, nor had he dined at an exclusive club. While he enjoyed his first few interactions with the CEO and was excited to be talking to such a powerful man who ran the very company he had worked for, they needed to find common ground, or it would be a long night.

The CEO sensed the same distance but knew how to bridge the gap. He raised his glass for a toast. "Here's to the rabbi and Mia." They clicked as the CEO continued. "I wish I could spend more time with them like you do. They're fantastic. I'm thrilled Lake Paradise worked out for them."

Jacob smiled warmly. "Yep, they're great. The rabbi has become my closest friend out West. And Mia is so much fun."

Jacob told the CEO that he first met the rabbi at the synagogue when he was seeking guidance for a personal problem. *It's Wednesday night,* he thought. *And here I am dining in elite land instead of fearing a nightmare from Hades.* He asked the CEO, "How did a corporate chief link up with a rabbi?"

The CEO responded, "That sounds like the beginning of a lame riddle." He confided that he was an atheist with no interest in God or religion. "What do I need with genuflecting to decrees from thousands of years ago?" He explained in a matter-of-fact way that the real reason he joined BC and made friends with the rabbi and Mia was the same as always. "They could help GoldOrb. There are influential people at BC. Plus, the place boasts a fourteen hundred members to advertise to."

Jacob looked incredulous as the third martini sloshed in his gut, emboldening him to square off with the CEO. "Let me get this straight. You don't believe in God. You don't buy Judaism. Yet you work tirelessly for an institution devoted to those ideals. How can you do that with an indifferent heart?" His tone was replete with curiosity, not animosity or scorn.

While many people would have turned defensive, the CEO loved the interchange. "Look, Jacob, here's the thing. I bleed GoldOrb blood. So, I'm being true to my convictions if I believe BC can help the company. Plus, legends, mysticism, and all that other religious jargon aside, BC does good deeds. They preach peace and brotherhood, spearhead charitable initiatives. What's wrong with joining forces for worthy causes?" He enjoyed cloaking capitalism with altruism.

The CEO paused to butter his roll. "BC also fights that cultural wreckage that you and Gabbing Gloria are so concerned with by focusing on family and values. Again, what's wrong with my helping them?"

Jacob looked perplexed by the CEO's rapid-fire rationalizations, but quickly regained confidence. "I'm not sure I see it that way, Geoffrey," he said. "I couldn't join an organization with a fundamental purpose I don't believe in. BC spends most of the time praising God, practicing rituals, and celebrating holidays. Aren't you using them for your own ends?" Before the CEO could answer, Jacob rolled out the heavy artillery. "And I wonder how innocent the whole scene really is. Religion divides people along mythical borders, causing wars and atrocities throughout the ages. Would you join the KKK if it furthered the company's aims?"

The CEO reddened slightly, but then chuckled, enjoying Jacob's honesty. It was so seldom that anyone stood up to him. He jabbed back in a gentle voice. "Jacob, when you worked for GoldOrb, were your views always in line with those of the big, bad corporation? How about when we closed factories or transferred jobs to a foreign country? I knew that, on balance, these were the right moves, but did you? Weren't you just the least bit compromised to make a buck?" He took a sip of his martini to let his points sink in. "And come on! Being part of BC and the Klan are not comparable. That one's out of bounds, and you know it."

Jacob squirmed in his chair, but then settled and looked contemplative. He admitted to the CEO that he had felt conflicted during his long career with GoldOrb but needed to provide a good life for his family. "Taking care of Lizzy and the twins was my primary goal, and I'm thankful GoldOrb enabled me to do that."

He was about to make a finer point, understanding that he had fallen into the CEO's trap, when the waiter interrupted. Suddenly the table was overflowing with food. Rare cuts of steak and lamb, twice baked potatoes with sour cream and chives, and a special mixture of farm-fresh vegetables sautéed in a scrumptious curry sauce made for an epicurean delight. Another round of martinis was served. The waiter left them with this wisdom: "Bon appétit."

The men took a break from sparring to enjoy their bounty. Jacob no longer felt self-conscious in the posh surroundings as he delighted in the cuisine. The CEO expressed how nice it was to make a new friend who would challenge him instead of pander. He hesitated as if to convey that the next topic was delicate. "I have a difficult one for you now. Why do you think the rabbi really left BC for his new life at Lake Paradise? I know he was out of gas and demoralized about Hannah, but there had to be more to it."

Jacob was intrigued by the conversational shift back to the rabbi. He too was thinking about their common friend, but for a different reason. The rabbi had continued to work at BC for twelve excruciating years after losing his faith from his parents' murder-suicide. And Jacob had consoled his friend, advising that regardless of his altered beliefs, he was performing good deeds for the community. He recalled telling the Rabbi, "To me, what's most important is the effect of your actions, not your mindset in carrying them out." Perhaps he was being too hard on the CEO for his mixed motives.

But Jacob felt slightly manipulated by the CEO's question and did not want to betray his friend's confidences. He gave the CEO an unreadable look. "You need to ask the rabbi, I guess. He's one in a million."

The CEO was impressed again. Jacob was trustworthy. It was nice to spend time with a man of such high integrity. "You're a good friend to the rabbi," he said. "Let's drop it and work on our own friendship." Was this a guy he could confide in about Gabbing Gloria, even let him know who the blogger was? Tempting as it was to share his secret pleasure, he remained quiet.

Jacob then surprised the CEO by raising his glass for another toast. "Here's to new friendships," he said. "And I'm sorry if I was out of line about your motives. Sometimes it takes me too long to wrestle out the right answer. The charitable work you do is terrific."

They spent the rest of the evening devouring their meals while enjoying each other's company. At times, the CEO felt like he was being interviewed. But he never doubted Jacob's sincerity. *There's no agenda*, he thought. *He's just unusually curious with a genuine need to tackle impossible issues.*

The CEO also continued to sense a high level of anxiety in Jacob. He noticed Jacob's eyes twitched on several occasions and speculated that his fervent need for answers and solutions might explain the nervous body language. *Better than the overconfident barracudas I'm forced to swim with at GoldOrb.*

The two men rambled on about the state of the country, and the flaws of capitalism and democracies. "But what system is superior?" asked the CEO. This reminded Jacob of *Manifest Misery*. He told the CEO about his childhood friend, the professor, and the book's harsh revelations. Despite his doubts about the book, Jacob took pride in his long friendship with an Ivy League author.

The CEO shook his head in disagreement with the professor's ideology. "It can't be that we got this far as a country without doing anything right," he said with irritation in his voice. "We in the business world make things happen while scholarly clerics luxuriate in vaunted sanctuaries playing with themselves, then whining. I'll take a doer over a make-believer any day of the week."

Jacob remembered that he too had reacted negatively to *Manifest Misery* long ago on his fortieth birthday. But he usually fought his instincts against academia. "I hear you, I really do," he told the CEO. "But there's a need for both the practical and theoretical. Sometimes, I wish I had devoted more of my life to the esoteric. I know so little at this point."

"Aging's a bitch," replied the CEO. The weariness he had begun to feel, and Sandra's restlessness, crept into his consciousness. But the waiter arrived to rescue the mood with the general's famous strawberry cheesecake. Jacob and the CEO fell silent, savoring the sweetness even as they aged a little more.

Despite Jacob's initial hesitation in this exclusive setting, he had a fantastic time. And the CEO was likewise exhilarated. He enjoyed Jacob's companionship and looked forward to a budding friendship. *Better yet, the guy's a thinker,* he reflected. *He's sure to provide loads of fodder for Gabbing Gloria.* The CEO scolded himself. *There I go again with mixed motives.*

CHAPTER VII – THE MAYOR

I had the bastard right where I wanted him. Ready to hemorrhage cash and snivel out a public apology to the good citizens of Chicago. Better yet, to show the hardworking voters from Main Street that their mayor takes no shit from Wall Street.

The CEO waltzed into my office like we were old buddies. A strong handshake while staring me straight in the eye, some wry jokes. He wanted to beat around the bush forever, making all varieties of small talk. He even peered at my shelves and spotted *Manifest Misery*. Next thing you know, the guy wants to chat up a storm about the author, of all things. "I have a good friend who has known the professor since they were boys," he said. "We have several reservations about the book. What do you think, Mr. Mayor?"

I responded that the professor and I attended graduate school together, that he was delusional on a good day, and that his book was academic crap. Not exactly an invitation to keep the superficial party talk going.

The CEO nodded sagaciously, and his tone turned serious. He sat straight up at the edge of his chair with his hands clamped together as if to signal it was time for me to listen up to the grand business visionary. Frowning, he told me that he'd heard rumors that my office thinks GoldOrb polluted the Chicago River and should pay up. "Nothing could be further from the truth, Mr. Mayor. This happened so long ago that Sid Luckman was still chucking touchdown passes for the Bears."

"The Bears suck," I said, again rejecting the chumminess and awaiting a real discussion.

He looked like he was mildly disappointed in a good friend. "Everyone believed that GoldOrb ran the plant by the book," he pitched. "The City's regulators were on board, not only with us, but the other factories along the river. And then we went ahead and sold the property, got out of the watchmaking business altogether long ago. I don't think there's a problem with the water. But if there is, GoldOrb isn't responsible."

With that second-rate propaganda, the CEO was officially annoying me. Typical little man trying to compensate for his physical inadequacies by flaunting make believe power. I would tolerate none of it and swatted the fly. "Look, Geoffrey, or whatever you want me to call you. I am Mayor of a great city. If Chicago is harmed, I stand up for the people. The river's full of dangerous chemicals doing the backstroke that trace directly to your factory. Someone needs to clean up the mess. And that someone should be the company that polluted the water, don't you think?"

Truth be told, my experts were unsure whether the old watchmaking plant even did it. They also warned that dredging up chemicals from the bottom of the river where some might escape capture to float around again could cause more harm than cure. Who knows? Certainly not the clueless scientists.

The reality is that this is about politics, not science. I could care less about the river. No one swims in the blasted water anyway. If they do, they should have a lobotomy.

My goal is simple: Bring corporate America to its knees for all to see. My constituents need reminding that I'll fight for what's right. And if that means we can limp along with our pension morass, and me still at the helm, that's a pretty good outcome.

The CEO droned on with rehearsed arguments. Statute of limitations. The new owner of the premises is responsible, not GoldOrb. Blah, blah, blah. He could see this was going nowhere fast, so he tried to engage me by asking about the other companies with factories near the water. As if poor little GoldOrb Diversified was being singled out, a victim of unfair treatment.

"Other polluters aren't your concern," I responded. "You're here to answer for the actions of GoldOrb, are you not?"

My strategy was to force GoldOrb to cave first. Then, we could go after smaller players, one by one. They'll fold like bad poker hands once they see mighty GoldOrb succumbing to Mr. Mayor. Each new concession will attract more voters as I emerge victorious in the public eye time and again.

The CEO's face reddened. He gripped his hands together until he was near breaking his knuckles and tightened his designer tie to the point of asphyxiation. Maybe he was cutting off his own circulation as a negotiating ploy to gain my sympathy. I was enjoying the scene as he whined and coughed up an offer. "We need to work this out. GoldOrb is innocent, but we love Chicago and are prepared to open a plant here with a thousand new jobs. Or perhaps there are some GoldOrb products the City prefers at a discount. What's your pleasure, Mr. Mayor?"

I must admit that the twirp's offers were tempting, so long as he wasn't planning to pander for tax breaks in the small print. But my gut told me that they weren't what I needed at the polls. Jobs and price breaks wouldn't excite my base as much as humbling a titan of industry.

"Okay," I countered. "If you don't want to link this up to polluting the river, the cost is three billion in concessions." You should have seen the pipsqueak's expression. Priceless.

I then laid my trap. "Look, Geoffrey, this isn't personal. But big business must take responsibility for its actions. You talk about bringing in a thousand jobs. But what about all the work you ship to India and Mexico, devastating the towns you abandon? Can Chicago trust you? Somebody has to stand up and do what's right."

The CEO looked exasperated. But he quickly reengaged, and his voice turned calm and unapologetic. "Mr. Mayor, sending work around the globe gets lower prices for your fair citizens. I don't hear them complain about paying less when they shop. And they sure aren't rejecting their growing 401(k) balances. Look, I'm offering you jobs in a world where the work can be performed cheaper elsewhere, places where we are raising people out of poverty on a massive scale." He then tried to boost my ego. "You're sophisticated enough to know there are two sides to the globalization debate."

"You are spinning a carefully calibrated tale of pseudo intellectualism," I countered. "Stories crafted to justify the rape and pillage of America." I didn't really believe this, not all of it. But it sure put him back on the defensive.

And then I sprung. "Mr. CEO, you too are smart enough to understand that pigs get fat while hogs get slaughtered. Don't feed me your contrived arguments concocted by disingenuous think tanks. The fact is, sir, that you are paid four hundred times as much as the average GoldOrb worker." My staff uncovered this nugget in the company's proxy. My voice rose in moral indignation. "For every day you tool around in elite class on your company jet, it takes Joe sixpack more than a year of working his ass off to make the same money. That's the appalling reality on the ground, not your fanciful theories about how you make the world a better place with layoffs."

I was feeling it and decided to launch a trial balloon, watching the CEO for his reaction. "I also strongly suspect that there's a smoking gun somewhere deep in the bowels of GoldOrb. We'll come for everything if we don't get this settled." This wasn't a complete shot in the dark. Tommy Mack, my head of special ops, got wind of an ancient memo written by the plant manager that just might help us. We're trying to land a copy from our mole inside GoldOrb.

I didn't think the little man was a match for me, but his reaction to my attack was surprising. The CEO smiled like this was nothing but good-natured ribbing between pals. And now it was his turn. "I admit it Mr. Mayor. I'm not worth what I'm paid, but I think you will find that I'm effective. And perhaps you are paid more than the good people of Chicago understand." He paused to let that sink in. "As for the company's bowels, be my guest. We'll flood you with millions of pages of rotting documents in a damp, dark corner any time you wish at the taxpayers' expense."

He shrugged and shifted back to working the issue like nothing happened, professional and calm. He was unflappable now and threatening in his own right. The redness on his face had disappeared.

When the meeting concluded, the CEO asked when we should get together again. I hesitated, doing some calculations in my head. "Let's make it several months from now," I said. "Maybe that'll give you time to come back with a real proposal."

He seemed to be processing what I said, then stared at me with an air of superiority. "I'm looking forward to my flight back home, 'elite class,' as you put it." On his way out the door, he winked at me like we were coconspirators. "You know, I think it's good public policy that my perks like the jet show up in the company's proxy, so that everyone can see and judge for themselves if I'm paid too much. I bet you wouldn't mind a little more transparency, Mr. Mayor."

This guy worries me. I'll have Tommy Mack take a closer look under his hood.

CHAPTER VIII - THE CEO

He arrived at the Timberwolves game just in time to witness Chloe Calypso sing the National Anthem. The local diva wore a sparkling cowboy hat atop pink hair, matching jewels piercing her ears, eyebrows, and naval, and a designer dress that resembled a bikini. Cheering fans drowned out the words, emphasizing the disconnect between patriotism and the game. "Beat the Lakers!" a short man wearing a wolf mask screamed over the rockets' red glare. "Kick their asses back to LA!"

Sandra greeted her husband at their courtside seats. From this vantage point, they could see subtle expressions on the players faces and the manufacturer's emblem on the ball. They could also hear the game. Shoes squeaking, shots swished and clanked, players talking trash, screaming, "Foul! Dammit, make the call ref!"

Sandra loved it when the graceful giants leapt over her, trying to save a basketball from jetting out of bounds. But the CEO preferred less tumult. "I can live without sweat dripping on my head and into my drink," he complained, a problem only the rich and famous must endure.

The game was exactly what the CEO needed to improve his sour disposition. On the company plane back from Chicago, he was fuming. Mayor Dumars was a bully, and this was personal. The CEO was convinced that the politician didn't care one iota about protecting the environment. He needed a scapegoat and thought he'd found one in GoldOrb.

The CEO worried that his lieutenants at headquarters were not up to this brand of warfare. They'd play strictly by the rules, worrying endlessly about legalities, subtleties, and niceties at the urging of the general counsel. None of that would matter with this adversary. He needed a different point of view to devise a winning strategy.

The final score was Lakers, 107; Timberwolves, 101. After the game, the CEO and Sandra shook hands with several players, shouting over the crowd noise, "Good game. Next time will be different." Their limousine was waiting outside the VIP exit to whisk them to the General's Club for a nightcap.

Sitting across from her husband at their usual table where the CEO had dined with Jacob, Sandra could see that he was preoccupied. Again, his tired look worried her.

"What happened, Geoffrey? You seem off and I know it's not from the final score."

"The mayor is a flaming prick and I've got no leverage," he replied. "The good news, if you can call it that, is that he wants me to get back to him in several months, not tomorrow."

"Why so slow?"

"He's likely waiting until the next election, which is still a few years off. He'll move slower now and go for the jugular then."

"But he's making you miserable now. For what?"

"He's trying to keep us off balance, probing and working public opinion for a later kill. For now, the ass wipe is having fun toying with us."

Sandra listened carefully as the CEO gave a blow-by-blow account of the mayor's rudeness. She was the silent partner, but deadly. After the CEO finished, her advice was succinct. "Geoffrey, right now, we have squat other than your hunch he's on the take. You can't win if your hands are tied by too many corporate rules of conduct that the mayor ignores. The good news is that with this SOB, there'll be skeletons in his closet, maybe his entire basement. To find them and gain control, you need to be creative."

The CEO listened carefully, full of respect and love for this capable woman, lucky to have her on his side. He placed his hand over hers. "Creativity is more in your bailiwick, Sandra. Out with it. I can tell you've got an idea."

Sandra looked pleased. She had been feeling bored earlier in the day and welcomed the stimulation. "I don't know if you remember her, but back at Harvard, there was this renegade kid I was friends with, Skylar Sharpe. She became a private investigator and made a fortune going after fat cats who were unfaithful to their aging queen honeybees. If Skylar is anything like she was in college, she's the superstar of snoops. Get her on your team."

The CEO cocked his head. "I hope you weren't looking into PIs for any particular reason."

Sandra smirked. "I know you'd be very equitable, dear."

He held her hand tighter. "You're my better half Sandra. You aren't going anywhere except to Xanadu with me. Let's continue the conversation at home, but without talking." Sandra blew a kiss and rose from her chair.

The next morning, the CEO convened his team in the board room. *They're all in their places with bright shiny faces,* he thought. The mood degenerated as he generically debriefed them. "My meeting with the mayor was rocky," he said. "As suspected, the problem is serious and won't go away anytime soon. I want each of you to continue scouring the earth for solutions. Keep me posted with developments."

This, of course, was Plan B, the conventional approach of endless corporate protocols that would likely yield nothing. But the CEO still needed his captains for backup. He would launch Sandra's Plan A, an unorthodox strategy to protect their unconventional lifestyle, the next day in Cambridge.

Skylar's office was in the basement of a martial arts gym a few blocks from their alma mater. Only the best combatants in the Northeast were admitted and the action was furious and violent. Skylar sparred daily with some of the toughest warriors. Her office was spacious and swank, despite its location beneath the gym.

When the CEO entered, she was still wearing workout clothes which accentuated her muscular physique. Her eyes had an unusual yellow tint, and she moved with the stealth of a feline. *Feels like I'm interviewing the Cat Woman to help a Fortune One Hundred company,* he thought. *I Hope Sandra is right about this one.*

Skylar began the conversation by offering the CEO a power shake made of kale, hazelnuts, and organic yogurt from New Zealand, but he declined. While she drank her potion, they relived their days at Harvard. Skylar then inquired about Sandra. "You better be keeping her happy, Geoffrey." The CEO smiled and nodded affirmatively, but silently worried about his wife's state of mind. *Something is missing. Maybe it's middle age, but what to do?*

Skylar finished her power shake and signaled that it was time for business. "Take as much time as you need to lay out the problem, Geoffrey. One warning. I only take cases that intrigue me. So, before you start, know that I might reject you. Nothing personal." The CEO found her behavior audacious. People customarily kowtowed to the chief. His world seemed topsy-turvy. *First Mayor Dumars, now Cat Woman, feel free to throw their weight around.*

Still, he was impressed by Skylar's moxie. He took a calculated risk and conveyed his story, while screams and thumps wafted down to the basement from the boxing rink.

Skylar listened attentively without taking notes. The CEO noticed how quickly she processed information, her yellow eyes moving rapidly from side to side. Her questions were insightful. As for her intangibles, they screamed off the charts.

He wanted Skylar to take the job, unsure what levers to pull to convince her. But when he mentioned that the mayor of Chicago was his foe, her eyes sparkled, and she tilted her head up in fascination. Her body language signaled everything the CEO needed to know. "You'd have one objective," he said. "Dig up dirt on the bastard so I can get him under control." Skylar smiled.

When the CEO finished, she laid out the terms of their engagement. "First, I want assurances you are authorizing me to take any measures I deem necessary. Legal or otherwise."

The CEO agreed without hesitation, remembering how the prima donna mayor made clear that anything goes. He would confront the mayor on his own terms.

Skylar pursed her lips and shrugged as if to signal that her next request was minor. "Second, I want a little skin in the game. No cash, retainer fee or signing bonus. I'll pay all expenses. If I fail, it'll cost you nothing and it's adios amiga. But if I succeed, GoldOrb stock will soar. I want part of the action. My fee is seventy-five thousand stock options that trigger upon the mayor's defeat."

The CEO was flabbergasted as Skylar made clear that her terms were nonnegotiable. But, relying on Sandra's endorsement and his own instincts that he was securing an exceptional talent to fight a dangerous adversary, he told Skylar they had a deal. But first she needed to prove her wares with a small favor. He called it "a delicate situation" as he described the smoking gun memo from the old plant manager that the mayor hinted about. "I want you to wipe out any trace of its existence. Our general counsel is clutching to a copy like it's the Hope Diamond. There's no way I can pry it from him."

Skylar looked pleased. "Ah, a warmup. Just grant me access to your email and the HQ building after hours. Piece of cake."

He arranged for her clearance the next day. That night, an email was waiting for him. "Like I said, piece of cake."

"Your seventy-five thousand stock options have been awarded," the CEO responded. "May they grow in value with your success."

CHAPTER IX - SANDRA

I forgot what it's like to have fun. Our last good time was two years ago at the Timberwolves game.

Since then, the mayor continued his assault. As Geoffrey predicted, he didn't conflagrate to full-scale warfare. It was more like water torture designed to torment us, keep us off balance. But Chicago elections are approaching now, and D-Day is too.

Unfortunately, GoldOrb remains penetrable. There were no changes to the general counsel's dour legal prediction. And, as the CFO put it, "The price tag for cleaning the river won't budge. It is what it is." Worst of all, our secret weapon, Skylar Sharpe, went missing.

We were certain that Skylar's performance would match her swagger. But as time elapsed, she seemed to vanish. She never contacted Geoffrey with a progress report. And when he called, her response was vanilla, uninspiring. "I'm working it, but the sledding is slow," she claimed. "This takes time GG. Do you want results or speed?" It sure didn't sound like the superstar we thought we hired.

My GG, *Mr. get going*, was exasperated. He lost confidence, complaining, "Her Cat Woman act was bravado not substance. I'm glad we didn't pay cash."

I wasn't ready to throw in the towel, not until Skylar admitted defeat. After all, her foe was formidable. And she had a reputation for taking her sweet time, meticulously lining up her ducks in a perfect row before pouncing.

Well, as usual, I'm droning on about GoldOrb and the mayor as if they're our big problem. Actually, I welcome the distraction. I don't know why Geoffrey and I always talk business first, as if work is more important than life itself. Unfortunately, I have far worse news.

My indestructible, iron-willed husband is sick. Of course, Geoffrey ignored the symptoms, thinking determination alone was enough to triumph. "I've never taken a sick day in my life and I'm not about to start," he bragged. "I play hurt."

After months of ignoring body signals, he called me from headquarters with a weak voice I barely recognized. "I think I'm dying." His very trait that propelled him to the top, his fierce determination, was now working against him.

After several misdiagnosis, the doctors concluded that Geoffrey suffered from a rare blood disorder that was fatal a disturbing percentage of the time. "Eleven out of twelve survive," reported the doctor, positively spinning the statistics. Those odds got our attention. "You mean one in twelve don't," Geoffrey clarified in a calm voice while I took notes of the doctor's feedback, hoping to mask how scared I was. The formal name of his malady sounded like a long cuss word in Latin, so we called it the "grim reaper."

As the disease progressed, Geoffrey became increasingly tired. On some days, he couldn't rise from bed without my help. Normal tasks required monumental effort, his heart beating in overdrive. And, at nighttime, he'd fall apart.

We secured an all-star team of doctors. They tried experimental drugs, some with harmful side effects, others that seemed to temporarily stem the tide of the disease. But we had no idea what the future held. I guess we never did, but it took the grim reaper to remind us.

Doctor Margaret Paine, Geoffrey's chief hematologist, was brilliant and compassionate. She looked anxious when she summed up his condition. "GG, the disease may vacate your body in the stealth of the night, just like it arrived, but to be honest, that's unlikely. It's also possible that your drug won't hold, and you slip until we find another. Unfortunately, there's no proven treatment, but we'll do everything possible."

When we got home, Geoffrey joked that his diagnosis sounded like advice from the general counsel. "Years of preparation in medical and law schools are worthless," he complained. "They only teach these vaunted professionals to opine that there are no answers." But he knew that Dr. Paine was the best.

I was sympathetic, understanding how difficult the diagnosis was for an impatient man like my husband, and tried to stay positive. "Listen, Geoffrey, the doctor is a kind woman and renowned authority. And don't forget, your likeliest scenario is recovery. You'd pull the trigger on a business deal every time if the odds were eleven out of twelve."

I was optimistic for his sake, but terrified on the inside. I didn't want to be alone, a widow wandering the hallways of Xanadu without my best friend.

Geoffrey needed my help to weather the storm. Our royal lifestyle was at stake. Here's the thing. I was unsure if I even wanted it anymore. But now wasn't the time for dramatic change. So, I stepped up my game from behind the scenes.

Of course, GG never stopped fighting, not for a minute. I love him for his force of will. There were difficult days when he had no business marching into the GoldOrb frying pan. He remained gifted and effective.

But the grim reaper extracted its toll, rendering him vulnerable and compromised as hell. That's where I came in. I'd go through Geoffrey's emails early in the morning and late at night, responding in his name. On rough days, he'd stay home, and we collaborated. We debated how to handle large customer complaints and complicated offers by suppliers. I even chose which country to plant a new factory in. Tiebreakers went to me as we struggled to keep the corporate behemoth on course.

To my husband's credit, he accepted the help. "Two is better than one, Sandra, especially when it's you and me," he said with both conviction and melancholy. "We need to keep GoldOrb afloat. Employees, shareholders, and customers depend on us." We weren't exactly saints. The two of us depended on *G.O.D.* more than anyone.

Nobody suspected a problem. Geoffrey's physical absences were barely noticeable in these days of virtual communication. And when a face-to-face meeting was required, my resolute husband put on a show, suffocating necktie and all. But afterwards, he'd return home depleted, and I'd step up. Our plan was to limp along until he improved. Not exactly a brilliant strategy, but there was no other choice.

We had a few good stretches. Geoffrey felt near normal for a month after taking an experimental drug. But it caused a severe irregular heartbeat, and he was forced to abandon the medicine. Another time, for no reason at all, he regained strength for weeks. We were on a roller coaster of good days and bad, like the frantic up and down sketching from a cardiogram.

During the respites, Geoffrey itched to board the company jet and visit the rabbi, Mia, and Jacob at Lake Paradise. "They're my real friends, not business colleagues who consider me a means to an end. Listen Sandra, they'll help me get through this."

"There's not a snowball's chance in hell you're going alone," I countered. "Not in your condition."

I'm sure you can guess that Geoffrey's illness provoked intense philosophical discussions about how we were living our lives, where we were headed with our remaining days. There we were, the king and queen of Xanadu, having climbed the Himalayas, only to discover the obvious truth that was there all along. That we were mere flesh and blood, vulnerable and confused despite our stature.

We had chosen a life of materialism. There was no religion to fall back on during this time of fragility. In the past, we took pride in our clearheaded, sober view that upon death, we would simply cease to exist. But when the rubber hits the road and you are forced to stare mortality in the eye, this vision of nothingness did not prove to be comforting. And our wealth couldn't help us. *A lot of good money does when the grim reaper knocks,* I ruminated. *All we can do with it is pay for grand funerals as new occupants move into Xanadu for short stints of sunshine.*

Geoffrey argued that this was another reason to visit Lake Paradise. "The rabbi and Jacob spend day and night thinking about the human condition, about life, about death," he said. "I need to join the conversation because right now, I'm holding on for dear life with nothing to grasp onto."

I mostly hid my gloom. But I told Geoffrey, "When you get better, we need to chart out where we're headed. I want to live more intentionally in the time we have left." I hoped that the grim reaper was our wakeup call, not our last act.

I'm proud to report that we also kept the conversation going on Gabbing Gloria. Again, I acted behind the curtain helping Geoffrey any way that I could. I loved the surreptitious thrill of GG's secret pleasure. Make that our secret pleasure.

When Geoffrey felt up to it, we'd meet in bedroom nine. I wore bracelets that matched his necklace in a show of unity and typed the postings. Geoffrey reviewed them before I hit the submit button. It was exhilarating to watch our opinions jet into the universe, memorializing our very existence.

Our blogging continued to attract a vociferous crowd, especially the episode we called "Privilege from the Perspective of the Lucky Ones." The idea originated from a conversation Geoffrey had with Jacob. In the post, we told the story of an older White man named Jack who felt condemned by his success. The White guy complained:

> *I didn't create the system. I just worked hard, had a little skill, followed the rules, and was rewarded. Why must you diminish my efforts?*

The number of comments was staggering. Some condemned Jack with extreme profanity. Juno the Millennial gave a scathing rebuke:

> *Silence is the greatest crime of all, you jackass. You behaved worse than the schmucks in white hoods. You didn't take a stand, speak up, did you? Just lined your pockets choosing not to notice your privilege.*

A few likened Jack's silence to the passivity that enabled the atrocities in Europe during World War II. "You Nazi bastard," posted Horace Herzl. Others were tamer, accusing him of being "complicit," the label du jour, or snively and out of touch.

But plenty sided with the old White guy. Renaldo from Harlem posted:

> *I'm a Hispanic who struggled to build a small business that makes me proud. Amigo, I congratulate you on your efforts and honesty. People can't expect you to self-destruct. We all do*

*everything we can for our families. Of course, you better have
voted on the side of the angels.*

Racists also emerged to support Jack. Some included links to
supremacist sites that we quickly removed.

As I read on, an interchange between Night Train Lenny and JH
caught my eye:

> Night Train Lenny: *Oh Jack, you poor clueless "victim." Do you
> really think your privileged feelings, your damn ego, matter
> in the face of real suffering? Why can't you people for once
> in your goddamned lives say I'm sorry, accept that you
> benefitted from a rigged system and then shut the hell up!*
> JH: *I'm sorry Night Train. God should be too.*

I nudged Geoffrey. "That's a loaded exchange. What do you make
of it?"

Geoffrey stared at the screen in concentration. "Well, I bet it's from
our very own JH," he finally responded. "Jacob Hart." He quietly read
the exchange a few more times. "Jacob likes to peruse the site. And who
else would bring God into it?"

We put a wager on it, and I dared Geoffrey to call Jacob to find
out. Geoffrey put me on the speaker phone to listen in. Jacob sounded
surprised to hear from us, but soon confessed, "You know this topic
weighs on me."

Geoffrey responded, "But what are you sorry for Jacob? The system
may have been flawed, but you didn't do anything."

"Well, I'm sorry for the state of the world, not for anything I
personally did," Jacob explained. "I'll go to my grave questioning if I
should be sorry for what I didn't do."

Geoffrey's voice filled with exaggerated confidence. "For my two
cents, you sound like Don Quixote tilting at windmills. It was beyond
your power. Not only do you ask impossible questions, my friend, you
hold yourself to unfeasible standards."

I nudged Geoffrey to be nice. "That's what I like about you," he
added.

"We like about you," I corrected.

There was a pause on the line while Jacob digested the feedback. Of course, he couldn't see Geoffrey's face. If he did, he'd know that the CEO's cavalier tone belied his bewildered expression. Geoffrey looked completely unsure of himself, and so was I.

Jacob unexpectedly began chuckling, which caused a cracking sound on the speakerphone. "I might be Don Quixote, but I have a new observation." Now it was his voice filling with bravado. "You're Gabbing Gloria, aren't you Mr. CEO?"

"Busted," I whispered in Geoffrey's ear.

Geoffrey repeated, "You ask impossible questions, my friend."

I added, "That's what we like about you."

Jacob said, "Good night, folks. I look forward to *gabbing* with you again real soon."

After a good laugh, Geoffrey and I talked long into the night, sharing Jacob's uneasiness. We first tried denial, hoping to rationalize the problem away. "Think of Martin Luther King," I said. "'The arc of the moral universe is long, but it bends toward justice.' We've improved. There's more opportunity. We even elected an African American President."

"GoldOrb has gotten better too," Geoffrey responded. "We recruit Black hires where we can, and ties go to them. *G.O.D.* also donates to African American causes."

We fell silent, knowing it wasn't enough. Finally, I admitted, "The problem is that slavery and Jim Crow existed for most of our nation's history and the poison persists."

"You're right," Geoffrey responded. "There's a wealth gap the size of Texas and disparities in education as big as Florida."

I can't say that we felt guilty or "diminished," as Jacob calls it. This wasn't our fault, nor did we see ourselves as racists. We had sacrificed and were proud of our achievements. But we empathized with a people who had suffered a vast unfairness. I wanted to deploy our wealth and power to help tackle this problem but didn't know how, certainly not now with Geoffrey so ill.

While the topic was painful, I think you can see that Gabbing Gloria helped keep our focus where it belonged. On life, even with its flaws, and away from the grim reaper.

I was proud to help run the blog, to air these views, but then I slipped up. During a bad stretch when Geoffrey was sick as a dog, I snuck behind his back and posted my own Gabbing Gloria episode. I convinced myself that I was just being helpful, that Geoffrey needed to rest. But really, I craved my own time in the spotlight without playing second fiddle. And my heart yearned for answers as I trudged on through the storm anonymously trying to hold everything together. My husband was livid.

CHAPTER X - GABBING GLORIA

Post 43: Time For Change?

Greetings my sweets. This is personal, so let's forget about politics, sports, and commerce. Nothing from headline news that makes us hot and bothered. Picture me instead on a leather couch having the chat of a lifetime with Sigmund. Deep breath in. Exhale fully. Here goes.

> *Yours truly is in a bad place! Somebody I love is sick. Not a cold or flu, but the real deal. It's making me reflect. Am I where I should be? Are things still working? Should I take a chance or stay the course? I'm not going to get weepy and blab details about Gabby's trivial story. But I want to know what I should be considering, what I should look for, before leaping. How do I decide if it's time to make a big change to my life?*

You've no idea how much your ideas can help your forever grateful patient.

And don't forget. One of you will take home moolah for being a faithful reader. $1,000!

Till we meet again! I love you!

Gabbing Gloria

Likes: 4300
Dislikes: 1274
Comments: 566

Monster of the Midway: "I use my Ouija board. My dead mama's spirit visits to help me make the tough calls. Try it, Gloria."

Lance: "God will show you the way. Don't torture yourself honey. It's all preordained."

Phil: "Follow your heart baby. That's all you need to do."

Jeanne: "Yep, follow your ticker. And if it's strong enough, go bungee jumping. The rush will open your brainwaves."

Surfing Rebel: "We aren't fucking robots, Lance. How is it all preordained? Why bother using our brains or raising a finger if fate is fixed. Make it happen, Gloria, ACT!"

Tera: "When I get stuck, I write all my pros and cons on a single sheet and weigh them before making my choice. Stay logical."

Loving Lucy: "You know it when you see it. I found my husband in bed with a tramp. It was an easy call to dump his stinking ass."

Tambourine Man: "My body sends signals. My boss gave me an ulcer. I told him where to stick it and quit. Don't wait too long, Gloria."

The Terminator: "Follow your heart. That's where God resides. Jesus lights the path."

Toenail Lady: "Gloria, what's up with you? This is sappy. If I see a post like this again, I'll make my own change."

Rocket Man: "I make changes to my life whenever I get bored. Like I feel right now reading this mushy post. Hey, Toenail Lady, let's hook up."

Spock: "Gloria, go Vulcan. Do a cost benefit analysis. Assign weights. The numbers will make your decision obvious."

Topless: "Listen dearie, consult your astrology charts and let the stars guide your journey. I bet you're Aquarius."

Big Chris: "Go on a long hike in the woods where solitude gives your heart a chance to open up and speak. Good luck. I hope the bum didn't cheat on you."

Temple Mount: "Astrology? Ouija? What's next, tarot cards?

Dear Abby? I say follow God. Ask your clergy for help. My priest is like a prophet."

CHAPTER XI - THE CEO

The CEO was shellshocked. GoldOrb was mired in a political war while the grim reaper pummeled his health. And now his wife betrayed him.

Time For Change? Time For Change? Sandra's burning question that she so thoughtlessly aired with the universe echoed in his mind. He knew that she was unhappy, dissatisfied. Maybe she even wanted a divorce. *I'm not half the man I used to be,* he worried. *I'm holding her back, making her live in this cesspool.*

He tried to break out of his funk, to get going, as only GG can. But he had no energy. He was fatigued and demoralized, a wicked one-two punch that left him flailing in quicksand.

Sandra apologized for going behind his back. "I just got carried away," she said. "I'd never leave you, Geoffrey, are you fricking kidding?"

He looked stubborn and hurt. "There's more. Say it to my face, Sandra."

"Oh, stop it, you already know. I never should've kidnapped Gabbing Gloria. But yes, something's missing. I feel an emptiness and we, as a couple, must confront it."

She admitted that it had become difficult living in his shadow. And she confessed feeling lonely. She recognized how lucky she was to live a life few could dream of, but it was no longer working. "I'm a spoiled brat Geoffrey, but I can't help how I feel. Your illness has focused me on the future like never before. What should we be doing with the rest of our lives, our very finite lives?" She started to weep, furious at herself for being weak, for unloading on her husband while he was sick.

GG felt powerless to make things right. But it could have been worse. While upset, he was also relieved that Sandra wanted to work things out, to create a vision for their joint future. He knew she was right. *I felt a heaviness even before I got sick.* His collision with the grim reaper, with mortality, made change impossible to ignore any longer.

He put his arms around Sandra. "For all these years, we knocked it out of the park with our unconventional lifestyle, so now we need a new game plan. I don't know if that means tinkering or blowing it all to smithereens."

But his nature was to fight, not concede and slither away in the stealth of night. "With the grim reaper and Mayor attacking, I've got no energy to spare," he said in a pleading voice. "Can you hold on just a little longer?"

Sandra looked dejected. "We're trapped. I don't know why we needed to wait for a sledgehammer as our wakeup call."

"You're being too hard on us. We aren't the first people to experience an eye-opening emergency. Let's deal with the manure and regain control, then turn to new beginnings."

Sandra reluctantly agreed but looked defeated. The crisis had taken its toll for too long. And, while she didn't like to go there, she silently worried that it might never pass. *One in twelve. Oh my God, one in twelve.*

They visited Lake Paradise the next time the CEO's symptoms eased. During the daytime, Sandra ventured out with Mia while the CEO joined the rabbi and Jacob. Their experiences could not have been more different.

Mia made sure that the ladies had fun. They went antiquing, picked wild blueberries, and rode inner tubes down a winding river, munching on fresh pastries from a local bakery as they lazily floated along. Sandra was grateful for the break, knowing that her husband was in good hands with the rabbi and Jacob. And she became better friends with Mia, admiring her positivity and sparkling personality.

During a rare moment, the women turned serious. Sandra complimented Mia on her amazing transition from rebbetzin to innkeeper. She asked the question that had been plaguing her. "How did you know it was time to make the leap from religion to hospitality? You two are my role models." As she waited for Mia to answer, her anxiety grew. *Will Geoffrey and I have what it takes when our time comes? If our time comes.*

Mia laughed, agreeing that her journey wasn't the ordinary glide path for clergy. She then fell quiet, reflecting on the gruesome deaths of the rabbi's parents that he kept secret for twelve years, their flight to the groundskeeper's house in the middle of a cemetery, and their leap of faith buying the Paradise Inn from the eccentric old innkeeper. All this while their daughter Hannah remained lost.

She teared up. "I'm afraid the rabbi and I aren't exactly role models. The real story is that we hung on far too long to something that no longer worked, ignoring all warning signals. We then acted out of desperation when calamity struck. Fortunately, Aaron and I had enough love to weather the storm. Mix that with barrels of dumb luck and that's how we landed on our feet."

Mia shrugged as if to emphasize the randomness of it all and softly cried. She then inhaled deeply and forced a smile, her dimples appearing like sunrays through the storm clouds. "So, let's celebrate love and good fortune, that's what I say." It was time for paddle boating on a beautiful inlet that only the locals knew of.

Mia had no idea how important her story of love and luck was to Sandra. The whole conversation took ten minutes, but Sandra would replay it time and again when she was being too hard on herself. She thanked Mia for her honesty and sang out, "Party on!"

The men, of course, focused on deliberating, not celebrating. The CEO, Jacob and Rabbi conversed endlessly over the meaning of life, of death, first over hot cups of coffee and then moving on later in the day to cold refreshing beer.

The CEO was a novice, playing catchup to masters in the arena of the impenetrable. Given his confrontation with the grim reaper, he was an eager student. He learned from their wisdom and silently applied it to his personal dilemmas. Their conversations yielded no ultimate answers. But he found their theories provocative and relevant. *I feel less lonely somehow, more in tune to life. Maybe not from their deep ponderings, but just being together.*

The CEO felt healthy enough for an easy walk on a trail boasting world class scenery. The three men ambled along until they reached an overlook where they could gaze out into infinity. In the distance, there was a rainstorm. The dark and potent clouds seemed to touch the ground. They were bordered by a breathtaking rainbow that extended in a perfect arch from one end of the horizon to the other. On the side of the colorful border, closer to the men, was sunlight and blue sky.

The CEO sensed that his companions were spiritually moved by nature's spectacle. In the case of the rabbi, it was palpable. "Out here in the open air, the snow-covered peaks, the sounds, the wildlife, I'm certain of a benevolent God. Just look at the colors. This is our gift. To be part of His perfection." *My friend the rabbi, turned innkeeper, is still, well … the rabbi,* thought the CEO.

Jacob also seemed inspired, although his praise was measured. "Gentlemen, it's conceivable that this paradise was not an accident. If so, I think I can find my way to God." He looked out at the dark storm far away and the bright landscape nearby, separated by the colorful arch. "I just can't figure out why tempest and tranquility always seem to mingle." He blinked rapidly a few times, but the CEO ignored the tick. Jacob seemed fine, just anxious, and introspective, as usual.

Observing his friends, the CEO felt a gaping hole. Yes, Lake Paradise was indeed beautiful and the rainbow breathtaking. But he couldn't raise that to a higher level. He yearned to be uplifted by spirituality, to feel in his heart what the rabbi experienced and Jacob was wrestling toward.

But to the CEO, towering mountains were to be climbed and conquered and volatile weather signaled price changes in commodities. Nature was to be mined and exploited to create products and lift the stock price. The fittest in his capitalistic order were destined to profit from Mother Earth.

In nature, the CEO feared that something was fundamentally wrong with his nature, that he suffered a disorder even worse than the grim reaper. Gazing at the beauty, he admitted to his friends, "I wish I could feel God here like you two are getting at. My lot in life is to rumble on in the dark as a myth buster, a cynical businessman, and nothing more. I don't see what you see, my soul isn't moved. I don't even know if I have a soul."

Jacob looked like he understood the CEO's problem. "Geoffrey, you can't just flip it on and off. It takes hard work. Even then, you only get so far." He blinked rapidly.

The rabbi said, "You are who you are. Please accept that, Geoffrey. You feel other things we can only dream of."

The CEO broke down for the first time in his life. There were no tears, his voice was firm. But his friends could see that he was tormented. "I always enjoyed the thrill of the hunt, winning and grabbing the spoils. I smugly convinced myself that my triumph was masterfully designed to also help society. Win, win. Everybody should be happy with the invisible hand, nobody harmed, right?" He lowered his head, wondering if the rabbi and Jacob were even following his economic dogma, whether they wished to hear him prattle on about rising tides lifting boats. *I can barely stand listening to myself speak,* he thought. *How can they?*

But when he looked up, he saw kindhearted expressions on his friends' faces. They were riveted, not because of any business logic, but because they cared about him. This gave him the strength to continue. "Well, thirty years in, I want what's hiding at the top of the pyramid, not to be smothered by the treasures buried within. Sandra says something is missing and she's right. Maybe … what's missing … is my soul."

The CEO looked embarrassed. He was a strong leader who eschewed showing emotion and vulnerability. He felt inferior and weak. But his friends didn't seem to share that view.

The rabbi said, "We all feel as you do at some point. I ruthlessly questioned my past, Geoffrey. Surely, you know that." Jacob silently nodded his strong concurrence.

No further words were spoken. But as they walked the final leg of the trail, majesty ahead of them, grandeur behind, each friend extended an arm around the CEO. If only for a moment, humanity was perfected in paradise. The CEO felt a radiance stirring from a deep and mysterious place.

CHAPTER XII – THE PRIVATE INVESTIGATOR

The CEO had to be right. There was something crooked about Mayor Dumars. But what?

His defenses were elite, far too elaborate for a normal politician trying to hide the usual graft. Most of these bags of wind are sloppy and hire retired cops, friends on the take and government hacks for protection. Not the mayor of Chicago. He convened an arsenal of supervillains. With a payroll like that, he clearly was up to no good.

The mayor's leader of "special ops," whatever that meant, was Tommy Mack, an ex-Navy Seal who brought his talents to the evil empire. Tommy was smart and cruel. Worse yet, the goon was meticulous.

Insulated by this merry band of thieves, I knew that I had a long road ahead to deliver the mayor's head on a platter. The CEO wasn't happy. But I assured him, "GG, in the end, only results matter." CEOs love speaking truisms like that, but they hate hearing them.

I admit that my feedback was annoying. I even irritated myself. I decided it was better to shut up, take my sweet time, and make the CEO smile later.

But the case dragged on far longer than even I expected. I ran down a million leads about the mayor. I won't bore you with the details. Just know, I left no stone unturned. Not for a crack at that bastard and seventy-five thousand stock options. Still, I made no progress.

Finally, out of ideas, my attention turned to Tommy Mack. I thought maybe, just maybe, he expended so much energy protecting the mayor that he let his personal defenses down. Like the brilliant doctor who regularly sneaks Oreos dipped in gelato, or the ace policeman whose house is ransacked because he didn't lock the front door on the way to the Memorial Day picnic. If I could find dirt on Tommy, it might implicate the mayor. Easier said than done. The thug wasn't slurping sugar or frolicking on holidays.

I couldn't wear sunglasses and tail Tommy like in the movies. He would've spotted me in seconds. And I sure wasn't going to sleep with the numbskull. But I still began feeling intimate with him. I came to know everything about the crook. Where he went to grammar school, his friends, second cousins, godparents, barber, dentist, hobbies, and church seats. It turns out he was a religious man, belting out prayers on Sunday mornings with the best of them.

The picture that emerged from my snooping was bizarre. Tommy was the type of guy who attended holy mass in the morning, then donned a fedora to trot in circles with his groomed poodle at the afternoon dog show. In between, he was happy to bludgeon a poor schmo with his hammer to extract information. But I couldn't connect him to the mayor. I was getting frustrated. Make that nauseated.

Looking back, I should have known sooner that there was a better way. In today's world, you can't seal the deal without hacking a computer. I got in touch with Jimmy McVee to help.

I met Jimmy when I volunteered to interview candidates for admission to Harvard. He came from a small farming community in Nebraska with perfect SAT scores. Harvard coveted his demographic to add to its exotic collection.

At the interview, Jimmy slouched on the sofa without making eye contact. I finally asked what he did for fun, and he responded "VV," making the victory sign with each hand. When he saw the confused look on my face, he explained, "I mean virtual voyeurism. Hacking is epic!" The glow in his eyes told me it wouldn't be a passing fancy. I decided to keep in touch with the kid. He had potential.

Jimmy was bored out of his mind at college. What did he need with a liberal arts education when virtual sirens beckoned? He dropped out and started a computer security firm near my gym, bagging half a billion dollars when it went public. He was a twenty something cash-out who never needed to work again. "I'm the embodiment of capitalism," he bragged. "Epic!" I wondered what the CEO would think.

Since Jimmy's very early retirement, he has gone by a new name: the "Sunshine Kid." He works a few cases a year for fun, only choosing what interests him. Kind of like me. Most of the time, he hangs out with a frisbee and suntan lotion at his beautiful home off the beach in Kawaii.

The Sunshine Kid's ears rose to attention when he heard that my prey was Chicago's mayor. Frankly, he also likes working with little ole me. Unlike Tommy Mack, I find him adorable and visit him in the tropics when I get the itch.

Tommy's computer defenses were top notch. Even the Sunshine Kid couldn't break into his encrypted documents. But what we could do was peer over Tommy's shoulder, sharing his screen whenever he went online.

The Sunshine Kid set me up so that each night, from the comfort of my home in Cambridge, I could sit with my l-Pad and watch Tommy's screen along with him as he webbed it up. Wherever Tommy went on his computer, I was sure to follow with claws ready to rip.

I detected a pattern. On the last day of each month, Tommy prepared a spreadsheet that he labelled "Manna." As he updated it, I watched over his shoulder from my easy chair halfway across the country.

Tommy used Manna to record his investments to the last penny. Like I said, he was meticulous. He was also loaded, squirrelling it away to the tune of fifteen million dollars. Tommy had stocks and bonds all over the place. But what caught my eye was an entry for "RR real estate," totaling well over two and a half million dollars. What the hell was "RR?"

Looking closer, I saw six addresses under RR real estate, with dollar amounts assigned to each:

55 Wilson Avenue	*$530K*
99 Hampton Street	*$620K*
89 Ridgeland Lane	*$475K*
41 Piccolo Drive	*$425K*
9 Harper Blvd.	*$320K*
21 Spangler Street	*$240K*

I racked my brains, spying on Tommy each month as he recalculated his loot.

Finally, it was New Year's Eve. I felt pitiful, such a loser. There I sat in my living room having a virtual date with a lowlife in Chicago who didn't even know me.

I wondered if Tommy would stick to his practice and update Manna on the last day of the month instead of hitting the town to celebrate like normal people do. Shortly before midnight, I got my answer. My screen sprang alive with pulsating electricity, like the ball dropping in Times Square. As I peered over his shoulder, Tommy ushered in the new year by adding another investment under "RR real estate:"

58 Marshall Dr. $280K ($560K in a year)

I puzzled over this new development into the wee hours of the morning. Finally, I grabbed a chilled bottle of Dom Perignon from the fridge, popped the cork, and whispered, "Happy New Year, you asshole."

CHAPTER XIII – THE CEO AND SANDRA

During their flight back home, the CEO and Sandra rehashed their visit, congratulating themselves on their good fortune to have the rabbi, Mia, and Jacob as close friends. The CEO snuggled close to his wife. "I'm even luckier to have you." Sandra responded with a silly look, batting her big brown eyes. "You romantic fool." But she understood her husband's sincerity and reciprocated with heartfelt emotion. "You're the love of my life, Geoffrey. We need to heal you. Then we fly to the moon." For the remainder of the flight, they held hands. Only on the company jet can passengers enjoy such intimacy high in the sky.

Thirty thousand feet above the Great Plains, the CEO told Sandra what she longed to hear. "Life's too short. We can't let the grim reaper or mayor stand in our way of change any longer. Let's grab control, right now." Sandra hugged him.

Back at Xanadu, Sandra threw herself with abandon into the task of recreating their lives. She dug up her old Harvard philosophy books stashed in the basement that hadn't seen daylight for thirty years. She once again pondered the teachings of Aristotle, Sophocles, Confucius, Kant and even Freud. "These voices from the past offer clues," she told Geoffrey. "Might as well consult the best minds of all time to forge our future."

The scholars raised eternal quagmires for her to untangle. Was she reacting to a fear of dying, or perhaps of living? Was it her duty to pursue justice for the masses, or to keep focusing on personal gratification? Was a repressed trauma from childhood emerging from her subconscious, creating her feeling of instability?

Surrounded by her books, she turned to her husband. "What does it all mean? What? Just tell me!"

"You sound like the rabbi and Jacob."

Sandra ignored him and continued researching. She slowed down when she got to Abraham Maslow, one of her favorites in college. Placing Maslow's book on her lap, she said, "We need to be self-actualizing, that's what's missing. If you haven't noticed, our material needs have been met. It's time to live a life of purpose at the apex." Her face held a mixture of excitement and confusion. "Fulfillment will be our reward. How great is that, Geoffrey?"

"I'm relieved. This isn't about sexual hang ups, or dear mommy, after all."

She still didn't crack a smile. "Look man, don't derail my progress."

"I'm just baffled by the heavy jargon."

The CEO silently weighed Sandra's thoughts about fulfillment. He recalled that radiant feeling when Jacob and the rabbi put their arms around him during the final leg of their walk. *I wouldn't mind more of that sensation, whatever it was.*

"Yes, fulfillment should be our priority," he said. "Let's self-actualize."

"Exactly!"

"So, what should we do?"

"I don't know."

While Sandra studied wisdom from the past, the CEO turned to modern teachings when he had enough energy. He read self-help books topping the best seller lists that people devoured and soon forgot. The CEO discovered that they needed to empower themselves. To lean in. To let go. To trust God. To follow their guts. To find their voices. To listen. To be present. Meditate. Contemplate. Modulate. Feng shui. Live for joy. None provided a eureka moment.

In the midst of their journey, the grim reaper rebounded with disdain for all philosophies, forcing the CEO to focus solely on essential GoldOrb tasks. Sandra responded by intensifying her efforts. She even revisited her rogue post on Gabbing Gloria, reading the latest comments to "Time For Change?" There were scores of new entries containing pearls of down-home wisdom. The predominant view remained, "Follow your heart." Ringo from Richmond summed it up best:

Move with the rhythm of your heart. Dance to the beat.

She remained immobilized. At an abstract level, these perspectives made perfect sense. But they still didn't help her create a concrete plan of action that responded to the uniqueness of her own life. "I obviously want to follow my heart, who can argue with that?" she complained to Geoffrey. "But it's an organ, not a navigation system. It doesn't pump out explicit directions."

Sandra was inundated with ideas and out of them at the same time. She began suffering from nightmares where she roamed from room to room at Xanadu. Each time she stopped she heard the soft voice of a small girl chanting what sounded like a nursery rhyme from the room next door. She couldn't make out the words but knew that the child needed her.

She pursued the girl through the vast halls of the mansion into countless rooms, feeling responsibility, even love, for the defenseless wanderer. Finally, the chants led her down a long stairway to the basement. The lights flickered and then went out. Standing in complete darkness, the chanting stopped. Sandra felt a sense of dread that she had failed the child.

A white glow began to seep into the basement. It flowed from a crack under a door leading further down to a subterranean level. *I didn't even know there was another room in this house,* Sandra thought. *Where does it lead?* The girl's chanting resumed, this time from behind the subterranean door. It grew louder, and the voice turned deeper. In place of the wandering child was a vague, sinister presence. Sandra stood paralyzed as the subterranean door crept open.

Petrified, Sandra forced herself awake to avoid the awful moment of truth. She never glimpsed the being on the other side. Instead, she spent the rest of the night dissecting the nightmare. The child's chants permeated her thoughts. *My subconscious is torturing me. I made a fatal mistake not having children and emptiness is my punishment.* In the dark of the night, Freud, not Maslow, controlled the conversation.

The next morning, the CEO saw the dark shadows beneath his wife's eyes. "It was just a dream, Sandra. We all have them." He kept his guilt to himself wondering, *Did we make a pact with the devil? Am I to blame for my ambition?*

Sandra called Mia, seeking a boost from her limitless reservoir of positivity. She told Mia about the dream and her fateful decision to forego having children. "I'm childless and hopeless. I deserve this for not devoting my life to raising another human being."

There was a heavy silence on the line. Finally, Mia spoke, but she sounded defeated. "I understand, Sandra, oh I do. Imagine having a daughter and then losing her." The phone went quiet again. Mia was crying.

Sandra was disgusted with herself. She knew that Mia's wound over Hannah was forever raw. *Yet I selfishly reopened the laceration, blinded by my own problems.*

In a shaky voice, she said, "Mia, I'm so sorry. I'm a self-centered prima donna. It's just that you're so upbeat that sometimes I forget the pain you've endured."

Mia's voice remained barely audible. "No worries, Sandra. Let's talk later."

Sandra was torched with regret. *I'm self-destructing and hurting my friends and husband in the process.*

Earth didn't stop rotating during Sandra's agonizing soul-search. The CEO improved but relapsed yet again. Another month, a new experimental drug. And Sandra continued to help him each step of the way despite her troubles. In her darker moments, she wondered why she was wasting time planning the future. *It's futile. There is no future. I'm doomed to loneliness.*

And then came the breakthrough. Not philosophically, but physically. An experimental drug took hold and the CEO's strength returned. After an onslaught of pricks, prods and scans, Doctor Paine announced the verdict with two short sentences that changed the world. "Your results are phenomenal, GG. You're cured!" Doctor Paine wiped tears from her eyes as she watched Sandra and the CEO embrace, then call her over for a group hug.

Before leaving, the CEO asked, "What about recurrence?"

"Unlikely," replied the doctor. "But we'll be monitoring you. If it returns, it'll be a long time from now and we'll fight again with new treatments."

When they returned to Xanadu, Geoffrey looked concerned about relapse, but Sandra took his hand. "We all live under the cloud of uncertainty, so you're not so different. Let's make the best of this second chance. Let's get going!" Her eyes danced with unbridled joy. The CEO didn't think he ever loved her more.

The CEO's recovery was in the nick of time. He would require all the vitality he could muster. Chicago's elections were fast approaching and GoldOrb was on the brink of a full-scale war.

CHAPTER XIV - THE PRIVATE INVESTIGATOR

I spent a deplorable New Year's Eve hanging out online with Tommy Mack the slimeball. But I was ecstatic. After watching the goon add a new property to his precious Manna, the clock struck twelve and I set to work hatching my plan.

I flew to Chicago two days later in the freezing cold and hopped a taxi to the Registrar of Deeds. And there it was. The official record of Tommy's purchase of 58 Marshall Drive for $280,000. Bingo. This squared with his spreadsheet. But Tommy seemed to think the price would double. Why was that?

I decided to dig deeper and pull the deeds for his other properties. In each case, the purchase price from the official records was a mere fraction of the current value listed on Manna. For God's sake, he bought his first property at 55 Wilson Ave. for only $75,000, but it was now booked at $530,000 on Manna. The guy was making out just like the bandit I knew he was.

I was officially hot on his trail. I drove to each of Tommy's properties to see them with my own eyes. Maybe this would trigger a revelation. Except for the newest entry, the locations seemed normal. Nice neighborhoods, each gentrified with all the amenities. But 58 Marshall Drive was in a sketchy part of town. A few blocks away, I noticed a large sign which announced, "Site For New Train Station."

My mind shifted to "RR real estate" again, Tommy's mysterious entry on Manna. "RR" had to mean something important. But what? It wasn't Ronald Reagan or Robert Redford. Too bad.

That night, holed up in my downtown hotel room with deep-dish pizza, I studied a detailed map of the city. I circled the locations of Tommy's other properties and, lo and behold, just like 58 Marshall Drive, each was located at the end of a train line. I researched when he made the purchases and when the new stations were built. The dates lined up across the board. Tommy was buying properties shortly before new tracks were constructed. And then it hit me. "RR" stood for Railroad. He was calling his booty "Railroad real estate." YES!

I was on track now, make it the green line, barreling down on these hoodlums. If the CEO's goal was to nail Tommy Mack alone, my work would have been finished. But we needed to connect what Tommy was doing to the mayor.

I took a break from the paperwork and grabbed my laptop for some raunchy entertainment, courtesy of the Sunshine Kid. Peering over Tommy's virtual shoulder, he grabbed my attention with something new. He was gathering information about the CEO from any site he could find. Hours later, he moved to a blog called "Gabbing Gloria" and spent the remainder of the night with that provocateur. I didn't mind the strange diversion. Gabbing Gloria was a stitch. But what the hell was Tommy up to?

With so much work ahead, I filed the mystery away for another day. I needed to do a complete inventory of the city, looking back twenty years for patterns. My goal was to find all track extensions coupled with nearby real estate purchases. I wanted to know if anyone else had a habit of buying property just at the right moment like Tommy Mack.

After painstaking research and too many pizzas to count, three names popped up time and again. They were playing the same rigged game as Tommy. If any of these profiteers could also be linked to Mayor Dumars, we'd have the evidence we needed to pounce.

I couldn't connect the dots for two of the suspects. They had nothing to do with Chicago's head thief, no connection whatsoever. But I hit the jackpot on the third guy. He was Samuel Lerner, an Ivy League history professor of all things. The guy even wrote a book. I quickly discovered that he and the mayor were old pals from graduate school in Chicago. And, like Tommy, he made a killing buying real estate ahead of track extensions. Now, two of the mayor's closest allies were implicated. It was finally time to update the CEO.

We met at the CEO's home turf, not my office beneath the gym. It looked like the Taj Mahal. The CEO seemed different, frazzled at the edges, beat up. But he still was formidable. Sandra also joined, looking like her old self from our college days but distracted.

The CEO seemed upset. He was obviously mad at me for taking too long, but told me something else was rattling him. "The mayor is threatening me with going public about a blog site. I have no idea how the swine discovered it."

I took a shot in the dark. "Does the site happen to be Gabbing Gloria?"

He and Sandra looked like a tornado had just struck. "Lucky guess," I said.

They were all ears as I spun out my story, two of the best listeners I ever met. Let me tell you, the CEO and Sandra were riveted by my long, complicated tale of infiltration and intrigue.

By the time I finished, they looked rejuvenated. "There are cavities that still need filling," I said. "But the bottom line is that two of the mayor's closest allies used inside information from Chicago to buy properties. Connect the dots folks. He's snared."

The CEO plotted next steps like a five-star general in the war room. "We need to leak this to the Chicago press," he directed. "Let them run with it and find more dirty links to the mayor before our hands get too muddy. The mayor won't believe what hit him, nor will he ever know that it came special delivery from G.O.D."

If there's one thing to understand about guys like the CEO, it's that they have connections scattered to the four corners of the Earth. He directed me to reach out to Connor Duffin, III, Chief Editor at the Chicago Star. "We served on a board together," he said. Sandra added, "He's a pit bull. Tell him everything but be sure he knows it's off the record." Both wanted me to jump on this yesterday.

The CEO asked me to repeat the names of the mayor's two allies. Tommy Mack meant nothing to him. But when I mentioned the professor, his brow furrowed with concentration. "Samuel Lerner ...

Sam Lerner... hmm." He looked like he was onto something, but then lost the thread. "Doesn't ring a bell."

Before we concluded, Sandra had a passing thought. She asked for the identities of the two other matches who purchased Chicago property the same way Tommy Mack and the professor did. I couldn't remember their names, but assured her, "They have no connection to the mayor. These two won't make our case." The CEO shrugged. "No rush. We just want the info for the sake of completeness. But get moving with Editor Duffin. We're in crisis mode."

I forgot about the other two names until weeks later, when I was scrolling through Gabbing Gloria, just for the hell of it. The site captivated me. I alternated between visions of the capitalist CEO and gossiping Gloria time and again, always with the same fractured thought pattern. *Crazy, insane, nutso, true.* When I surfed to a post about "Cultural Wreckage," I noticed that a viewer named "Jacob" commented and my mind flashed back to their request. That was the name of one of the other Chicago investors. No sweat that I dropped this ball. They said I could take my time and Jacob didn't matter anyways.

But I sure didn't drag my feet about calling Editor Duffin. He saluted and opened his schedule wide for me when I name dropped the CEO and hinted that the mayor was on the hook. There was no love lost between Editor Duffin and Mayor Dumars. The Star relentlessly reported on the city's pension deficit, housing inequities, and cronyism in doling out contracts. The mayor dismissed all of it as fake news, which infuriated the editor.

Editor Duffin told me, "Come right away." The call ended without a goodbye, although I could hear him excitedly issuing directions to his underlings as I hung up the phone.

We met at the Chicago Star building the next morning. My first words were, "This is off the record."

As I conveyed the sordid affair, I could almost hear Editor Duffin's heart palpitating. The Chicago Star was officially on the case, ready to deploy its vast arsenal. They'd stop at nothing. The kill was at hand.

Editor Duffin brought in his ace reporter as a second set of ears, arms, and legs. She was sharp and eager. They both had a million questions. Once they pumped me dry, he turned to the kid. "Get on the calendar to meet with the mayor pronto. Tell him you want to talk about the pension quagmire, that you understand where he's coming from. Then ambush him with ... let's call it ... 'Traingate.' See how he reacts. He might slip up. It's time to knock that lowlife off his throne."

The reporter wrote furiously on her notepad as Editor Duffin continued to rev his engine. "Get the team to scrutinize Tommy Mack and that professor," he ordered. "And uncover every connection that exists between them and the mayor, as well as the mayor and the rail division."

The reporter smiled with excitement. If she played her cards right, Train-Gate could be her Pulitzer.

CHAPTER XV - THE CEO

The CEO was euphoric over his recovery. His mood ascended to rapture when Skylar Sharpe reported in. "GG's back in the saddle," he proclaimed to Sandra. "I'm riding high, my boots in the stirrups."

Sandra glanced at him sideways like he was ten years old. "You aren't mounting a horse dear." But she too brimmed with enthusiasm. "The tide has turned, Geoffrey. I feel it. Let's get going on our new lives."

Adding to the merriment was their upcoming trip to Colorado to celebrate the rabbi and Mia's seventh anniversary running the Paradise Inn. After a long cold winter, everything was perfect.

A few hours before their flight, the CEO received two emails from Skylar, one right after the other. The first was labelled "Chicago News!" It transmitted the very same article from the Chicago Star that had sent Walter into a tailspin and Jacob into dreamworld. The clip reported that the mayor was accused of real estate fraud. As the CEO read on, he learned that the investigative reporter was missing. He was thrilled with the public allegations against the mayor but felt an uneasy responsibility for the reporter's fate.

The CEO clicked on Skylar's second email, which she labelled, "Two Other Matches:"

> *Dear GG.*
>
> *Sorry for the delay. I was so wrapped up with dealing with Editor Duffin and nailing Mayor Dumars to the cross that I let this slip.*
>
> *Anyways, the others who bought Chicago property with suspicious timing are Jacob Hart and Walter Hart, a father and son. Again, they were not*

connected to the mayor. But I expect the police will investigate them.

It has been a pleasure doing business and my best to Sandra.

Till we meet again ...

Skylar Sharpe, PI

In the few moments it took to digest the email, the CEO's bliss nosedived to nuclear panic. His thoughts were scattered. *How many father and son combos can there be with the same names as my Jacob and Walter? No way, not a chance.... But wait ... wasn't the mayor in cahoots with a damn professor? No ... oh no, NO!... Manifest Misery was on the mayor's shelf. OH SHIT! That idiot author ... Jacob's friend. OH MY GOD!"*

The CEO tried to convince himself that this was a scary coincidence, a strange misunderstanding. In sheer desperation, he prayed without believing in who he was praying to.

Still in denial, he called his private investigator to learn where Jacob Hart lived. Skylar quickly responded, "Lake Paradise, out in the Colorado boonies."

He smashed his fist against his desk. *What have I done?!*

The CEO knew that Jacob and Walter were innocent. Jacob was a virtuous man, end of story. He took pride in doing things the right way, no matter the level of difficulty. He was a seeker of truth, not a criminal. And Walter was sure to be guiltless too, simply investing alongside his father.

The CEO also understood that the media frenzy would burn Jacob beyond recognition. Everything he stood for would be attacked in public. His son's involvement worsened the situation to the breaking point for this introspective, anxious man.

He needed to reach Jacob fast. *I'll calm him down, assure him he'll have the best legal and PR teams in his corner. I'll spare no expense.* He phoned Jacob but was placed in voicemail. "Press four if your message is urgent, star for normal delivery." Jacob, always available in a nanosecond, was nowhere to be found. No options remained but to call the rabbi.

The Rabbi answered on the first ring from the reflection pool. He was readying the Paradise Inn for that night's anniversary celebration and excited to hear from his friend.

The CEO's voice was calm but grave. "Sit down, Aaron."

PART V

The Circle

"Some of you say, 'Joy is greater than sorrow,' and others say, 'Nay, sorrow is the greater.' But I say unto you, they are inseparable."

—Kahlil Gibran

CHAPTER 1 - JACOB AND THE PROFESSOR

The professor's mind raced. How much time did he have before the police discovered his self-incriminatory email to the mayor? Had Jacob also heard the Chicago news? That would explain the funk of the century happening in the bedroom.

When Jacob emerged hours later, his eyes twitching furiously and his face conspicuously contorted into a forced smile, the professor had his answer. *He knows.*

Jacob wanted to talk about the meaning of life, of death. This led to the strangest, most disjointed conversation of their long friendship. Nothing the professor said mattered as Jacob paced the living room. It was as if he was speaking to himself, and the professor was a mere fly on the wall witnessing a fractured soliloquy.

The topics were the same as always. But the vibes were deadly negative, Jacob's voice cutting like a knife as the professor tried to placate him.

"God, God, God," Jacob repeated. "Paradise is proof."

"Maybe Jacob. Just look at this place. You're living the dream. You deserve it."

"NO! It doesn't work like that. NO!"

"Okay, calm down man."

"I just flitter, flutter, ricochet, and collide. Serendipitous reward and random punishment, that's our lot in paradise. My fucking lot."

"Listen, you've been rewarded tenfold living here."

"My country... my career... *this... me!* Hubris. I butted to the front of the line with the worst imaginable privilege. Diminished.... Shrunk to nothing.... I'm a mosquito.... Lizzy, Lizzy."

The professor took a deep breath and told Jacob to sit down as if he was starting class. "Look Jacob. There's an elephant in the room. I need to tell you something and it's not good. My friend, the mayor of Chicago, was accused of a serious crime and it might involve our investments. I have no idea what it's all about."

"Walter told me. Oh God, my son."

"He'll be fine. We all will."

Jacob peered at the professor from a faraway place. But he began to sound more sober. "All my life, I chose the straight and narrow. Sacrificed for tomorrow without shortcuts. Paid the price. Now what?"

The professor calmly responded, "I get it, but you've got to have faith. We're both innocent. We didn't know."

"Faith," repeated Jacob with a look of scorn. "Faith in what?"

"The system, our laws. I trusted Mayor Dumars. He's my second oldest friend. The press is just in a feeding frenzy to bring him down. Things will work themselves out in court, you'll see."

"Trusted?"

"I mean trust."

Jacob stared at the professor for a long time while making an unreadable calculation. When he spoke again, the edge in his voice was tempered. "Okay, you're right. Like you say, I'm innocent. So is Walter. I need to get a grip."

The professor struck his Thinker pose. "Right. They're after the mayor for political reasons, not us small fries. And even if they come looking for us some day, so what? The police or a smart judge will figure out we've got nothing to hide."

Jacob nodded in agreement. "Okay, okay. I'm not going to let this ruin tonight or tomorrow's party at the Paradise Inn. We'll cool it, grab dinner, and go out on the lake as planned."

The men fell silent. Each considered the long years of their unlikely relationship, bound together by a chemistry and gravitational pull from childhood. The professor looked at Jacob as if he had a critical point to make. "We've been at this a very long-time buddy."

Jacob nodded. *Too long,* he thought.

The sun set exactly on schedule as it has done since the beginning of time, and the North Star took its rightful place in the evening sky. A few hours later, the men walked to the shore and untied Jacob's canoe. The crisp air caressed them while the sound of crickets echoed encouragement from all directions. They were ready to launch into Lake Paradise under that full moon that Jacob had beamed about earlier in the week.

The view improved with each stroke as Jacob steered them away from the shore, gliding over the calm, black water. While they rowed, Jacob and the professor admired the shadowed outlines of the mountains with their distinct formations. The moon lit the panorama to shaded perfection while stars from unfathomable distances twinkled gently, camouflaging their enormous force and breadth. The night sky was alive, in everlasting unity, despite the chaos below.

The lifetime friends stroked in unison, each lost in thought. When they reached the middle of Lake Paradise, Jacob suggested a breather. It was as if the tumult of the day had vanished. "Look in all directions," he said. "We are part of an infinite grand design. This place proves everything if only we're willing to accept our role."

The professor was happy that Jacob seemed to have regained traction. "This stillness would be ideal for a few moments of meditation," he said. "Have you ever tried it out here?"

"Go for it," Jacob encouraged.

"It would be amazing to be, just be, in this place. I could use a break from rowing."

"We should both appreciate this in our own way. You're on vacation. I'll sit back and take it all in, feel it, while you do your thing."

Jacob had to hand it to the professor and the power of meditation. Even after all the angst from the day, the man was able to attain peace within moments. *How does he flip the switch like that?*

He let the professor "just be" as the academic slipped into a deep state of contemplation, gazing within, centered on his core, unaware of anything but his breath. Just when his inward focus seemed unshakable, Jacob tapped him softly on the shoulder and whispered in a voice that was barely audible, if not for the venom. "Pay the price!"

The professor turned around to find Jacob towering over him. Before he could react, Jacob viciously kicked him in the face, causing the craft to tip wildly from side to side. The professor's face was frozen in astonishment as he lost consciousness and slipped from the boat into the dark cool water.

It all appeared to be happening in slow motion to Jacob. He knew that he also was in danger of falling overboard, but somehow managed to fall back into his seat and steady the craft.

Was it a random coincidence that this friendship began and expired the same way, with a swift kick? Or was it fate instigated by a higher power with a master plan?

Jacob wrestled with these questions while the professor fought for his life. He was knocked out, bleeding from his wound and dreaming that his father had once again fallen on top of him on the family room floor. He was suffocating, but this time from swallowed water.

The choking caused the professor to regain consciousness. "Pull me back in," he pleaded. "Have you lost your mind? We've known each other our entire lives. My sister, mother. Help me, brother!"

Jacob responded with the same malevolent whisper, quoting again from his own dark hallucination. "Pay the price, sacrifice."

The professor was petrified, comprehending the madness of the moment. He was about to scream for help when he sensed that the moon beams had impossibly pierced the water and were now shining down to the bottom of the lake, instead of reflecting off the surface, as if pointing the way to his doom. A flock of black and white birds appeared overhead. The professor thought from a far corner of his mind, *They've come to witness my demise.* He didn't know if this was real or panic setting in.

Jacob watched expressionlessly, thinking that the moonbeams pointed to where Lizzy had receded after their latest kiss in paradise. He began to paddle away in silence, contemplating all the sacrifices he had made in his life, all the times he had paid the price. It was the professor's turn.

But there was still a powerful alchemy deep within Jacob. His conscience continued to navigate his path, despite the ruined chemistry and extinguished gravitational pull of the broken friendship. In the end, Jacob was a righteous man, not to reap any reward from God, nor to meet a sacred text. From a place of profound mystery came a directive.

Jacob abided. He turned the canoe around and returned to the professor as he was going under. Not a word was spoken as he pulled the injured man in while the boat rocked dangerously, nearly tipping again. The professor laid on the bottom of the craft in shock, gasping for air.

Jacob soon forgot about his passenger. There were far more important things to do. He rowed back to shore with vigor as the stars continued their eternal rotation through the evening sky.

CHAPTER II – THE PROPHET

When Jacob reached shore, he rose from the canoe and walked swiftly to his cabin, leaving the dazed professor to drift back into Lake Paradise. There was no time for trivial matters like docking the vessel and storing equipment. The professor could worry about that later when he revived and made his way back to land.

Once home, Jacob sat comatose on his bed staring into space, his eyes shining with ageless wisdom. He was now a prophet delivering the words of God, or of something paramount, even paranormal, that were written on a golden parchment.

He found himself transported to places of great importance. The Vatican in Rome. The Temple Mount in Jerusalem. And atop a towering stage at the fifty-yard line during halftime of the Super Bowl. It was from these landmarks, and everywhere else, that Jacob orated to the masses his answer to every problem, solution to every issue. He raised the golden parchment high over his head and proclaimed:

> *Countless tales, metaphors, myths galore*
> *My imperceptible, imperfect mites*
>
> *Dwarfed by time, space, omniscience*
> *Scurrying, scampering beneath my master plan*
>
> *Do your stories light the way my little ones?*
> *Fables that guide, divide*
>
> *None capture the essence*
> *But flip it on if you can, flip it off if you may*

The lucky ones
They accept, embrace my gifts

Grandeur, majesty
Ageless rhythms, eternal order

To the beat of searing indifference
About life, about death

Dream on, dream, oh dream
My seekers

All are part of the splendor
Perpetual renewal awaits!

Jacob trembled from the veracity of his vision. But the answer was rejected by the masses at the Vatican as blasphemy. "Crucify him!" they raged. The solution was refuted by the throngs at the Temple Mount as the rantings of an infidel. "Behead him!" And Jacob's holy message was blared into rubble at the Super Bowl by the belligerent rap idol who kicked him off the towering stage while the mob below screamed profanities. "Waste him!"

Scorned, Jacob retreated to beneath the weeping willow in his backyard with Lake Paradise in the distance. He had returned alone to God, or something paramount, even paranormal. "I tasted the sting not the honey," he lamented to the higher power. "Please, I beg of you, give me another bite of the red orb."

He staggered to the shore of Lake Paradise before sunrise, that perpetual time for new beginnings. There was a glow emanating from the center of Lake Paradise that illuminated a flock of black and white birds hovering in unison. Jacob waded in and was pushed along by waves that had reversed course. In the distance, he glimpsed the old innkeeper with his arms extended in welcome, translucent with a billion trillion stars shining through. As the innkeeper faded, Lizzy appeared, glowing with love, beckoning to him, with Hunter at her side.

Jacob's Early Warning System wailed. He swam toward them as the inescapable pressure on his chest escalated to explosive pain.

CHAPTER III - THE RABBI

The rabbi awoke before dawn brimming with anticipation. After a quick breakfast, he scurried about with Mia, preparing the Paradise Inn for their anniversary bash. *Seven years an innkeeper,* he marveled to himself. *A number with profound significance.* He was excited to host Jacob, the CEO, and professor. *Finally, we can all meet. Jacob will be thrilled.*

He walked outside to decorate the reflection pool. He planned to spread photographs of the guests throughout the area. Each picture was a treasured memory, sure to add to the festivity.

As he began to work, birds sang in the background to welcome the new day. His phone rang, cutting through the symphony with a metallic alert. It was the CEO and the tone in his voice was sobering. *Please don't let this be a relapse.*

"Sit down, Aaron."

The rabbi complied holding the pictures in his lap. "How're you doing, Geoffrey? Preparing to board the company jet, I hope?"

"Aaron, we have a crisis. Jacob's in trouble."

The rabbi stared blankly at the pictures while the CEO updated him. He heard the details but, like the CEO, couldn't accept their implication.

"Jacob? No way. Not a chance he did it," said the rabbi. "I've never met a more honest man. It's a colossal misunderstanding."

"Of course, Rabbi. Agreed."

"This is a catastrophe," continued the rabbi, instantly arriving at the same conclusion as the CEO. "Jacob isn't up to this."

The CEO took control. "Find him immediately. I'll supply Jacob with the best lawyers, the top publicity team. Call me back when you're together."

Like the CEO, the rabbi first tried to phone Jacob. Again, no answer. He sprung from his chair as the pictures tumbled from his lap, some scattering on the pavement and many landing in the water to fade away at the bottom of the reflection pool. He left the scene in disarray and raced past Mia.

The rabbi knew that Jacob was hosting the professor. He would interrupt the reunion and do the best he could to help his friend. *The professor will provide added support,* he reasoned. As he hurried to Jacob's cabin, he assured himself that things would turn out fine. *The CEO is formidable, and I'm just a short distance away. Whatever Jacob needs, he'll get.*

A few minutes later, he arrived at Jacob's cabin, but nobody was home. Jacob's car was parked in front, so the rabbi knew that he was nearby. With nowhere else to look, he headed toward Lake Paradise with the sun rising in the sky.

It was there he found Jacob face down in the water. The rabbi attempted to revive him. Nothing. He screamed for help and called an ambulance. The medics arrived minutes later and frantically tried resuscitation. No response. They pronounced Jacob dead from a massive heart attack and gave the rabbi their condolences.

The rabbi stood motionless as the medics carried Jacob's body away on a gurney. The ambulance drove off without a siren or flashing lights. As endless waves lapped the shore, Jacob's infinite questions about life, about death, bombarded him. *Where is he now? Why did this happen?*

The rabbi turned toward Lake Paradise as if he might find answers in the clear blue waters, in God's natural splendor. The very place where he, and Jacob too, had gained insights and inspiration under majestic skies.

What he saw instead was Jacob's canoe floating in slow motion toward the shore with the professor curled in a heap on the bottom. The rabbi pulled him out and both men fell into the sand.

CHAPTER IV - DISCOVERIES

Mia stood at the front door waiting for the rabbi. Her expression overflowed with worry, but there was hope in her eyes as well. The rabbi wished he could protect his beautiful, optimistic wife, but that would be impossible. As he spoke the words, Mia broke down, unable to do anything but hug him. He hadn't suffered such sorrow since the morbid scene with his parents at Sunnyside Nursing Home. At least this time, he would not grieve alone.

Mia stood beside her husband as he phoned the CEO. "I can only hope that Jacob has finally found the answers he's been searching for," the CEO said in a stoic voice. "Sandra and I will miss him." In the background, the rabbi could hear Sandra crying.

The last calls were the hardest. The rabbi phoned Walter and Michelle, steeling himself to give the news about their father. It took his final ounce of strength to utter a single sentence to each twin. "Your Dad was the best friend a man could ever have."

The twins dropped everything and rushed to Lake Paradise. Gracie planned to join Michelle a few days later for the funeral, but Walter's wife chose to remain home with the children. They needed to attend to daily life, and she despised flying.

When the twins arrived, they regressed into familiar patterns, bickering whenever possible. And in a morbid display of pent-up energy, they moved at warp speed, throwing out most everything in Jacob's cabin with little examination. Jacob's prized possessions were expeditiously transformed to garbage. The place settings for "dinner for two" with his dear departed Lizzy, his favorite books about the meaning of life, awards from GoldOrb, treasured Polaroid photos, even the yellowing marriage certificate signaling the beginning of their family unit, were unceremoniously tossed into a crate ticketed for the dump.

"Only the person ever really matters in the end," observed Michelle.

"Whatever," replied her brother.

After a short break, the twins entered Jacob's bedroom. The first thing they saw was the yellow legal pad lying on the floor with an uncapped sharpie next to it. Walter moved to reflexively crumple Jacob's manifesto inscribed on the golden parchment, but Michelle slowed him down. "It might be some kind of message, maybe Dad's last words," she said.

Each child read it several times as their confusion grew. Finally, they could agree on something. This message of "Countless tales, metaphors, myths galore" did not sound like Dad. But it clearly was his handwriting. Of course, the twins' agreement ended there. They argued about what the message meant. They could not concur whether it was profound wisdom or folly, sacrilege or spiritual.

Michelle kept her greatest concern to herself. *Dad's note reflects poorly on his state of mind. Even his sanity.*

Walter suggested that they share the text with the rabbi. "He was Dad's best friend. Maybe he can clue us in." Walter harbored his own unexpressed fear that his father's last words were instigated by the horrible news from Chicago. He wondered where the professor went, strongly suspecting that their investment partner was involved.

The twins brought the yellow legal pad to the rabbi later that day. He read it several times and wept. "To his last breath, your father sought meaning. He was a good man with a burdened soul wrestling with paradise."

The rabbi chose not to discuss his darker worries. Did Jacob find peace or was something else at play? What was he doing in the water? Like the twins, the tone of Jacob's message distressed him. And he too speculated that the Chicago investments were linked to this strangeness.

Back at the cabin, the twins reminisced about their father as they continued their ghoulish romp through his possessions. While sifting through mounds of old bank statements, utility bills, meaningless paper that seemed important enough to store years earlier, they found solace from the rabbi's words.

"Dad was a good man," Walter agreed. "Isn't that the ultimate grade we all strive for on our final report card?!"

Michelle nodded. "I was always proud of him. He had a conscience to fill the universe and wonderment to examine it."

With that spark of common ground combined with raw emotions from their father's demise, they shared secret regrets. Both admitted that they should have made more time for Jacob. And they felt an emptiness over unresolved issues. Holding a balled up generic sweater that she had given Jacob for his birthday, Michelle looked helpless. "Dad loved me, but the truth is he was squeamish about who I really am. I should have confronted him and forced a resolution. Our relationship would have been more honest."

Walter sounded frustrated. "He never got on board with my passion for religion. He was so wrapped up in his own quests that he ignored mine. Belittled mine." He stopped sifting through papers as if to emphasize that his next point was important for Michelle to hear. "Funny, we seem to have adopted Dad's biases against each other."

"Maybe we need to rethink things," Michelle responded.

On the morning of the funeral, the twins were still busy emptying the cabin when the doorbell rang. It was the professor, but he didn't look like the suave Ivy League academic they were accustomed to. He sported a huge purple protrusion on his forehead and his eyes were encircled by dark rings.

Walter's jaw tightened. "I ought to kick your ass to get to the bottom of what happened with those investments."

The professor stiffened but asked to come in. "I've been hiding like a coward in Denver," he said. "I'm here to tell you everything. I'll turn myself in to the police after I leave."

Michelle caught sight of her brother clenching his fist. "Walter and I think it's up to Jesus to judge you, Professor, not us. What did you come here to say?" Walter regained his composure, soothed by Michelle's subtle gesture of peace and respect for his beliefs.

The professor spared no detail. "Your father was furious," he concluded. "The biggest mistake he ever made was befriending me. He was honest to his last breath. I want you kids to know that." He whispered his next words in an unrecognizable humbled state. "Your dad always sought the truth. I mocked him while I loved him. Now I have to live with what I've done. I beg your forgiveness."

Walter and Michelle said nothing. Their silence was his cold rebuke.

The professor looked stricken but held his ground. There was another reason for the visit. He removed a check from his pocket and handed it to Michelle. "Here's money to take care of my sister and mother. Take it, please."

Michelle gave him an icy stare as she accepted the money. "I'm doing this for them, not you. Leave. Now."

The look on Walter's face was even harsher. There would be no reconciliation. The professor departed in disgrace, a new emotion for the Thinker.

The twins were deeply agitated by the professor's report. They could only imagine their father's devastation from his oldest friend's deception.

"Dad, of all people, tried to do things the right way," said Michelle. "Instead, he profited from a big-time fraud. The professor corrupted his ideals."

Walter cringed. "I committed the same felony. You can bet Dad felt responsible."

Michelle gave him a kind, forgiving look but said nothing. She retreated to that dark place, speculating again over her father's sanity, blaming herself for not being more assertive. She continued to play psychologist, as if she was in her office diagnosing a complicated and fragile patient. *What were those colorful pills doing in Dad's dresser? Did he hallucinate about our hike? The move to Lake Paradise was sudden. What else was going on with him that I missed?*

Her ruminations were mercifully interrupted by a phone call from Gracie. The sweet sound of her voice lifted Michelle's spirits. "My flight is delayed," Gracie reported. "But I should make it in the nick of time and will meet you at the funeral. Be strong!"

CHAPTER V - THE INTERRUPTION

Twenty-six mourners gathered near the graceful weeping willow in Jacob's backyard. The weather was brilliant. *A proper sendoff from heaven for a good man on Earth,* thought the rabbi.

He was joined by Mia, the twins, the CEO and Sandra, Mr. Wang, members of Jacob's drum circle, and his Paradise Donuts crowd. The CEO brought along John Shepard, Jacob's long-time boss. Hunter, buried a short time ago, lay a few feet away in the shade of the magnificent tree.

Undertaker Judd arranged the logistics for Jacob's memorial service masterfully. It was on the house as a favor to the rabbi.

The rabbi leaned on a podium and scanned the crowd. He tried to calm himself for the hardest service he would ever conduct apart from the memorial for his parents. As he cleared his throat, signaling that it was time to begin, he caught sight of a straggler who had just arrived and waited for her to find a seat.

The rabbi often glanced at Mia before commencing a funeral, gaining confidence from her presence, her shining light. He would need all the strength she could send his way. But something seemed terribly wrong with his wife. Mia was gasping for air and holding onto the CEO as if she was about to collapse.

The rabbi's mind was spinning. *What's happening? Should I go to her?*

Mia seemed to be gesturing toward the latecomer. As Gracie made her way closer to Michelle, the rabbi noticed her striking features. She looked just like his wife. *Dimples the size of the moon.* And then he too gasped.

He was no longer in control of his actions. His mind froze, but his body moved on pure instinct. He abandoned the podium and rushed to his daughter, holding her for dear life. Mia soon joined, hugging them both. The rest of the mourners looked on in complete confusion.

Michelle was the first to understand. She whispered a question to the rabbi, and he nodded, confirming what she already knew. She had just enough composure to announce to the assembly, "I'm sorry, but something extraordinary has happened. We need to delay my father's funeral for three hours." She assured the crowd that everything was fine, but the postponement was imperative. "You can make yourselves comfortable in the cabin or walk around town in the meantime," she said. The rabbi motioned for the crowd to disperse, still unable to talk.

When he could speak again, the rabbi apologized to Michelle and Walter for interrupting their father's funeral. With Mia at his side, he asked Hannah to accompany them to the Paradise Inn for a quiet conversation. His daughter gently told him that her name was now Gracie and requested that Michelle accompany them. Mia, her eyes staring directly into her daughter's soul, assured her, "We would have it no other way. Both of you must come."

Once at the inn, it was impossible for the reunited family to verbalize anything without a fresh outbreak of tears. And when words could be uttered, they were unimportant. Everything that mattered had already happened.

CHAPTER VI - THE FUNERAL

The rabbi stood erect before the reassembled mourners, forcing himself to concentrate, to focus on Jacob and give him the sendoff that he deserved. Each time he thought he had his emotions under control, he caught a glimpse of his daughter, wrapped in Mia's arms while hugging Michelle as she mourned. He had no choice but to lower his eyes and read from notes. He needed the crutch.

The rabbi spoke solemnly. "Jacob was a man of integrity seeking the same blunt honesty from God. May he be at peace in paradise."

He read passages from various prayers that he hoped could provide insight and consolation. While reciting, he imagined Jacob questioning the words, the irrational or unproven premises, ideas that missed the mark. *Rabbi, Psalm 23 makes little sense to me. It's outdated, but people recite it like lost sheep.*

The rabbi's voice gained strength as he reflected on their countless interchanges in search of knowledge. "The time I spent with Jacob was paradise," he said. Choking up again, he asked if anyone wished to speak. To his surprise most hands shot up. They took turns celebrating Jacob's life, many confessing more love for the man following his death than they ever expressed to him while he was alive.

The CEO went first, followed by Sandra, each twin, the boss, and the leader of the drum circle. And for the first time the rabbi could recall, even the rebbetzin spoke. "Oh, Jacob, soulful Jacob," she said. "He was my husband's best friend, my dear companion too. And somehow, for reasons only God can explain, he brought our precious daughter back to us. I wish he could be here to see this." The Rabbi could hear Jacob's voice in his head, questioning Mia's assumption about God's role in what might have been a colossal coincidence.

Finally, it was Gracie's turn to praise a man she barely knew, who awkwardly kept his distance from her. "He had to be special to have raised such a caring daughter," she said. "He would have made a wonderful father-in-law. I'll miss that."

The rabbi and Mia were on an emotional roller coaster. Amidst Jacob's funeral, a new family was blooming, and they were part of it. Tears of joy mixed with tears of sorrow. *The good, the bad, each is part of a full life to be grateful for,* thought the rabbi. He recalled Jacob's belief that death was part of life too. He wished he could explore these connections further with his friend.

Again, the rabbi needed to force himself to refocus if he was to complete the service. He was appreciative that the other mourners spoke, relieving pressure while adding dimensions about Jacob that he could not capture alone. He took a deep breath and told the mourners, "Let me leave you with the words of a brilliant philosopher:"

> *Dream on, dream, oh dream*
> *My seekers*
> *All are part of the splendor*
> *Perpetual renewal awaits*

"If you haven't guessed, these poetic words are from Jacob," the rabbi continued. "He was right. We are all part of something bigger and perhaps death is not the end, but another beginning."

When the service concluded, the CEO sought out Walter among the scattering crowd. He put his hand on Walter's shoulder like a father to a son. "I have insights I'd like to share with you about Chicago and a few other things," he said. "Now isn't the time. But I'd like to call you in a few days if you'll hear me out." Walter hesitated but gave the CEO his phone number.

The next day at sundown, a small contingent met at Lake Paradise. The rabbi, Mia, Gracie, the CEO, and Sandra all stood respectfully on shore as they watched Walter and Michelle row Jacob's canoe toward the middle of the lake. On the floor of the boat, where the injured professor had lain just a few days earlier, was an urn.

The twins reminisced as they coasted through the healing water. Michelle said, "I know this sounds weird, but I wish Dad could see us, working together." Walter replied in a friendly tone she hardly recognized. "He's watching with Mom."

As the sun met the horizon at that moment of sheer predictability yet immeasurable wonder, the twins lifted the urn and slowly scattered Jacob's ashes into the welcoming waters of Lake Paradise while his beloved mountains bore witness to the enactment of his final wish. The ashes floated on the surface as if to enjoy a last glance at the apexes before receding into mystery. A large flock of black and white birds flew overhead, singing a somber farewell.

CHAPTER VII - THE WEDDING

One year after Jacob's funeral, the Paradise Inn hummed with anticipation. Excitement filled the air as wedding guests adorned in colorful gowns and formal tuxedos assembled at the reflection pool.

The rabbi watched intently as the wedding party began its progression down a plush white carpet leading from the labyrinth. He loved weddings, captivated by the vibrant expressions of newlyweds as they proclaimed their love and publicly launched their new identity as a couple. The events were also profound milestones for parents, a time to celebrate as they too entered a new phase. The rabbi was thankful to God for the miraculous reconciliation with Gracie, for his mended family. The future was bright.

He had scrupulously prepared to marry his daughter to Jacob's child, to say just the right things from his heart. What he would have given for Jacob to be there, to share this extraordinary moment as their families merged.

Mia glowed as she walked Gracie down the aisle. They had spent countless hours selecting just the right dresses and meticulously planning the affair. The rabbi loved that they worked as a team, bonding after years of acrimony. *They look so alike, so beautiful.*

When mother and daughter arrived at the canopy, it was the rabbi's turn to escort Michelle. He was honored that she selected him, sad that Jacob could not do it. Mia stepped to the side letting her daughter bask in the limelight while they waited for Michelle.

In all his years on the pulpit, the rabbi had never done a better job officiating. But he became confused when it was time for the groom to smash the glass, not anticipating whether Michelle or Gracie should perform this final ritual. As he hesitated, Michelle whispered, "We asked Walter to bring two glasses, so we'll each have a shot." Walter smiled and placed them under their feet. Stomp, stomp, "Mazel Tov!"

Michelle and Gracie raised their arms in jubilation as they left the reflection pool. They carved out a quiet moment for themselves at a romantic spot overlooking Lake Paradise while the guests mingled. "Let's appreciate this to the fullest," said Gracie. "Our dream is now reality."

When the newlyweds returned, Walter introduced them while the crowd gave a standing ovation and clapped to a celebratory beat set by the drum circle. At precisely the right moment, the drumming was interrupted by a loud guitar wail as a high-energy, six-piece, rock and roll band from Boulder called The Peaks began to perform. The dance floor was mobbed.

Walter was best man and made a pitch perfect toast. He started with a short, good-natured roast. "My sister and Gracie will need to rein it in if they have a child. With two shrinks for parents, that poor little creature will need all the help he can get." But mostly, he praised them for their perseverance and good judgment in finding one another. He also mentioned his parents. "We miss Mom and Dad and know they're smiling, watching over us from heaven. They're part of us."

Food and drinks flowed while The Peaks performed all the hits. The drum circle reappeared to accompany them for a few songs, adding to the revelry on the crowded dance floor. Gracie could not believe her eyes as she watched her father, the rabbi, hammering away at his bongos, the CEO right behind him marching in place to the beat, his arms waving from side to side over his head.

Finally, it was time for the last song. The Peaks slowed the pace with a reflective Harry Chapin melody that Jacob had loved and passed on to the twins:

> *All my life's a circle; Sunrise and sundown;*
> *Moon rolls through the nighttime; 'Til the daybreak comes*
> *around.*
>
> *All my life's a circle; But I can't tell you why;*
> *Season's spinning round again; The years keep rollin' by.*

It seems like I've been here before; I can't remember when;
But I have this funny feeling; That we'll all be together again.

The guests joined hands, swaying in time to the tune while encircling Michelle and Gracie.

Gracie beamed as she surveyed the room one last time, surrounded by the people who meant the most to her. She took the microphone and asked if they would indulge her just a little longer, that she had something important to announce before they said their goodbyes.

Sparklers were distributed and the guests held them high while Gracie spoke. Magic again filled the air. Gracie thanked everyone for making the occasion so special and toasted Michelle. She then told the gathering that she had two small tidbits to share. "First, I'm changing my name back to Hannah to honor my parents. Hannah is who I am, who I've always been." The rabbi and Mia nodded their thanks and put their arms around each other. "And second, Michelle and I will be meeting our new baby son on our honeymoon. He was born this morning! On our wedding day! His name is Jacob, after his grandfather!"

Michelle let out a scream of pure joy. "We love him already!" The guests cheered as the sparklers burnt down.

CHAPTER VIII - THE CEO

The CEO sat erect behind his desk at six o'clock in the morning, the usual time for GG to get going. His hands were clenched in a vicelike grip with his tie knotted as tight as ever. He felt healthy and intended to lead GoldOrb Diversified forever. *They'll have to carry me out with my boots on.*

He and Sandra had left no stone unturned planning their future. But in the end, he chose to stay put. *Being CEO is all I know,* he concluded. *And I'm good at it.* His days continued to fly, filled with outsized challenges, still making his mark in the commercial world.

Facing the CEO from the other side of his desk was a young man who had quickly climbed the ranks at GoldOrb over the last several years. Walter Hart was a budding star. The CEO was impressed by his combination of grit and intelligence, traits inherited from his father. It just took a little mentoring for Walter to hit his stride.

Walter was updating the CEO on negotiations with Chicago. The city agreed to drop the pollution charges for twelve hundred jobs at a new manufacturing site. The only remaining step was for the CEO and Chicago's new mayor to formalize the agreement.

"This is the optimal solution," Walter assured the CEO. "It took a while to get her up to speed, but the mayor agrees that dredging the river may do more environmental harm than good. They've prioritized boosting the local economy instead to help fill their pension hole."

"What's in it for us besides escaping liability?" asked the CEO, already knowing the answer.

"We tap into a skilled labor pool and get a publicity boost."

The CEO was proud. "Great job, kid. I'll phone the mayor to let her know GoldOrb is thrilled to be partnering with them."

Walter said a silent prayer thanking Jesus for this opportunity. He intended to make the most of it. All charges against him over the real estate fraud had been dropped. The CEO made sure of that, providing the best defense money could buy. Once his legal team discovered the professor's email proclaiming Jacob's and Walter's innocence, the case was over. Walter could devote his full attention to his new career.

Although the CEO remained at GoldOrb's helm, the rest of his unconventional lifestyle was unrecognizable. Sandra was relentless in executing their sparkling new vision with complete support from her husband. "You've got the keys to the kingdom," he said. "I'm behind you all the way."

The transformation began with Sandra selling Xanadu to the creator of a popular online gaming business that went public for a cool billion without a penny of profits. She located a cozy new home with three bedrooms and a small yard overlooking a pond. "Less is more," she told the CEO. "We'll survive without the castle and moat."

She was just warming up. Sandra took 99 percent of their investments and, with the help of an army of professionals, established Hart College in honor of Jacob. Walter and Michelle attended the opening celebration to cut the gold ribbon. Walter, recently divorced, was unaccompanied, but Hannah looked on with pride.

When they pulled into the driveway of their modest home following the ceremony, the CEO teased, "Sandra, where's the gate? You gave away the kingdom."

Sandra's expression was resolute. "Nope. I kept the keys."

Hart College was designed to be unique. Students were provided Hart Scholarships for a free world class education. In return, they pledged to work for two years after graduation in community service and to spend a lifetime healing the world.

The admissions committee recruited exceptionally talented students from all social classes with a special emphasis on impoverished neighborhoods, hoping to ensure fairness. "It's not enough to do good deeds if we stay locked in different silos of rich and poor, all White, only Black, just Christian, solely Jewish," Sandra explained. "If we don't share vicinity, we'll remain at each other's throats."

Sandra was not a Pollyanna. *Breaking down barriers is hard, maybe impossible,* she thought. *It can also make us exceptional.*

The curriculum was unconventional. Instead of offering a broad array of electives to supplement a major, extra courses were required in social responsibility, civil discourse, justice, critical thinking with fact finding, and philanthropy. "Our students need to know the truth without feeling personally blamed or victimized," Sandra instructed her staff. "Focus on coexistence with shared ideals for moving forward." Students also attended classes from a spiritual resources department, so aptly named by Mia years earlier. The rabbi was a frequent guest lecturer.

Sandra was chancellor and worked from a small office located in the middle of campus. Like the CEO, she was the first to arrive and the last to leave.

The CEO loved Sandra's vision, remembering how troubled Jacob became later in life by societal privilege and cultural wreckage, how fascinated he was with spirituality. He recalled Jacob's complicated lament: "I'll go to my grave questioning if I should be sorry for what I didn't do." He hoped Hart College would make him proud.

Sandra and the CEO understood there'd be criticism. They were not saints, having accumulated more wealth than a whole city needs. And they maintained control over the money, diverting it to purposes of their choosing.

In an interview of the couple aired on several major networks, Sandra responded to the doubters. "Our mission is noble. The world requires repair, and the answer is in our youth. We'll equip the next generation with skills they need to help themselves ... and the rest of us."

The CEO was blunter when asked to weigh in. "We won the capitalistic lottery wearing blinders. This is the right thing to do unless we want to drop bags of cash from an airplane or fork over our fortune to the government to squander." This was his only remark during the entire interview. He let Sandra take center stage.

Sandra was fulfilled. She no longer questioned her decision to remain childless. "The students are my kids," she said.

"Maslow would salute," responded the CEO. "Your heart found its navigation system."

The CEO no longer needed his secret pleasure to let off steam. Instead, he spent his free time behind the curtain supporting his wife in running a major university. "Besides," he told Sandra. "Podcasts are replacing blogs. Gabby might go obsolete fast."

Sandra smiled. "Well, I suppose Gabby can't evolve to podcasts. Her voice would sound ridiculous."

Shortly after Jacob's death, Gabbing Gloria entered a final post:

Post 51: Farewell

I am grieving, my loves. A dear friend died far too soon, and it shocked my world.

So, farewell to Jacob. I miss you but know that you're still here, part of this grand universe, inside my heart.

I'm sad to also bid farewell to you, my little munchkins. It's time for Gabby to make that change we talked about. To get going with something new.

By the way, I hope you like the final cash prize. You should because I'm tripling it to 3 grand. $3,000!

Chao. auf Wiedersehen. Shalom. Adieu.

Kiss, kiss, kiss.

I'm out of here.

Gabbing Gloria

The site was swamped by an outpouring of emotions among complete strangers, sharing their lives for a split second in the age of the internet. Readers expressed their digital remorse that Gloria was calling it quits. They offered virtual heartfelt condolences for Jacob, a man they never met.

Private investigator, Skylar Sharpe, an avid follower, felt the loss on a more personal level. She circled a copy of the farewell post with a red heart and wrote, "Dear GG. Thank you for your wisdom and mirth. Gloria touched my soul and I'll miss 'her.'" She mailed her message to the CEO in the slow, old-fashioned way. The CEO framed Skylar's note and hung it in the third bedroom of their new home.

The CEO and chancellor kept in close contact with the rabbi and rebbetzin, often flying on the company jet for visits. While hiking with the rabbi, the CEO recalled how agitated he had been for failing to feel inspired by the raw power of nature. Nowadays, he felt a spark. But at this moment, it was extinguished by guilt, and he decided to seek counsel. "Rabbi, I'm the one who set everything in motion that killed Jacob. If I hadn't gone after the mayor, he and that reporter would still be here."

The rabbi frowned. "You never intended to hurt them, just like Jacob never meant to invest in sour property. Nobody can anticipate what happens as butterflies ripple around the globe."

The rabbi paused, weighing whether he should keep the conversation going and share his own concerns. Like the CEO, he needed to get it off his chest. "Jacob had problems that we overlooked. Call it what you will. Diminishments, disappointments, combined with something else. Something I should have ...'"

"Nonsense," the CEO interrupted. "Jacob was wrestling with paradise, just where he belonged, and I sucker punched him, cutting his feet out from under him for the bottom line. This is my fault!"

Tears filled the rabbi's eyes, followed by a long bout of the sacred stroke. "Focus instead on how you and Sandra responded to the inexplicable with Hart College. With helping Walter. You must know that Jacob would be grateful. You're my heroes."

The CEO was stone-faced. "There are consequences to my actions that I'll have to live with. It is what it is, Rabbi. It is what it is."

The men walked on in silence. When they finished the hike, they found a spot to rest in a beautiful clearing. The rabbi's praise for Hart College reminded the CEO of another topic he was struggling with. "Rabbi, you know I'm an atheist. But something deep inside me wants to be a good man. I care about living an ethical life, now more than ever." There was no bragging in his tone, only curiosity, even embarrassment. "Sandra feels it too. Our only explanation is that our species evolved by hardwiring this need into our DNA for the collective good. It helps humanity survive, keeps us fittest."

The rabbi was unsure whether the CEO's scientific explanation made greater sense than the ancient myths but was relieved to move off the topic of culpability. "Geoffrey, call it whatever you wish. Accept the explanation that makes the most sense to you. Religious people also hear a voice from within to do the right thing. They call it God." The rabbi felt an undefinable luminescence as his inner spirit rose. *This conversation reminds me of my times with Jacob. Intellectual gymnastics, metaphysics ... most of all friendship.*

Two months later, the CEO relapsed. The grim reaper imposed a vice like grip on his body, indifferent to guilt or innocence. "I feel cornered," he told Sandra in a weak but steady voice. "Out of options."

On days when he could do little else, the CEO weighed the rabbi's words. In lighter moments, he felt a sense of fulfillment from helping Sandra with Hart College and assisting Jacob's son. He was also proud of his long tenure at GoldOrb. His life was not a waste, and he felt that undefinable glow.

But he also suffered darker times. *These are fruitless rationalizations to escape the void. The rubber is hitting the road and I've nothing to anticipate but worms feasting upon my sorry flesh.*

The forces of light and darkness battled within his mind to his last breath. The CEO departed GoldOrb Diversified with his boots on and Sandra at his side. She remained chancellor of Hart College for twenty more years.

CHAPTER IX - THE PROFESSOR

The professor entered his sixth year of captivity at Capon Correctional Center. Time crawled at a glacial pace. Monotony washed over the academic relentlessly, like the never-ending waves of Lake Paradise.

Each detail of his life was regimented. Schedules were enforced for awakening, exercising, showering, and eating. Cells went dark at nine o'clock sharp. Even the mice and roaches seemed to patrol his miniscule living space at prescribed times. *I never kept to a routine, didn't wear a wristwatch,* he vaguely observed. *Now this.*

He wore the same drab uniform as the other convicts instead of his expensive tweed jacket. His cell was cramped, muted, and depressing, housing a rusty toilet as its centerpiece. Privacy was out of the question. *At least I can flush whenever I want.*

Food from the prison cafeteria was tasteless. The professor was forced to dine with other inmates, but seldom spoke as he picked at the bland offerings. Nobody was interested in anything the Ivy League scholar had to say.

When the boredom lifted, it was usually replaced by raw pain. There was the time the professor received a letter from Michelle advising him that his mother had died. The professor grieved in silence and worried about his sister. On another occasion, Tommy Mack appeared in the exercise yard. He gave the professor a shove. "Hey asshole, I know what you did." But Tommy was soon transferred to a higher security prison for punching a guard.

The professor endured confrontations with other inmates. *Bulls inevitably lock horns in close quarters,* he thought. He understood that the conventional wisdom was to stand his ground, fight back, but this baffled him. *Exactly how am I supposed to do that when the guy stealing my square of butter is half my age and built like a linebacker?* He succumbed, staring down, surviving to another day.

His sharp mind was numbed by the tedium and indignities. Sometimes, a flicker of an idea would spark. *Most of the inmates here are Black, while most of the guards are White.* He tried to connect this dynamic to *Manifest Misery* but lost focus, too inundated with his own misery to pursue the insight.

He often thought of Jacob. When he did, that guilt which he masterfully tamped down for most of his life would swarm over him. *I killed my oldest friend,* he brooded. Fortunately, the never-ending fog blunted this emotion too.

The professor was in a dull meditative state when a guard approached his cell holding a package. "I don't know what you're up to," he mumbled under his breath. "It's from a Jewish rabbi, whatever the hell that is."

The package was already opened. All deliveries to the jail were routinely inspected for compliance with hundreds of pages of regulations. Food was not allowed. Liquids were banned. Cell phones and other electronic gear forbidden unless specified on a short schedule and shipped by an approved vender. But there was no prohibition against books, so long as each page was inspected for hidden razors, racy pictures, or white powder. The guard smirked, "Your package was clean."

The professor reached inside the box. There were three books. The first thing he noticed was that they were colorful: bright red, sunlight yellow, and Caribbean aqua. *How festive,* he thought. *Glitter for the grayness.*

There was no accompanying note, but the professor didn't expect one. *Not after what I did.*

The professor had written the rabbi after reading the Bible twice in his cell, cover to cover. He wanted to learn more. Knowing that the rabbi and Jacob obsessed over such topics, he made his plea:

> *Dear Rabbi:*
>
> *The only time we met was on the beach of Lake*

Paradise where Jacob died. I am profoundly sorry and will suffer for my sins for the rest of my days.

I know that I don't deserve your help but have nowhere else to turn. If you can find it in your heart, please send literature "about life, about death." I think you know what I mean.

Perhaps your service will result in a better man at this late stage in life.

Sincerely and in repentance,

Samuel Lerner

The rabbi's first instinct was to tear the letter to shreds. But he resisted the urge and gave the professor's request careful consideration. He also consulted Jacob's children. Michelle said, "It's your call, Rabbi, but I guess it's relevant that I'm still helping the professor's sister." And Walter responded, "Jesus teaches forgiveness with repentance." Emblazoned in the rabbi's mind were similar edicts from Judaism. It took him several more days to choose which books to send.

The professor clutched the rabbi's esoteric offerings like rare jewels. He read the summaries on the back covers, nodding with approval. He also skimmed several pages of each book, noting with interest the rabbi's extensive red markings in the margins. And he thought, *I want to escape this suffering.*

He placed the books in the corner of his cell. *The red, yellow, and aqua add prophetic pizazz,* he mused. That would be his last observation for hours. He struck his Thinker pose and stared into space as heavy fog rolled in.

CHAPTER X - THE RABBI

After Michelle and Hannah returned from their honeymoon with their newborn son, Mia suggested a family tradition. "When a birthday and anniversary happen on the same day, it's huge and we need to celebrate together. Let's make it a holiday at the Paradise Inn." Her wish came true. As the circle spun around again while the years rolled by, the family made it a priority to come together on this special day.

The rabbi woke up at the crack of dawn on Michelle and Hannah's seventh anniversary and young Jacob's seventh birthday. They were expected to arrive later that morning. That gave him time for his customary walk at Lake Paradise. Much like his morning prayers at the synagogue, this had become his daily ritual, his path to the Divine cleared by Occam's Razor.

The air was intoxicating, the scenery brilliant and the birds mellifluous as they greeted the rising sun. The rabbi doubted whether Jacob's technicolor dreams that beckoned him to paradise were more vivid. After all this time, Jacob remained on his mind.

The rabbi strolled to the shore and stared at his reflection in the blue waters. He saw a loving, wrinkled face gazing back. *I've become my father,* he thought. Time had transformed them into mirror images. *I miss you, Dad. I'm carrying on for both of us, Mom too.*

He cast his eyes toward where the old innkeeper took them fishing and Mia had made her miraculous catch. As if on cue, a trout jumped clear out of the water. The rabbi smiled, basking in radiant light that had been missing from his life for so long, choosing it, inhaling it. Paradise was part of him, and he was part of it. *Yes, indeed. Yes, indeed,* he thought, as joyous laughter bubbled up from deep within.

On the walk back home, a biblical passage that fascinated him in his youth entered his mind. It was from Jacob's famous dream about a staircase to heaven. Upon awakening, Jacob said, "Surely the Lord is in this place, and I did not know it." The rabbi looked in all directions and raised his gaze to the limitless sky, embracing the wisdom. He yearned to share these words with his own Jacob, to dissect their meaning together.

When he returned to the Paradise Inn, the family gathered at the reflection pool and lit sparklers, reenacting the electric farewell scene from the wedding. The four adults toasted the day with the finest champagne, courtesy of Sandra, who shipped several bottles each year to mark the event.

When the sparklers burned down, Mia wrapped young Jacob in a warm hug. "Seven years ago, we learned that you'd be our wonderful boy and the whole wide world opened up to us." The rebbetzin beamed as she watched the precocious child roast marshmallows at a massive stone firepit, the newest addition to the inn. The boy liked to dip his burnt delicacy in a bowl of melted chocolate and crushed wafers. This was his favorite treat, and his parents allowed him to eat as much as he wished on this single day of the year.

After young Jacob had his fill, he opened his gifts. He then climbed into his grandfather's lap for a well-deserved rest. As he nestled in, he felt an object protruding from the rabbi's pocket. "What's this, Grandpa?" The rabbi pulled out a beautiful antique pocket watch that Mia had given him and read the inscription: "I believe in You and am grateful." After several sacred strokes, he told his grandson, "This sums up everything there is to know, my boy."

Young Jacob inspected the timepiece. He began to squirm and giggle. "Why do you touch your beard so much, Grandpa? Does it itch?"

The rabbi hugged him. "I do this when I'm deep in thought, thanking God for you, my family, this paradise. And for the privilege of having known your other grandfather. He was special, like you."

Young Jacob's brow furrowed as he tried mightily to work something out. "Why did he die? Did God mean for it to happen? Where is God? I don't see Him."

ACKNOWLEDGMENTS

I want to give special thanks to a few of you who rolled up your sleeves and worked with me on the book. First, last, and always, to my wife, Dena Wald. Thank you for encouraging me to write during challenging times, and for your boundless patience to discuss the impenetrable, anytime, anywhere. Your wise, positive outlook, and overwhelming goodness, keep me on course.

I'd also like to express gratitude to Joel and Debra Wald and Naomi and Scott Warren (Xander too) for the bright and vibrant light you shine my way. You are amazing people with deep reservoirs of insight. You inspire me with faith in the future. Thank you for the help you provided in writing this book.

Special thanks to Sheldon Siegel, Sally and Stuart Gold, Ron and Betsy Rooth, Gary and Marla Goldstein, David Gibbs, Lee Meyer, and Paul Shindell for reviewing early drafts. As usual, each of you was brilliant and kind. Your insightful comments improved the book far beyond anything I could have managed alone. And thank you also to Ira Wald for reviewing my book and your stellar work in creating my website.

There are many other exceptional people who mean the world to me and have helped me along the way. I'd like to thank the rest of my family and friends in Massachusetts, Illinois, Connecticut, Israel, Minnesota, Florida, Virginia, New York, Vermont, Colorado, California, Ohio, Texas and beyond. You know who you are. Our relationships make life worth living.

I also want to recognize Teri Rider, Chelsea Robinson, and the rest of the staff at Top Reads Publishing and Torchflame Books for your remarkable help in designing the cover for my book, insightfully editing it, and getting me to the finish line. Your guidance was invaluable.

After suffering a horrible trauma, Rabbi Friedler rediscovers his need to be grateful to a higher power, something beyond his miniscule everyday existence. I too choose God, in whatever form He might reside. I thank Him for the good, the bad, for everything that comprises this precious opportunity called "life."

ABOUT THE AUTHOR

Jerry Wald received his undergraduate degree in accounting from the University of Illinois. He is also a graduate of the University of Chicago Law School. He practiced law for 34 years specializing in employee benefits.

Jerry lives in the greater Boston region with his wife, Dena, and Goldendoodle, Maui. But he has retained his Midwest roots as a die-hard Chicago Bulls and Bears fan and hopes that, someday soon, fate will finally smile upon these teams – if fate exists.

Jerry is a new grandfather and author. He recently wrote a children's book for his amazing grandson, Xander.

If you've enjoyed this book, please consider leaving a review for me.

Please visit Jerry's website at www.jerrywald-author.com.

Printed in the USA
CPSIA information can be obtained
at www.ICGtesting.com
CBHW021143190724
11674CB00001B/51

9 781611 535938